IVAN BUNIN
COLLECTED STORIES

Ivan Bunin

Collected Stories

TRANSLATED FROM THE RUSSIAN
AND WITH AN INTRODUCTION BY
GRAHAM HETTLINGER

Ivan R. Dee

CHICAGO 2007

IVAN BUNIN: COLLECTED STORIES. Copyright © 2007 by Ivan R. Dee, Inc.
English translations copyright © 2002, 2005, 2007 by Graham Hettlinger. All rights
reserved, including the right to reproduce this book or portions thereof in any form.
For information, address: Ivan R. Dee, Publisher, 1332 North Halsted Street,
Chicago 60622. Manufactured in the United States of America and
printed on acid-free paper.

www.ivanrdee.com

Library of Congress Cataloging-in-Publication Data:
Bunin, Ivan Alekseevich, 1870–1953.
    [Short stories. English. Selections]
    The collected stories of Ivan Bunin / Ivan Bunin ; translated from the Russian,
and with an introduction by Graham Hettlinger.
        p. cm.
    Includes bibliographical references and index.
    ISBN-13: 978-1-56663-758-9 (cloth : alk. paper)
    ISBN-10: 1-56663-758-9 (cloth : alk. paper)
    1. Bunin, Ivan Alekseevich, 1870–1953—Translations into English. I. Hettlinger,
Graham. II. Title.
PG3453.B9A2 2007
891.73'3—dc22
                                                            2007011830

For Mila, gratefully

Acknowledgments

I WISH TO THANK the many people who made helpful comments and suggestions on these translations, including Daniel Collins, Irene Masing Delic, Karen Hettlinger, Mary Hettlinger, Jared Ingersoll, Maria Lekic, and Holly Stephens.

I am indebted as well to many of my workplace colleagues, including Alissa Bibb, Sheila Dawes, Cristina Dinu, Timothy O'Connor, Darya Shakhova, Vladka Shikova, and Margaret Stephenson, all of whom provided me friendly support and much needed time away from the office in order to finish this book.

I am particularly grateful to Angela Brintlinger and Terrence Graham, who read and commented extensively on earlier versions of many of these stories, and to Richard Davis, whose teaching on the craft of translation has been invaluable to me over the years.

Finally, I wish to express once more my enormous gratitude to my wife, Mila Medina. This work would never have been completed without her insights into the author, his language, and his writings; her careful review and correction of each translation; and her unwavering support for this project over the years. In many ways these translations are hers as much as they are mine.

G. H.

April 2007

Contents

Acknowledgments   vii
Introduction   xi

The Scent of Apples   3
Sukhodol   18
Summer Day   74
The Gentleman from San Francisco   75
Ida   95
Light Breathing   103
Cranes   109
Chang's Dreams   111
Ballad   126
Mitya's Love   132
Calf's Head   187
Sunstroke   189
Sky Above a Wall   197
The Elagin Affair   198
Old and Young   233

CONTENTS

Styopa   237
Muza   243
Old Woman   249
Late Hour   251
Zoyka and Valeriya   257
The Eve   269
In Paris   270
The Hunchback's Affair   279
Caucasus   281
Calling Cards   286
Rusya   292
Wolves   302
Antigone   305
Little Fool   313
Tanya   315
First Class   334
Cold Fall   336
Raven   340
Cleansing Monday   346
On One Familiar Street   360

Notes to the Stories   363

Introduction

THIS BOOK combines two earlier collections of works by Ivan Bunin, *Sunstroke* (2002) and *The Elagin Affair* (2005), and adds new English translations of four stories that did not appear in those books: "Chang's Dreams" (1916), "Light Breathing" (1916), "Calling Cards" (1940), and "Wolves" (1940). *Collected Stories* is intended to provide English-language readers a comprehensive sampling of Bunin's works, including three of his major novellas ("Mitya's Love" [1924], "The Elagin Affair" [1925], and "Sukhodol" [1911]) and many of his most acclaimed stories, including "The Gentleman from San Francisco" (1915), "Sunstroke" (1925), and "Ida" (1925), as well as seventeen works from his final collection, *Dark Avenues* (1946).

Ivan Bunin (1870–1953) was born into the Russian rural gentry in the midst of its decline. The emancipation of the serfs in 1861 had begun a process of economic disintegration that would eventually eliminate most of the country's large family estates in the fashion of Chekhov's *Cherry Orchard*. Bunin's early life was deeply bound to such places. Like the narrator of "Sukhodol" and the title character of "Mitya's Love," he spent his boyhood exploring estate gardens and forests, threshing barns, and the ramshackle rooms of an aging manor house. For him, the disappearance of such places meant the eradication of his childhood and the elimination of a way of life that had defined his family for generations.

Consequently many of Bunin's best early writings are filled with elaborate images of Russian rural life and shaded by an elegiac sense of loss. Indeed, in many ways, such early stories as "The Scent of Apples" (1900) seem at times an attempt not simply to record the histories of those who occupied the old lands but to preserve through language and memory the actual physical experience of those bygone days—to make timeless and indestructible through words the white blossoms and rich black dirt of the author's early life. The goal, in other words, is often more poetic than prosaic, as Bunin, like Proust and Nabokov, seeks not so much to tell a story as to recreate experience. For this reason Bunin's prose, like poetry, often resists retelling. Its meaning lies not in events that can be summarized but in the action of specific language, in the delicate chain of sensations produced by words in a sentence, and in the rhythm of our reading.

This is not surprising, given that early in his career Bunin was best known as a poet, between 1898 and 1909 publishing six highly acclaimed books of verse. It was primarily Bunin's poetry and his translations of poetry (most notably Longfellow's "The Song of Hiawatha") that brought him the Pushkin Prize, one of Russia's most important literary awards, in 1903, 1909, and 1915. Writers as prominent and diverse as Aleksandr Blok, Russia's leading symbolist, and Maksim Gorky, the so-called founder of Soviet literature, placed him among the country's most important poets at the turn of the century.[1]

By 1910, however, Bunin's prose had begun to eclipse his verse with the publication of *The Village*, an austere and controversial depiction of the peasantry. Although critical and public reaction focused largely on the book's political rather than its artistic importance, the novel's wide readership brought Bunin new notice as a writer. *The Village* was followed by several of Bunin's most important early works, including the novella "Sukhodol" and such acclaimed short stories as "The Gentleman from San Francisco" and "Light Breathing," which broadened the scope of his work to include such themes as love, sexuality, and materialism and served to solidify his position as one of Russia's greatest prose writers. From this point forward, prose would continue to occupy an in-

1. Julian Connolly, *Ivan Bunin* (Boston: G. K. Hall, 1982), 9, 11.

creasingly important place in the author's works, while Bunin's poetry largely faded from the public view.[2]

Bunin's rise to literary prominence occurred in the midst of wracking, violent change in Russia. The strikes, mass demonstrations, and bloodshed that began to spread throughout the country as it lurched toward revolution left Bunin terrified and distraught, and the outbreak of World War I only confirmed his dreadful forebodings about the future of humanity. The Bolshevik Revolution of 1917 was the last and most shattering of these cataclysmic events. As an aristocrat and a staunch opponent of the new regime, Bunin soon decided that he could not remain in Russia. After eight months under Soviet rule, the author and his future wife, Vera Nikolaevna Muromtseva, fled to Kiev and then to Odessa, where for two years Bunin edited *The Southern Word*, a newspaper supporting the cause of the White Army in the civil war.[3] During those years Bunin also kept a detailed diary, later published under the title *Accursed Days*, in which he recorded a montage of slogans, conversations from the streets, and his own impressions of life during the war. In 1920, with the White Army on the verge of its final defeat, Bunin and Muromtseva joined a crowd of desperate refugees on a steamer bound for Constantinople. From there they traveled through Europe to France, where they eventually settled in Grasse, in the Maritime Alps. Bunin was fifty years old when he left his homeland; he would never return to the Soviet Union and would never adopt foreign citizenship. For the remainder of his life he was a man without a country.

Despite the pain and disruption of his forced emigration, Bunin soon began to work productively. By 1925 he had completed several of his most successful stories and novellas, including "Mitya's Love" (1924), "The Elagin Affair" (1925), "Sunstroke" (1925), and "Ida" (1925). He also began work on his autobiographical novel, *The Life of Arsenyev*, excerpts of which first appeared in 1927.[4] Bunin was a prominent figure in the Russian émigré community, which numbered some 400,000 in France.[5] His fellow exiles viewed the author's ability to write successfully on foreign soil as an important rebuke to the Bolsheviks' claims that they were

---

2. Robert Woodward, *Ivan Bunin: A Study of His Fiction* (Chapel Hill: University of North Carolina Press, 1980), 13.

3. Ibid., 15.

4. Thomas Gaiton Marullo, *Ivan Bunin: From the Other Shore, 1920–1933* (Chicago: Ivan R. Dee, 1995), 24.

5. Woodward, *Bunin*, 14.

the new arbitrators of Russian culture.[6] The true heir to Tolstoy and Chekhov, they argued, had fled the Soviet state and now existed—and thrived—in direct opposition to those who had seized his homeland.

While living and writing in France, Bunin also began to gain recognition beyond the Russian diaspora. In the 1920s a wide array of important Western literary figures, including André Gide, D. H. Lawrence, Thomas Mann, and Rainer Maria Rilke, became champions of his work, and critics writing in English-language newspapers periodically expressed an almost breathless excitement over this newly discovered émigré author. "When 'The Gentleman from San Francisco' first appeared (in English), we felt as if a new planet had swum into our ken," a British reviewer wrote in 1922. "It is . . . without a doubt one of the finest short stories . . . of modern times."[7]

Bunin's acclaim reached its apogee in 1933, when he became the thirty-second writer in history to receive the Nobel Prize for literature.[8] For years he had dreamed of receiving the prize, only to suffer bitter disappointments; now, at last, he'd achieved his highest aspirations, and after years of struggle and obscurity the exiled author was an international celebrity. Publishers throughout the world sought new manuscripts and new translations of his work; photographers crowded around him like a film star on the streets, and more than eight hundred congratulatory telegrams were delivered to his home in France in the days following the announcement of the prize.[9] For the Russian émigré community, Bunin's victory was particularly sweet. "In these days, when it seems we have lost everything, is not our Russian language the only treasure we have left?" wrote Zinaida Gippius, another well-known Russian writer in exile. "Bunin personifies for émigrés the last and most valuable part of a Russia that can never be taken away from us. That is why his victory . . . is so close to the heart of the emigration; that is why it has caused so much universal joy."[1]

Sadly, however, the benefits of the prize for Bunin proved fleeting in many ways. The surge in demand for manuscripts and translations failed to produce a sustained readership in the West, and the author's largest audience, the millions of Russians living in the Soviet Union, re-

6. Ibid., 16.
7. Quoted in Marullo, *Bunin: From the Other Shore*, 84.
8. Ibid., 270.
9. Ibid.
1. Ibid., 284.

mained inaccessible. Indeed, Joseph Stalin's effort to eradicate Bunin from the consciousness of his compatriots reached Orwellian heights after 1928, when the author's books were removed from Soviet libraries and destroyed, and reference to Bunin by name became a punishable offense.[2] At the same time, after 1933 Bunin's relationship with the émigré community grew increasingly complex. While still a favorite son, the Nobel laureate disappointed many of his fellow exiles by refusing to make himself a full-time figurehead for the cause of "Russia Abroad." More and more, his need for a quiet place outside the limelight set him at odds with more active émigrés, who sought—indeed, often demanded—his constant participation in their war of public relations with the Soviet Union. Perhaps most significantly, Bunin soon spent or gave away almost all the money he had been awarded in Stockholm. Deeply distressed by the plight of Russian émigrés, he donated large portions of his prize money to refugee assistance funds.[3] And, like a true aristocrat, he gave substantial sums to needy friends, made numerous bad investments, and repeatedly fell victim to swindlers. As early as June 1934 he wrote to a friend, "No one believes me when I tell them I have no money, but I am telling the truth: I do not have any. . . ."[4]

World War II would plunge the Bunins back into cruelly familiar conditions of deprivation. Bunin ardently opposed the fascists and, as an act of protest, refused to publish during the occupation of France. Consequently he and Vera Nikolaevna had almost no income,[5] surviving for several years on meager rations and the few vegetables they managed to grow in their garden. (A writer living in France at the time recalls being told of Bunin "wandering on the slope alongside his home, cutting the grass with scissors to make soup."[6]) Despite this, they sheltered and fed several friends and writers, aided Russian prisoners of war brought by the Germans to Grasse, and protected Jews from arrest and deportation by hiding them in their home throughout the war.[7] Bunin believed it was immoral to be silent before the evil of fascism and denounced Hitler and Mussolini repeatedly in public, to the considerable alarm of friends

---

2. Yury Maltsev, *Bunin* (Frankfurt, Moscow: Possev-Verlag, 1987), 6.
3. Thomas Gaiton Marullo, *Ivan Bunin: The Twilight of Emigré Russia, 1934–1953* (Chicago: Ivan R. Dee, 2002), 46.
4. Ibid., 51.
5. Woodward, *Bunin*, 17.
6. Quoted in Marullo, *Bunin: Twilight*, 214.
7. Ibid., 21.

and family.[8] Remarkably, he also continued to write. Cold, malnour-ished, weak, and long ago cut off from his homeland, he huddled over his desk, often wearing a hat and gloves, and described not the horrors of humanity or the end of civilization but rather a Russian girl whose whole body seemed to sway under a yellow *sarafan* when she walked, quail calling cheerfully from sopped rye after a thunderstorm, and jack-daws perched on the blood-red walls of a convent in Moscow. "How do I live?" he had written earlier in his diary, "I keep remembering and re-membering. . . ."[9]

In retrospect it almost seems that "The Scent of Apples," one of Bunin's first, great renderings of a disappearing life, was actually a kind of model—a trial run or a practice exercise—for the greater challenge of preserving even larger and more diverse components of Russia—its great cathedrals, city streets and squares, its riverboats, railroads, and cafés, its peasant speech and popular sayings—in equally vivid, regenerative lan-guage that could withstand the vagaries of exile and the horrors of an-other world war. For often this is what it seems Bunin set out to do after fleeing Russia: depict his homeland with such intensity and precision that his words could bring it back in true, physical form despite the time and distance that lay between the author and his subject. It is perhaps this remarkable ability to call up and distill the past, to preserve experi-ence in the alembic of language that prompted André Gide to write in a public letter to Bunin, "Your inner world . . . has triumphed over the ex-ternal one. For you, it is the true reality."[1]

The final result of these efforts would be thirty-seven stories, most of which depict intense, fleeting, and often erotic affairs. Bunin titled the collection *Dark Avenues* and finally published it in its entirety in 1946. "It is the best and most original thing I have written," he declared,[2] and today most critics and scholars agree that these stories mark the cul-mination of Bunin's art. Tragically, however, *Dark Avenues* received vir-tually no serious critical attention during Bunin's lifetime. While a few friends and fellow writers recognized the book's originality, many of Bunin's previous admirers were too shocked by its bold depictions of sex-uality to consider any of the work's literary merits. The failure of *Dark*

---

8. Ibid., 20.

9. Quoted in Thomas Gaiton Marullo, *Ivan Bunin: Russian Requiem, 1885–1920* (Chicago: Ivan R. Dee, 1993), 243.

1. Quoted in Marullo, *Bunin: Twilight*, 357.

2. Connolly, *Bunin*, 134.

Avenues was a final, heavy blow for the author. He and Vera Nikolaevna had never recovered financially from the war, and soon both began to suffer chronic illnesses that added mounting medical bills to their troubles. When *Dark Avenues* failed to generate even a modest income, Bunin was reduced to begging friends and admirers for help, his shame and humiliation mounting with each plea for money. Seven years after the publication of his last collection of short stories, the Nobel laureate died in Paris, impoverished and largely forgotten.

Since his death, Bunin has found a lasting place in Russia's literary canon. The author was posthumously "rehabilitated" in 1955, and his works were subsequently read and studied throughout the Soviet Union. Today his stories remain a standard feature of any Russian school's curriculum, and his major writings are as well known as those of Chekhov and Turgenev among his countrymen. One can only imagine how pleased and gratified Bunin would have been to see this lasting recognition of his work in the country he loved so passionately and missed so painfully through thirty years of exile.

Despite his stature in Russia today, Bunin remains relatively unknown in the West. Several new translations of his stories and numerous insightful studies of his work have appeared in recent years, but in the United States Bunin's readership remains largely limited to specialists and students of Russian culture. In significant part, I would argue, this stems from the problems of translation. Many of the most compelling aspects of Bunin's writings are deeply resistant to English-language renderings of his work.

In this regard it is difficult to overstate the importance of poetry. Although it was his prose that made him famous, Bunin referred to himself as a poet throughout his life and claimed never to recognize a sharp distinction between the two forms. He once boasted to another writer that he could have written all his stories in verse,[3] and he insisted that one must find the proper register, the correct sound in order to compose in prose. ". . . The general sound of the piece is created in the very beginning phrase of the work," he notes in an essay titled "How I Write." "Yes, the first phrase is decisive. If you don't manage to capture that primordial sound correctly, then you . . . get all tangled up and set aside what you started, or just throw it away as useless."[4] Not surprisingly, Russian

3. See Marullo, *Bunin: From the Other Shore*, 136.
4. Ivan Bunin, *Kak Ya Pishy (How I Write)*, in I. A. Bunin, *Sobraniye sochineny v chetyrekh tomakh* (Moskva: Pravda, 1988) v. 1, 18.

critics invariably point out the musicality of Bunin's prose as one of its most striking features.

Further, Bunin is a deeply imagistic writer. It could be said that images rather than events or characters are the driving force behind most of his narratives. Even such novellas as "Mitya's Love" and "Sukhodol," replete with murder, sex, and madness, derive their greatest force and energy from the author's heady recreations of sensory experience and his lyrical descriptions of weather, land, and light. Similarly, the great power of "The Gentleman from San Francisco" stems not from the story's single dramatic event but from its deeply resonant descriptions of everything from a caged parrot to an ocean liner; "Sunstroke" is a highly detailed account of its protagonist wandering alone through an unnamed town on the Volga, and "Late Hour" is a loosely structured, impressionistic meditation on young love. While other, later works such as "Tanya" (1940), "Rusya" (1940), "Cleansing Monday" (1944), and "Zoyka and Valeriya" (1940) are rich in drama, their specific images— Moscow streets on a winter evening, cranes in a marsh in late summer, a dacha's grounds at night—remain more powerfully stamped in the reader's memory than any single plot line. All this means that language is of utmost importance throughout Bunin's work, for it is only with this raw material that compelling images are created. And unlike Chekhov or Tolstoy, Bunin calls attention to his words. He wants the reader to be aware of them, to feel them on the tongue, to recognize their weight and resonance. Consequently Bunin's stories suffer badly if we preserve in translation their major events but lose their manner of depiction.

This dilemma becomes particularly acute with the stories of *Dark Avenues*, where the structure of Bunin's prose is perhaps most deeply linked to its meaning.[5] At their core, almost all the stories in this collection are concerned with the human struggle to preserve moments of happiness against the relentless, forward march of time (a struggle described by the captain some twenty-five years earlier in "Chang's Dreams"). Throughout the collection, Bunin's protagonists undergo moments of intense joy and fulfillment, only to see these pleasures eradicated by death or other tragic changes in their circumstances. In portraying these moments, Bunin often inserts extensive descriptive detail between the key grammatical components of his sentences. A thirty-word phrase containing information only tangentially related to the

5. See Woodward, *Bunin*, 218.

main clause, for instance, may separate a participle from its object or a subject from its predicate. In Russian, as in Latin and German, a word's form rather than its position in a sentence indicates its grammatical function, so this intervening information does not create confusion for Bunin's native audience. Rather, these passages unfold during a kind of lull—the Russian reader knows he will return to finish the clause that has begun, but in the meanwhile he can comfortably absorb the new information as it plays out during a break in the sentence's main action. It is an effect that some have compared to retardation and resolution in music,[6] and Bunin uses it with enormous skill, creating an extended pause in the normal, forward movement of key sentences in order to dwell on particularly rich and important moments in the lives of his protagonists. In doing so, he seems to lift these instances out of time; they occur in a space between clauses, separated from the usual linear rush of events, closed off in a kind of syntactic harbor. Here, in other words, Bunin's writing mirrors precisely the content of his stories: just as the protagonist longs to suspend a moment in time, the author's syntax frees it from the normal forward push of language on the page. Conversely, later Bunin uses short, impersonal sentences to undercut this effect of timelessness by announcing the story's (invariably) tragic denouement with clipped, impersonal neutrality. Thus, just as Bunin's phrasing briefly allows his protagonist to linger outside time, so too does the author's language later embody the silence and oblivion of time's ultimate incontrovertibility.

Elements such as these in Bunin's artistry confound his translator. How does one preserve the musicality and resonance of the text if one can no longer use words that sound like the Russian original? How does one recreate narrative structures that are inherently linked to the formal properties of the author's native language? And if these elements are lost entirely, to what degree can we say Bunin has been translated?

In the translations that follow, I have attempted to resolve these questions through constant compromise, weighing the demands of literal accuracy with the need to preserve, in some fashion, the more elusive but equally important stylistic elements of Bunin's writing. In doing so, I have allowed myself at times to break up and rearrange sentences in order to create linguistic effects in English that resemble those of the

---

6. See Werner Winter, "Impossibilities of Translation," in *The Craft and Context of Translation* (Austin: University of Texas Press, 1961).

original, even if the forms producing these effects vary considerably from the original forms. Where a literal translation of a Russian phrase would result in a flat English cliché—a cliché that does not mar the original—I have attempted to find a close alternative that remains true to the spirit of the Russian. In instances where the repeated use of multiple modifiers would transform a richly textured Russian sentence into something ungainly and overwrought in English, I have tried to redistribute the weight of the modifiers or to use one adjective that may adequately substitute for two. All of this means that readers will not find an exact replica of Bunin's prose in the pages that follow. I hope, however, they will encounter some slight echo of its music and its grace that has previously gone unregistered.

IVAN BUNIN
COLLECTED STORIES

The Scent of Apples

T HE EARLY DAYS of a lovely autumn come back to me. In August there were warm and gentle rains—rains that seemed to fall deliberately to help the sowing, coming in the middle of the month, near the holiday of St. Lavrenty. People in the country always say that fall and winter will not quarrel if the water's still and the rain is soft on St. Lavrenty's Day. During the warm days of *babye leto*, the gossamer was thick in the fields, and this too is a good sign—another promise of fine weather in the fall. . . . I remember a fresh and quiet morning. . . . The big garden, its dry and thinned-out leaves turning golden in the early light. I remember the avenue of maples, the delicate smell of the fallen leaves, and the scent of autumn apples—*antonovkas*, that mix of honey and fall freshness. . . . The air's so clear it seems there is no air at all. The sounds of squeaking carts and voices drift distinctly through the garden: it's the traders from the city. They've hired some of the local *mouzhiki* to pack up apples that they'll send to the city during the night—invariably the trip is made at night, when it's so wonderful to lie on a pile of apples and stare at the stars, smell the scent of tar in the fresh air, listen to the cautious squeaking of the loaded carts as they move in a long line through the darkness on the big road. The *mouzhik* who loads the apples eats them one after another with a crisp and succulent crunching, but the trader never tries to change such habits. Instead he says, "Go ahead, eat your fill! Everyone deserves a little of the extra honey!"

The morning's cool silence is broken only by the sated, throaty calls of thrushes from a mountain ash that's turned as red as coral in the garden thicket, and the muffled rumbling of apples being poured into measuring boxes and barrels. Through the thinned-out trees you can see far down the big road that's strewn with straw. It leads to the hut where the trader has set up an entire household for the summer. The scent of apples hangs everywhere, but there the smell's especially strong. They've set up beds inside the hut. A single-barreled shotgun leans against a wall not far from a tarnished samovar. Dishes are stacked in the corner. In the yard outside lie bits of matting, crates, and tattered cloth; a fireplace for cooking has been dug into the ground. Here a splendid pork-fat stew simmers at midday, and the samovar is heated in the evening, its long ribbon of blue smoke stretching out among the trees. On holidays the yard beside the hut is like a market square; every minute customers in bright attire flit past the trees. Wearing *sarafans* that smell of dye, the daughters of the *odnodvortsy* gather in a lively little group; servants from the manor houses come dressed in coarse and pretty, almost atavistic suits. The young wife of the village elder appears as well. Pregnant, with a wide, sleepy face, she projects the self-importance of a pedigreed cow. Each of her two braids has been wrapped around the sides of her headdress, then covered with several scarves. It's a style known as "horns," and it makes her head appear enormous. Wearing half-boots with strips of steel along the heels, she plants her feet and stands with dumb placidity, her figure draped in a long apron and a sleeveless gown of velveteen, a violet skirt with brick-red stripes and golden lace (which she pronounces "lice") along its hem.

"Now there's a little lady with real presence!" the trader says of her, shaking his head. "You don't see many like that anymore. . . ."

Hatless, towheaded boys in short pants and white canvas shirts come steadily in groups of twos and threes, shuffling their feet in rapid, light succession while watching from the corners of their eyes the shaggy German Shepherd tied to a nearby apple tree. Only one of them, of course, buys anything, and even he spends just one kopeck, or offers up an egg as barter. But there are many customers, and the buying's brisk: in his red boots and long frock coat, the consumptive trader is happy.

His brother, a burring, lively semi-imbecile, lives with him "out of charity," and together they trade jokes and silly phrases as they sell their wares; sometimes the trader even "fingers out a tune" on his accordion. And so a crowd remains all day around the hut, and you can hear among the garden trees the laughter and the voices, sometimes the rhythmic tread of dancing until dusk. . . .

In fair weather the air turns sharply colder as night comes on; dew weighs down the grass. Having breathed your fill of the rye scent that rises from the new straw and the chaff in the threshing barn, you head home to dinner, walking briskly past the garden's earthen wall. Voices in the village, the squeak of a closing gate—everything resounds with rare and sharp precision in the freezing final glow of dusk. Then full dark falls. And still another smell: someone's lit a fire in the garden. The sweet smoke of burning cherry limbs wafts heavily toward you. And in the darkness, in the depth of the garden, you witness something from a childhood tale: crimson flames blaze like a corner of hell near the hut, surrounded by the gloom. And like something carved from ebony, the black silhouettes of people move around the fire while their gigantic shadows lurch across the apple trees. One's almost completely covered by a massive arm that's several meters long; then the shadows of two legs appear like huge black columns. And suddenly it all slips from the trees—the shadows seem to merge and fall straight down the avenue, stretching from the trader's hut to the front gate. . . .

Late at night, when all the village lights are out, and the seven stars of the Pleiades hang like gems in the sky, you run once more into the garden. Rustling among the fallen leaves, you blindly make your way toward the hut. In the clearing there it grows a little lighter; the whiteness of the Milky Way spreads out overhead. . . .

"Is that you, *barchuk?*" someone calls out from the dark.

"Yes, it's me. . . . Aren't you sleeping, Nikolay?"

"Sleep's not for us, sir. . . . But it must be late already. . . . Seems the night train's coming now."

We listen for a long time, eventually discern a trembling in the ground. The trembling turns into a noise, and soon it seems the train wheels are pounding out their rapid measure just beyond the garden: rumbling and knocking, the engine flies toward us . . . closer, closer, ever louder and more furious . . . until its roaring suddenly subsides, dies off, as if the cars had sunk into the earth. . . .

"Where's your gun, Nikolay?"

"Here, sir, beside the crate. . . ."

You point the single-barreled shotgun up—it's as heavy as a crowbar—and pull the trigger on an impulse: a crimson flame shoots toward the sky with a deafening bang, blinds you for a moment, puts out all the stars—and then a cheerful echo comes crashing out, rolls along the horizon like a wheel, slowly, slowly fades away in the sharp, clean air. . . .

"Well done!" says the trader. "Give them a jolt, *barchuk*! Give them a good scare! That's the only thing they understand! They shook down all the pears already at the garden wall!"

Falling stars etch their paths with burning streaks into the sky's blackness. For a long time you look into its blue-black depths, its dense array of constellations—and then the earth begins to drift beneath your feet. You rouse yourself. Hide your hands inside your sleeves, run fast along the avenue toward the manor house. . . . How cold it is! How heavy the dew! How good it is to live on earth!

II

"Good *antonovkas* bring good years." Everything's in order in the village if there's a healthy crop of *antonovkas*: it means the wheat is also healthy, and the coming harvest will be plentiful. . . . I remember a year of rich harvests.

In the early dawn, while roosters are still crowing and black smoke rises from the chimneys of the peasant huts, you throw open the window that looks out onto the garden: it is filled with a lilac shade, through which falls the morning sun in random, brilliant spots. It's impossible to wait: you order that a horse be saddled, then run down to the pond to wash. The willows on the banks have lost almost all their leaves, and now their limbs are visible against the turquoise sky. The water below them is icy, limpid, somehow heavier than usual: immediately it takes away the sluggishness of night. And then—after washing, after joining the workers in the servants' hall to eat black bread and hot potatoes with large, damp grains of salt—how good it is to feel the leather saddle shift beneath you as you ride through Vyselki on your way to hunt. Autumn is a time of many holidays and festivals. People put on their best clothes; they appear well kept and satisfied. The village looks completely different than it does at other times of year. And if the harvest has been good, if mounds of grain have risen on the threshing floors like golden cities on a plain while the early-morning cackling of geese continues sharp and clear upon the river, village life is far from bad. And Vyselki has been known throughout the ages as a place of great prosperity; since grandfather's days it's been famous for its "riches." Old men and women lived long lives there—the first true sign that a village is well off—and they were always tall and strapping, their hair as white as down. "Oh yes," you'd overhear a person saying. "Agafya just finished off her eighty-third year." Or a conversation along these lines:

"When will you die, Pankrat? You must be getting on toward a hundred."

"What's that you say, sir, if you'll permit me?"

"I was asking your age—how old are you?"

"I don't know, sir."

"Well, do you remember Platon Apollonych?"

"Oh yes, of course. Like yesterday."

"Then—you see?—you have to be at least a hundred."

A sheepish smile passes briefly across the old man's face as he stands rigidly before the master. What can he say, after all? He's guilty. He's lived far more than his fair share. And if he hadn't stuffed himself with onions on St. Peter's Day, he'd probably go on living even longer.

I remember his old wife. She always sat on a little bench on the porch, hunched over, shaking her head, gasping for breath as she clung to her seat with her hands—and always, it seemed, thinking about something. "About her valuables, I'll bet," the village women liked to say, for she did indeed have quite a few possessions locked away in trunks. She would act as if she hadn't heard a word, stare blindly off into the distance with her eyebrows sadly raised, shake her head and struggle, evidently, to revive some distant memory. She was tall and dark. Her skirt was almost from another century; her rope shoes were strictly for the dead. The skin around her neck had turned dry and yellow, but she always kept her blouse—with its little, inlaid triangles of colored linen—a perfect, flawless white. "Good enough for getting buried in." A large stone lay near the porch: she'd bought it herself for her grave, just as she had bought a shroud, a lovely one, with angles and crosses, prayers inscribed along its edges.

The peasant houses in Vyselki were well suited to those older residents, for they'd been built of brick back in the days of our grandfathers. It wasn't customary for married sons to split off land from their fathers' plots in Vyselki, and therefore wealthy peasants—Savely, Ignat, Dron—had cottages comprised of two or three large sections to hold their growing families. They raised bees, kept their estates in careful order, took pride in their steel-grey stallions. Their threshing floors were often packed with thick bundles of rich, dark hemp. They had barns and sheds with well-thatched roofs, storerooms with iron doors protecting bolts of canvas, spinning wheels, new sheepskin coats, harness plates, and barrels bound with copper rings. Their sleds and gates had crucifixes burnt into their wood. There was a time when I found nothing more alluring than the life of a *mouzhik*. Riding through the village on a sunny morning, you'd think, how good to take a scythe into the fields, to thresh the wheat, to sleep on sacks of straw on the threshing floor, to get up with the sun on holidays as church bells ring, their weighty and melodic notes pouring through the village. How good to wash from a barrel, dress in a shirt and pants of simple linen, wear those indestructible boots with steel along the heels. And if you add to this a pretty, healthy wife dressed in holiday attire, a trip to Mass, then lunch at the home of your bearded father-in-law—a lunch of hot mutton served on wooden plates with sifted-flour bread, with honey from the comb, and homemade beer—one could wish for nothing more.

Until quite recently (in days that even I recall), the rural household of an average noble family resembled that of the wealthy peasants in its economy, prosperity, and rustic, old-world charm. Such was the estate of my aunt, Anna Gerasimovna, who lived twelve *versts* from Vyselki. . . . Riding at a walk to keep from wearing out the dogs you take along, you never reach her house much before midday. . . . And you don't want to hurry—it's lovely in those open fields on a cool and sunny day! You can see far into the distance across the level plains. The sky is light—a deep, expansive blue. Carts and carriages have smoothed out the road since the rains, and now its oily-looking surface gleams like metal rails in the bright sun that slopes across it. All around you spreads the winter wheat in triangulated fields of rich, green shoots. A young hawk rises out of nowhere, hovers over something, fluttering its small, sharp wings in the transparent air. Telegraph poles lead far into the clear distance; like silver strings their wires curve along the sloping edge of the sky. Merlins perch on them in rows like sharp black notes written on a sheet of music.

I never knew or witnessed serfdom, but I remember feeling it, somehow, at Aunt Anna Gerasimovna's. As soon as you ride into the courtyard, you feel it there—feel it vividly. The estate's not large, but all of it is aged and solid, surrounded by willow trees and birches that are at least a century old. Many buildings stand inside the courtyard, small and neat, with uniformly dark oak walls and roofs of thatch. Only the servants' house, its walls going black with time, stands out from the other buildings because of its size—or more precisely, its length. The sole remaining household serfs of Russia peep out from its entrance like the last of the Mohicans: a few decrepit men and women, and a retired, senile cook who looks like Don Quixote. They draw themselves up very straight, then bow low, almost to the ground, as you ride into the yard. Coming for your horse, the grey-haired driver removes his hat while still beside the carriage house, then passes through the entire yard with nothing on his head. He was once my aunt's postillion, but now he drives her to church in a covered sleigh in winter, or a rugged little trap with metal bracing—like those preferred by priests—in summer. My aunt's garden is well known for its neglected state, its nightingales, its turtledoves, and its apples; her house is famous for its roof. The house stands at the top of the courtyard, just before the garden, encircled by the limbs of linden trees. Its walls are thick and rather small, but the roof—a hardened, dense, and blackened layer of thatch that had been pitched at an extraordinarily steep angle—gives the house an air of indestructibility: it seems impervious to time. I always had the sense it was alive: the front façade resembled an old face staring out from under an enormous hat with sunken, nacreous eyes—years of rain and sun had made the windows iridescent. Two porches jutted out from either side of that façade— large, old-fashioned porches with tall columns. Well-fed pigeons squatted on their pediments while thousands of sparrows moved like sudden bursts of rain from one roof to another. . . . It's comfortable there, in that nest beneath autumn's turquoise sky.

You notice first the scent of apples as you go into the house, and then the other smells: old furniture made of mahogany, dried-out linden flowers that were scattered on the windowsills in June. . . . In all the rooms—the entranceway, the drawing room, the dining hall—it's dark and cool, for the house is surrounded by the garden, and the windows' upper panes hold glass that's colored blue or violet. The rooms are quiet and clean, though you have the odd impression that all the armchairs, the inlaid tables, the mirrors in their narrow, twisted frames of gold might never had been moved from the places they now occupy. You hear someone coughing, and your aunt comes in. She's small, but, like everything around her, solid. She wears a large Persian shawl around her shoulders. She approaches you with both formality and friendliness, and soon, amid the steady stream of talk about bygone days and legacies, she begins inviting you to eat: pears at first, and then four kinds of apples—*antonovkas, plodovitkas, borovinkas,* and *belle barynyas.* All of this is followed by a remarkable meal: pink ham with peas, stuffed chicken, turkey, pickled vegetables, red *kvass*—strong, sweet *kvass.* The windows are open on the garden. . . . The cool and bracing air of fall drifts in. . . .

III

The spirits of the disappearing, landed gentry have been buoyed by just one thing in recent years: hunting.

In earlier days, estates like Anna Gerasimovna's were no great rarity. And there were noble families with larger holdings—huge manor houses, fifty-acre gardens—who kept on living lavishly even while descending toward bankruptcy. To be sure, a few of these estates still exist today, but all of them are lifeless now. . . . There are no *troikas,* no Kirghiz saddle horses, no borzois or hunting hounds, no household serfs, no owners to command it all—no landed devotees of hunting like Arseny Semyonych, the late brother of my wife.

At the end of September our threshing floors and gardens emptied out, turned bare; the weather changed dramatically. For entire days the wind battered and tore at the trees; rain poured down on them from morning until night. Sometimes toward evening the low sun's trembling, golden rays broke through the gloomy clouds in the west; then the air seemed particularly sharp and clear, and the light was blinding when it fell among the last few leaves and branches, which jumped and twitched like nets the wind had brought to life. The sky's damp blue shone cold and clear above leaden clouds in the north while white clouds slowly surfaced from beneath them like a snowy mountain crest breaking into view. . . . Standing at the window, you think that with a little luck it may turn clear. But the wind does not subside. It harries the garden, tears apart the ribbons of smoke rising from the servants' hall, drives together ashen, ragged, and foreboding clouds that sail in low and fast and soon obscure the sun—blot its light like heavy smoke, close that little window of blue sky. . . . Once more the garden seems abandoned, sullen. . . . And then the clouds begin to scatter drops of rain. . . . Quietly they fall at first, uneasily. . . . Then steadily they gather weight, turn into a driving stream, a storm that shakes the trees and makes the sky go even blacker. A long, uneasy night begins.

After such a thrashing, the garden trees are almost bare, quiet and resigned among the wet and scattered leaves. But how beautiful they are when clear weather comes again, when those cold transparent days begin October, that final marvel of the season. Any leaves remaining on the trees will now last until the first snow. The black garden will shine beneath a cold and turquoise autumn sky while waiting peacefully for winter days and warming itself in the distant sun. And already the fields are turning black beneath the plows or green with brilliant shoots of winter wheat. . . . The time for hunting has begun!

And so I see myself at the estate of Arseny Semyonych, in the dining hall of his large house. It's filled with sunlight and smoke from countless pipes and cigarettes. All the people in the crowd have tanned and wind-chapped faces, wear warm vests and high-cut boots. They've just had a filling lunch. They're flushed from loud and animated talk about the coming hunt, and though they've finished with their food, they make a point to drink until the vodka's gone. Someone blows a horn outside in the courtyard; dogs begin to howl in varied tones. Arseny Semyonych's favorite dog, a black borzoi, climbs onto the table and begins to eat leftover rabbit meat and sauce from the plates, but then lets out a terrified yelp and scrambles from the table, turning over plates and glasses: carrying a pistol and a hunting crop from his study, Arseny Semyonych deafens the hall with a sudden shot. Even more smoke fills the room as he stands before the guests and laughs.

"Missed. Too bad," he says, his eyes flashing.

He's tall and lean but broad-shouldered, graceful, strongly built. He's dressed comfortably in a shirt of crimson silk, tall boots and wide-cut velvet pants; he has a handsome gypsy's face. Something wild gleams in his eyes. Having startled his dog and all his guests with the pistol shot, he begins to recite in a deep baritone, his voice both earnest and amused:

> Let us saddle now our waiting horses,
> Sling our horns across our shoulders . . .

And then breaks off, says loudly: "But let's not waste our time—the day is short!"

I still remember how greedily I breathed, how capaciously my young lungs inhaled the cold and damp, clean air as I rode late in the afternoon with Arseny Semyonych's noisy hunting party, excited by the scattered barking of the dogs set loose to rove through some stretch of land known as Red Knoll or Rustling Copse, place names that alone could stir a hunter's blood. . . . You ride a Kirghiz saddle horse; he's powerful, thick-set, ill-willed, and you keep the reins in tight; it feels as if your body's al-most joined to his. He snorts, urges you to let him trot, his hooves loudly stirring loose beds of blackened leaves, every noise resounding dimly in the empty, cold, damp woods. A dog yelps somewhere in the distance, another answers it with anguished zeal, a third—and suddenly the woods reverberate as if they're made of glass with shouts and fervid baying. A shot rings out amid the uproar, and everything breaks loose, goes tearing, rolling off into the distance.

"Look sharp!" someone shouts through all the woods in a despair-ing voice.

"Look sharp"—the words pass through your mind like a drunken thought. You let out a shout to the horse, go flying through the woods as if you've snapped free from a chain, discerning nothing in the blur but trees that flit before your eyes and mud that flecks your face from the churning hooves. You burst out of the woods and see a mottled, strung-out pack of dogs running through the plains, and spur the Kirghiz even harder, race to cut the quarry off, storming over plots of plowed-up earth and stubble, fields of new green wheat—and then plunge into another woodland, lose the pack and all its frenzied noise. You're damp with sweat; your body trembles with excitement and exertion as you rein in the foaming, wheezing horse and breathe the icy dampness of the forest valley. The baying dogs and hunters' shouts drift off into the distance. Dead silence spreads around you. The forest floor's uncluttered; the tall trees stand motionless. It's as if you've entered some forbidden hall. The heavy scent of mushrooms, rotting leaves, wet bark rises from the gullies. And the dampness rising with that scent grows ever more perceptible. . . . The woods are turning dark and cold. . . . It's time to find a place to spend the night. But gathering the dogs is hard. For a long time the horns blow forlornly in the woods; for a long time yelps and shouts, curses drift among the trees. . . . And finally, already in full darkness, the hunting party streams into the estate of some bachelor you barely know, the riders' noise filling up the courtyard, which now is lit by lamps and candles carried out to greet the guests.

Sometimes a hunting party would stay for several days in the home of a generous host. At early dawn the hunters would go out again in an icy wind and the first wet snow, ride through the forests and fields, and then, as dusk approached, return, covered in grime, red-faced, smelling of their horses' sweat and the hide of the slaughtered prey. Then the drinking bouts began. The bright and crowded manor house was always warm after a full day spent in the open cold. . . . Everyone wanders from room to room with their thick vests unbuttoned. They drink and eat without ceremony, noisily exchanging impressions of the slain, full-grown wolf that now lies in the middle of the hall, its teeth bared and its eyes rolled back, its thick and airy tail lying to one side, its cold, pale blood darkening the floor. After vodka and a meal, you slip into a state of such sweet somnolence, such languid, youthful drowsiness, that all the conversations seem to drift to you through water. Your face burns from the wind. If you close your eyes, the earth begins to float beneath you. And when you finally lie down in some corner room in the ancient house—a room with icons and icon lamps and a soft feather bed—a horse still seems to run beneath you, all your body aches, and dogs with flaming coats drift before your eyes. And yet you don't notice that you're drowsing off with these strange sights and feelings, don't realize that you're slipping into a healthy, restful sleep, forgetting even that this room was once a chapel for the owner of the estate, an old man whose name is bound to grisly legends from the days of serfdom, and who died here, in this room, quite likely in this very bed.

Sometimes it happens that you oversleep and miss the hunt. And then your rest is particularly pleasant. You wake up and lie in bed for a long time. All the house is quiet. You can hear the gardener as he walks carefully from room to room, heating up the stoves; you can hear the pop and sputter of the burning wood. The estate's been boarded up for winter, and now a completely idle day spreads before you in the silence. You dress slowly, wander in the garden, find a cold, wet apple that's been forgotten among the leaves. For some reason it's remarkably delicious; it seems unlike any other apple. . . . And then you settle down among the books—books from our grandfathers' days, with thick leather bindings and little gold stars on their Moroccan spines. How wonderful they smell! Like prayer books from a church with their yellowed, rough, and heavy pages! A pleasant, slightly sour mustiness laced with old perfume. . . . And how good it is to see the notes written in their margins, a large and gently rounded script from a goose quill pen. . . . You open up a volume, read: "An idea worthy of ancient and new philosophers, the light of reason and true feeling . . ." And inadvertently you find yourself caught up in the book—*The Gentleman Philosopher*, an allegory printed some hundred years ago by the state board of charity with funding from "a highly decorated citizen." It tells the story of a gentleman philosopher who, "possessing time and the ability to reason well, set out to test those heights to which the human intellect might ascend, and built a model of the universe on his land. . . ." Then you come across the *Satirical and Philosophical Writings of M. Voltaire*, and for a long time relish the quaintly mannered style of the translation: "My sovereign lords: Erasmus was pleased to compose a tribute to buffoonery in the 16th century [semi-colon—an affected pause]; now you command that I extol reason and its virtues here before you. . . ." Then you move from Catherine's time to the Romantics, to almanacs, and finally to long and sentimental, slightly pompous novels. . . . The cuckoo darts out of the clock and sings above you with a mix of ridicule and sorrow in the empty house. A strange, sweet sadness starts to gather in your heart.

Here you come across *The Secrets of Aleksis*; then it's *Victor, or a Child in the Forest*. You read: "The clock strikes midnight. A sacred silence takes the place of the day's noise and the peasants' happy songs. Sleep spreads dark wings above the surface of our hemisphere, shakes dreams and darkness down from them. . . . Dreams. . . . How often are they a mere continuation of suffering for the forsaken. . . ." And cherished, time-worn words begin to flash before your eyes: crag and oak, pale moon and loneliness, spirits, specters, *eroty*, roses and lilies, "the pranks and gambols of misbehaving youths," arms as white as ivory, Lyudmilas and Alinas. . . . And here are journals with the names of Zhukovsky, Batyushkov, Pushkin in his student years. With sadness you remember your grandmother, how she played a polonaise on the clavichord, how she languidly recited lines from *Evgeny Onegin*. And that dreamy, antiquated world rises up before you. . . . How lovely they were, the women and girls who lived on those estates! Now they look down at me from portraits on the wall: aristocratic, beautiful, their hair arranged in old-world styles. With diffidence and grace, they lower their sad and tender eyes behind long lashes. . . .

IV

The aroma of *antonovkas* is disappearing from estates and country houses. We lived those days not long ago, and yet it seems a hundred years have passed since then. All the old people of Vyselki have died off.

Anna Gerasimovna is dead. Arseny Semyonych shot himself. Now begins the age of petty farms, owners on the verge of abject poverty. But even those impoverished lives are good!

And so I see myself once more in the country. Deep fall. Cloudy, dove-grey days. Mornings I ride into the fields with a dog, a gun, a hunting horn. The wind blows hard, head on, whistling and humming in the barrel of the gun, dry snow swirling in its stream at times. All day I wander among the empty plains. . . . Hungry, chilled to the bone, I return toward dusk, and when the small lights of Vyselki begin to flicker in the distance, when I smell the smoke of kitchen fires from the manor house, happiness and warmth begin to rise in me. I remember how they liked to sit and talk with the lamps unlit, watching the dusk fade away as evening spread throughout our house. Coming inside, I notice that the double panes have been put back in all the windows in anticipation of the growing cold, and this adds even more to the mood of quiet winter calm. A worker is heating the stove in the hall. I squat the way I used to as a child beside a mound of straw, smell its winter freshness, watch the blazing fire, watch the window where the bluing dusk is sadly dying out. Then I walk into the servants' kitchen. Here it's bright and crowded: girls are chopping cabbage. I listen as their flashing knives tap out a fast and friendly rhythm, and they sing their poignant village songs in harmony. . . . Sometimes the owner of a small estate comes to take me to his farm for several days. . . . And the life of the petty landowner is also good!

He wakes up early, stretches soundly, rises, rolls himself a thick cigarette of cheap tobacco. The pale November dawn reveals a simple study; other than a pair of stiff and yellowed fox hides nailed above the bed, the walls are bare. A stocky figure in wide-cut pants and a long, unbelted shirt stands before the mirror, his sleepy face with slightly Tatar features hanging in the glass. Dead silence fills the warm and half-dark house. The old cook who's lived here since her childhood lies snoring in the corridor beyond the door, but this does not prevent my host from shouting in a hoarse voice that penetrates every corner of the house:

"Lukerya! Samovar!"

Having pulled on boots and wrapped a vest around his shoulders, he walks out to the porch, the collar of his shirt still unfastened at the side. It smells heavily of dogs behind the closed door to the *sentsy*. They rise lazily and stretch when he comes in, yawn with little squeals, smile, crowd around his legs.

"Go on, go on," he says in a slow, indulgent, low-pitched voice and starts walking through the garden to the threshing barn. He draws deeply into his lungs the dawn's sharp air and the smell of the bare garden under frost. His boots pass noisily through fallen leaves, black and curled with rime, as he walks along his avenue of birches, half of which have been chopped down. Jackdaws doze on the barn roof's ridge, their ruffled feathers sharp and clear against the low sky's gloomy backdrop. . . . A fine day for hunting! The owner stops in the middle of the avenue, looks for a long time at the autumn fields, the abandoned plots of green winter wheat where calves now roam. Two hunting dogs whine at his feet, but Zalivai has already raced beyond the garden: leaping over plots of sharp stubble, he seems to plead and beg to go out on a hunt. But what can you do with a pack of hunting dogs at this time of year? The quarry's in the field, keeping to the open spaces and the plowing, too frightened by the rustling of wind-blown leaves to go into the forest now. . . . Without borzois you won't catch a thing!

Threshing has begun in the barn. The drum drones as it slowly gathers speed, and the horses lazily pull their traces, swaying as they walk a circle strewn with their own droppings. The driver sits on a little bench at the center of the wheel, turning as the horses walk and shouting at them in a monotone, his whip falling constantly on the same brown gelding, which moves more sluggishly than all the rest: his eyes are covered; he might well be walking while he's sound asleep.

"Well, now—girls, girls!" sternly shouts the operator, a staid man wearing a wide sackcloth shirt. The girls scatter with their brooms and barrows, hurriedly sweep up the threshing floor.

"With God's grace . . .," the operator says, releasing a small, test bundle of rye. It flies into the buzzing, squealing drum, then rises up and out of the machine like a tattered fan. The drum drones more and more insistently, the work begins in earnest, and soon all the separate noises merge into the pleasant, even sound of threshing. The owner stands in the entrance and watches as hands and rakes, straw, red and yellow headscarves flicker in the darkness of the barn, and all the bustling movement's made rhythmic, measured by the drone of the drum, the whistling and monotonous shouts of the driver. Clouds of chaff drift toward the door and cover the owner in grey dust. . . . He glances at the fields again. . . . Soon, soon they'll be white. Soon the first snows will cover them. . . .

First frost, first snow! Without borzois it's impossible to hunt in November, but when winter comes, the real work starts with hounds. And as they did in earlier times, the owners of small estates go to visit one another, drink away the last of their money, disappear for entire days in the snowy fields. And on some distant farm the lit windows of a hunter's hut burn far into the dark winter night. Smoke fills the hut; the tallow candles burn wanly. Someone tunes a guitar, begins to sing in a deep tenor:

At dusk a violent wind began to blow,
It flung the garden gate wide open . . .

And the others join in clumsily, with sad and hopeless bluster, pretending that it's all a joke:

It flung the garden gate wide open,
And buried all the roads with drifting snow . . .

[1900]

Sukhodol

W E WERE always amazed by Natalya's attachment to Sukhodol.

She grew up there with our father. She was the daughter of his wet nurse and lived with him in one house. And for a full eight years she lived with us in Lunyovo — lived with us as a relative, not a former slave, not a house serf. She herself called each of those years a reprieve, a rest from Sukhodol and all the suffering it had caused her. But there's a reason why they say a wolf is always looking to the woods no matter what you feed it: as soon as she had finished raising us, Natalya headed back to Sukhodol.

I remember bits of our childhood conversations with her.

"You're an orphan, aren't you, Natalya?"

"An orphan, sir, an orphan. Just as my master was. Your grandmother, Anna Grigoryevna, after all, was practically a girl when they folded her fair arms across her breast. . . . My father and my mother were no different."

"Why did they die so young?"

"Death came, and so they died."

"But why — why did it happen so early?"

"God made it so. . . . The masters wanted to punish my father, so they sent him to be a soldier. And then my mother died early on account of turkeys—newborn turkeys. I don't remember any of this myself, of course—where would I have been at such a time? But this is how the other serfs in the household said it happened. She was the birdkeeper. And there was no counting all the hatchlings she was to care for. One day a hailstorm caught them in the open pasture, beat them all to death. Killed them all. She ran out to save them there, and when she looked and saw them dead, her soul flew out from terror."

"Why didn't you get married?"

"My groom's still growing up."

"But really . . . seriously."

"They say the young mistress, your aunt, made it so I'd never marry. And that's how it got started in the household—the teasing. They began to call me 'miss,' just like her—as if I too was a young lady."

"What do you mean? How could they say you're a lady?"

"But I am sir, I am indeed a lady," she said, a slight smile creasing her lips. She ran her dark, old woman's hand over her mouth. "My mother was your father's wet nurse, after all. The milk we shared makes me his sister. I'm your second aunt."

Growing up, we listened ever more attentively to any talk of Sukhodol at home. And as it grew easier to explain those things that had once perplexed us, all the oddities of life at that estate became more and more conspicuous. We had once been convinced that Natalya was one of us—that she too was a Khrushchyov of ancient noble lineage! No one could have believed this more earnestly than we did, for we knew that she had lived a life identical to our father's during the past half-century. But now we learned that members of our noble family had driven her father into the army and terrified her mother so intensely that the woman's heart exploded at the sight of some turkey hatchlings killed by hail.

"Of course!" Natalya had said. "Who wouldn't die from terror, seeing such a thing? They'd have sent her somewhere next to hell."

And then we learned even more strange facts about Sukhodol. We learned that there was "no one on this earth" as kind and simple as the owners of that estate—but there was also no one "more explosive." We learned that the old manor house at Sukhodol was dark and gloomy. We learned that our deranged grandfather, Pyotr Kirillych, was killed in that house by his bastard son, Gervaska, Natalya's cousin and a friend of our father. We learned that a tragic affair had driven our aunt Tonya out of her mind, and that she now lived in a serf's old hut near the decaying manor house, ecstatically playing country dances on a piano so old its keys rattled and droned. We learned that even Natalya had suffered a period of madness, for as a young girl she fell inexorably in love with our late uncle, Pyotr Petrovich, who banished her to the farm at Soshki. . . . Our passionate dreams of Sukhodol were understandable: for us it was a poetic image of the past. But what could such a place be for Natalya? As if answering a question she'd been mulling over silently, she once said to us with great bitterness:

"Well, what more is there to say?. . . They used to carry whips with them to meals at Sukhodol. Just the memory brings me terror."

"Whips?" we asked. "Do you mean hunting crops?"

"It's all the same, sir."

"But why?"

"In case a fight broke out."

"Did everyone fight at Sukhodol?"

"God save us, sir, not a day passed without some kind of war! Everyone was ready to explode—every day was pure gunpowder."

We glanced ecstatically at one another as Natalya spoke. Her words enthralled us, and the scene that then took shape in our imaginations remained for many years: a huge estate and garden, a house of rough oak beams beneath a thatch roof turned black with age—and meals in the dining hall, everyone sitting at the table, everyone eating and throwing bones on the floor for the hunting dogs, everyone watching from the corners of their eyes, whips lying in their laps. We dreamed of that golden age when we would be adults, when we too would dine with whips in our laps! But we also understood full well that those whips had never brought Natalya any joy. And still she left Lunyovo for Sukhodol, that source of her dark memories. She had nowhere to live there, no family, no corner to call her own. And since ownership of Sukhodol had changed, she couldn't serve Aunt Tonya after her return. Instead she had a new mistress—Klavdiya Markovna, Pyotr Petrovich's widow. But it didn't matter: Natalya couldn't live away from that estate.

"What can you do, sir?" she said modestly. "Habit. The thread must follow the needle. . . . You're needed where you're born. . . ."

She was not alone in suffering a deep attachment to Sukhodol. Everyone who'd ever lived there seemed to be enthralled. My God, what fervent acolytes they were! How ardently they loved their memories of that place!

Aunt Tonya was completely destitute. She lived in a peasant hut. Her happiness, her sanity, her chance to live a normal life had all been lost to Sukhodol. My father tried repeatedly to talk her into joining us in Lunyovo, but she refused to hear of it. She would not give up her ancestral home: "I'd rather hack the stones out of a quarry!"

Our father was a carefree man. For him, it seemed, there were no bonds, no troubling attachments. But you could hear a deep sadness in his stories about Sukhodol. He'd left it long ago—moved to Lunyovo, the country estate of our grandmother, Olga Kirillovna. But he complained until the very end:

"Only one Khrushchyov left on this entire earth—just one! And still he doesn't live at Sukhodol!"

But then, of course, he often fell to thinking after making such pronouncements. He'd pause and look at the fields outside the window, and taking a guitar down from the wall, he'd add:

"Sukhodol. A lovely place, all right—may the earth swallow it whole!"

And these words were no less sincere than those he'd spoken just before them.

But the soul inside him came from Sukhodol—a soul immeasurably affected by the weight of memory, the steppe and its inertia; a soul shaped by an ancient sense of clan that merged the village huts and the servants' rooms with the manor house of Sukhodol. It's true that we can trace our lineage back to early history—the name Khrushchyov is entered in the Sixth Book of noble families, and among our legendary ancestors there were many noblemen of ancient Lithuanian descent as well as a few little Tatar princes. But the Khrushchyov blood has also mixed with that of household serfs and laborers since time immemorial. Who gave life to Pyotr Kirillych? There are many different versions of this legend. Who fathered his killer, Gervaska? We had heard from early childhood that it was Pyotr Kirillych himself. Why were there such sharp differences between my father and my uncle? We'd heard many different stories about this as well. My father nursed at the same breast as Natalya. He traded crosses with Gervaska. . . . It was long past time for the Khrushchyovs to face the fact that they had relatives among the village serfs and household menials.

My sister and I lived for a long time in the steady tow of Sukhodol, lived under the spell of its antiquity. Together with the owners of the manor house, the domestic serfs and villagers formed one large family there. But it was always our ancestors, of course, who ruled that family, and we felt this through the ages. The history of family, kin and clan, is always subterranean, convoluted, mysterious, often terrifying. But it's that long past, those dark depths and legends, that often give a family strength. Sukhodol had no more written record of its ancient history than some Bashkir encampment in the steppe, for legends took the place of all such writing in those early days in Rus. But legends and old songs are a sweet poison for the Slavic soul! Our former serfs from Sukhodol were ardent idlers and dreamers—and where could they indulge their souls more freely than they did on our estate at Lunyovo? Our father, after all, was the last, true heir to Sukhodol. The first words we spoke were words of Sukhodol. The first songs and stories that moved us were those our father and Natalya brought from Sukhodol. And who could sing "My True Love's Airs" the way my father had learned to sing it from the household serfs? Who could match those notes of idle sorrow and tender reproach, that tone of unresisting candor? Could anyone tell a story like Natalya? Was anyone closer to us than the *mouzhiki* of Sukhodol?

Like so many families living over generations in close isolation, the Khrushchyovs gained notoriety in history through their fights and brawls. When we were still quite small, a particularly violent quarrel erupted between my father's house at Lunyovo and our relatives at Sukhodol. As a result, my father didn't cross the entrance to his boyhood home for almost an entire decade. And thus we didn't know Sukhodol as children. We were there only once, briefly, while en route to Zadonsk. But sometimes dreams are more powerful than any reality: our memories of that long summer day were dim, but they remained indelible. We remembered undulating fields and a large, overgrown road that fascinated us with its broad expanse; we remembered the hollow trunks of a few surviving white willows that rose occasionally along its side—and one that stood farther off in the fields, a beehive hanging in its limbs above the wheat, a beehive left completely to the will of God near a road buried in the weeds. We remembered a wide turn in the road and a long, slow rise; a huge plain dotted with little huts that had no chimneys. We remembered the rocky yellow ravines that opened beyond those huts, and the white crushed stone lying at the bottom of those barren cliffs. . . . It was a part of Sukhodol's past—Gervaska's murder of our grandfather—that first acquainted us with horror. And when we heard that story, we were haunted by the yellow ravines we'd seen that day—those ravines leading to some secret place. We were convinced Gervaska had used them to escape, having carried out his terrible crime and vanished "like a key flung into the sea."

Like those who served inside the manor house, serfs who worked the fields at Sukhodol came periodically to visit us at Lunyovo. They were driven by a need for land rather than nostalgia, but they still entered the manor house as if arriving at a relative's. They bowed below the waist to my father, kissed his hand, straightened their hair, then kissed each of us—my father, me, my sister, and Natalya—three times on the lips. They brought honey, eggs, and homespun towels as gifts. Having grown up in the fields, we were well attuned to the scents of country life; indeed, we craved such smells the way we longed for Sukhodol's songs and its legends, and thus we savored the unique and pleasant, slightly hempen scent of Sukhodol's *mouzhiki* as they kissed us. Their gifts were also laced with the smells of an ancient village in the steppe: we tried to learn them, tried to keep them in our memories—the heavy scent of haylofts and smoke-filled huts that came from the towels, the aroma of blooming buckwheat and beehives in rotting oaks that lingered in that honey. The *mouzhiki* who came from Sukhodol never told us any stories. After all, what stories could they tell? Even legends did not exist for them. Their graves were anonymous, their lives almost identical. Traceless. Gaunt. All their labor and their struggles brought only bread—bread that's eaten up. They dug out ponds in the rocky riverbed where the Kamenka once flowed. But ponds are unreliable—they too go dry. They built huts and shacks. But these cannot last for long: the smallest spark will burn them to the ground. . . . So what was it, then, that so stubbornly drew us all toward that barren pasture, to those huts and ravines, the ruined manor house at Sukhodol?

II

We were well into our adolescence when we finally reached that estate we'd heard so much about, that estate which stamped Natalya's soul and ruled her life.

I remember it like yesterday. As we approached Sukhodol toward evening, a torrential storm broke out with violent claps of thunder and lightning bolts that snaked across the sky in sudden, blinding streaks. A black-and-violet thunderhead drifted ponderously into the northwest and blocked out half the sky. The fields of green wheat covering the plain turned smooth, precise, and deathly pale beneath its mass, while the sparse grass along the road became fresh and unusually bright. The horses looked emaciated from the rain as they slopped down the road, the *tarantass* splashing behind them, their iron shoes glinting in the dark blue mud. . . . And suddenly, at the turn to Sukhodol, we saw a strange figure in the tall, wet rye—a figure that at first seemed neither male nor female. Wearing a bathrobe and a headscarf like a turban, it was beating a skewbald, hornless cow with a switch. As we approached, the beating grew more vigorous and the cow, flicking its tail, jogged clumsily onto the road while the old woman shouted something, ran toward the *tarantass*, and thrust her pale face toward us.

We glanced apprehensively into her black madwoman's eyes as this strange figure kissed us, the sharp, cold tip of her nose touching our cheeks, the heavy scent of a peasant hut rising from her clothes. Could she be the witch Baba-Yaga? But then, a grimy scarf rose like a turban from this Baba-Yaga's head, and her naked body was wrapped in a wet bathrobe so badly torn it didn't even cover her thin breasts. She shouted as if she were deaf, as if she wanted to curse and berate us—and from that shouting we understood: Aunt Tonya had come to meet us.

Plump and short, with a few grey whiskers and unusually animated eyes, Klavdiya Markovna shouted too—but hers were happy shouts, like those of an excited schoolgirl. She'd been knitting a cotton sock as she sat by an open window and now, with her glasses perched on her head, she looked past the house's two large porches, toward the courtyard and the fields. Standing on the right side porch, Natalya made a low bow, smiling modestly: kindhearted as ever, darkly tanned, she wore bast shoes, a red wool skirt, and a grey blouse with a low-cut collar that revealed her wrinkled neck. And I remember how, looking at her neck and her sharp collarbones, her sad and tired eyes, I thought: this woman grew up with our father long, long ago in this very place, where in lieu of the great manor home that our grandfather built from oak—and which burned to the ground many times—an ordinary house now stands, where the garden's been reduced to this ordinary assortment of old birches, a few bushes and poplar trees, and where nothing remains of the servants' quarters and the outbuildings but a peasant hut, a barn, a clay shed, an icehouse buried under amaranth and wormwood. . . . Earnest questions and the smell of smoke from a samovar began to fill the air while from the hundred-year-old cabinets came crystalline dishes for jam and sugar biscuits specially kept for guests, gold spoons worn thin as maple leaves. And while the conversation warmed—it had been solicitous and friendly after such a long falling-out—we went to explore the house's dark chambers, search for the balcony with a view of the orchard.

Everything was black with age, simple, rough in those empty, low-ceilinged rooms; they'd been built from the remains of chambers that our grandfather himself once occupied, and they were arranged according to his original plan for the house. In one corner of the servants' quarters hung a large dark icon of St. Merkury, the same saint whose helmet and iron sandals lie before the iconostasis in the ancient cathedral in Smolensk. We had heard the story: Merkury was a man of great renown; a voice from the icon of the Guiding Virgin called on him to free the lands of Smolensk from the Tatars. When he had driven out the Tatars, Merkury slept, and was beheaded by his enemies. The saint then rose and, with his head in his hands, came to the gates of Smolensk to tell of these events. It was terrifying to look at that scene, painted by an icon-maker, long ago, in the ancient city of Suzdal: it showed a decapitated man holding in one hand the icon of the Guiding Virgin and, in the other, his own lifeless head, still helmeted and blue. This image of St. Merkury was said to be our grandfather's most cherished icon; heavily encased in silver, it had survived several terrible fires, one of which had cracked its board. The genealogical table of the Khrushchyov family was written out in Old Church Slavonic on its back. The painting's aura seemed to be matched perfectly by the large iron deadbolts that secured the top and bottom halves of the heavy divided door leading to the dining hall. Although it had been built to replicate that room where the Khrushchyovs once gathered to eat meals while holding whips in their laps, the current hall was only half the size of the original. It had small sash windows and inordinately wide, slick, dark floorboards. We passed through it on our way to the drawing room. There, across from the balcony doors, once stood the piano that Aunt Tonya played when she was in love with the officer Voitkevich, a friend of Pyotr Petrovich. Farther on, the doors had been left wide open to the den, which in turn led to the corner rooms of the house where our grandfather once had his private apartment. . . .

It was a gloomy evening. Summer lightning flashed in the distance, revealing thunderheads that hung like pink and gold mountains beyond the remnants of the orchards, the silver poplars, and the stripped-out barn. Evidently the storm had not passed over Troshin Forest, which now was going dark far beyond the orchard, on the hillsides past the ravines. From there descended the warm, dry smell of oaks mingled with the scent of green leaves, and a light, damp breeze that passed across the tops of the remaining birches in the avenue, the tall nettles, the over-grown weeds and shrubs near the balcony. Over everything reigned the deep silence of evening, the silence of the steppe and all the distant, un-known lands of Rus. . . .

"Come for tea now, please," a quiet voice called out to us. It was she — the witness and survivor of this entire life, the vital narrator of its events — Natalya. And behind her came Aunt Tonya, Natalya's former mistress: her back was slightly hunched as she glided ceremoniously across the smooth, dark floor, peering around the room with her mad-woman's eyes. She still wore her grimy headscarf, but the dressing gown had been replaced by an old-fashioned *barege* dress and a shawl of faded gold silk.

"*Ou etes-vous, mes enfants?*" she shouted, smiling affectedly. Sharp and precise as a parrot's, her voice echoed strangely in the empty, dark rooms.

III

The sad remains of that estate which gave Natalya life still retained a delicate allure, just as she herself possessed a natural charm with her peasant's candor and simplicity, her pitiable and lovely soul.

It smelled of jasmine in the old drawing room with sloping floors. The decaying balcony had turned blue-grey with time and now was sink-ing into the tall nettles, the honeysuckle, and the staff shrubs. If you wanted to get down from it, you had to jump, for it had no steps. On hot days, when its wood baked in the sun and the sagging doors were left open, their shimmering glass reflected in the dingy oval mirror that hung inside the drawing room, we always thought of Aunt Tonya's piano, for it once stood below that mirror. She used to play it, reading yellowed sheets of music with titles written in elaborate script, while *he* stood behind her, clenching his jaw and frowning, his left hand resting firmly on his waist. Wonderful butterflies flew into the drawing room, their bodies and their wings like something made from Japanese ki-monos, bright cotton prints, or shawls of black-and-lilac-colored velvet.

Before he left, he crushed one with his palm—lashed out in rage as it alighted timidly on the piano lid. Only a silvery dust remained, but when the maids stupidly wiped it away several days later, Aunt Tonya grew hysterical. . . . We went out onto the balcony, sat on the warm floorboards—and thought, and thought. Wind rose in the orchard, brought to us the sound of birches rustling like silk, their green branches spread wide, their trunks like white satin paper flecked with black · enamel; wind blew in from the fields, whispering and sighing loudly. A gold-green oriole cried out sharply, joyfully, then shot like an arrow above the white flowers, following a flock of chattering jackdaws that lived with all their relatives in the ruined chimneys and dark lofts, where it smelled of old bricks and sunlight fell through the dormer windows, sloped in golden strips across mounds of grey-and-violet ash. The wind settled down. Bees crawled sleepily among the flowers by the balcony, carrying out their measured work. And only the poplars' silvery leaves stirred amid the silence—lightly, evenly, like a small and constant rain. . . . We roamed through the orchard and wandered to its outskirts where the undergrowth was wild and heavy, bordering the fields of wheat. And there, in the bathhouse that our great grandfather built—that bathhouse where Natalya once hid a mirror that she'd stolen from Pyotr Petrovich, and which now lay in ruins, its ceiling half collapsed—we discovered white rabbits. How softly they leapt out to the steps. How strangely they sat there, twitching their whiskers and their divided mouths, squinting with their wide-set, bulging eyes at tall spring onions and nightshade, blackthorn and cherry trees choked by high nettles. . . . And an eagle owl lived in the stripped-out threshing barn. He'd searched for the gloomiest place he could find and settled on a pole for holding haystacks; perched there with his ears stuck up like horns, his blind and yellow pupils aimed fiercely at the world, he resembled a small, pugnacious demon. . . . The sun descended far beyond the orchard in the sea of wheat; a bright and peaceful evening settled in. A cuckoo called in Troshin Forest; the birch-bark pipes of the old shepherd, Styopa, sounded plaintively somewhere above the meadows. . . . The eagle owl sat and waited. Night came and sleep descended on the fields, the village, the manor house. And then the eagle owl screeched and cried. Noiselessly he'd sail around the barn and through the orchard, softly settle on the roof of Aunt Tonya's hut—and begin to wail as if in pain, waking Aunt Tonya on her bench beside the stove.

"Jesus. Beloved. Dearest. Pity me," she'd whisper.

Flies buzzed with sleepy dissatisfaction along the ceiling. Something woke them every night. Sometimes a cow scratched its flank against the hut. Sometimes a rat ran fitfully across the rattling keys of the piano, then toppled with a crack into the pottery shards that Aunt Tonya carefully stacked in the corner of the room. Sometimes the old black cat with green eyes returned late from one of its outings and lazily called to be let in—and sometimes that owl flew onto the roof and began its screaming like a prophet of doom. Then Aunt Tonya would overcome her drowsiness, brush away the flies that crawled around her eyes as she slept, grope her way past the benches to the door, throw it open with a bang, and step outside. And then, aiming by sheer guesswork, she would fling a rolling pin into the starry sky. The owl's wings would rustle softly against the thatch as he launched himself into the darkness, descending almost to earth as he glided back toward the barn, then shooting up to settle on its roof. And from there, once more, his cries would reach the manor house and drift through the estate. He'd sit as if remembering something, let out a startled wail, and pause, go silent. Then, without the slightest warning, he'd launch into a frenzied laughing, hooting, squealing—only to break off, go silent once again—but not for good: he'd soon burst out with moans and sobs and keening cries. . . . And the warm, dark nights, with their lilac-colored clouds, were calm, calm. The steady, drowsy stirring of the poplars' leaves was like a languid stream. Summer lightning flashed cautiously above dark Troshin Forest, and the warm, dry scent of oaks lingered in the air. Near the forest, drifting in a glade of sky between the clouds, Scorpio hung above the plains of wheat like a silver triangle, like the little roof they put above a graveyard cross to protect it. . . .

We often came back late to the manor house. Having breathed our fill of dew and wildflowers, grass and fresh air from the steppe, we'd carefully cross the porch and enter the dark foyer. And there we'd often find Natalya praying at the icon of St. Merkury. Barefoot, small, her hands clasped together, she stood and whispered, crossed herself, bowed low before the saint, who was hidden by the dark. All of it was simple, as if Natalya were engaged in conversation with someone no less gracious and benign than she.

"Natalya?" we called out quietly.

"Yes, it's me," she answered softly, simply, breaking off her prayers.

"Why are you still up so late?"

"The grave will give us all the time we need to sleep."

We sat on a large chest while she stood before us, her hands clasped together. Summer lightning flickered in the distance and secretly lit up the darkened chambers of the house. We opened a window. A quail was calling far away in the heavy dew of the steppe. A duck stirring on the pond began to quack uneasily.

"The two of you have been out walking, sir?"

"Yes."

"And so it ought to be. Walking's for the young. We used to walk all night as well. Dusk would bring us out, and dawn would send us home."

"Did you live well back then?"

"Yes, sir. It was good, our life."

A long silence fell.

"*Nyanechka,* why does the owl shout so much at night?" my sister asked.

"For no good reason, dear. There's no getting at him, though. Gunshots, even. Nothing makes him stop. And he brings us all a terror. Everyone believes he's promising some doom. How your aunt is terrorized by him! And it takes almost nothing, after all, to stop her heart with fear."

"What made her ill?"

"Well, everybody knows, sir—it was tears and tears, black grief. . . . Then she started praying. She grew fierce with us—with all the girls in the house. And she was always angry with her brothers. . . ."

Remembering the whips, we asked: "It wasn't very friendly then, among the family?"

"Friendly? There were no friends anywhere! Especially once your aunt was taken ill and your grandfather died. That's when the young masters came into their own, and Pyotr Petrovich wed. Everyone was hot—pure gunpowder!"

"Did they whip the house serfs often?"

"No, sir, that was not the custom here. I was guilty in so many ways! And all they did to me—all Pyotr Petrovich ordered—was to cut my hair with sheep shears and dress me in a shirt of twill, then ship me to the farm. . . ."

"What was it you were guilty of?"

But there was no guarantee of a quick and simple answer. Sometimes Natalya told her stories with surprising detail and directness. But at other times her speech grew halting; she fell to thinking and lightly sighed. And even though we couldn't see her face in the darkness, we knew from her voice that she was smiling sadly.

"Well, I was to blame. . . . I've told you before . . . I was young. Foolish, sir. *'In the garden sang a nightingale—a song of sins and suffering.'* Everyone knows, sir. It was a girl's foolishness. . . ."

"*Nyanechka*," my sister said tenderly, "tell us that poem all the way—to the end."

Natalya was embarrassed. "It's not a poem, dear, it's a song. . . . I don't remember all the words now."

"That's not true—you do know all the words."

"Well then, all right. Here you are," Natalya said, and quickly ran through the refrain without emotion: *"'In the garden sang a nightingale—a quiet song of sins and suffering; and in the dark of night, her head still full of dreams, a foolish girl lay listening. . . .'"*

"Were you very much in love with uncle?" my sister asked, overcoming her embarrassment.

"Very much, dear."

"Do you always remember him in prayers?"

"Always."

"They say you fainted when they took you away to Soshki."

"I fainted, yes. . . . All of us who served the house—we were awfully tender. Couldn't take real punishments. Our skin was soft—nothing like those *odnodvortsy* who have leather hides. . . . When Yevsey Bodulya drove me away in the cart, fear and sorrow were like a fog in me. . . . He brought me to a town, and I felt like I was suffocating there—I'd never breathed such air! And then we drove out to the steppe, and I felt so sad and helpless. An officer who looked like him rode past: I shouted, fainted dead. And when I came back to myself, still lying in that cart, I thought: 'Everything is better now. . . . It's like I've gone to heaven now.'"

"Was he strict?"

"God preserve me! He was strict."

"But Aunt Tonya was the most difficult of all?"

"She was, sir. I'll tell you: they even took her to a saint's remains. What we've gone through with her! She could live now, live just fine—it's time, after all. But she was proud, and wound up touched. . . . How he loved her, that Voitkevich! But what can anybody do!"

"Well, and grandfather?"

"Well, what of that?. . . His mind was weak. But he could blow up too. They all were flint and fuel. . . . But for all that, the old masters didn't act like we were grime. They didn't wipe us from their hands. Sometimes your father would punish Gervaska for something at dinner—punish him with good reason—and then, in the evening, you'd look outside and see them playing balalaikas in the yard together. . . ."

"But tell us, was he handsome, that Voitkevich?"

Natalya thought it over. "No, sir, I don't wish to lie: he looked a bit like a Kalmyk. And so serious! Insistent. Always reading poems and scaring her—'I'll die,' he'd say, 'I'll die and then come back for you.'. . ."

"But then, grandfather lost his mind from love as well, didn't he?. . ."

"It was because of your grandmother. But that was a different kind of story. And the house was gloomy. . . . Not at all a happy place. . . . I'll tell you, if you want to listen. If you want to hear about it in my clumsy words."

And Natalya began a long narrative, whispering unhurriedly.

IV

According to legend our great grandfather, a rich man, moved from somewhere near Kursk to Sukhodol in his later years. He didn't like the place—its isolation and its endless forests. It's become a cliché to say that there were forests everywhere in the old days, but evidently it was true two hundred years ago, when people traveling our roads fought their way through dense woodlands. Everything was lost in those forests—the Kamenka River and its upper banks, the village, the estate and all the hilly fields surrounding it. But it wasn't like this in my grandfather's time. By then the picture had already changed: bare hills and rolling steppe, fields of buckwheat, rye, and oats; a few hollow white willows along the big road; and on the rise where the manor house stood, nothing but flat white stones. Only Troshin Forest remained of all the woodland. But, of course, the orchard and the garden were still lovely: a wide avenue of seventy spreading birches; cherry trees sinking in the nettles; dense thickets of raspberry cane, acacia, and lilac; and almost a full grove of silver poplars at the orchard's edge, bordering the fields. The house had a thick, dark, solid roof of thatch. It looked out on a courtyard with long outbuildings and servants' quarters extending in sections along its sides. Beyond the courtyard sprawled the estate's village—large, poor, ramshackle—amid an endless expanse of green pastures.

"The village was all of a piece with the master," Natalya would say. "And the master didn't pay much mind to things. Couldn't handle money well. Didn't follow farming. Semyon Kirillych, your grandfather's brother, had already taken for himself whatever was largest and best in their inheritance, including their father's house. All he left your grandfather was Soshki and Sukhodol, and another four hundred souls, half of which ran away."

Our grandfather died at around the age of forty-five. Our father always said that he'd lost his mind when a sudden storm caught him sleeping on a carpet in the garden and rained an entire treeload of apples down on his head. But among the menials, Natalya told us, there was another explanation. They said that Pyotr Kirillych lost his mind from grieving over the loss of his beautiful wife, who died the day after a huge thunderstorm passed through Sukhodol. Pyotr Kirillych had dark hair, sloped shoulders, and black eyes that looked out at the world with affectionate attention; he looked a little like Aunt Tonya, and he lived out his life in a quiet, peaceful state of madness. According to Natalya, the family had more money in those days than anyone knew what to do with; and so, wearing boots of Moroccan leather and a florid caftan, Pyotr Kirillych wandered noiselessly through the house, nervously looking around him and stuffing gold coins in the cracks between the oak beams that formed the walls.

"It's for Tonya's dowry," he muttered when they caught him. "This is far more reliable, my friends. Far more reliable. . . . But even so, it's a matter of your will. If you don't want me to, I won't. . . ."

And then he went right back to hiding coins inside the cracks. Some days he would rearrange the heavy furniture in the drawing room, expecting, all along, some kind of visit despite the fact that the neighbors almost never came to Sukhodol. On other days he would complain of hunger and prepare *tyurya* for himself—inexpertly crushing and grinding green onion in a wooden cup, crumbling bread into the mush, then pouring in a foamy mix of water and fermented flour, and, finally, adding so many large, grey grains of salt that the *tyurya* was bitter, impossible to eat.

Life on the estate slowed to a halt after lunch, and all the people in the manor house wandered off to some quiet napping place where they would doze for hours. During those long afternoons, Pyotr Kirillych was at loose ends: he slept little even during the night, and now had nothing to do. And so, unable to endure his loneliness, he would quietly approach the bedrooms, the foyers, and the female servants' hall and call out to the sleepers:

"Arkasha, are you asleep? Tonya, are you sleeping?"

Upon receiving an infuriated shout—"For the love of God, *papenka*, leave me in peace!"—he would hurriedly begin to soothe his listener—"Well then, sleep, sleep, my soul, my dear. I'm not going to wake you"—and then proceed to the next room, avoiding only the footmen's quarters, for the lackeys at Sukhodol were extremely churlish. Ten minutes later, however, he would appear again in the doorway and call out in a still more cautious voice, pretending that he'd just heard the harness bells of a private cab passing through the village—"Maybe Petenka has come home on leave from his division?"—or seen a massive thunderhead looming in the distance.

"And the master truly was terrified of thunderstorms, poor lamb," Natalya told us. "I was still a girl, still young enough to go without a headscarf then, but I remember well, sir. There was a kind of blackness to the house. . . . An unhappy place, God be with it. And a summer day was like a year. There were more serfs tending to those rooms than anyone knew what to do with. . . . Instead of one footman, they had five! And everybody knew—the young masters, after lunch, they go to sleep—and we, loyal serfs and upright servants, we went along to nap ourselves. And Pyotr Kirillych better not come to wake us! Especially not Gervaska. 'Lackeys! Hey, lackeys, are you sleeping?' he calls out. And Gervaska lifts his head from the trunk where he's been dozing, says: 'Would you like me to stuff your crotch with nettles?' And Pyotr Kirillych starts: 'What! Who do you think you're speaking to, you damned idler, you do-nothing!' Gervaska answers back: 'I was talking to the house spirit, sir—I was half asleep. . . .' And so Pyotr Kirillych again goes roaming around the hall and the drawing room, all the time peering out the windows, looking at the garden: isn't there a cloud out there? It was true, though—thunderstorms came often then. And those were powerful storms. Sometimes after lunch it would happen—an oriole begins to shriek, and suddenly, over the orchard, thunderheads come rolling in. . . . The house goes dark inside and all the weeds, the thick beds of nettles, they start to rustle and sway. The turkeys and their poults go to hide under the balcony. . . . And you feel such a menace in the air. Such black loneliness! And he, the old master, how he sighs and crosses himself, climbs up to light the wax candle in front of the icons, hangs up the towel from his father's burial—that towel I feared like death itself. Either that, or he throws a pair of scissors out the window. That helps, of course. Scissors—just the thing for turning back a thunderstorm!"

Sukhodol was happier when it was home to two citizens of France. First there was a certain Louis Ivanovich, a man with a long moustache and dreamy blue eyes, strands of hair combed carefully from ear to ear across his balding pate, and pants that ballooned around his hips in extraordinary ways, then tapered past his knees. He was followed by the middle-aged, forever cold and shivering Mademoiselle Sizi. And everything seemed livelier when they were there; when Tonya had piano lessons; when Louis Ivanovich's voice rumbled through all the rooms as he shouted at Arkasha, "Go, and do not returning be!"; when in the class-room could be heard, "*Maître corbeau sur un arbre perché.*" The French contingent stayed at Sukhodol for a full eight years. Even after the children had been sent to school in the province's main town, they remained at the estate to save Pyotr Kirillych from ennui. It was only when the children were about to come home for their third holiday of the year that the French finally departed. And at the end of that school holiday, Pyotr Kirillych decided it was more than adequate to send Petenka back alone: Tonya and Arkasha were to stay with him. And so they stayed for good, untended and untaught. . . .

Natalya used to say, "I was younger than all the rest. But Gervaska was almost the same age as your *papasha*, and that made them best friends from the start. Only, it's right what they say: 'Wolves and horses can't be in-laws.' They befriended each other, swore for all time on their friendship, even traded crosses—and then Gervaska almost right away does this: he almost drowns your papa in the pond! He was just a dirty scab of a thing, but he was full of fiendish little plans. A nasty little plotter. 'So,' he says to your papa, 'you going to beat me when you grow up?' 'Yes,' your papa answers, 'I am.' 'Oh no,' Gervaska says. 'Why not?' asks your papa. 'Just because,' he says. And then he thinks up something. We had a barrel on the hill near the pond. He saw it, made a little note inside his head. And then he gave Arkady Petrovich the idea—climb inside and roll right down. 'You sail it down here first, then I'll take a ride,' he says. And so the young master climbs inside, shoves off, and goes rolling, banging down the hill so hard he hits the water. . . . Mother of God, there was just a cloud of dust where he'd been! Thank God the shepherds were nearby. . . ."

The house still looked and felt inhabited when the French were there. During grandmother's day there had been authority and order. A master and an overseer. Power. Subordination. Formal rooms where guests were entertained, and private rooms where the family gathered.

Ordinary working days and holidays. All of this remained in evidence while those two citizens of France resided there. But when they went away the house was left without a master. When the children were still small, Pyotr Kirillych seemed to have the upper hand. But what could he really do? Who owned whom? Did he command the serfs, or did they rule him? Someone closed up the piano. The tablecloth disappeared from the dining room. They ate lunch at random at the bare oak table. The *sentsy* was so crowded with borzois that no one could walk through it to the porch. There was no one left to think of cleanliness, and the dark log walls of oak, the dark ceilings and floors, the dark and heavy doors and frames, the old icons that filled a corner of the house with their stark figures painted in the ancient Suzdal style—soon all of it had gone completely black. The house was frightening at night, especially during thunderstorms, when the garden raged under heavy rain, when the mystic visages of the icons were lit up every minute in the hall, when the pink and golden, trembling sky suddenly flew open, yawned above the garden trees, and then, in blackness, blows of thunder split the air. And during the day it was sleepy, empty, dull. Pyotr Kirillych grew weaker every year, went more and more unnoticed. His wet nurse, the decrepit Darya Ustinovna, eventually emerged as the house's overseer, but her power was just as minimal as his. And Demyan, the village head-man, knew only how to run the fields. He refused to be involved in the household, saying with a lazy smirk, "I'm not doing anything to put the master out." My father had no time for Sukhodol in his youth: he was completely carried away by hunting, balalaikas, and his love for Ger-vaska, who was counted among the footmen but disappeared for entire days with his young master to places like Meshchersky's Marshes, or to the carriage house where he gave lessons in the subtleties of birch-bark pipes and balalaikas.

"We knew perfectly," Natalya would say, "they used the house only for sleeping. And if they aren't asleep, it means they're in the village or the carriage house—or else they're out hunting: rabbits in the winter, foxes in the fall, quail and ducks and bustards in the summer. They climb into the *drozhky*, throw a gun over their shoulders, shout to Dianka—and that's it, they're gone: today it's Srednaya Mill, tomorrow it's Meshchersky's, the day after that the steppe. And always with Ger-vaska. Everywhere they went, it was always his idea. But he'd pretend the young master was dragging him along. Arkady Petrovich loved him, truly loved Gervaska, his enemy, like a brother. But that one—he just jeered at Arkady Petrovich. The more they were together, the more vicious was his jeering. Arkady Petrovich would say, 'Gervaska, come on, let's practice balalaikas. Please—teach me "Red the Sun Went Down."' And Gervaska looks at him, exhales cigarette smoke through his nose, says with a smirk: 'First, kiss my hand.' Arkady Petrovich goes all white, jumps up, and *bam!*—slaps Gervaska in the face with everything he's got. And that one, he just jerks his head back, turns even blacker, scowls like a killing brigand. 'Get up, you bastard!' your *papasha* shouts. He gets up, stands all straight, like a borzoi, but with his baggy pants hanging down. . . . Says nothing. 'Ask my forgiveness.' 'My fault, sir.' And the young master—he just chokes on anger, doesn't even know what else to say. 'You hear that—"sir"! That's right—"sir,"' he shouts. 'I try to get along with you like an equal, you bastard. Sometimes I even think, "I'd give up my soul for him." And you—what are you doing? You try to set me off! You want me in a rage!'

"It's enough to make you wonder, though," Natalya said. "Gervaska mocked the young master and your grandfather while your aunt, the young mistress, she mocked and jeered at me. But Arkady Petrovich—and really, the truth be told, your grandfather too—they worshipped Gervaska. They could forget their souls looking at him! And I was just the same with the mistress. I worshipped her . . . when I returned from Soshki, came back a little to my senses after those misdeeds. . . ."

V

They began to bring whips to the table after our grandfather died and Gervaska fled Sukhodol, after Pyotr Petrovich married, after Tonya lost her mind and declared herself a bride of "sweetest Jesus," and after Natalya returned from the farm called Soshki. It was love that made Aunt Tonya lose her mind; love that sent Natalya into exile.

The dull isolated days of our grandfather were being replaced with a time of young masters. Pyotr Petrovich returned to Sukhodol, having unexpectedly resigned his post. His homecoming proved to be the ruin of both Natalya and Aunt Tonya.

They both fell in love. They didn't notice when it happened. At first it simply seemed that life had grown happier.

As soon as he returned, Pyotr Petrovich brought a new order to Sukhodol, a festive, stately way of life. He came with a friend, Voitkevich, as well as a cook—a clean-shaven alcoholic who looked with contempt upon the tarnished, ribbed molds for jelly, the crass and ugly cut-lery of Sukhodol. Pyotr Petrovich wanted to appear generous, carefree, and rich before his friend, and he tried to come across this way through awkward, adolescent gestures and displays. And indeed he was, in many ways, a boy—a boy with both delicate and handsome features as well as a harsh, cruel temperament; a boy who seemed self-confident but who in fact was easily embarrassed to the point of tears—and then long har-bored bitter malice toward the cause of his discomfiture.

"Brother Arkady," he said on his first day back at Sukhodol. "I seem to recall us having a few bottles of Madeira that weren't bad."

Our grandfather flushed. He wanted to say something but couldn't find the courage, and instead began tugging at the front of his caftan. Arkady Petrovich was confused.

"What Madeira?"

Gervaska gave Pyotr Petrovich an insolent look and smiled.

"You forget, if you will permit me, sir," he said to Arkady Petrovich, making no attempt to hide his ridicule. "We did have a stock of that wine. More than anyone knew what to do with! But us drudges in the yard, we took care of it, sir. Fine wine, really—fit for a master. We gulped it down like *kvass*. . . ."

"What is this?" shouted Pyotr Petrovich, flushing darkly. "Don't open your mouth!"

Grandfather joined in ecstatically. "That's right, Petenka, that's right! Bravo!" he cried in a thin, joyful voice. "You can't imagine how he mocks me! So many times I've thought—I'll just sneak up right now and shatter his skull with a copper pestle! . . . God knows I've had that thought! I'll plant a dagger to its hilt in him!"

But Gervaska suffered no loss of words.

"I hear, sir, that the punishment for that kind of thing is quite painful," he answered with a scowl. "And besides, I have an idea too—it just keeps crawling into my head: the master's overdue in heaven!"

Pyotr Petrovich would later say that after such a shockingly impu-dent answer, he managed to control himself only on his guest's account. He spoke just three more words to Gervaska: "Leave. This instant." And then he even felt embarrassed for this flash of anger. He hurried to apol-ogize to Voitkevich, smiling as he raised to him those charming eyes that always lingered for a long, long time in the memory of anyone who knew Pyotr Petrovich.

For too long those eyes lingered in Natalya's memory.

Her happiness was stunningly brief. And who could have thought that it would end in a trip to Soshki, the most remarkable event of her entire life?

Soshki farm is still intact today, though its ownership long ago passed to a merchant from Tambov. It consists of a long peasant hut in the middle of an empty plain, a storehouse, a shadoof and a well, and a barn in the middle of some melon fields. It was just the same in grandfather's day; even the town along the road from Sukhodol has hardly changed over the years. Natalya's crime was theft: to her own surprise she'd stolen a small folding mirror in a silver frame from Pyotr Petrovich.

When she saw that mirror she was so astonished by its beauty—as she was by everything that Pyotr Petrovich owned—that she could not resist. And for several days, until they noticed that the mirror was missing, she lived in a daze, stunned by her crime, spellbound by her terrifying secret and her treasure, like the girl in the tale of the scarlet flower. Lying down to sleep, she asked God to let the night pass quickly, to let morning come as soon as possible: the manor house had come to life, turned festive; something new and wonderful had entered all the rooms since the arrival of the handsome master, so elegantly dressed and pomaded, with a high red collar on his military jacket, with a dark complexion and a face as tender as a girl's. A festive atmosphere had even filled the entranceway where Natashka slept, and where, at dawn, she jumped up from the trunk on which she made her bed and immediately remembered that the world contained great joy because a pair of boots light enough for the tsar's first son to wear now stood outside the door, waiting to be cleaned. That festive mood, together with her giddy fear, grew strongest out beyond the garden—there, in the abandoned bathhouse, where the double mirror in a heavy silver frame was hidden. While everyone was still asleep, she'd run there through the dewy brush, and in that secret place she'd savor her possession of this mesmerizing treasure—carry it out to the bathhouse steps, unfold it in the hot morning sun, stare at her reflection until her head began to spin—and then she'd hide it, bury it once more, run back to the manor house where all morning she would tend to him, that man to whom she couldn't raise her eyes, he for whom she stared so long at her reflection, hoping, crazily, that he might find her pretty.

But the fairy tale about the scarlet flower ended quickly, very quickly. It ended in disgrace and shame that had no names in Natashka's mind. . . . It ended in an order from Pyotr Petrovich that they cut off all her hair, make hideous that girl who used to wear her nicest things for him, who darkened her eyebrows in that little mirror, who created in her mind the sweet illusion that she had shared with him some secret intimacy. He discovered her crime himself and turned it into a simple theft, the stupid escapade of a serf girl whom they dressed in a shirt of coarse twill and whom—disgraced, suddenly cut off from everything she knew and cherished, her face still swollen from her sobbing—they sat on a manure cart and, with all the other house serfs gathered round to watch, drove away to some frightening and unseen farm somewhere in the distant steppe. She knew that there she'd have to tend to turkeys, chickens, fields of squash and melon; that she would burn in the sun, utterly forgotten by the world; that the long steppe days would be like years; that the horizons would sink in sheets of shimmering heat, and it would grow so silent, so sultry that she'd long to sleep a dead sleep for days but would be forced instead to listen to the careful crack of dried peas, the deliberate scratching of the brood hen in the hot dirt, the measured exchange of sad calls among turkeys—be forced to watch out for the cruel shadow of the hawk as it sailed across the land, and then leap up, scream "Shoo!" in a thin and drawn-out voice. There an old Ukrainian woman would have complete control over Natashka's life and death, and now, already, she was waiting impatiently for her victim to arrive! The only advantage that Natashka had over someone being driven to his execution was that she might still decide to hang herself. And this alone gave her comfort as they drove to her exile, which she assumed would be eternal.

The sights were endless as they traveled from one end of the district to the other. But none of it was for her. She thought, or rather felt, one thing alone: life is over. Your crime and your disgrace are far too great for you ever to hope for a return! For now there remained one person who was close to her: Yevsey Bodulya. But what would happen once he gave her into the hands of the old Ukrainian, spent the night, then left her behind forever in that strange land? She wept, and then she wanted to eat. To her surprise, Yevsey looked on this quite simply, and while they ate together he spoke to her as if nothing had occurred at all. Then she fell asleep and woke up in the town. It stunned her with its dreariness, its dry and stuffy air—and something else, something vaguely harrowing and mournful, like a troubling dream you can't explain. From that entire day she would remember only that the steppe is hot this time of year, that nothing on this earth is longer than the big district roads or more endless than a summer day; she would remember that there are places in a certain town where the wheels of a cart rattle strangely over the paving stones; she would remember that the town smelled of tin roofs in the distance, but in the middle of the square, where they stopped to rest and feed the horse among rows of closed-up eating sheds, the air was filled with the scents of tar and dust and rotting hay, which lay mixed with manure in clumps where other carts and *mouzhiki* had stopped. Yevsey unharnessed the horse and led it to the wagon to eat. He pushed his hat back on his head, wiped the sweat from his forehead with his sleeve, and, looking blackened by the raging heat, set off for an inn. He'd given Natashka the strictest orders "to look around" and, if anything went wrong, to raise the entire square with her shouts. Natashka stared at the cupola of a newly built cathedral, which burned like a huge, silver star somewhere far away, above the houses. She sat without taking her eyes from it, sat without moving until Yevsey returned. Looking livelier, still chewing something, he led the horse back into the cart shafts while holding a *kalach* under one arm.

"You and I are a little late now, my princess," he mumbled with new animation, addressing either Natashka or the horse. "No cause for hanging, though, I hope. It's not like there's a fire burning somewhere. . . . I'm not going to race back, either. The master's horse, brother, means more to me than your damn mouth," he said, already imagining Demyan, the village headman. "He opens that hole of his, starts talking. 'You watch it with me,' he says. 'Something happens — I'll see what you've got in your pants!' 'Akh,' I think. 'His insult is like a blow to my stomach. The masters never even dropped my pants. Never once beat me! And you? You're like a dog with black gums.' 'Watch it,' he says. What's for me to watch? I'm no slower than you. I won't come back at all if I don't feel like it. Take the girl to the farm, make the sign of the cross — and that's the last they see. . . . And really, I mean — I'm surprised at this girl! What's the little fool grieving for? Is all the world in Sukhodol? The cart drivers will come through, or some wanderers. They pass the farm — just say a word, and next thing you know, you're past Rostov. . . . And there, well, no one knows a thing. Let them try to guess your name!"

Plans for hanging herself were momentarily displaced by thoughts of flight in Natashka's cropped head. The cart began to squeak and shake. Yevsey stopped talking and led the horse to the well in the middle of the square. The sun was going down behind them now, slowly sinking past a large garden outside a monastery. Across from it stood a jail with yellow walls: all of its windows had turned golden in the fading light. The sight of the prison further spurred her thoughts of flight. People do it—run away and live! But they say the wanderers steal children and burn their eyes out with hot milk, then pass them off as cripples to help their begging. And the cart drivers, they say they take children to the sea, sell them to the Nogais. And it happens—sometimes the masters catch their runaways, bring them back in chains, lock them in the prisons. It's not animals locked up in there, after all—just like Gervaska said. Those are people in there too. . . .

The light disappeared from the jail's windows. Natashka's thoughts grew confused. No, running away is even more terrible. Worse than hanging yourself. . . . Yevsey's bold talk had stopped. He was silent now, pensive.

"We're a little late, my girl," he said, his voice already sounding worried as he jumped onto the side of the cart.

And again the cart began to roar over the paving stones, shuddering and knocking loudly as it made its way toward the district thoroughfare. "It would be best to turn this cart around," Natashka half felt, half thought. "Race back to Sukhodol, fall at the master's feet!" But Yevsey kept driving on. There was no star above the buildings anymore. Ahead stood bare white streets, white houses, white paving stones—all ending in that huge white cathedral with its new cupola of white tin beneath a dry and pale blue sky. But back there, at home, the dew had already fallen; fresh cool air lingered in the garden; the scent of a warming stove began to rise from the cook's quarters; far beyond the plains of wheat, beyond the silver poplars at the garden's edge, beyond the old and cherished bathhouse, the dusk was slowly dimming. In the drawing room the doors were open on the balcony, and a scarlet glow was mixing with the twilight in the corners of the room while a girl who resembled both grandfather and Pyotr Petrovich with her black eyes and her dark, slightly sallow complexion adjusted the orange silk sleeves of her light, wide dress. Sitting with her back to the sunset, she stared at the sheets of music, struck the piano's yellowing keys, filled the room with the solemn and melodious notes of Oginsky's polonaise—filled the room with all those sounds of sweet despair, and seemed to pay no attention at all to the stocky, dark-complexioned officer who stood behind her, his left hand resting firmly on his waist as he frowned and intently watched her quick, light hands.

"It's happened to us both . . . her and me," Natashka half thought and half felt on those evenings, her heart going still. She would run into the cold, damp garden, step into the deep underbrush, and stand, half hidden, among the nettles and strongly scented burdock, waiting for that moment that would never occur—that moment when the young master would come down from the balcony, start walking down the avenue, see her, suddenly turn from the path and draw close with quick steps—and she would not utter a sound from terror and joy. . . .

The cart was rattling down the street. She'd thought the town might hold something magical, but it was only hot and odorous. Natashka looked with painful wonder at the well-dressed people walking along the paving stones among the houses, the gates, and the small shops with open doors. . . . "Why did Yevsey come this way?" she thought. "Isn't he embarrassed to rattle past them all so loud?"

They left the cathedral behind and began to descend toward the river along a bumpy, dusty incline that took them past blackened smithies and the rotting little shacks of craftsmen. The air began to seem familiar again—it smelled of warm fresh water and silt from the river, a crispness from the fields as evening fell. The first light began to burn in a distant, lonely little house that stood on the opposite hill near the signal arm at the railroad tracks. . . . They were in the open now, completely on their own. They crossed a bridge and drove up to the signal arm—an empty road of white stones stared at them, its chalky surface receding far into the dark, fresh, and endless blue of evening in the steppe. The horse broke into a little trot until it passed the signal arm, then slowed back to a walk. Again you could hear how quiet it was, how silent the earth and sky became at night: only a little bell was ringing softly somewhere far away. It steadily grew stronger, more melodious, flowed into the rhythmic rattling of a *troika*, the steady clatter of carriage wheels as they raced along the road and drew near. . . . A young, free driver held the *troika*'s reins, and in the carriage sat an officer, his chin buried in the collar of his hooded officer's coat. He lifted his head for a moment as the *troika* drew level with the cart, and Natashka saw a red collar, a black moustache, a young man's eyes shining under the visor of a helmet. . . . She gasped, went numb, and fainted. . . .

The senseless thought that this was Pyotr Petrovich had flashed through her mind, and the sudden jolt of pain and tenderness that surged like lightning through her simple, nervous, menial heart suddenly revealed exactly what it was she'd lost: all proximity to him. . . . Yevsey rushed to douse her lolling head with water from a wooden jug they carried in the cart.

A wave of nausea brought her back to consciousness, and she hurriedly leaned over the cart's side. Yevsey held her cold forehead in his palm. . . .

And then, her collar damp, her body unburdened and chilled, she lay on her back and looked at the stars. Alarmed, Yevsey sat silently, thinking and shaking his head, believing she was asleep as he drove faster and faster. The shuddering cart raced forward, and the girl felt as if she had no body anymore, just soul. And that soul was content, "as happy as it would have been in heaven."

Her love had bloomed like that scarlet flower in the garden of a children's tale. And now she rode away with it, took it to the steppe, a place even more remote than the deep woods of Sukhodol, so that there she could overcome in solitude and silence the first sweet agony of that love—and then, for years, for all her life, for eternity—bury it within the soul that Sukhodol had given her.

VI

Love was strange at Sukhodol. And so was hate.

Our grandfather was killed in that same year. His death was as senseless as that of his killer—as senseless as the death of anyone who died at Sukhodol.

Pyotr Petrovich invited guests to celebrate the feast of Pokrov—always a big holiday at Sukhodol—and worried terribly: would the marshal of the nobility come as he had promised? Grandfather was overjoyed but also worried for some reason no one understood. The marshal came, and the dinner was a great success. It was lively and loud, and no one had a better time than grandfather. Early in the morning of October 2, they found him dead on the floor in the drawing room.

When he resigned from the military, Pyotr Petrovich had made no effort to conceal the fact that he was sacrificing himself to save the Khrushchyov family's honor and ancestral home. He did not hide the fact that he was taking the estate into his hands "against his will." But he thought it essential to become acquainted with those more educated members of the local gentry who might prove useful, while avoiding any kind of rift with the others. At first he met these obligations flawlessly, even visiting all the small estate owners and the farm of Aunt Olga Kirillovna, a monstrously fat woman who suffered from sleeping sickness and cleaned her teeth with snuff. By fall no one was surprised that Pyotr

Petrovich ran Sukhodol like an autocrat. He no longer resembled a handsome officer who'd come to visit while on leave; instead he looked like the true owner of an estate, a young master. He no longer flushed darkly when upset. He grew sleek, filled out, wore expensive caftans. He pampered his small feet with red Tatar slippers, adorned his small hands with turquoise rings. Arkady Petrovich was embarrassed to look into his brother's light brown eyes. He didn't know what to talk about with him. He went out hunting as much as possible and, at first, simply deferred to Pyotr Petrovich in everything.

At the feast of Pokrov, Pyotr Petrovich wanted to charm each and every one of his guests, show them all that he was master of the house. But grandfather bothered him terribly. He was blissfully happy but also tactless, garrulous, and pathetic in his velvet relic's hat, his new, inordinately wide, navy blue coat, which the family tailor had sewn. He too imagined himself to be the gracious host, and he fussed around the house from early morning, determined to turn the initial reception of the guests into some kind of stupid ceremony. Half the double doors between the vestibule and the main hall were never opened. But grandfather himself pulled up the iron catches—carried in a chair by himself and climbed onto it, his entire body shaking from the effort. With both doors now flung back, grandfather stationed himself on the threshold and, exploiting the silence of Pyotr Petrovich—who had resolved to endure all of this and now seemed paralyzed by embarrassment and rage—he remained there, in the entranceway, until the very last guests had arrived. With his eyes fixed constantly on the porch—where it was also necessary to open all the doors as if in keeping with some odd custom—he stood and shuffled his feet with excitement until he saw a new arrival, then rushed toward him, throwing one foot over the other as he leapt up and executed a little *pas de chat*, followed by a low bow and a breathless, sputtering stream of words, which he repeated before everyone:

"How glad I am! How delighted! It's been so long since you visited me! Please, please come in!"

It enraged Pyotr Petrovich too that grandfather informed each and every new arrival of Tonya's departure to Lunyovo, the estate where her aunt Olga Kirillovna lived. "Tonechka's fallen sick with melancholy. She's gone to her aunt's for the entire fall,"—what could the guests possibly make of this unsolicited announcement? Of course everyone knew the story of Voitkevich. He might have had truly serious intentions, sighing as he did, enigmatically, whenever he was near Tonya, playing duets with her on the piano, reciting "Lyudmila" in a muffled voice, or telling her with gloomy pensiveness, "Your sacred word has bound you to a dead man." But even his most innocent attempts to express his emotions—giving her a flower, for instance—sparked a rage in Tonya, and Voitkevich left abruptly. Once he had gone, Tonya stopped sleeping at night, sitting instead near an open window in the dark, waiting for a particular moment—known only to her—when it was time to burst out sobbing and rouse Pyotr Petrovich from his sleep. He would lie in bed for a long time, clenching his jaw, listening to those sobs and the constant patter of the poplars, which sounded like a small, incessant rain in the dark garden beyond the windows. And then he went to try to soothe her. Half asleep, the house girls came as well, and sometimes grandfather would come running in alarm, at which point Tonya would begin to pound her feet and shout: "Leave me alone! Savages! My enemies!"—and the entire business ended in shameful abuse, almost violence.

Pyotr Petrovich would drive out grandfather and the girls, slam the door, and stand there, still holding its handle. "Just imagine, you little snake," he'd whisper in a rage. "Just imagine how this looks to them!"

"Ahhh!" Tonechka would squeal furiously. "Papenka! He's shouting that I'm pregnant!"

And clutching his head in his hands, Pyotr Petrovich would fly from the room.

At the feast of Pokrov he was deeply worried about Gervaska: a few incautious words could trigger an embarrassingly rude response from him in front of the guests.

Gervaska had grown terribly. Huge, ungainly, he was both the smartest and most prominent of the servants, and now he too was dressed in a long, dark blue coat; wide trousers; and soft kid boots without heels; a worsted, lilac-colored scarf tied around his neck. His dark, coarse and dry hair was parted on the side, but Gervaska didn't want it cropped close to his scalp; instead he kept it in an even bowl-cut all the way around his head. There was nothing for him to shave other than two or three tough little curls on his chin and at the corners of his mouth, which was so big that people joked about tying it shut with ribbon. All bones and sharp angles, with an exceedingly wide, flat chest, with a small head and deep-set eyes, with thin, ashy-blue lips and large bluish teeth, this ancient Arian, this Persian of Sukhodol, had already been given a nickname: Borzoi. Looking at his bared teeth, hearing his intermittent coughing, many people thought to themselves: "Soon, soon,

Borzoi, you'll drop dead." But unlike all the other serfs, they dignified this overgrown child with a patronymic: Gervasy Afanasyevich.

Even the masters were afraid of him. Their mind-set was the same as that of their serfs: you either rule a man or fear him. Much to the surprise of all the other menials, Gervaska had received no punishment at all for his impudent answer to grandfather on the day of Pyotr Petrovich's arrival. "You're an absolute swine, brother," Arkady Petrovich told him succinctly, to which he received an equally concise response: "I can't stand him, sir!" But Gervaska went to Pyotr Petrovich of his own accord. He stood in the doorway, presumptuous as usual, one knee cocked forward while he leaned back on his disproportionally long legs in enormous, wide trousers, and asked to be flogged:

"I'm a lout, sir, and I have a terrible hot temper," he said nonchalantly, widening his gaze as he looked into the room.

Believing the phrase "terrible hot temper" to be a hint at something, Pyotr Petrovich took fright.

"There will be plenty of time for that, my friend, plenty of time," he shouted with feigned severity. "Now go away, I can't stand seeing your impudence."

Gervaska stayed where he was without speaking. Then he said: "As you wish."

But he continued standing there a little longer, twisting one of the tough little hairs above his upper lip, baring his bluish teeth like a dog, all emotion eradicated from his face—and then he went away. From that time on he was firmly convinced of the advantage such a manner afforded: show no expression and be as brief as possible in your answers. Pyotr Petrovich began to avoid not only talking to Gervaska but even looking him in the eye.

Gervaska behaved with the same inexplicable nonchalance at Pokrov. Everyone in the house was run ragged preparing for the holiday, giving and receiving instructions, cursing, arguing, washing floors, cleaning the heavy dark silver of the icons with bluing chalk, kicking the dogs away as they tried to crowd back into the *sentsy*, worrying that the jellies wouldn't set, that the pastries and the cakes would burn, that the forks would not suffice. Only Gervaska smirked calmly and said to Kazmir, the alcoholic cook, who was now in a frenzy: "Take it easy, father deacon, or your cassock's going to split a seam!"

"Watch you don't get drunk," Pyotr Petrovich said to Gervaska distractedly, worrying about the marshal.

"I haven't drank since I was born," Gervaska shot back, as if speaking to a peer. "Not interesting."

And then, when all the guests had arrived, in a voice loud enough for everyone to hear, Pyotr Petrovich called out ingratiatingly:

"Gervasy! Don't disappear, please. It's like I have no hands without you near!"

And Gervaska answered with utmost courtesy and poise: "Don't worry for a moment, sir, I wouldn't dare to leave you."

And he served as never before, fully justifying the words that Pyotr Petrovich had spoken to the guests:

"You can't imagine the nerve of that gangly fellow. But he's an absolute genius! Hands of pure gold!"

How could he have known that these words would be the drops that overfilled the cup? Hearing them, grandfather began to pull at the breast of his coat and suddenly, across the entire table, he shouted at the marshal:

"Your Excellency! I beg your hand in aid! Like a child to its father, I run to you now with a complaint against my servant. Against that one, there! Against Gervasy Afanasyevich Kulikov! At every step he mocks me! He. . . ."

They interrupted him, implored him, calmed him down. Grandfather was distraught to the point of tears, but they began to soothe him with such affection and esteem—all of it, of course, tinged with a mocking irony—that he yielded to their supplications, was filled once more with the happiness of a child. Gervaska stood silently by the wall, his eyes lowered and his head turned slightly to the side. Grandfather saw that this Vulcan's head was extraordinarily small—and would be even smaller if the Vulcan's hair were trimmed; he noticed that the back of that head was pointed, almost sharp, and there the hair was particularly thick—coarse, black, crudely cut, it formed a kind of protuberance that stuck out over the back of his thin neck. All the sun and wind of his hunting trips had made Gervaska's skin begin to peel, and now his face was marked by several pale, violet-colored splotches. Grandfather cast his glances at Gervaska with fear and alarm, but all the same shouted joyfully to the guests:

"Very well, I forgive him! But for this I will not allow you to leave, dear guests, for three entire days! I won't let you leave for anything! Most of all, I beg you not to leave this evening. How disturbed I feel when the sun goes down! It's all so sad and lonely, so frightening. The sky starts to fill with storm clouds. And they say they caught two more French soldiers again—Bonaparte's men!—in Troshin Forest!. . . I'm bound to die in the evening—mark my words! Martyn Zadeka already predicted this in my future. . . ."

But he died early in the morning.

He insisted, and "for his sake" many guests stayed the night. They drank tea all evening. There were so many different kinds of preserves that you could come and go several times to try them all. Then they opened up the card tables, lit so many spermaceti candles that their reflected light spilled from all the mirrors, and the rooms of Sukhodol—filled with noise and conversation and the fragrant scent of Zhukovsky tobacco—took on a golden glow, like the incandescence of a church. But most important was the fact that many guests had decided to stay the night, for this meant not only another happy day but more chores, responsibilities. After all, if not for him, Pyotr Kirillych, they never would have managed such an entertaining party, such a rich and lively dinner, such a grand assembly of guests.

"Yes, yes," grandfather thought worriedly as he stood without his jacket late that night in his bedroom and looked at the blackening icon of St. Merkury, a row of wax candles burning on the lectern before it. "And death will be savage to the sinful. . . . Let the light of our anger burn without ceasing!"

But just then he remembered that he had wanted to think something else; hunched over, whispering the fiftieth psalm, he moved across the room, pausing to trim the pastille that smoldered on his nightstand, and picked up his Psalter. He opened it with a deep sigh of contentment and raised his eyes once again to the headless saint—and suddenly struck on the idea he'd been meaning to pursue. A smile lit up his face:

"They say, 'Have it—hate it; lose it—love it.' Well, it will be the same with this old man when he's gone. . . ."

Fearing he would wake up late and fail to issue some essential order, grandfather hardly slept. And early in the morning, when that silence that comes only after a holiday still hung with the scent of tobacco smoke in all the disordered chambers of the house, he stole into the drawing room with nothing but slippers on his feet, fastidiously picked up several small pieces of chalk that lay on the floor near the open green tables, and then let out a faint gasp of pleasure as he glanced at the garden through the glass doors, saw the bright cold light of the azure, the silver rime that had covered the balcony and the handrails, the brown leaves of the bare thicket below the balcony. He opened the door and sniffed deeply: a bitter, almost astringent scent of autumnal decay still rose from the bushes, but now it was mixed with a winter freshness. And everything was motionless, calm, almost solemn. The sun was just rising over the village, and it lit the tops of the birches that lined the main path to the house like a painting, revealing a subtle, joyful lilac tint that the azure sky created as it gleamed through the white, half-bare limbs and branches still flecked with golden leaves. A dog ran to the cold shade beneath the balcony, its feet crunching sharply over the brittle grass, which seemed to be laced with salt. That crisp sound reminded him of winter, and a shiver of pleasure passed through the old man's shoulders. Then grandfather came back into the drawing room, took a deep breath, and began to rearrange the heavy furniture, which scraped loudly along the floor as he worked, glancing occasionally at the mirror, where the sky was reflected. Suddenly Gervaska entered the room, moving noiselessly and quickly. He was without his coat, half asleep, and "evil as the devil," as he would later say.

"Quiet, you! Who told you to move the furniture!" he shouted in an angry whisper.

Grandfather raised his excited face and answered with a tenderness that had come to him the previous day and stayed through the entire night.

"You see what type you are, Gervasy," he whispered. "I forgave you yesterday, and you, instead of showing gratitude to your master. . . ."

"I'm sick of you, you slobbering fool. You're worse than fall," Gervaska interrupted him. . . . "Let go of the table!"

Grandfather looked with fear at the back of Gervaska's head, which jutted out even more than usual above the thin neck that rose from the collar of his white shirt, but that fear was not enough to stop him from flaring with anger. He stepped in front of the card table that he'd planned to move into the corner.

He paused for a moment to think it over. "You let go!" he shouted, but not loudly. "It's you who must defer to the master! You're going to wear out my patience! I'll bury a dagger in you!"

"Akh," Gervaska said with annoyance, baring his teeth—and hit the old man on the chest with a backhanded blow.

Grandfather slipped on the smooth oak floor, flailed his arms, and struck his temple on the sharp edge of the card table as he fell.

Seeing the blood, the old man's gaping mouth, his skewed and lifeless eyes, Gervaska tore from grandfather's still warm neck a small gold icon and an amulet on a worn-out cord. . . . He looked hurriedly around, tugged grandmother's wedding ring from the old man's pinky . . . and then Gervaska went quickly and soundlessly from the drawing room — vanished into thin air.

The only person from all of Sukhodol who saw him after that was Natalya.

VII

Two major events occurred at Sukhodol while she was still living at Soshki: Pyotr Petrovich married, and the brothers left as volunteers in the Crimean War.

She returned only after two full years had passed: they'd forgotten about her. And when she returned, she did not recognize Sukhodol, just as Sukhodol did not recognize her.

On that summer evening when a cart sent from the master's estate began to squeak outside the hut in Soshki, and Natashka hurried down the steps, Yevsey Bodulya exclaimed with surprise:

"Is that really you, Natashka?"

"Who else would it be?" she answered with an almost imperceptible smile.

Yevsey shook his head.

"You've turned out badly here."

But in fact she simply didn't look the way she had before. The round-faced girl with short cropped hair and clear eyes had turned into a calm, reserved young woman with a petite, graceful figure and a gentle manner. She wore a wraparound skirt of checkered wool and an embroidered blouse; although her headscarf was tied in the Russian style, it was dark, and Natashka's face, tanned from the sun, was covered in small freckles the color of millet. Born and raised in Sukhodol, Yevsey naturally objected to the dark headscarf, the freckles, and the suntan.

As they drove home, Yevsey said:

"Well now, my girl, you're old enough to have a husband. Do you want to marry?"

She only shook her head.

"No, Uncle Yevsey. I won't ever go to the altar."

Yevsey even pulled the pipe out of his mouth. "Why? What good could come of life alone?"

She began to explain unhurriedly: it wasn't meant for everyone to marry, after all. At Sukhodol they'd give her to the young mistress, most likely—and the young mistress had promised herself to God. She wouldn't want her servant girls getting married. And besides, she'd had many dreams lately. It was clear what they meant.

"What do you mean?" Yevsey asked. "What did you see?"

"No, well. . . . Nothing, really," she said. "Gervaska scared me to death then. He told me everything, and I started thinking. . . . And then the dreams came."

"Is it really true that he sat down and ate with you, Gervaska?"

Natashka thought for a moment:

"He ate breakfast. He came and said: 'I'm here on important business from the masters. Only, let's have a meal first.' We set the table for him as an honest man. He ate his fill, went outside the hut—and winked at me. I ducked out and he talked to me around the corner. Told me all of it in truth. And then he just went off on his own. . . ."

"Why didn't you call for the bosses?"

"No chance, no way. . . . He promised he would kill me. Said to keep quiet until evening. He told them he'd go down to sleep along the storehouse, and just kept on going."

All the house serfs looked at her with great curiosity at Sukhodol; her girlfriends from the servants' quarters pestered her with questions. But she answered with such brevity that Natashka seemed to be playing some kind of role that she had specially taken on.

"It was good," she told them repeatedly.

And once she said, like some kind of old pilgrim woman, "God's will is in everything. It was good."

And simply, without delay, she entered the daily working life of the estate, seemingly unsurprised by the fact that grandfather was gone, that the young masters had gone to war as volunteers, that the young mistress "had been touched" and now wandered among the rooms in emulation of her father, that Sukhodol was now controlled by a new, completely unfamiliar mistress who was lively, small, plump, and pregnant.

At lunch the new mistress shouted:

"Call in that one—what's her name? Natashka!"

Natashka came into the room quickly and noiselessly. She crossed herself and bowed to the icon in the corner, then to the mistress and Miss Tonya, and stood waiting for questions and instructions. Of course, only the mistress questioned her—Tonya, who had grown very tall, thin, and sharp-nosed, stared vacantly with her fantastically black eyes and never uttered a word. The mistress decided that Natashka should serve the young lady. Natashka bowed and said simply:

"Very well, ma'am."

The young mistress continued to stare at Natasha with the same indifferent attention, then suddenly attacked her that evening, her eyes crossed in a savage fury as she pulled out Natashka's hair with violent pleasure because the young serf had clumsily tugged on her leg as she removed her stockings. Natashka wept like a young child but said nothing, and later, as she sat on a bench in the servants' quarters and removed the many strands of hair that Tonya had torn loose from her scalp, she even smiled with tears still hanging on her lashes.

"She's a savage one!" she said. "And this will be a trial. . . ."

Tonya lay in bed for a long time after waking up the next morning. Natashka stood in the doorway with her head lowered, glancing sidelong at her mistress's pale face.

"What did you see in your dreams?" the young mistress asked. Her face and voice were so completely disengaged that someone else might have been speaking for her.

Natashka answered:

"Nothing, it seems, miss."

The young mistress leapt up as suddenly as she had attacked the night before, and flung her cup of tea at Natashka in a rage, then collapsed back onto the bed and began bitterly to sob and shout. Natashka managed to avoid the cup as it sailed toward her, and she soon learned to move out of the way of flying objects with unusual skill and speed. It turned out that the young mistress would sometimes shout, "Then make something up!" at those stupid girls who answered her questions about dreams by saying they'd seen nothing in their sleep the night before. But as Natashka was an ungifted liar, she was forced to develop a different skill: dodging.

A doctor was finally brought to see the young mistress. He left her with a wide array of pills and drops. Fearing they might poison her, Miss Tonya forced Natashka to try all her medicines first: she took them one after the other without a word of protest. Soon after her return to Sukhodol, Natashka learned that the young mistress had been waiting for her "like the light of day." Miss Tonya, it turned out, had remembered her for some reason, and she all but wore her eyes out looking for the cart on the road from Soshki while ardently assuring everyone that she would be completely well the moment Natashka returned. And Natashka did return—only to be met with absolute indifference. But perhaps it was her bitter disappointment that made the young mistress cry? Natashka felt her heart constrict with sorrow and regret when she realized this. She went into the corridor, sat down on a trunk, and wept again.

"Well now, feeling better?" the young mistress asked when Natashka came back into the room with swollen eyes.

The medicine had made her head spin and her heart skip beats, but Natashka whispered, "Better, miss," as she approached her, took her hand, and kissed it ardently.

For a long time after that she felt such pity for the young mistress that she couldn't look at her directly, and walked everywhere with her eyes lowered.

"There she goes—a little Ukrainian snake in the grass!" Soloshka shouted at her from the servants' quarters one day. More than any of her other girlfriends, Soloshka had tried to become the confidante of Natashka's innermost thoughts and feelings. But she repeatedly ran up against Natashka's brief and simple answers to her questions—answers that left no room for any of the charms and pleasures of girlish intimacy.

Natashka smiled sadly.

"Well, maybe so . . .," she answered thoughtfully. "It's true what they say—we bond to those we're near. I miss them, those Ukrainians. More than my own father and mother even."

At first she'd given no meaning to her new surroundings in Soshki. They'd arrived near morning. And nothing seemed strange that morning other than the fact that the peasant hut was very long and white and clearly visible from far away in the plains; that the Ukrainian woman greeted them in a friendly way as she heated the stove, while the Ukrainian man did not listen to Yevsey. And Yevsey rambled on and on without stopping. He spoke about the masters, about Demyan, about the blazing heat they'd encountered on the road, about the food he'd eaten in town, about Pyotr Petrovich, and of course about the mirror. But the Ukrainian man, Shary—or, as they referred to him in Sukhodol, the Badger—only shook his head and, when Yevsey finally fell silent, looked at him distractedly and began to sing under his breath in a happy, nasal tone: "Whirl, little snowstorm, whirl . . ." Then she began, little by little, to come to herself—and to wonder at Soshki, to discover more and more charm in it as well as ever more dissimilarities with Sukhodol. Even the

Ukrainians' hut was remarkable with its white walls, its smooth and level roof of thatch made from rushes. How clean and wealthy it seemed in comparison to the poor and slovenly huts of Sukhodol! What expensive foil icons hung in the corner! And how lovely were the bright towels displayed above them, the paper flowers arranged around their frames! And the patterned cloth on the table, the rows of dark blue pots on the shelf near the stove! But most remarkable of all were the keepers of that hut.

What it was that made them so exceptional Natasha couldn't say, but she felt it constantly. She had never seen a *mouzhik* who was so calm, well kept, and agreeable as Shary. He wasn't tall, his head was shaped like a wedge, and his thick, full, greying hair was cut short. He had no beard, only a narrow moustache, like a Tatar's, which was also grey. His face and neck were tanned and deeply creased from the sun, but even his wrinkles seemed agreeable, neatly defined, somehow necessary. He wore pants of coarse, bleached canvas folded into the tops of his boots, which were so heavy they seemed to weigh down his feet. His shirt, also made of bleached canvas, had a low-cut collar and extra width in the arms; he wore it neatly tucked into his trousers. He hunched his shoulders slightly as he walked, but neither this nor his deep wrinkles nor his grey hair made him seem old: his face had none of that weariness, that torpor that fills our men. His small, sharp eyes looked at the world with keen and delicate laughter. He reminded Natashka of an old Serb who once appeared at Sukhodol from out of nowhere with a boy who played the violin.

The Ukrainian woman was named Marina, but they always called her the Spear at Sukhodol, for she was tall, thin, and gracefully built despite her fifty years. She had wide-set cheekbones and a coarse face. Her complexion was much darker than that of anyone who lived at Sukhodol, and years of sun had added an even, slightly yellow hue to her fine skin. But the candor of her eyes, their unyielding ebullience, made her almost pretty: they contained the grey of both amber and agate, and they changed like a cat's eyes. A large black-and-gold kerchief with red polka dots covered her head, resembling a high turban; a short, wraparound skirt of black wool clung tightly to her long waist and legs, sharply accentuating the whiteness of her blouse. On her bare feet she wore shoes with steel strips lining their heels; her bare calves were shapely and thin, and the sun had turned them the color of light lacquered wood. Sometimes when she worked she would narrow her eyes and sing in a deep, strong voice about the infidels laying siege to

Pochaev, and the Mother of God defending the monastery as "the evening sunset burned above the walls," and there was such despair in her voice, such keening sorrow—and yet, at the same time, such majesty and power, such a mighty threat of retribution, that Natashka couldn't take her eyes from her for fear and ecstasy.

The Ukrainians had no children; Natashka was an orphan. If she'd lived with a family in Sukhodol they would have called her their adopted daughter, and they would have pitied her on certain days while denouncing her as a thief and wounding her with piercing looks on others. The Ukrainians were almost cold by comparison, but they treated Natashka with temperance and equanimity, saying little and asking almost nothing. In the fall, Russian peasant women from Kaluga were brought in for the harvest and the threshing, but Natashka stayed away from these "Kaluga girls," for they were known to be debauched and shamefully diseased. Busty, impudent, and mischievous, they wore bright *sarafans*, swore with pleasure and obscene proficiency, scattered flippant phrases throughout their speech, straddled horses like men, and rode as if possessed. Her grief might have been dispersed by daily life and new confidantes, by tears and shared songs. But to whom was she to tell her story? With whom was she supposed to sing? If one of the Kaluga girls began a song, all the others would immediately join in, erupt with their coarse, shrill voices, their whistling and their little yelps. Shary sang only humorous little songs that were meant for dancing. And even in her love songs, Marina was stern and proud, somber, meditative:

> *The willows that I planted*
> *Stir softly now*
> *Beyond the weir*

she'd sing, forlornly drawing out the words, and then, lowering her voice, she'd add with absolute despondency:

> *And still my darling love*
> *Is nowhere near.*

And so it was in solitude that Natashka slowly drank in the bittersweet poison of unrequited love, suffered through her shame and jealousy, the terrible and tender dreams that often came to her at night. Every day she struggled with the dead weight of her impossible hopes and expectations in the silence of the steppe. And the searing pain of her injury often gave way to tenderness within her heart; passion and despair

became humility—a simple desire for some modest and discrete existence close to him, a love that she'd conceal from everyone forever, a
love that demanded nothing, expected nothing. News and messages
from Sukhodol helped to sober her, but for a long time there was no
news, no sense of daily life at home—and Sukhodol began to seem so
wonderful, so necessary that she felt she couldn't bear her loneliness and
sorrow. . . . Then, suddenly, Gervaska appeared. He quickly and
offhandedly related all the news from Sukhodol, covering in half an
hour events that others might require entire days to describe, including
the fact that he had killed grandfather with a shove.

"And now—goodbye for good!"

He went out to the road and turned; his eyes seemed to burn right
through her as she stood there, stunned by his confession:

"And it's time for you to get the pap out of your head!" he shouted.
"He's getting married any day. And he won't need you at all, not even on
the side. Open your eyes!"

She did open her eyes. She lived through the terrible news, came
to herself—and opened her eyes.

Then the days began to pass steadily and slowly, like the pilgrims
who walked and walked on the highway past the farm and often carried
on long conversations with her as they rested. They taught her patience
and reliance on God, whose name they pronounced with dull despondency. Above all else, they taught her one rule: don't think.

"Think, don't think—nothing changes. Nothing will occur by our
will," the pilgrims would say as they retied the laces of their bast shoes
and squinted wearily into the distant steppe, their weathered faces creasing deeply. "God's will is in everything. . . . Now sneak us a little onion
from the garden, there, won't you dear?"

There were others, of course, who frightened her with talk of sin
and promised her far greater woe and suffering in the world that lies beyond this one. And then she had two terrible dreams, almost in a row.
She was thinking all the time about Sukhodol—at first it was so hard to
keep from thinking!—about the young mistress, about grandfather,
about her future. Sometimes she would try to guess when she'd marry,
and if she would, with whom. It was in the midst of such a reverie that
she slipped imperceptibly into a dream: with utter clarity she saw herself
running to a pond with buckets as the sun set on a sultry, dusty day, and
a troubling wind swept across the land. Suddenly a hideous dwarf with a
large head and torn-out boots appeared on a hillside of dry clay. He had

no hat; the wind blew his red, disheveled hair into clumps, and his un-belted fire-red shirt billowed around him. "Grandfather!" she shouted with alarm and horror. "What's burning!" "Now it will all be blown away! Not a trace will remain!" the dwarf shouted back, his voice drowned out by the hot wind. "An untold storm is coming! Don't dare to take a groom!" The other dream was even more terrible. She seemed to stand at noon on a hot day inside a peasant hut. The door had been bolted shut from outside. She was waiting for something, her heart going still—and suddenly a huge grey goat jumped out from behind the stove. It reared back onto its hind legs and came at her, obscenely aroused, with ecstatic and imploring eyes that burned like coal. "I'm your groom!" it shouted in a human voice, tapping its hind legs in shallow lit-tle steps as it awkwardly drew close, then toppled forward onto her, its front legs striking hard against her breasts. . . .

Lurching upright from her bedding on the floor, she almost died from the pounding of her heart in the aftermath of those dreams—almost died from the terror of the dark, and the thought that she had no one she could turn to.

"Lord Jesus," she whispered hurriedly. "Holy Mother of Heaven! Holy saints!"

But she imagined all the saints were dark and headless like Merkury, and thus they only added to her fear.

As she began to contemplate her dreams, she realized that her girl-hood years had passed. She became convinced that many trials awaited her and that her fate was already determined, for it was not in vain that something so unusual as love for the young master had fallen to her lot! She believed it was essential that she learn restraint from the Ukrainians and obedience from the pilgrims. And since the people of Sukhodol liked to play roles—since they convinced themselves that certain events were inevitable, even though they themselves had invented these events from the beginning—Natashka too took on a role to play.

VIII

Her legs went weak with joy when Natashka ran out on the steps and un-derstood that Bodulya had come for her; when she saw the dusty, bat-tered cart from Sukhodol stopped outside the hut on the eve of St. Peter's Day; saw the torn hat on Bodulya's shaggy head; saw his tangled, sun-bleached beard; saw his animated, weary face—prematurely aged and indistinct, almost enigmatic in its amorphous incongruity; saw the familiar shaggy dog that looked not only like Bodulya but all of Sukhodol, with dingy grey fur covering its back and black hair matted to its chest and neck as if stained by the heavy smoke of peasant huts. . . . Quickly she composed herself. As they drove home, Bodulya sang whatever came into his head about the war in the Crimea, seeming to rejoice one minute and grieve the next, while Natashka said in a judicious tone:

"Well, it's obvious—we've got to force them back, those French."

All day while they drove toward Sukhodol, she had an eerie feeling: she was looking at the old and familiar with new eyes; she seemed to reenter her former self as they drew closer to her home. Soon she noticed little changes that had taken place along the road, recognized the people they passed. At the turn from the big road into Sukhodol, a three-year-old colt was running in a fallow field overgrown with wart cabbage. Standing with one bare foot on a rope lead, a young boy clutched at the colt's neck and tried to climb onto its back, but the colt refused to let him, shaking and running. Natashka felt an odd thrill of joy when she recognized the child as Fomka Pantyukhin. They passed the old man Nazarushka, who was now at least a hundred, and so wasted away "there'd be nothing left to put in his coffin"; even his eyes were colorless and sadly faded. He sat in an empty cart like a woman instead of a man, his legs stretched straight out in front of him, his frail shoulders raised high and held tense. Hatless, he wore a long, threadbare shirt that had turned dove grey with ash from his constant lying on the stove. Natashka's heart contracted, went still as she remembered once again that the kind and carefree Arkady Petrovich had wanted to flog this Nazarushka three years ago when he was caught with a radish in the vegetable garden and stood weeping, barely alive from fear, among a crowd of house serfs who shouted with raucous laughter:

"No, no, old man—whining won't do you any good. You'll have to drop your pants for this one! There's no getting out of it now!"

But how that same heart raced when she saw the pastures, the row of peasant huts—and then the estate: the garden, the high roof of the manor house, the back walls of the servants' quarters, the storage sheds, the stables. Yellow fields of rye filled with cornflowers ran right up to those walls, ran up to the tall weeds and the spring onions. Someone's white calf with brown spots had waded deep into the oats and stood there now, eating tassels from the stems. All of the surroundings were peaceful, simple, ordinary; they grew ever more alarming and remarkable only in Natashka's mind, which now turned turbid as the cart rolled briskly into the courtyard, where white borzois lay sleeping like headstones in a country churchyard. For the first time after two years in a peasant hut, she entered the cool interior of the manor house with all its familiar smells—wax candles and linden flowers, the open pantry, Arkady Petrovich's leather saddle lying on a bench in the vestibule, empty cages in which quail are kept above the window. Timidly she looked up at St. Merkury, moved now from grandfather's room to a corner of the entranceway. . . . Sunlight from the garden was streaming cheerfully through small windows, as it had before, into the gloomy hall. A chick that had appeared inside the house for some odd reason wandered around the drawing room, cheeping forlornly. A sweet scent came from the linden flowers drying on the hot, bright windowsill. . . . Everything old that surrounded her seemed to have grown younger, as always happens in a house after a burial. In everything, in everything—but especially in the flowers' scent—she felt a part of her soul, her childhood, her adolescence, first love. And she was sorry for those who had grown up, those who had died, those who had changed—as she herself, and the young mistress, had changed. Her peers were now adults. Many of those old men and women who would occasionally appear in the entranceway of the servants' quarters and look uncomprehendingly at the world, their heads wobbling with decrepitude—many of them had disappeared forever from this earth. Darya Ustinovna had disappeared. Grandfather had disappeared—he who'd feared death like a child, believing it would slowly take him into its grip and prepare him gradually for that terrible hour, but was instead mowed down with lightning speed by its scythe. It was impossible to believe that he no longer existed, that it was he rotting beneath that burial mound near the village church in Cherkizovo. It was impossible to believe that this thin, black-haired, pointy-nosed woman—she who was indifferent one moment and furious the next; she who chatted openly with Natashka as she would with a girlfriend and then began ripping out her hair—was the young mistress Tonya. And it was impossible to understand why the household was now run by some Klavdiya Markovna, who was small, had a little black moustache, and tended to shout. Once, Natashka looked timidly into the new mistress's bedroom and saw the fateful little mirror in a silver frame—and it all came flooding sweetly back into her heart, the fear and joy she'd felt, the tenderness, the expectation of happiness and shame, the heavy scent of burdock wet with dew at dusk. . . . But she stifled all those thoughts and feelings deep within herself, snuffed them out. Old blood—old blood from Sukhodol ran in her veins. She had eaten too much bitter bread from the loamy soil of that estate. She had drunk too much brackish water from those ponds her ancestors dug in the dried-up river beds. She was not daunted by that ordinary, everyday life that exhausted her with its predictable demands—it was the unusual, the extraordinary that she feared. Even death did not frighten her. But dreams, the darkness of night, thunderstorms, fire—these things made her tremble. She carried within herself the vague expectation of some inevitable disaster the way another woman caries an unborn baby below her heart.

This expectation made her old. And she told herself every day that her youth had passed, looked constantly for proof of her old age. The year had not yet rounded out since her return to Sukhodol, and already not a trace remained of that youthful feeling with which she'd crossed the threshold of the manor house.

Klavdiya Markovna gave birth. Fedosya the birdkeeper was promoted to nanny—and Fedosya, who was still young, put on the dark dress of old age, became humble, God-fearing. The new Khrushchyov could barely bug out its milky, senseless little eyes; it produced streams of drool and bubbles, toppled forward helplessly under the overwhelming weight of its own head, screamed viciously—and already they called him *barchuk*, "little master"; already the old, old pleas and admonitions could be heard from the nursery:

"There he is, there he is—the old man with the sack. . . . Old man, old man! Don't you come to us. We won't let you take the little master. He's not going to shout anymore. . . ."

Natashka imitated Fedosya, considering herself a nanny as well—a nanny for the ailing young mistress. In the winter Olga Kirillovna died, and Natashka asked to go to the funeral with all the old women who were living out their final years in the servants' quarters. There she ate frumenty, and its bland, cloyingly sweet flavor filled her with revulsion; but later, when she returned to Sukhodol, she spoke sentimentally about Olga Kirillovna, saying that she'd "looked like she was alive," though even the old women hadn't dared to glance at that monstrous body in the coffin.

In the spring they brought to the young mistress a sorcerer from the village of Chermashnoe, the renowned Klim Yerokhin, a wealthy and appealing *odnodvorets* with a big grey beard and curly grey hair that he parted in the middle. He was a very capable farmer, and his speech was ordinarily simple and direct, except for those moments when, in the presence of the ailing, he transformed himself into a sorcerer. His clothes were unusually neat and well made: a tight little jacket sewn from coarse cloth the color of steel; a red sash and good boots. His little eyes were artful and astute; piously they sought an icon as he came into the house with his fine figure slightly hunched forward, and began a perfectly pragmatic conversation. He talked about crops, about rains and drought, and sat for a long time, meticulously drinking his tea. Then he crossed himself once more and finally asked about the patient, altering his voice the moment he spoke of her.

"Twilight. . . . Darkening. . . . Time. . . .," he said enigmatically.

The young mistress was shaking as if gripped by a violent fever. Sitting in the dusk in her bedroom, waiting for Klim to appear at the threshold, she was prepared to collapse onto the floor in convulsions. Natalya too was seized from head to foot with horror as she stood beside the young mistress. The entire house had gone quiet—even Klavdiya Markovna had ordered a crowd of servant girls into her bedroom, where she spoke with them in whispers. No one dared to light a single lamp, raise a single voice. The usually cheerful Soloshka was ordered to stand in the corridor outside Tonya's room and wait for instruction or a call from Klim. Her heart was beating in her throat, and her mind was going dark when he walked right past her, untying a little handkerchief that held some sort of sorcerer's bones. And then his loud, strange voice resounded in the deathly quiet of the house.

"Rise, slave of God!"

His grey head suddenly popped out of the doorway.

"A board." He threw the words out lifelessly.

Cold as a corpse, her eyes bulging out with terror, the young mistress was placed standing on the board as it lay on the floor. It was so dark that Natalya could barely make out Klim's face. Suddenly he began in a strange, distant sort of voice:

"Filat will come in. . . . Open the windows. . . . Open wide the doors. . . . Shout and say: 'Grief! Grief!'

"Grief, grief!" he exclaimed with sudden force and threatening power. "You must go now, grief—into the darkening forest—it's there you sleep—it's there you rest! On the ocean, on the sea," he muttered now, rapidly repeating the words in an ominous, muffled stream: "On the ocean, on the sea—on the Island of Buyan—lies a bitch, and on her back—there spreads a full grey fleece . . ."

Natalya felt there could be no words more terrible than these, which sent her back to the edge of some savage and fantastic world, some still unformed, primeval place. And it was impossible not to believe in the power of those words, just as Klim himself could not fail to believe in them, having brought about miracles among those possessed by disease—the same Klim who sat in the entranceway after his sorcery and spoke so simply, so modestly as he wiped the sweat from his forehead with a handkerchief and once more settled into his tea.

"Well, two more twilights now. . . . If God allows, it will ease a bit. . . . Did you sow buckwheat this year, madam?. . . They say it's good this year, the buckwheat. Strapping good!"

They expected the young masters to return from the Crimea in the summer. But instead Arkady Petrovich sent a registered letter with the news that they could not return before the end of the fall due to a wound that Pyotr Petrovich had suffered and which, though minor, required extensive rest. They sent someone to the soothsayer Danilovna, in the village of Cherkizovo, to ask if the wound would heal safely. Danilovna began to dance and snap her fingers, which meant, of course, that it would. Klavdiya Markovna was reassured. But Natalya and the young mistress had little time to think of the brothers. At first the young mistress had improved. But after St. Peter's it all began again: misery and fear—fear of thunderstorms and fires, and something else that she kept hidden. All of it was so consuming that she could think of nothing else. Nor could Natalya turn her attention to the men. Of course she asked for Pyotr Petrovich's health and salvation every time she prayed, just as later she would ask for his soul's repose as part of every prayer she uttered until she too reached her grave. But the young mistress was closest to Natalya now, infecting her more and more with her fears, her expectations of disaster, and that secret terror she explained to no one.

The summer was fiercely hot, dusty, windy; each day brought another thunderstorm. Dark, disturbing rumors spread among the people—rumors of some kind of new war, of riots and fires. Some said that any day now the *mouzhiki* would have their freedom; others said just the opposite—they'd all have their heads shaved and be pressed into the army. And as so often is the case, a countless array of vagabonds, monks, and fools appeared. Tonya almost came to blows with Klavdiya Markovna because of them, for the young mistress was determined to present them all with bread and eggs. Dronya came to the estate—he was tall, red-haired, exceedingly ragged. He played the role of a holy fool, but in fact he was just a drunk. He would become so lost in thought as he walked across the courtyard that he'd bang his head into the wall of the manor house, then jump back with a joyful look on his face.

"Birdies! My small birdies!" he would squeal in a falsetto, contorting his entire body and raising his right arm, as if to shield himself from the sun. "My birdies flew and flew across the sky!"

Emulating all the married women, Natalya watched him with the dull compassion one is supposed to show when looking at a holy fool. But the young mistress rushed to the window and cried out in a tearful, piteous voice:

"Holy Droniye! Little St. Droniye—pray to God for me, a sinner!"

Hearing such shouts, Natashka's eyes widened with terrible misgivings.

From the village of Klichin came Timosha Klichinsky: yellow-haired, small, effeminately fleshy with large breasts and the face of a cross-eyed baby, he labored both to breathe and comprehend beneath his suffocating bulk. Wearing a white calico shirt and short calico pants, he shuffled his ripe little legs in quick, mincing steps with the tips of his shoes pointed down, and as he approached the porch of the manor house his small narrow eyes looked as if he'd just surfaced from a deep pool of water, or saved himself from certain death.

"Ooful," he muttered and panted. "Ooful."

They calmed him down, fed him, waited for him to say something. But he didn't speak, just breathed noisily through his nose and made a chomping sound with his lips and tongue. And then, having chomped his fill, he tossed his sack back over his shoulder, looking anxiously for his walking stick.

"When will you come again, Timosha?" the young mistress called to him.

He answered with a shout, his voice an absurd, high alto:

"At holy week, Lukyanovna!" he called, mangling, for some reason, the mistress's patronymic.

And the mistress wailed mournfully:

"Holy Saint! Pray to God for me, a sinner, Mariya of Egypt!"

Reports of calamities—storms, conflagrations—came from all directions every day. The ancient fear of fire grew more and more extreme in Sukhodol. The moment storm clouds rose from behind the estate and darkened the sandy-yellow fields of ripening wheat, the moment the first gust of wind sailed across the pasture, all the women in the village rushed to carry the small, dark boards of their icons to the doorways of their huts, hurried to prepare those special pots of milk that everyone knew was best for pacifying flames. And at the manor house, scissors sailed through windows into beds of nettles; the dreadful, venerated towel made its appearance, and with trembling hands the people lit wax candles, covered up the windows. Even the mistress was consumed by some kind of fear, either genuine or contrived. She used to say, "Thunderstorms are natural occurrences," but now she crossed herself and squeezed her eyes shut, shrieked at the lightning. And in order to deepen her alarm and that of those around her, she spoke incessantly of some kind of fantastic storm that erupted over Tirol in 1771 and instantly killed 111 people. Her listeners would then join in, hurrying to tell their own stories about a white willow burnt to nothing on the highway, about a woman in Cherkizovo knocked dead by a thunderbolt a few days earlier, about a *troika* so deafened on the road that all three horses fell to their knees. . . . And then a certain Yushka—"a wayward monk," as he liked to call himself—began to join these revelries of fear and panic.

IX

Yushka had been born a peasant. But he never dirtied his hands with work. Instead he lived where God provided, paying for his bread and salt with stories of his constant loafing and his "waywardness." "Brother, I'm a *mouzhik* with brains, and I look like a hunchback," he would say. "Why should I work?"

And he really did look like a hunchback; there was a kind of caustic intelligence to his completely hairless face, and he kept his shoulders slightly raised from the rickets in his chest. He chewed his nails; his fingers—which he used constantly to push his long strands of reddish-brown hair back from his face—were thin and strong. He considered plowing both "boring" and "obscene." And so he entered the Kiev Monastery, "grew up there," and was soon thrown out "for an offense." Then Yushka realized that posing as a man who seeks to save his soul—a pilgrim wandering among the holy sites—was old and tired, and often quite unprofitable. He decided to adopt a different guise: without removing his cassock, he began to boast of his idleness and lust, to smoke and drink (there never seemed to be enough to make him drunk), to ridicule the monastery, and to explain exactly how, by means of obscene gestures and body movements, he'd had himself thrown out.

"It's no surprise," he'd tell the *mouzhiki* with a wink. "No surprise at all they slapped me, slave of God that I am, square on the neck for that! So I headed home, to Rus. . . . I'm not going to waste away, I said. . . ."

And indeed, he didn't waste away: Rus took him in, a shameless sinner, with the same consideration that it gave those pilgrims struggling to save their souls: it fed him, gave him drink, let him stay the night, listened to his stories with delight.

"Did you really swear off work for good?" the *mouzhiki* always asked, their eyes shining with the expectation of some new and poisonous revelation.

"The devil couldn't make me work," Yushka answered back. "Not now. I'm spoiled, brother! And I'm rutting like a monastery goat. I don't need women—even if it's offered up for free, I don't care much about those older ones—but girls, well, they're afraid of me like death, and they love it. And why wouldn't they? You don't come across my type just anywhere! Maybe my feathers aren't the prettiest, but my bones are shaped just right. . . ."

Already savvy to the world, Yushka came straight through the main entrance to the manor house when he appeared at Sukhodol. Natasha was there, sitting on the bench and singing to herself, "As I swept I found a piece of sugar." She leapt to her feet in terror when she saw him.

"Who are you?" she cried.

"A man," Yushka said, quickly looking her over from head to foot. "Go and tell the mistress."

"Who's there?" the mistress called out at that moment from the hall.

But Yushka immediately reassured her: he told her he was a former monk, not at all a runaway soldier, as she quite likely feared. He explained that he was returning to his native land and asked that they search him, then let him stay the night and rest a little. His directness so disarmed the mistress that she allowed him to move into the servants' quarters the next day, and he soon became a regular member of the household. Thunderstorms came ceaselessly, but he never tired of entertaining the mistress; he thought up a way to block the dormer window and better protect the roof from lightning; he even ran onto the porch during the loudest claps of thunder just to prove that they were not so terrible. When he helped the house girls heat the samovars, they watched him from the corners of their eyes, feeling his quick, lascivious glances passing over them, but they still laughed at his jokes, while Natashka—whom he had already stopped more than once in the dark corridor with the whispered words, "I'm in love with you, girl!"—could not bear to raise her eyes to him. The stench of shag tobacco that had seeped into his cassock made him foul to her, and he was terrifying, terrifying.

She knew what would happen. She slept alone in the corridor, near the door of the young mistress's bedroom, and Yushka had already told her point blank: "I'll come to you. You can stick me with a knife, and I'll still come. And if you scream, I'll burn this whole place to the ground." Above all else, her strength was sapped by the knowledge that something *inevitable* had been set in motion, that the realization of her dream—that terrible dream about a goat in Soshki—had now drawn near, and she was clearly destined to suffer ruin with her mistress. Everyone understood by now: the devil dwells in the house at night. Everyone knew exactly what it was besides thunderstorms and fires that drove the young mistress from her mind, what it was that spawned in her those shameless and voluptuous moans as she slept, then drove her to leap up with a wailing cry, a howling beside which even the most deafening blows of thunder seemed like nothing. "I'm being strangled!" she would scream. "By the snake of Eden! By the serpent of Jerusalem!" And who was that snake, if not the devil, if not the grey goat that came into the rooms of girls and women at night? And is there anything in the world more terrifying than his appearance on those nights when storms rage, when thunder rolls ceaselessly above the house, and lightning flickers constantly across the blackened surface of the icons? The urgency, the lust with which that charlatan whispered to Natashka—it too was inhuman. How was she to fend it off?

In the corridor at night, contemplating her fateful, inevitable hour as she sat on a horse cloth on the floor, Natashka peered into the darkness with a pounding heart, listened for the faintest creak, the slightest rustling in the sleeping house. Already she felt the first attacks of that painful illness that would torment her far into the future: suddenly an itch began in her foot, followed by a sharp, prickling spasm that bent all her toes toward her cramping sole, and then—painfully, sweetly twisting all her sinews—traveled up her legs, spread through her entire body, came right up to her throat until Natashka longed to scream, release a cry even more frenzied, even more voluptuous and tortured than the wails of her young mistress.

The inevitable occurred: Yushka came, precisely during one of those terrifying nights at the end of summer. It was the eve of St. Ilya, the

ancient fire-thrower's day. There was no thunder that night, and no sleep
for Natashka. She dozed—and suddenly woke up, as if she had been
pushed. The insane beating of her heart told her that it was the dead of
night, the latest hour. She jumped up and looked to one end of the corridor, then to the other: the taciturn sky was filled with fire and secrets;
from all directions it flashed, burst into trembling flames, swelled with
blinding sheets of pale blue and gold lightning. Every few seconds the
entranceway turned as bright as day. She began to run, then stopped,
rooted to the floor: the cut logs of aspen that had been lying for a long
time in the courtyard now turned a blinding white with each flash of
lightning. She stepped into the hall: one window was raised, and she
could hear the steady rustling of the garden. It was darker there than in
the entranceway, but this made all the brighter those flames that flashed
beyond the windows, and as soon as blackness poured back into the
room, everything would jump and twitch once more as another random
flare began to burn, and the garden rose, trembling in its momentary
light, the sky's massive backdrop—gold one instant, violet-white the
next—gleaming through the lacy edges of the foliage, through poplars
and pale green birches that loomed like ghosts. "On the ocean, on the
sea—on the Island of Buyan," she whispered, rushing back, certain she
would utterly destroy herself with this sorcerer's incantation, "Lies a
bitch, and on her back—there spreads a full grey fleece . . ."

And as soon as she spoke those dreadful, primordial words, she
turned and saw Yushka standing two steps from her with his shoulders
raised. The lightning lit up his pale face, the black circles of his eyes. He
lunged silently toward her, seized her waist with his long arms, locked
his grip; he flung her to her knees in a single motion, then shoved her
onto her back on the cold floor of the entranceway. . . .

Yushka came to her the next night as well. He came to her for many
nights, and she, losing consciousness from horror and revulsion, gave herself submissively to him. She didn't dare to contemplate resisting, or appealing to the masters or the other serfs for help, just as the young mistress
did not dare resist the devil as it satisfied itself with her at night—just as,
they said, even grandmother, a powerful and beautiful woman, had not
dared to resist her house serf, Tkach, an utter villain and thief who finally
was banished to Siberia. . . . At last Yushka grew bored with Natashka,
grew bored with Sukhodol—vanished as abruptly as he'd appeared.

A month later she felt that she was with child. And in September,
the day after the young masters returned from war, the manor house

caught fire: for a long and terrifying time it burned. Her second dream had come to pass. The fire began at dusk, under a heavy rain. According to Soloshka, it was caused by a golden ball of lightning that flew out of the stove in grandfather's room and bounded through the house. But Natalya would later recount how, seeing the flames and smoke, she bolted from the bathhouse—where she'd spent several days and nights in tears—and began to race toward the house, only to run into a stranger in the garden, a man in a red jerkin and a tall Cossack hat with a galloon. He too was running as fast as he could through the wet bushes and burdock. . . . Natalya could never say with complete certainty if the man was real or some kind of vision, but one fact was clear: the horror that seized her when she saw him had freed her from her future child.

After that she faded. Her life began to run along the rails of simple, quotidian existence, and she did not veer from those tracks until her final days. They took Aunt Tonya to a saint's remains in Voronezh. Afterward the devil no longer dared come close to her, and she grew calmer, began to live like everyone else. Only the gleam of her almost feral eyes, her extreme slovenliness, her violent irascibility, and her mournful sadness during thunderstorms revealed the disturbance of her mind and soul. Natalya was with her during the visit to the saint's remains, and from that trip she too gained a certain calm, a release from everything in her life that seemed inescapable. How she had trembled at the mere thought of meeting Pyotr Petrovich once again! She'd lacked the strength to think about it calmly, regardless of how long she tried to steel herself. And Yushka, her shame, her ruin! But the very singularity of that ruin, the unusual depth of her suffering, the apparent ineluctability of her misfortune—for surely it was not a mere coincidence that the shock of the fire would so closely follow her ruin and disgrace—all of this, together with the pilgrimage to the saint's remains, gave her the right to look simply, calmly into the eyes not only of those around her but even into the eyes of Pyotr Petrovich. God himself had marked her and the young mistress with the tip of his annihilating finger: why should they fear people! When she returned from Voronezh, Natalya entered the manor house at Sukhodol as placidly as a nun, like a simple and humble servant of everything light and good, like a woman who'd received her final communion before death. She approached Pyotr Petrovich calmly, and her heart contracted with tender, youthful, girlish sentiment only for a moment as she touched her lips to his small, dark hand with its turquoise ring. . . .

Life became mundane at Sukhodol. Rumors spread again about emancipation—rumors that seemed weightier than the earlier talk. They triggered alarm among the house serfs and the field hands: What lies ahead? Will it all be worse? How easy it is to say, "Begin your new life!" The masters too were confronted by the prospect of a new life— and they had managed poorly with the old one. Grandfather's death, followed by the war, the comet that plunged the entire country into terror, the fire, and finally rumors of emancipation—all of this changed the masters' faces and their souls, deprived them of their youth and their insouciance, their quick tempers and their readiness to make amends, while fostering ennui, malice, a constant captiousness with one another. "Disharmonies began," as our father said, and eventually they led to whips at meals. Necessity stubbornly reminded the young masters that they had to find some means of reviving the estate, which their long absence at the war, the fire, and the family's debts had utterly destroyed. But the brothers only bothered each other as they sought to manage their affairs. One was ridiculously greedy, stern, and suspicious; the other was ridiculously generous, kind, and trusting. Finally they managed to agree on a venture that was sure to bring big gains: they mortgaged the estate and bought nearly three hundred bedraggled horses, gathering them from almost every corner of the district with the help of a certain Ilya Samsonov, a gypsy. They hoped to get the horses fat and healthy over the winter, then sell them at substantial profit in the spring. But after consuming huge quantities of flour and straw, the horses for some reason began keeling over one by one; almost all of them were dead by spring. . . .

The discord between the brothers now grew more and more severe. At times it reached a point where they would snatch up guns and knives. There's no saying how it would have ended if a new misfortune had not befallen Sukhodol. In the winter, four years after his return from the Crimean War, Pyotr Petrovich went to visit Lunyovo, where he had a lover. He spent two days on the farm, drinking constantly, and then, still drunk, left for Sukhodol. There was a great deal of snow on the ground; two horses were harnessed to the wide sledge, which was covered with a heavy rug. Pyotr Petrovich ordered that the outrunner—a young, high-strung filly that sank to her belly in the loose drifts—be unharnessed and tied to the back of the sledge. Then he stretched out to sleep, his head apparently lying back toward the horse in tow. A misty, dove-grey dusk began to fall. As he often did, Pyotr Petrovich had taken Yevsey Bodulya with him on the trip instead of Vaska Kazak, the regular driver, for his constant beatings had embittered all the house serfs, and Pyotr Petrovich feared that Vaska would one day kill him. Settling back to sleep, Pyotr Petrovich shouted, "Get going!" at Yevsey and kicked him in the back. The shaft horse, a strong bay, its belly wheezing, its coat already damp and steaming, went plowing through the loose, deep snow and the murky gloom of the empty fields, carrying them into the winter night as it grew ever darker and more lowering. . . . But at midnight, when everyone at Sukhodol was already sleeping like the dead, an anxious rapping at the window of the entranceway woke Natalya. She leapt up from the bench and ran out barefoot to the porch. The dark forms of the horses and the sledge stood out dimly; Yevsey was standing there with a whip in his hand. "Disaster, girl—disaster!" he muttered indistinctly, strangely, as if he were asleep. "The horse killed the master. . . . She was tied . . . she ran up, stumbled—and her hoof . . . His face is all smashed. . . . He's already cold. . . . It wasn't me. Not me. By Christ, not me!"

Silently she descended from the porch and approached the sledge, her bare feet pressing down the snow. She crossed herself and fell onto her knees. She cradled the icy, bloody head in her arms and began to kiss it, began to shriek and fill the house with a savage, joyful wailing, struggling to breathe between her laughter and her sobs. . . .

X

Whenever we happened to leave the cities behind and came to rest in the quiet, impoverished backwoods of Sukhodol, Natalya repeatedly unfolded the narrative of her broken life. Sometimes her eyes darkened and stared blankly; sometimes her voice became a sharp and clear half-whisper. I always remembered the crude icon that hung in a corner of the lackeys' quarters in our old house: the decapitated saint sought out his countrymen; he carried his lifeless head in his own hands to demonstrate his story's truth.

Even those slight physical traces of the past that we briefly glimpsed at Sukhodol have vanished now. Our fathers and our grandfathers left us no portraits, no letters, not even the mundane artifacts of their everyday existence. And those few small possessions that did remain were ruined in the fire. Some kind of trunk stood for a long time in the entranceway: a hundred years ago it had been covered in sealskin, but only a few stiff rags and worn-out clumps of that upholstery remained. It belonged to our grandfather once, and its movable drawers of Karelian birch were stuffed with charred French dictionaries and church books spattered in candle wax. Eventually, however, it too disappeared, just as the heavy furniture that once stood in the living room also broke apart and disappeared. More and more the old house sagged and wore away. And all the long years that followed the events depicted here—those years saw nothing but the slow and steady dying of the house. . . . Its past seems more and more a myth.

The residents of Sukhodol led remote and gloomy lives, but they still seemed substantial, wealthy, intricate. And judging by the sheer inertia in that way of life, judging by the people's fierce adherence to its principles, one could easily believe there'd be no end to it. But those descendants of the nomads from the steppe proved weak and pliant, ill-prepared for punishment! And so the sheltered homes of Sukhodol's inhabitants disappeared as tracelessly, as quickly as those little mounds of earth above the hamsters' passageways and burrows vanish under the plow when it cuts across the field. The occupants all died or scattered; only a few hung on and struggled to live out their last remaining days. We did not witness their true lives and mores; we encountered, instead, the memory of that earlier time combined with some stark, half-savage existence. And we visited that region of the steppe less and less often over the years. It seemed more and more remote to us; we felt more and more removed from both the blood and custom that once gave shape to us. Many of our fellow noblemen, like us, were born of heralded and ancient families. Our names are entered in the history books and chronicles; our ancestors were courtiers and governors in ancient Russia, "distinguished gentlemen," close associates and even relatives of the tsars. Had we been born farther to the west, had our ancestors been known as knights, how much more conviction would have come into our voices when we spoke of them, how much longer would our way of life have persevered! No knight's descendant could ever say that in half a century an entire class of people vanished from the earth. He could never speak of such great numbers of people who deteriorated, who committed suicide and drank themselves to death, people who went mad, let go of everything, just disappeared. He could never admit, as I confess here, that the lives of not only our ancestors but even the lives of our great grandfathers are a complete and utter mystery to us now, and every day it grows more difficult for us to gain the vaguest understanding of events that happened only fifty years ago!

Long ago they plowed over and seeded that place where Lunyovo once stood, just as many other estates have been plowed and seeded. Somehow Sukhodol held on. But after chopping down the last birches in the garden and selling off the last of the arable land in small plots, its owner, Pyotr Petrovich's son, abandoned the estate and went to work as a conductor on the railroad. The last, old inhabitants of Sukhodol—Klavdiya Markovna, Aunt Tonya, and Natalya—lived out their final years in hardship. Spring became summer, summer became fall, fall became winter. . . . They lost track of the many changes. They lived on memories, dreams, quarrels, worries about daily meals. Those grounds on which the estate once spread expansively now sank beneath the peasants' rye in summer, and the house was visible from far away, surrounded by those plains. All that remained of the garden were bushes, and they grew in such a riot that quail called directly from the balcony. But what is there to say of summer! "Summer is our paradise," the old women would declare. Long and hard were the rainy falls, the snowy winters in Sukhodol. Cold and hunger gripped the ruined house. Blizzards mounded snow across its walls; the freezing wind of Sarmatia blew right through its rooms. And the heat—they heated it very rarely. In the evening a tin lamp burned dimly in the window of the mistress's room, the only inhabitable space in the house. The old mistress wore a short fur coat, felt boots, and glasses as she leaned toward the lamp and knitted a sock. Natalya dozed on a cold bench by the empty stove. And Aunt Tonya, like some Siberian shaman, sat and smoked a pipe inside her peasant hut. When they were not quarreling, Klavdiya Markovna would place her lamp on the windowsill instead of the table. And on those nights Tonya sat in a strange, weak half-light that reached her from the house, reached inside her freezing hut, cluttered with broken furniture and pottery shards and the great mass of the piano that had heaved onto its side. The hut was so cold that chickens, whose care consumed all of Tonya's strength, would often suffer frostbite to their feet while sleeping on those ceramic shards and ruined bits of furniture.

And now the Sukhodol estate is completely empty. All those mentioned here have died, as have their neighbors and their peers. And sometimes you think: Is it true? Did they really live on this earth?

It's only at the graveyard that you feel they really did exist—feel, in fact, a frightening proximity to them. But even for that you must make an effort; you must sit and think beside a family headstone—if you can find one. It is shameful to say, but impossible to hide: we don't know where the graves of grandmother, grandfather, and Pyotr Petrovich lie. We know only that their place is somewhere here, near the altar of the old village church in Cherkizovo. You won't make it there in winter: the drifts are waist deep—just the tops of a few bushes, some branches, an occasional cross can be seen sticking out from the snow. In the summer you ride along a hot and dusty, quiet street in the village, tie your horse up at the churchyard fence. Spruces stand baking in the heat beyond it, dense as a dark green wall. And behind the open gate, behind the white church with a rusty cupola, you find a whole grove of small and spreading ash trees, elms, and lindens—it's cool and shady everywhere. For a long time you wander among the bushes, the small mounds and hollows covered by a thin graveyard grass, the stone slabs sinking into the earth, porous from the years of rain and overgrown by black, crumbling moss. . . . Here there are two or three monuments of iron. But who are they for? They're tarnished such a heavy green and gold that it's impossible to read the inscriptions. Under what mounds lie grandmother, grandfather? God alone knows! You know only that they're somewhere here, somewhere close. And so you sit and think, try to imagine all those forgotten Khrushchyovs. At one moment their time seems endlessly far away; at the next, impossibly close at hand. And then you say to yourself:

"It's not so hard. . . . It's not so hard to imagine. You only have to remember that the same crooked, gold-plated cross rose into the blue summer sky when they were here. Then, just as now, there were hot and empty fields of rye that yellowed and turned ripe, while here the bushes and the shade were cool. . . . Then, just as now, a white nag like this one wandered grazing in the bushes, with slightly green and scruffy withers, with pink and broken hooves."

[*Vasilyevskoe, 1911*]

Summer Day

A SETTLEMENT on the outskirts of Russia. An endless summer day. And all day a bootmaker sitting barefoot on a rotting bench near a tumbledown shack, his belt unbuckled and his long shirt hanging loose, the sun beating down on his shaggy head. He sits there killing time with a red dog.

"Shake!"

The dog doesn't know the command.

"I said 'shake!'"

Still the dog doesn't offer his paw. The bootmaker slaps his muzzle. The dog bats his eyes in shock and disgust, turns away, bares his teeth — a bittersweet smile. Then he lifts one paw uncertainly, drops it back to the ground. Another blow to the face. And again —

"I told you to shake, you son of a bitch!"

[1930]

The Gentleman from San Francisco

T HE gentleman from San Francisco—no one really learned his name in Naples or Capri—was traveling with his wife and daughter to the Old World for two whole years, strictly for the sake of entertainment.

He was firmly convinced that he had every right to rest, enjoy himself, take a trip of utmost excellence in all regards. This conviction rested on two points: first, he was rich; second, despite his fifty-eight years, he had only just begun to live. He hadn't lived before—he had only existed. True, he had existed well, but always with his hopes put off to the future. He'd worked ceaselessly—the Chinese laborers whom he enlisted by the thousands understood exactly what that meant!—until at last, seeing that much had been accomplished and he'd drawn almost level to those he held as paragons, he decided it was time to rest. It was customary for his kind of people to begin enjoying life with trips to Europe, India, and Egypt—now he proposed to do the same. Of course, he wanted first and foremost to reward himself for all his years of work, but he was also happy for his wife and daughter. Although his wife's sensitivity to the world had never been particularly remarkable, all middle-aged American women love travel passionately, and for his daughter—a girl of poor health and increasing age—the trip was quite essential. After all, regardless of their beneficial health effects, don't such voyages often lead to happy meetings? One day you're dining or looking at a fresco, and right beside you there's a billionaire.

The gentleman from San Francisco worked out a vast itinerary. In December and January he would enjoy the sun of southern Italy, the ancient monuments, the *tarantella*, the songs of wandering minstrels, and that delicacy which people of his age were particularly well suited to appreciate in all its subtlety, even if it wasn't offered in a purely altruistic spirit: the love of Neapolitan girls. Carnival he planned to spend in Nice and Monte Carlo, where members of the most select society gather at that time of year, and one group ardently devotes itself to racing yachts and cars, another plays roulette, a third engages in a practice known as flirting, and a fourth shoots pigeons as they're released from cages, rising beautifully, for a moment, above the emerald lawns and the forget-me-not background of the sea, before plummeting in little white clumps to the ground. Early March he would devote to Florence, and for Holy Week they'd go to Rome to hear the *Miserere*. Venice, Paris, bullfighting in Seville, swimming off the British Isles—these were also in his plans, along with Athens, Constantinople, Palestine, Egypt, and even—on the journey home, of course—Japan. Everything went wonderfully at first.

It was the end of November, and they sailed through icy fogs or storms of wet snow all the way to Gibraltar. But they traveled comfortably. There were many passengers, and their ship, the renowned *Atlantis*, was like a huge hotel, with every comfort and convenience—a late-night bar, Turkish baths, even its own newspaper. Life on board flowed in perfect measure. They rose to bugle notes resounding sharply in the corridors at that early, gloomy hour when daylight was still spreading sullenly above the waves and the surging sea resembled a grey-green desert in the fog. They put on flannel pajamas, drank coffee and cacao or hot chocolate, bathed, did morning exercises in order to feel hungry and invigorated. Then they dressed and went to breakfast, after which it was customary to play shuffleboard and other games on deck or walk briskly around the ship, inhaling the cold freshness of the sea and stirring up an appetite again. At eleven the passengers fortified themselves with sandwiches and bouillon, and then, well fortified, they read the newspaper with pleasure or waited patiently for lunch, which was even more filling and diverse than breakfast. The two hours following their second meal were set aside for resting: wrapped in warm blankets, the passengers lay on cane-back couches specially arranged along the decks, dozing peacefully or staring at the cloudy sky and the foaming swells that flashed beyond the ship's sides. Some time after four, feeling cheerful and refreshed, they were given cookies and strong, fragrant tea; and at seven, trumpet notes announced the key event of their existence — its crowning glory: immediately the gentleman from San Francisco would hurry to his wealthy cabin in order to get dressed for dinner.

Evenings, the many portals of the *Atlantis* shone like countless glowing eyes in the gloom while a vast multitude of servants labored below deck in the galleys, the sculleries, and the wine cellars. The ocean passing outside the walls was terrifying to them, but they rarely thought of it, believing firmly in the powers of their captain, a red-haired man of monstrous height and weight who always seemed slightly sleepy, rarely left his secret cabin to appear among the passengers, and resembled a massive pagan idol in his uniform with broad gold stripes across its sleeves. Every few minutes, a siren on the forecastle would yelp as if enraged and start to howl with desolate despair, but few passengers could hear it: an orchestra played ceaselessly in the festive, two-toned dining room, and the delicate sound of its strings drowned out the siren's wailing while throngs of women in revealing gowns and men in tails and dinner jackets were served by trim waiters and obliging *maitre d's*, one of whom wore a little chain around his neck like a lord mayor and specialized exclusively in wines.

His starched white linen and his dinner jacket made the gentleman from San Francisco look younger than his age. Short and slightly withered, strongly built but somehow ill proportioned, he sat in the golden, pearly light of the hall with a bottle of wine, goblets of the finest glass, and a rich bouquet of hyacinths before him. There was something Mongolian about his sallow face and neatly trimmed silver moustache. His large teeth gleamed with gold fillings, and the outlines of a strong, hard skull were visible beneath his hairless scalp, which glistened like old ivory. His wife, a large woman with wide hips and a peaceful disposition, was dressed expensively but in keeping with her years. Tall and thin, his daughter wore a light, transparent, elaborate, and revealing dress with innocent immodesty, her splendid hair charmingly arranged, her breath freshened by the scent of violet lozenges, a few pink and tender pimples near her lips and between her lightly powdered shoulder blades.

Dinner lasted for more than an hour; then dancing began in the ballroom, and the men—including, of course, the gentleman from San Francisco—put their feet up in the bar, smoked Havana cigars, and drank liquor until their faces were as red as beets while being waited on by Negroes in red waistcoats, their bulging eyes like large, peeled eggs. The ocean's massive black hills boomed beyond the walls, a blizzard whistled shrilly in the burdened rigging, and the entire ship shuddered as it forged through the storm and those hills—like a plow it parted the ocean's seething mass, toppling the waves onto their sides as they boiled and rose and flung huge tails of foam high into the air. Muffled by the fog, the siren moaned in dire misery, the men on watch began to freeze and grow hysterical from the overwhelming strain of following the storm, and in the underwater belly of the ship, which resembled hell's ninth and final circle with its hot, dark depths, huge furnaces cackled indistinctly, consuming mounds of coal flung roaring into their molten jaws by men stripped to the waist, their bodies streaked with soot and acrid sweat, purple in the light of the flames. But there in the bar, men casually draped their legs over the armrests of their chairs, savoring their cognac and liquor while their heads grew light in pungent clouds of cigar smoke. In the warm and joyful ballroom, everything was flooded with bright light; the couples spun through waltzes or bowed and swayed to tangos, and with sweet shamelessness the music continued its sad, insistent pleading—always its entreaties were the same. The brilliant crowd included a great tycoon who was tall, clean-shaven, and dressed in old-fashioned tails; a celebrated Spanish writer; a world-renowned beauty; and a graceful, loving couple whom everyone observed with curiosity. The two of them made no effort to conceal their happiness as he danced exclusively with her, and everything they did was so delicate and charming that no one but the captain knew they'd been well paid by Lloyds to feign their love and sail on different ships for years.

In Gibraltar the sun made everyone happy: it felt like early spring, and a new passenger appeared on the deck of the *Atlantis*, attracting universal interest. A small, wooden man with a wide face and narrow eyes behind gold-rimmed glasses, he was the crown prince of some Asian country, traveling incognito. There was something disconcerting about the long, sparse strands of his moustache, which—like the facial hair of a corpse—revealed the skin above his lip, but the prince was generally quite pleasant, very modest, down-to-earth, and kind. In the Mediterranean they sailed among large waves as colorful as peacock tails, which the *tramontana* blew apart with savage glee as it rushed head-on toward the ship beneath a cloudless, brilliant sky. And then, on the second day, the sky began to whiten and a cloudiness appeared on the horizon: they were approaching land. Ischia and Capri came into view, and with binoculars one could see Naples scattered like sugar cubes at the base of a blue-grey mass. Many gentlemen and ladies had already donned light winter coats trimmed with fur while the cabin boys—soft-spoken, timid Chinese teenagers with bowed legs, coal black braids that reached their heels, and thick, girlish eyelashes—unhurriedly began to carry suitcases, walking sticks, blankets, and overnight bags to the stairs. The gentleman from San Francisco's daughter stood on deck beside the prince, who'd been introduced to her by lucky happenstance the night before, and pretended to look intently at something he was pointing out in the distance. He was explaining something, telling a story quietly and quickly, but the girl was so excited that she listened without understanding any of the words he spoke. With his spectacles, his bowler, and his English overcoat, the prince looked truly odd and unattractive. He was no taller than a boy; the strands of his moustache resembled horsehair; and the dark, delicate skin across his level face seemed to have been pulled taut and lightly varnished. But in his presence the girl's heart throbbed with inexplicable ecstasy: everything, everything about him—his dry hands, his clear skin, his ancient royal blood—made him unlike any other, and even his remarkably neat but simple European clothes seemed to hide some secret charm. Meanwhile, the gentleman from San Francisco, who had donned grey spats, was looking at the world-renowned beauty—tall and blond, with a surprising build and eyelids painted in the latest Paris fashion, she stood nearby, talking ceaselessly to a tiny, scruffy, bow-backed dog, which she held on a silver chain. Vaguely embarrassed, the gentleman from San Francisco's daughter made an effort not to notice her father.

He'd been quite generous on the journey and therefore had no doubts about the solicitude of those who'd given him food and drink, anticipated his slightest whim from morning until night, preserved his cleanliness and peace, carried his possessions, called for porters, delivered all his luggage to hotels. It had been this way everywhere he went; it had been this way on board the ship, and it would be this way in Naples. Naples was growing large and drawing close; with their brass instruments gleaming in the sun, musicians had already gathered on the deck, and now a festive marching song deafened the crowd. The giant captain appeared in full uniform on the bridge and waved graciously to the passengers, like a beneficent god. And when the *Atlantis* finally entered port with throngs of passengers spread among its decks, when its massive, multistoried frame gently pulled alongside the dock and the gangplanks dropped with a bang, what a crowd of porters and their assistants wearing peaked, gold-braided hats, what a crowd of assorted salesmen and whistling boys and robust urchins with packs of colored postcards in their hands rushed toward him, offering their services! But the gentleman from San Francisco only smirked at them as he approached a car dispatched from a hotel where royalty might stay, and calmly repeated through his teeth in English and Italian: "Go Away! *Via!*"

Life in Naples quickly fell into a set routine: early-morning breakfast in the gloomy dining room; a cloudy, discouraging sky and a crowd of tour guides near the vestibule doors; the first smiles of a warm and pinkish sun; a moment on the high balcony, where one could see Vesuvius still fully cloaked in a shimmering haze, the silver-pearly ripples of the bay, the delicate outline of Capri on the horizon, and lower down, tiny donkeys pulling two-wheeled carts along the shoreline at a trot, little regiments of soldiers marching off somewhere to upbeat, rousing music; then the leaving for the car; the slow ride through damp and crowded streets that wound like narrow corridors among tall buildings with many windows; a tour of some lifelessly clean museum where the light was pleasant, flat, and dull, like the light that rises from snow; or a visit to another cold cathedral, where always it was the same: a majestic entrance covered by a heavy leather curtain, beyond which one discovered a huge emptiness; silence and the smell of burning wax; the quiet, red little flames of a seven-branched candelabrum on a distant altar adorned with lace; a lonely old woman among the dark wooden pews; slick tombstones underfoot; and another invariably renowned rendition of Christ's descent from the cross. At one o'clock they lunched on San Martino, where many first-class people could be found midday, and where the gentleman from San Francisco's daughter almost fainted after thinking that she saw the prince sitting in the hall, even though she knew from the newspapers that he was touring Rome. At five they had tea in the elegant drawing room of their hotel, warmed by carpets and a blazing fireplace; and then, once more, preparations for the evening meal began: again the imperious crashing of a gong on every floor; again the lines of women in revealing gowns, the rustling of silks as they descended the stairs, the reflections of their figures in the mirrors as they passed; again the welcoming, palatial dining room, the red jackets of musicians on a little stage, and the black uniforms of waiters gathering around a *maitre d'*, who with unmatched artistry ladled thick, pink soup into the dinner bowls. And again the meals were so rich and varied, there was so much wine and mineral water, so many sweet desserts and so much fruit that some time near eleven the maids would bring hot-water bottles to the rooms so that all the guests could warm their burdened stomachs.

All the same, December wasn't perfect: when discussing the weather, the porters only shrugged their shoulders guiltily and claimed that no one could remember such a year, although this was not the first time they'd had to mutter such phrases and allude to something terrible occurring everywhere: unheard of storms and downpours in the Riviera; Athens under snow, and such big drifts on Aetna that the mountain shined at night; tourists abandoning Palermo to escape the freezing cold. . . . The morning sun deceived them every day: by afternoon the sky invariably turned grey and a light rain began to fall, quickly turning cold and heavy. Then the palms outside the hotel entrance glistened like wet tin; the town seemed especially crowded and dirty, the museums exceedingly monotonous. On those rainy afternoons, the rubber cloaks of fat cabbies fluttered in the wind like wings, the stench of their cigar butts became unbearable, and the energetic whip-blows they delivered to the air above their wretched, thin-necked nags looked absurdly fake. There was something terrible about the shoes of the *signori* who swept the trolley tracks during those showers, something offensive and absurd about the short legs of the women who slopped through the mud, their dark hair uncovered in the rain. And about the dampness, about the stink of rotting fish that rose from the foamy sea along the shoreline, there was simply nothing to be said.

The gentleman from San Francisco and his wife began to quarrel in the mornings. Their daughter was either pale and troubled by an aching head or wildly animated and enthusiastic about everything she saw. At such moments she was particularly sweet and beautiful—as were those complex, tender feelings that her meeting with an ugly man whose veins contained rare blood had stirred in her, for in the end it doesn't matter if it's money, glory, fame, or lineage that stirs a young girl's soul. . . . Everyone assured them that things were different in Sorrento and on Capri: it was warm and sunny there, they said, and all the lemon trees were blooming; the locals were more honest, the wine more natural. Thus the travelers from San Francisco decided to set out with all their trunks and luggage for Capri, so that after they'd explored the island—walked around the ruins of Tiberius's palaces, visited the caves of the fantastic Azure Grotto, and listened to the bagpipes of those Abruzzian highlanders who roam the island singing praises to the Virgin Mary for a full month leading up to Christmas—they could begin their stay in Sorrento.

On the day of their departure—a day the family from San Francisco would remember well—there was no sun at all, even in the morning. A heavy fog blanketed Vesuvius and hung low over the lead-grey ripples of the sea. Capri was completely hidden from view—it seemed that such a place had never existed on this earth—and the small steamer bound for the island rocked so violently from side to side that the family from San Francisco lay motionless on the couches in the tiny passengers' lounge, their legs wrapped in blankets and their eyes pressed shut from nausea. The gentleman from San Francisco's wife believed she was suffering the most; indeed, the certainty that she was dying overcame her several times. But the ship's attendant—a woman who had tirelessly endured such waves for years in both the freezing cold and the scorching heat— merely laughed as she ran toward her with a bowl. Terribly pale, the daughter traveled with a slice of lemon held between her teeth, and the gentleman from San Francisco never once unclenched his jaw as he lay on his back in a long overcoat and a large, peaked cap, his head throbbing, his face darkening, and his moustache turning white: lately the bad weather had led him to drink too much in the evenings and to enjoy too frequently the *tableaux vivants* of certain haunts. Rain beat against the rattling windowpanes and dripped onto the couches; the wind howled as it tore through the masts and from time to time, in combination with a sudden, rising wave, set the small steamer completely on its side, at which point something crashed and rolled around the cargo space below the passengers. During stops in Castellammare and Sorrento there was some relief, but the ship continued pitching violently, and everything on shore—the cliffs and gardens; the Italian pines and pink and white hotels; the smoky, leafy hills—flew up and down outside the window like something on a swing. Boats banged against the walls, a damp wind blew through the open doors, and there was no reprieve from the constant, slightly garbled, piercing shouts of the boy who stood beneath a banner for the Hotel Royal on a rocking barge nearby and exhorted all the passing travelers to join him. Fittingly enough, the gentleman from San Francisco felt like a very old man, and he thought with bitter misery about those greedy little garlic-eaters called Italians who surrounded him. During one of the stops he rose up on the couch, opened his eyes, and saw a wretched mass of little stone houses with mildewed walls stacked on top of one another at the water's edge below a rocky slope, saw boats and piles of rags, tin cans, brown nets—and fell into despair, remembering that this was the authentic Italy to which he'd come in order to enjoy himself. It was already dusk when the island began to draw closer, like a black mass pierced by little red lights at its base. The wind settled down, grew warm and fragrant, the waves flowed like black oil, and wide bands of golden light snaked across their surface from the pier. . . . Then the anchor rattled on its chain and splashed into the water; the eager shouts of boatmen vying for passengers resounded from all directions; and immediately their spirits rose: the cabin seemed brighter, they felt like eating, drinking, moving once again. Ten minutes later the family from San Francisco boarded a big barge; five minutes after that, they climbed the stone embankment on the shore and entered a bright cable car that carried them up the mountainside, droning as it passed over the staked grapevines in the vineyards, half-collapsed walls of stone, and wet, gnarled orange trees, sheltered here and there by awnings made of straw—all of which slid slowly down the incline, the oranges shining, the broad leaves glistening as they drifted past the open windows of the car. The earth smells sweet in Italy after rain, and the scent of every island is distinct.

The island of Capri was dark and damp that evening. But now it came to life, grew light in places. Already a crowd had gathered on the little platform where the cable car would stop on the mountain top—a crowd of people charged with meeting the gentleman from San Francisco in proper fashion. There were other passengers as well, but they didn't warrant much attention—a few disheveled, bearded Russians who had settled on the island, all of them wearing glasses and looking absent-minded, the collars raised on their threadbare coats; and a group of German youths with remarkably long legs and very round heads: dressed in Tyrolean suits and wearing canvas bags on their backs, they clearly had no need of assistance and were wholly unprepared to pay for it. The gentleman from San Francisco calmly kept his distance from both groups, and the waiting crowd soon noticed him. He and his women were hurriedly assisted from the car, people ran ahead to show them the road, and the gentleman from San Francisco was surrounded once again by boys and those robust peasant women who carry the suitcases and trunks of respectable tourists on their heads. Their wooden shoes tapped across the little square, which resembled an opera stage with one electric bulb swaying above it in the damp wind; the crowd of boys whistled like birds and did somersaults—and as if he were part of some performance, the gentleman from San Francisco walked among them toward a medieval arch below a group of buildings that had merged into one structure, and there, a little echoing street sloped toward the hotel's shining entrance, a palm tree with its fronds hanging like a forelock over the flat roofs to the left, dark blue stars in the black sky overhead. And it seemed that all of this was in honor of the guests from San Francisco—it seemed this damp, stony little town on the cliffs of an island in the Mediterranean had come to life on their account; that they alone made the hotel's owner happy and content, and the Chinese gong that began to ring on every floor the moment they arrived had been waiting all this time for them before summoning the guests to dinner.

The hotel's owner, a remarkably elegant young man who greeted the family with a refined and courteous bow, startled the gentleman from San Francisco: suddenly he remembered that among the senseless dreams that had beleaguered him all night, he'd seen this very gentleman, exactly him, with the very same morning coat, the very same hair combed to a mirrorlike sheen. Surprised, he almost faltered in his steps. But since every trace of so-called mysticism had long ago been eradicated from his soul, his amazement quickly passed, and he told his wife and daughter lightheartedly of the strange coincidence as they walked along the corridor. But his daughter looked at him with alarm when he spoke: suddenly her heart was gripped with sorrow and a terrifying loneliness on that strange, dark island. . . .

An important figure, Prince Reus XVII, had very recently checked out of the hotel; now his suites were given to the family from San Francisco. And the new guests were served by the most striking steward, a coal-black Sicilian with fiery eyes; the most able and attractive of the chambermaids, a Belgian who wore a starched white cap resembling a crown with little teeth and a corset that kept her waist firm and thin; and the very best of bellhops, the short and plump Luigi, who in his time had worked in many fine establishments. Soon the French *maitre d'* knocked lightly on the door of the gentleman from San Francisco's suite: he'd come to ask if the new guests would dine and, in the event he should receive an affirmative answer—of which, of course, he had no doubt—to inform the gentleman that tonight rock lobster would be served, along with pheasant and asparagus, roast beef, and so on. That wretched little Italian steamer had so thoroughly discomposed the gentleman from San Francisco that the floor still seemed to sway beneath his feet, but he didn't falter as he reached out with his own unpracticed, slightly awkward hand and closed the window that had banged open upon the *maitre d's* entrance, momentarily releasing into the room the smell of cooking smoke from the distant kitchen, the scent of wet flowers from the garden. And he answered with leisurely precision that the family would dine, that their table should be set far back from the entrance, that they would drink the local wine—and in response to each of his words, the *maitre d'* made little sounds of assent in varying intonations, all of which were intended to express the thought that there could be no doubt about the absolute correctness of the gentleman's desires, and that everything would be fulfilled precisely as he ordered. Then the *maitre d'* tilted his head at a slight angle and politely asked, "Is that all, sir?"

And having received a drawn-out "yes" in answer to his question, he added that the *tarantella* would be performed that evening in the hotel vestibule by Carmella and Giuseppe, who were famous throughout Italy and "the entire tourist world."

"I've seen her on postcards," the gentleman from San Francisco said in a voice devoid of all expression. "That Giuseppe, is he her husband?"

"Her cousin, sir," answered the *maitre d'*. And after pausing for a moment, after contemplating something silently, the gentleman from San Francisco released him with a nod.

And then he started getting ready once again, as if preparing for a wedding. He turned on all the lamps, flooded every mirror with reflected light and glare, images of furniture and open trunks; he began to shave and wash and ring the bell for the attendant constantly, competing all the while with equally impatient calls that rang out from his wife and daughter's rooms. Grimacing with horror, Luigi raced toward each ringing bell with that lightness that many people who are fat possess, and all the maids running down the corridors with porcelain jugs in their hands laughed so hard they almost cried as he tore past them in his red apron, rapped lightly with his knuckles on the door, and in a voice so full of feigned timidity that it bordered on the imbecilic, asked: *"Ha sonato, Signore?"*

And from behind the door, a slow, rasping, and insultingly decorous voice replied: "Yes, come in."

What did the gentleman from San Francisco think and feel that evening, which was so significant for him? Like anyone recovering from seasickness, he simply wanted very much to eat, and he imagined with great pleasure the first spoonful of soup, the first swallow of wine. These thoughts excited him so much that he finished his usual preparations for the meal in a somewhat agitated state, which left no time for any other feelings or reflection.

Having shaved and washed and comfortably inserted his false teeth, the gentleman from San Francisco stood before the mirror with several dampened silver brushes and straightened the last pearly strands of hair across his dark yellow scalp; stretched a pair of silk, cream-colored briefs over his firm, old man's body with its waist grown large from overeating; and slipped his flat, withered feet into black silk socks and evening shoes. He briefly bent his knees in order to adjust his black pants, held high by silk suspenders, and to straighten out his billowing, snow-white shirtfront; then he adjusted the cuff links at the edges of his brilliant sleeves and began struggling to fasten the top stud on his stiff collar. The floor still rocked beneath him, his fingertips throbbed, and the stud bit painfully into the loose, thin skin lying in a little recess just below his Adam's apple. But he persisted, and at last—his eyes shining from the effort, his face a bluish-grey from the exceedingly tight collar that now constricted his throat—the gentleman from San Francisco completed his toilet and sat exhausted before the pier glass, his reflection multiplied by all the other mirrors that surrounded him.

"Oh, this is awful," he muttered, lowering his bald head and making no attempt to contemplate exactly what was awful. Out of habit, he began to carefully inspect his short fingers: their stiffened, gouty joints; their large and prominent almond-colored nails. "This is awful," he repeated with conviction.

But just then the second gong rang out like something in a pagan temple, and the gentleman from San Francisco quickly rose. He pulled his collar even tighter with his tie, girded his stomach even more firmly with his waistcoat, donned his dinner jacket, straightened his cuff links, looked at himself in the mirror again. . . . "That Carmella," he thought, "there's something kittenish about her eyes. And such dark skin. She looks like a mulatto, especially in that bright orange costume. I bet her dancing is extraordinary." Cheerfully he left the room, walked along the carpet to his wife and daughter's suites, and asked in a loud voice if they'd be ready soon.

"In five minutes," a girl's voice rang out happily and clearly from behind the door.

"Excellent," said the gentleman from San Francisco.

Then he leisurely set out along the corridors and the red-carpeted stairs, looking for the reading room. Servants whom he met quickly turned away and pressed themselves against the wall—he passed as if not seeing them. And he quickly overtook an old woman who, late for dinner, was doing all she could to hurry down the hall: she wore a low-cut evening gown of light grey silk, but her hair was white as milk, her back was hunched, and all her efforts to move quickly only had a comical effect, for she looked like a bustling chicken. Near the glass doors of the dining room, where all the guests had already gathered and begun to eat, he stopped before a table loaded down with Egyptian cigarettes and boxes of cigars, picked out a large Manila, and tossed down three lire. Crossing the winter veranda, he glanced at an open window: a gentle breeze from the darkness passed over him; he saw the top of an old palm tree, vague as something in a dream with its huge fronds spread among the stars; the unfaltering sound of the distant sea reached his ears. . . . A grey-haired German who resembled Ibsen with his round, silver-framed glasses and his crazy, startled eyes stood leafing through a newspaper in the comfortable and quiet reading room, where the only lamplight lay neatly on the tables. The gentleman from San Francisco looked him over coldly, then settled into a plush leather armchair in the corner near a lamp with a green shade, placed his pince-nez on the bridge of his nose, craned his neck away from his suffocating collar, and disappeared completely behind his newspaper. He skimmed a few headlines, read a few sentences about the endless Balkan War, turned the page just as he always did—and suddenly the lines of newsprint flashed like glass before him, his neck went taut and his eyes bugged out, the pince-nez flew from his nose. . . . He lunged forward, tried to draw a breath, and snorted violently. His jaw dropped open, and his mouth filled with the golden glow of light reflected from his fillings. His head fell to his shoulder and began to roll from side to side; his shirtfront jutted out, as if a shoebox had been thrust beneath it, and his entire body writhed as he slid to the floor, digging at the carpet with his heels, struggling with someone desperately.

If the German hadn't been inside the reading room, the hotel staff would have quickly and discreetly put an end to this unpleasant display; they would have grabbed the gentleman from San Francisco by his head and feet and quietly hauled him out the back, and not a single guest would have known what he'd been up to in the reading room. But the German burst into the hallway with a shout, roused the entire building and the dining room. Guests jumped up from their meals and ran into the reading room, turning pale. "What? What happened?" they asked in every language, and no one answered their murmuring, for even to this day death astounds us more than anything, and no one wants to believe in it. The owner rushed around among the guests, trying to stop them as they ran into the room, and to calm them down with hurried assurances that it was nothing at all—just a fainting spell suffered by a certain gentleman from San Francisco—but no one listened to him, and many saw how the stewards and the bellhops tore off the gentleman's tie, his waistcoat, his crumpled jacket, and even, for some reason, pulled the evening shoes from his flat feet in their black silk socks. And he was still fighting: he struggled stubbornly with death, refusing to submit to such a crude and unexpected attack. He shook his head and snorted like an animal at slaughter, rolled his eyes like a drunk. . . . When they hurriedly carried him away to a bed in room 43—the hotel's smallest, coldest, dampest room, which stood at the end of the ground-floor corridor—his daughter came running, her hair undone, her half-uncovered breasts raised high by a corset, and then his heavy-set wife arrived, fully dressed for dinner, her mouth round with horror. . . . But the gentleman from San Francisco had already stopped shaking his head.

Fifteen minutes later some semblance of order had been restored in the hotel. But the evening was damaged beyond repair. Some of the guests returned to the dining room to finish their meals, but they all ate silently and looked offended while the owner, who felt to blame despite his innocence, went from one table to another, shrugging his shoulders with just the right degree of helpless indignation, assuring everyone he understood perfectly "how unpleasant" this had been, and promising to use "all means at his disposal" to correct the situation. They were forced to cancel the *tarantella*, and all the extra lights were turned off. Most of the guests went to a tavern in town, and it grew so quiet in the hotel that one could clearly hear the clock ticking in the vestibule, where a parrot muttered something woodenly to itself in its cage, fidgeting as it senselessly contrived to sleep with one foot awkwardly raised on its upper roost. . . .

The gentleman from San Francisco lay on a bed of cheap cast iron, light from a single bulb falling dimly on the coarse wool blankets wrapped around his body. An ice bag sagged on his damp, cold fore-head. His lifeless, blue-grey face was gradually stiffening, and the rasp-ing, gurgling sound of his breath was weakening as it rose from his open mouth, where a golden light still glimmered. And already it was not the gentleman from San Francisco who snored, it was someone else, for the gentleman from San Francisco was gone. His wife and daughter, a doc-tor, and some servants stood and watched. And then the thing they'd feared and waited for with dread took place: the wheezing stopped. And slowly, slowly, before the eyes of all who watched, a pallor spread across the dead man's face while his features lightened and grew finer. . . .

The owner came in. "*Gia e morto,*" the doctor told him in a whis-per. The owner's face remained impassive; he shrugged his shoulders. Tears quietly rolling down her face, the gentleman from San Francisco's wife approached him and said timidly that it was time to return her hus-band to his suite.

"Oh no, Madame," the owner objected quickly and correctly. He spoke French, instead of English, and his voice lacked all its former courtesy, for he had no interest in the trifles that these visitors from San Francisco would now leave inside his register. "That's utterly impossible, Madame," he said, explaining that if he carried out her wish, all Capri would learn of it, and future tourists would refuse those rooms, which he valued very highly.

The daughter, who'd been looking at him strangely while he spoke, sat down in a chair, pressed a handkerchief to her mouth, and began to sob. The wife's tears dried immediately. An angry look flashed across her face; she raised her voice and began to make demands, speaking her own language, refusing to believe that all respect for them was lost for good. But the owner silenced her with dignified civility: if Madame did not care for conditions in the hotel, he had no right to detain her. And then he added sternly that the body must be removed today at dawn, that the police had been informed of the situation, and that their representa-tive would soon arrive to complete the necessary formalities. . . . Could they at least find a simple coffin for sale on Capri? the Madame asked. Unfortunately, that was quite impossible; and no one would have time to make one. They would have to take some other course of action. . . . English soda water, for example, was delivered to the hotel in long, large boxes. . . . The dividers could be taken out. . . .

All the guests had gone to sleep. In room 43 they opened a window— it looked out onto a corner of the garden, where a sickly banana tree stood beside a high stone wall topped with broken glass—turned out the lights, locked the door, and left. The dead man remained in darkness; dark blue stars looked down on him from the sky. A cricket on the wall began to chirp with melancholy aimlessness. . . . Two maids sat on a windowsill, darning in the dimly lit corridor. Luigi approached them, wearing slippers, a stack of dresses slung over one arm.

"*Pronto?*" he asked in an anxious voice, casting his eyes toward the frightful door at the end of the hall. He gently waved his free hand in that direction. "*Partenza!*" he shouted in a whisper, as if seeing off a train—for this is what they shout in Italy as the cars begin to move—and the maids dropped their heads on one another's shoulders, choking on their stifled laughter.

Then he softly skipped down the hall to the door itself, knocked lightly, cocked his head to one side, and asked in the most courteous whisper:

"*Ha sonato, Signore?*"

And constricting his throat, thrusting out his lower jaw, he answered himself in a drawn-out, sad, and rasping voice that seemed to come from behind the door: "Yes, come in."

At dawn, while it grew white outside room 43; while a damp wind rustled the torn leaves of the banana tree and a light blue morning sky rose and spread out over the island of Capri; while the clear, precise peak of Mount Solaro turned golden in the sun as it ascended over the distant blue mountains of Italy, and the masons who repair stone paths for tourists on the island left for work, a long box for English soda water was carried to room 43. Soon the box became very heavy, and it pressed hard against the knees of the junior porter who rode beside it in a horse-drawn cart, quickly descending to the sea along a white highway that wound back and forth among the slopes and stone walls and the vineyards of Capri. The driver, a scrawny little man in worn-out shoes and an old jacket with sleeves too short for his arms, had been playing dice all night in a cheap café, and now, red-eyed and hung over, he incessantly whipped his small, strong horse, who was adorned Sicilian style with little bells that jingled earnestly on the points of his bronze-plated saddle-strap pad and on his bridle, among pompoms of bright wool, while a yard-long feather, rising from the horse's clipped forelock, trembled as he trotted down the road. The driver sat silently, weighed down by thoughts of his bad habits and his dissipation, and by the fact that he'd lost his last lira the previous night. But the morning was fresh, and in such air—surrounded by the sea, beneath the morning sky—the haze of a hangover quickly clears, an easy calm comes back, and the driver was comforted by the unexpected work that he'd received from a certain gentleman from San Francisco, whose lifeless head now rocked back and forth in the box behind him. Far below, a small steamer lay like a beetle on the delicate and brilliant blue that so thickly fills the Bay of Naples; the ship's horn was sounding its final calls, and they echoed cheerfully across the island, where every hillcrest, every contour, every stone was so clearly visible that it seemed there was no air at all. Near the docks, the junior porter saw his senior counterpart race by in an automobile with the dead man's wife and daughter, both of them pale, their eyes sunken from sleeplessness and tears. Ten minutes later the ship left port, stirring the water once more as it headed for Sorrento and Castellammare, and carried the family from San Francisco forever from Capri. . . . Quietude and calm settled on the island in its wake.

Two thousand years ago that island was inhabited by a man who somehow held power over millions of people. He gratified his lust in ways that are repugnant beyond words, and carried out immeasurable atrocities against his subjects. Humanity has remembered him through time, and now countless people come from all around the world to see the ruins of his stone house on one of the island's highest peaks. The tourists who had traveled to Capri with this aim were still asleep on that lovely morning, although small, mouse-grey donkeys with red saddles were already being led to the entrances of their hotels, so that all the old and young American and German guests could clamber up onto their backs after a big breakfast and a good night's sleep, and once again old, impoverished women would run behind them on stone paths with sticks in their sinewy hands, driving those donkeys all the way to the top of Mount Tiberius. Relieved that the dead old man from San Francisco— who'd planned to make this trip with all the others, but wound up only frightening them with an unpleasant reminder about mortality—had now been sent away to Naples, the guests slept very soundly; it was quiet on the island, and everything in town was closed except a small outdoor market on the square, where simple people sold fish and vegetables, and, as usual, Lorenzo stood without a care. He was a tall old boatman, an aimless wanderer, and a handsome model, well known throughout Italy for the many pictures in which he'd appeared. Having sold for next to nothing a pair of lobsters that he caught the night before—they were rustling now in the apron of the cook from the very same hotel where the family from San Francisco had spent the night—he was free to stand placidly on that square until the sun went down, smoking a clay pipe and looking at his surroundings like a king, preening in his shabby clothes, a red wool beret tugged down over one ear. Meanwhile, high among the cliffs of Mount Solaro, two Abruzzian mountain dwellers were following a Phoenician road down from Anacapri, descending ancient steps cut into the crags. One had a bagpipe made of a large goatskin and two reeds under his leather cloak; the other carried an ancient wooden flute. They walked and the entire country—joyful, lovely, bathed in light—spread out before them: almost all the island and its stone mounds lay at their feet, surrounded by a pure, fantastic blue; a mist shimmered over the sea to the east as the hot and blinding sun rose higher and higher; and the azure haze of the Italian mountain mass still wavered in the morning light, the beauty of its near and distant peaks beyond the power of the human word. Halfway down they paused: above the road, in a grotto cut into the mountainside, the meek and gentle Holy Mother stood in pure white plaster robes, her halo flecked with a golden rust from years of rain. Resplendent in the strong, warm light of the sun, she held her eyes toward the sky, toward the eternal, blissful dwelling place of her thrice-blessed child. They took off their hats, and with humble, innocent joy they praised the morning and the sun, praised her, the pure protector of all who suffer in this beautiful and evil world, praised the child born from her womb in a cave in Bethlehem, in a poor shepherd's hut, in the distant land of Judea.

The body of the dead old man from San Francisco was going home, returning to a grave on the shores of the New World. For a week it wandered from one port shed to another, suffering great degradation and neglect, until at last it wound up on the same celebrated ship that had only recently brought it to the Old World with such consideration and regard. But now they hid the gentleman from San Francisco from the living: they lowered him in a tarred coffin deep into the blackness of the ship's hold. And again, again the ship set out on its distant route across the ocean. It sailed past the island of Capri at night, and its lights, slowly disappearing into the dark sea, seemed sad to those who watched from the shore. But the ship's halls were filled with people and the festive glow of chandeliers that night, for as usual a ball was being held.

There was dancing on the second night, and on the third as well—again in the midst of a raging storm, the deep moaning of the sea like a mass for the dead, its black hills fringed with silver foam like the cloaks of passing mourners. The devil could barely see the ship's countless, glowing eyes through the falling snow as he stood on the cliffs of Gibraltar, the stone gate between two worlds, and watched the *Atlantis* sail off into the darkness and the storm. The devil was as huge as a mountainside, but the ship was also huge, with its many stories and its smokestacks—all of it born from the arrogance of the New Man, whose heart is old. The storm tore at its rigging and the wide-mouthed smokestacks as they turned white with snow, but the ship was hard, unyielding, majestic, terrible. At the top of its uppermost story, a comfortable, dimly lit cabin jutted up into the whirling snow, and there the ship's massive driver sat like a pagan idol, reigning over the vessel, alert and anxious in his unremitting somnolence. He could hear the siren's muffled howls and bitter shrieks through the wind, but just beyond the wall of his living quarters, another cabin stood—it seemed to be plated in armor, and it filled again and again with a secret hum, a blue flickering, a dry crackling flame that flared up and burst, illuminating the pale face and the metal headset of the telegraph engineer—and although this room was ultimately an utter mystery to the captain, its close proximity reassured him in the storm. At the very bottom of the *Atlantis*, deep in its underwater belly, twenty-ton cauldrons of steel shone dimly as they rasped with steam, as they dripped boiling water and oil, hulking among various other machines in a kind of kitchen where hellish furnaces heated everything from below and made the ship move: terrifying in its concentration, all the seething force contained within those cauldrons bubbled and surged toward the keel, traveling an endless passageway, a circular, dimly lit tunnel, a gaping maw with its entire length filled by a massive shaft that lay like a monster in an oily bed, slowly and continuously turning with such inexorable regularity that it would wear away the human soul. But in the middle of the ship—in the dining rooms and the ballrooms, everything was filled with joy and light, filled with the murmuring of the well-dressed crowd and the scent of fresh flowers, filled with the songs of the stringed orchestra. And once again, beneath those brilliant chandeliers, among the silks and jewels and the bared flesh of female shoulders, that delicate pair of graceful hired lovers spun and swayed, and ground against each other fitfully, with anguished passion: a sinfully modest young woman with lowered eyes and the hairstyle of an innocent girl, and a strapping young man in a narrow tuxedo with long tails and the most elegant patent leather shoes, his face powdered white, his black hair so perfectly combed it seemed to be glued to his scalp—a beautiful man resembling a giant leech. No one knew that this pair had long ago grown tired of faking their tormented bliss while the shamelessly sad music played on, nor what lay deep, deep below them, in the blackness of the hold, beside the hot, dark innards of the ship as it toiled to overcome the darkness, the sea, the storm.

[1915]

Ida

F OUR OF US — three old friends and a certain Georgy Ivanovich —
had breakfast at the Bolshoy Moskovsky at Christmastime.

The restaurant was empty and cool on account of the holiday. We
passed through the old hall, which was filled with a pale light from the
icy, grey morning, and stopped at the entrance to the new dining room.
The tables there had just been set with fresh, trim white cloths, and we
looked them over carefully, wondering which would suit us best. Then
the *maitre d'*, who was so well scrubbed and courteous he seemed to
shine, made a refined and humble gesture toward a round booth in the
corner. We followed his suggestion.

"Gentlemen," the composer said as he moved around the table and
settled his solid frame firmly on the couch. "For some reason I'd like to
treat you all to a real feast today. Do you remember the magic tablecloth
from all those fairy tales you read as a child?" he said, turning his wide
peasant face and narrow eyes to the waiter. "We need a tablecloth like
that. And a meal even more generous than those it produced for the
hungry prince. You know my regal habits."

"Of course, Pavel Nikolayevich," answered the waiter, an intelligent old man with a clean silver beard. "In fact, we've learned your habits by heart," he said, smiling with restraint as he placed an ashtray on the table. "Relax and enjoy yourself. We'll do our best."

A moment later the table was set with champagne flutes, goblets, and shot glasses, an assortment of flavored vodkas, pink salmon, cracked oysters on ice, filets of smoked and salted sturgeon, an orange block of Cheshire cheese, a black glistening square of pressed caviar, and a frosted silver tub of champagne bottles. . . . We started with the pepper vodka. . . . The composer enjoyed filling our glasses himself. He poured three shots, then paused:

"Most holy Georgy Ivanovich, may I indulge you?" he asked jokingly.

A quiet, invariably good-humored man whose only occupation consisted of befriending well-known writers, artists, and actors, Georgy Ivanovich blushed—as he always did—before speaking.

"You certainly may, most sinful Pavel Nikolayevich," he said with slightly excessive familiarity.

The composer poured him a drink, lightly touched glasses with each of us, tossed back his vodka with the words "gracious God," then exhaled through his moustache and set to work on the hors d'oeuvres. The rest of us turned to the food as well; it held our attention for quite a long time. Then we ordered *ukha* and paused in the meal to smoke. A sad, tender song began to play indistinctly on the phonograph in the old hall. The composer leaned back in his seat and drew on his cigarette. Then he raised his chest high and took a deep breath, as was his habit before speaking.

"Despite the pleasure my belly is enjoying, I'm sad today, friends," he said. "I'm sad because this morning, just as I was waking up, I remembered a trivial little story that took place exactly three years ago on the second day of Christmas. It involved a friend of mine who, in the course of events, was shown to be a complete ass."

"A trivial story, but no doubt an amorous one," said Georgy Ivanovich, with his girlish smile.

The composer cast a sidelong glance at him. "Amorous," he said sardonically. "Georgy Ivanovich—my dear Georgy Ivanovich, how will you ever answer for your salaciousness and your merciless wit on Judgment Day? May God be with you then. *"Je veux un trésor qui les contient tous, je veux la jeunesse"*— he raised his eyebrows as he sang along with the phonograph, which was playing *Faust*, and then continued to address us:

"Well, here is the story, friends. . . . Once upon a time, in an unknown land, a certain girl visited the home of a certain gentleman. A university friend of his wife's, she was so pleasant and unassuming that the gentleman referred to her simply by first name—Ida. Just Ida. He wasn't even completely sure of her patronymic or her last name. He knew that she came from a respectable but modest family, that she was the daughter of a musician who was once a well-known conductor, and that she lived with her parents while waiting, in the customary manner, for a groom to appear—and that was all.

"How can I describe this Ida to you? The gentleman was very well disposed toward her, but I repeat, he paid her no particular attention. She comes to the house and he says, 'Ah, Ida my dear, hello, hello. I'm very glad to see you.' She only smiles in response, hides her handkerchief inside her muff, and looks at him with the clear, slightly thoughtless eyes of a young girl. 'Is Masha here?' she asks. 'Of course, of course,' the gentleman answers, 'please come in.' 'Can I see her?' Ida asks, and casually walks through the dining room to Masha's door. 'Masha, can I come in?' Her voice rises from somewhere low in her chest. It's deep and velvety and it stirs him to his bones. Add to that voice all the vigor of youth and good health, the fresh scent of a girl entering a room from the cold. She's tall and slim, her figure's exquisite, and she moves with a rare, completely natural grace. Her face is particularly unusual: at first glance it seems completely ordinary, but look closely and you're lost. Her complexion is warm and even, like the slight blush of a fine apple. Her eyes are almost violet, bright, and full of life.

"Yes, look closely, and you're lost. And that ass—I mean, the hero of our story—he looks at her and goes into raptures: 'Ida, dear Ida,' he sighs. 'You don't know your own worth.' He sees her smiling as he says these words, and her expression is sweet but somehow slightly distracted. So the damn fool leaves—goes back to his study and occupies himself with some bit of nonsense that he calls a work of art.

"Time moved steadily along, and the gentleman never once thought seriously about this Ida until one fine day she disappeared. As you might imagine, he didn't notice in the least. Ida's gone. She's gone and he never thinks to ask his wife, 'Where has our friend Ida disappeared to?' Occasionally he feels something missing. He imagines the sweet anguish he would have suffered if he'd slipped his arms around her waist. He recalls the squirrel fur muff she carried, her English skirt, her delicate hands and pure complexion, her violet eyes. He remembers these things, feels a momentary pang of longing, and then forgets again. Two years went by that way.

"And then one day the hero of our story had to make a journey to the western regions of that mythical land in which he lived. It was Christmastime, but he had to go, regardless of the holiday. So he said farewell to his family and his subjects, rode off on his finest stallion. He rides all day and rides all night, until at last he reaches the regional station where he has a connection to make. But I should add that he arrives very late, and as soon as the train slows at the platform, he jumps off and grabs the first porter he sees by the collar. 'The express to so-and-so, has it left yet?' he shouts. The porter smiles politely. 'It just left, sir,' he says. 'You were pleased to arrive almost two hours late, after all, sir.' 'What?' The gentleman shouts. 'Are you joking? You fool! What am I supposed to do now! I'll send you to Siberia! To hard labor! I'll have you on the chopping block!' 'You are right, sir,' the porter answers. 'I'm obviously at fault. But as the saying goes, "those confessing sins are spared the sword." And there will be a local train, sir, that goes to that destination. Perhaps you'll be so good as to wait for it.' Our distinguished traveler bowed his head and plodded off to the station.

"It was pleasant and warm inside, crowded but comfortable. A blizzard had been blowing through the area for a full week, and the entire line was a mess—all the schedules had been shot to hell, and the transfer stations were jammed. Here it was just the same—people and luggage scattered everywhere, meals served at the counters all day, the smell of cooking smoke and samovar coals heavy in the air—all of which, as you know, is far from unpleasant in the midst of a blizzard and the freezing cold. Furthermore, this particular station was quite well appointed—clean and spacious—and the traveler realized right away that it would be no great tragedy to wait there, even for a day. 'I'll clean myself up, then have a few drinks and a good meal,' he thought with pleasure as he entered the passengers' hall, and immediately set about completing his plan. The gentleman shaved, washed, put on a clean shirt, and fifteen minutes later he left the washroom looking twenty years younger. At the buffet he drank two shots, following the first with a *pirog* and the second with some Jewish pike. He was ready to order a third when suddenly, from somewhere behind him, he heard a female voice that was both terribly familiar and beautiful beyond words.

He turned—'with a pounding heart,' of course—and whom do you think he saw? Ida!

"At first he was so overwhelmed with astonishment and joy that he couldn't utter a word. He just stared at her like a sheep studying a new gate to its pasture. But she—and this, friends, is what it means to be a woman—she didn't bat an eye. Of course she couldn't help being somewhat surprised, and even a certain joy was evident in her expression, but all in all, I tell you, she stayed remarkably composed. 'My dear,' she says, 'what fates have produced this happy meeting!' Her eyes revealed that she meant what she was saying, but she spoke, somehow, too simply, and the tone of her words was nothing like it used to be. It had become, somehow, ironic, even slightly mocking. Our gentleman was amazed by the many other ways in which she'd changed as well. It was overwhelming—she'd bloomed like some kind of exotic flower kept in a crystalline vase with the cleanest water, and now she was virtually unrecognizable as she stood before him in a sable cloak worth a thousand rubles and a hellishly expensive winter hat, both of which combined pure modesty with sheer coquettishness. Dazzled by the rings on her fingers, he timidly kissed her hand, and Ida tipped back her head, said nonchalantly, 'By the way, please meet my husband': a student stepped out from behind her and neatly presented himself in military fashion."

"What insolence!" exclaimed Georgy Ivanovich. "An ordinary student!"

"But that's just it, dear Georgy Ivanovich," the composer said with a bitter smile. "There was nothing ordinary about him. In fact, our gentleman had never in his life seen such a striking example of what is called nobility as this young man, whose features were as white and smooth as marble. He wore a double-breasted jacket. It was sewn from that light, grey cloth that only the most stylish gentlemen wear, and it was tailored perfectly to his trim waist. The rest of his wardrobe was equally refined and elegant—stirruped trousers, a dark green military cap in Prussian style, a luxurious overcoat with a beaver collar. But despite all this, he seemed completely unpretentious. Ida muttered the name of one of Russia's most famous families, and he quickly took off his hat (it was lined, of course, with red *moire*), removed one of his white suede gloves to reveal a delicate, milky blue hand that felt as if it had been lightly dusted in flour, then clicked his heels together and respectfully lowered his painstakingly groomed head to his breast. 'What a sight!' the gentleman thought to himself, feeling even more amazed. He looked stupidly at Ida again and immediately understood from the glance she aimed at the student that she, of course, ruled his life, and the student was a slave—not at all an ordinary slave, however, but one who bore his bondage with utmost pleasure and even pride. 'I'm very, very glad to meet you,' the slave said with utter sincerity, lifting his head with a pleasant, cheerful smile. 'I'm a longtime admirer of yours, and Ida has told me a great deal about you,' he continued, looking at our hero affably. He was clearly ready to begin a conversation, but Ida cut him short. 'Be quiet, Petrik. Don't embarrass me,' she said hurriedly, turning to the gentleman. 'My dear, it's been a thousand years since I saw you. I'd like to talk endlessly, but not with him here. Our reminiscences will mean nothing to him. He'll be bored, and because of his boredom, we'll feel awkward. Let's go for a walk, instead.' And having spoken thus, she took our traveler by the arm and led him out of the station. They walked almost a full *verst* on the platform, where the snow was nearly knee-deep, and she suddenly confessed to being in love with him."

"What do you mean, in love with him?" we all asked at once. Instead of answering, the composer took another deep breath, filling his chest and straightening his shoulders. He lowered his eyes, then rose up clumsily in his seat. Ice rustled as he took a bottle from the silver tub and filled a wine glass with champagne. The skin over his cheekbones was flushed, and his short neck had turned red. Slouching in his seat, trying to hide his confusion, he drained his glass and began to sing once more with the phonograph—"*Laissez-moi, laissez-moi contempler ton visage! . . .*" but immediately broke off and resolutely looked at us with narrowed eyes:

"Yes, her love. . . . It was . . . her confession was, unfortunately, completely real and genuine. Sudden, stupid, absurd, unbelievable—yes, of course, it was all these things. But it remains a fact. Everything happened just as I am telling you. They walked onto the platform and right away she started talking quickly, started asking questions with contrived cheerfulness: How was Masha? How were their mutual friends in Moscow? What was new in the city? Etcetera, etcetera. And then she announced that she had been married for more than a year, that she and her husband had spent some of that time in Saint Petersburg, some of it abroad, and the rest at their estate near Vitebsk. . . . The gentleman hurried along behind her, sensing, already, that something was wrong—that in a moment something stupid and unbelievable would occur—and he stared as hard as he could at the whiteness of the snow lying everywhere around them, heaped in endless drifts across the platforms and the rails, piled thickly on the roofs and the tops of all the red and green cars left standing on the tracks. He looked and with a terrible sense that his heart had gone still, he understood one thing: for years and years he had been completely, madly in love with this Ida. . . . You can imagine the rest of the story yourselves, I'm sure. It goes like this: Ida walked up to a row of crates left on some remote platform far from the station. She brushed the snow from one of the crates with her muff and sat down. She raised her slightly pallid face and her violet eyes toward the gentleman. And without the slightest pause, without the slightest warning, she said: 'Dearest, I want you to answer a question: Did you know that I was in love with you before? Do you know now that I'm in love with you still— that I've been in love with you for five entire years?'"

The music from the phonograph, which had been rumbling softly in the background, suddenly swelled into a grandiose, disturbing roar. The composer fell silent and raised his eyes to us—they seemed to be filled with fear and surprise.

"Yes," he continued quietly. "That's what she said to him. And now, let me ask you a question: How can one describe that moment with stupid human words? What can I tell you, other than cheap clichés, about that face turned toward him in the pallid light that only the snow of a recent storm produces? How can I describe that face which was itself as white as the snow, or the tender, ineffable emotions it expressed? How can I speak at all about the features of a beautiful young woman who walks in the snow and breathes the fresh, cold air, then suddenly stops to confess her love for you, and waits for you to respond? How did I describe her eyes? Violet? No, no—that's wrong, of course! And the way her lips were slightly parted? And the expression— the expression created by all her features combined—by her eyes, by her face and her lips? What can be said about the long sable muff in which her hands were hidden, or the outline of her knees beneath a checkered blue-green skirt? My God, who can even touch these things with words! And most important, most important—what answer could be given to that astounding confession which made him feel such dread and joy? What could he say as she trustingly looked up at him, waiting for an answer, her face drained of all color and distorted by a strange, uneasy smile?"

Not knowing how to respond, we stared with mute surprise at our companion's red face and glittering eyes. He answered his questions himself:

"Nothing, absolutely nothing. There are moments when a person must not make the slightest sound. And fortunately—to the great honor of our traveler—he said nothing at all. And she understood the way he froze before her, she saw his face. She waited there for a little while; she sat motionless in the absurd, cruel silence that followed her terrible question. And then she stood up, removed her warm, sweet-smelling hand from her muff, slipped it around his neck, and kissed him with both tenderness and passion. It was one of those kisses a man remembers not only on his deathbed but in the grave itself. And that was all—she kissed him and left. That's how the story ends. . . . And really, we've talked enough about this," the composer said, suddenly changing his tone. "In honor of my story, let's add to the fog in our brains," he continued loudly, trying to appear amused. "Let's drink to everyone who loved us and whom we—idiots that we are—didn't value. Let's make a toast to those who blessed us and made us happy and then were discarded forever from our lives, but remained forever linked to us by the most terrible link on earth. And let us agree, gentlemen, that I will smash this champagne bottle across the skull of anyone who adds even a single word to my story. Waiter!" he roared across the hall. "Bring the *ukha*! And sherry! A barrel of sherry! One big enough for a cuckold to douse his head with its horns!"

Our breakfast that day lasted until eleven at night. When it was over, we went to the Yar, and from there to the Strelna, where we ate *blinis* before dawn, ordered cheap vodka in bottles with red caps, and in general behaved scandalously: we shouted, sang, even danced the *kazachok*. The composer moved silently to the music—his dancing was violent, ecstatic, and surprisingly graceful for a man of his build. The morning sky was already pink when we raced home in the bitter cold. As our *troika* sailed past the Strastnoy Monastery, an icy, red sun rose from behind the roofs, and the first shuddering blow of the bells broke loose from the belfry—and all of frozen Moscow seemed to shake. The composer tore off his hat and with all his strength shouted tearfully across the square:

"My sun! My beloved! Hurrah!"

[1925]

Light Breathing

T HERE'S A NEW oak cross over a mound of freshly turned clay in the graveyard. It's solid, heavy, smooth.

April. Damp days. You can see the headstones and the monuments of the spacious district graveyard from far away through the stripped trees. A cold wind rings and rings through a porcelain wreath at the foot of the cross.

And set into the cross itself is a rather large, porcelain medallion. It bulges forward from the center. It bears the photograph of a schoolgirl whose eyes are stunningly alive and full of joy.

This is Olya Meshcherskaya.

As a young child, nothing set her apart from that crowd of little girls wearing identical brown dresses to school. What was there to say of her? She belonged to the ranks of rich and pretty, happy girls; she was bright but mischievous—and blithely indifferent to the admonitions of the *klassnaya dama*, that teacher charged with making future ladies understand the points of proper conduct.

But then she began to bloom. Her figure seemed to mature by the hour rather than the day, and by the age of fourteen, along with graceful, slender legs and a thin waist, she'd developed full breasts and all of those other contours whose charms remain beyond the power of the human word. At fifteen, her beauty was renowned. How diligently her girlfriends brushed their hair! How fastidious they were! How carefully they studied each deliberate movement that they made! But she was not afraid of any-thing—not disheveled hair or ink stains on her fingers, not a heavy blush reddening her face or a knee exposed while falling as she ran. Those qualities that distinguished her so clearly from her classmates during her last two years of school—her elegance and style, her grace, the radiance of her eyes—all came to her almost unnoticed, and without the slightest effort or concern. . . . No one danced the way Olya Meshcherskaya danced; no one skated with such poise. No one found so many suitors at the balls, or so much admiration, for some reason, among the children in the younger classes. It wasn't clear exactly when her body grew into a woman's, or when her fame became a part of daily life within the school, but once those changes had occurred, rumors started spreading. They said that she was fickle, that she could not live without admirers, that a student by the name of Shenshin was half insane with love for her, and that she too, apparently, loved him, but treated the young man with such capriciousness that he'd attempted suicide.

It was also said in school that Olya Meshcherskaya had gone com-pletely mad with happiness during her last winter. It was a cold and snowy winter, with heavy frosts and bright days, the sun setting early be-hind the tall grove of firs in the school's snowbound garden, its sharp, clear rays invariably promising that tomorrow the weather would again be good, that there would be more sunlight and frost, more walking down Cathedral Street, more skating in the city park, a pink sky in the evening, music, and that crowd gliding endlessly in all directions in the rink—that crowd among which Olya Meshcherskaya seemed the very most carefree, the very happiest of all. And so it was that one day during the major recess, as she flew like a whirlwind through the assembly hall and a group of blissfully squealing first-graders followed in hot pursuit, Olya Meshcherskaya was suddenly called to the director's office. She stopped in mid-stride, released a single, heavy sigh, and with the quick, practiced movements of an adult woman, patted her hair in place and tugged the corners of her pinafore toward her shoulders before running up the stairs, her eyes shining. The director, a woman whose young looks were belied only by her grey hair, sat calmly with her knitting at a desk beneath a portrait of the tsar.

"Hello, Mademoiselle Meshcherskaya," she said in French, not raising her eyes. "This, unfortunately, is not the first time I have found it necessary to call you here in order to discuss your behavior."

"I am listening, Madame," Meshcherskaya answered, approaching the desk and looking at the director with bright and animated eyes, though the rest of her face lacked all expression. She curtsied with that easy grace that she alone possessed.

"You will listen to me poorly; of that, unfortunately, I am completely convinced," the director answered as she pulled on a thread from a ball of yarn now spinning on the lacquered floor. Meshcherskaya looked at it with curiosity. "I won't repeat myself," the director said, looking up from her work. "I won't make a long speech."

Meshcherskaya had always liked that unusually clean and spacious office, which on days of heavy frost was so pleasantly filled with the fragrant warmth of a gleaming tiled stove and the fresh scent of Lilies of the Valley, which stood on the director's desk. She looked at the young tsar, portrayed in full length, standing in some resplendent hall, then studied the straight part that ran through the director's milky, carefully crimped hair, and held her silence, waiting.

"You're already no longer a girl," the director said significantly. In secret she was beginning to feel annoyed.

"Yes, Madame," answered Meshcherskaya, her expression forthright, almost happy.

"But not yet a woman," the director continued, giving even greater weight to these words, a slight flush beginning to suffuse her otherwise colorless complexion. "First of all—just look at the way you style your hair. It's like a grown woman's!"

"It's not my fault, Madame, that I have good hair," Meshcherskaya answered, lightly touching with both hands her hair in its lovely arrangement.

"Oh, that's it then—I see. You're not to blame!" said the director. "You're not to blame for your hair. You're not to blame for those expensive combs. You're not to blame for bankrupting your parents with shoes that cost twenty rubles! But all the same, I repeat: you have completely lost sight of the fact that you are still just a schoolgirl . . ."

But here Meshcherskaya politely interrupted. "Forgive me, Madame," she said, ingenuous and calm as ever. "I am a woman. And do you know who is to blame for that? My father's friend and neighbor—your brother, Aleksei Mikhailovich Milyutin. It happened last summer in the country . . ."

A month after that conversation, a Cossack officer—an ugly, pedestrian-looking man who had absolutely nothing in common with that circle to which Olya Meshcherskaya belonged—shot her at the train station, among a crowd of newly arrived passengers still standing on the platform. And that confession with which Olya Meshcherskaya had so stunned the director was completely borne out. The officer declared to the court investigator that Meshcherskaya had lured him on, grown intimate with him, and then sworn to be his future wife. But on the day of the murder, while seeing him off from the station on a trip to Novocherkassk, she suddenly said that it had never entered her head to love him and declared that she'd merely been mocking him whenever they spoke of marriage. She even gave him her diary so that he could read the very page where she had written of Milyutin.

"I read those lines and right there on the platform, where she was walking, waiting for me to finish—I shot her," the officer said. "That diary—look at what she wrote on July tenth of last year."

The following was written in her diary:

"It's after one. I fell sound asleep but woke up almost right away. . . . Today I became a woman! Papa, Mama, and Tolya all went to town, and I stayed here alone. I was so happy to be alone! I walked in the garden in the morning, went into the fields and the woods. I felt completely alone in the world—and I thought that nothing in my life has been as good as this. I even ate lunch alone. I played the piano for an entire hour, and with the music came a feeling that I'd live forever, that I'd be happier than anyone has ever been. Then I fell asleep in papa's study. Katya woke me up at four, saying that Aleksei Mikhailovich had come. I was very glad to see him—to have a guest to welcome to the house and entertain. He'd driven two of his best horses. They were very pretty, and he hitched them to the porch—they stood there the entire time. It had been raining, and he wanted to wait until evening to drive home so that the road would dry out. He said how sorry he was he'd missed papa. He was very boisterous, joking that he'd fallen in love with me a long time ago, and acting like a young man who'd come to call on me. The weather had already cleared when we went into the garden before tea, and the sun shone everywhere through the wet leaves, but it had turned completely cold, and he gave me his arm as we walked, saying he was Faust with Margarita. He is fifty-six but still very handsome, and always well dressed—only, he came in an old-fashioned cloak that I didn't like. He always smells of English cologne. His eyes are black and look like those of a young man, while his beard's very carefully combed into two long, completely silver strands. We had tea on the sunporch and I began to feel as if I were unwell. I lay down on the ottoman while he smoked; then he moved over to me and started telling me all sorts of compliments again. He held my hand and looked at it for a long time; then he started kissing it. I covered my face with a scarf and he kissed me on the mouth several times through the silk. . . . I don't understand how this happened! I've lost my mind! I never thought I was anything like this! Now there's only one way out. . . . I feel such revulsion for him. . . . I can't bear it!"

These April days have left our town clean and dry; all the paving stones are white again—pleasant, easy walking. Every Sunday after mass a small woman wearing mourning clothes with black kid gloves and an umbrella with a handle made of ebony sets out along Cathedral Street toward the edge of town. She follows the paved road through a dirty square where all the many forges have turned black with smoke and the breezes bring fresh air from the open fields. Farther on, between the monastery and the palisade, you can see a cloudy sky hanging over the grey fields of spring. If you continue on—if you pick your way among the puddles by the monastery wall, and then turn left, you'll see something like a large, low-lying garden surrounded by a white fence. A painting of the Assumption of the Holy Virgin hangs above the gate. The small woman crosses herself lightly and with routine familiarity walks down the center lane to a bench that faces the oak cross, and here she sits for an hour or two in the wind and the raw spring air until the cold has seeped right through her light boots and her thin gloves. Listening to the birds still singing sweetly in that cold air, listening to the wind as it rings in that porcelain wreath, she thinks sometimes that she would give up half her life if only she could make it disappear—if only that lifeless wreath were not before her eyes. That wreath, that mound of clay, that cross! Can it be she who lies beneath this cross—she whose eyes now shine from a porcelain medallion bulging at its center and seem so free of death? And how can all the purity of that expression ever be united with the horror that is now a part of Olya Meshcherskaya's name? But deep in her soul the small woman is happy, as are all those who have devoted themselves to some passionate dream.

This woman was Olya Meshcherskaya's *klassnaya dama*. She has been living a fiction in place of her real life for a long time, and now her youth is gone. At first the fiction was built around her brother, a poor and utterly unremarkable ensign. She invested all her soul in him and his future, which for some reason she believed would be brilliant. When he was killed at Mukden, she convinced herself that she should dedicate her life and soul to some other ideal, and the death of Olya Meshcherskaya created a new dream for her enthrallment. Now it is Olya Meshcherskaya who lies at the center of all her urgent thoughts, all her importunate emotions. She visits the grave on every holiday, staring for hours at that oak cross. She remembers Olya Meshcherskaya's small, pale face as she lay in her coffin among flowers. And she remembers the words she overheard when Meshcherskaya was quickly, quickly talking to her best friend—a tall, large girl named Subottina—as they walked one day in the school garden during the long recess.

"I read in one of papa's books what kind of beauty a woman ought to have. He has a lot of funny old books! There was so much written there, well, you know—there's no way to remember it all. But—black eyes, of course—black eyes like boiling pitch. That's what it said—boiling pitch! Eyelashes that are black as night. A slight flush that plays tenderly on the cheeks. A thin waist. Arms that are longer than usual—did you hear that?—longer than usual! Delicate legs. Large but proportional breasts. Calves that are symmetrical and slightly rounded. Sloping shoulders. Knees the color of a sea shell. I learned a lot of it by heart— all of it's so true! But do you know what's most important? Light breathing! And I have it—listen to me breathe—it's true, isn't it?"

Now that light breathing spreads out, once more, into the world. In the cloudy sky, in the cold spring wind, again, it is dispersed.

[1916]

Cranes

O N A CLEAR, cold day in late autumn, I'm riding at a steady trot down a big country road: low sun and brilliant light, bare fields, the expectant hush of fall. But then, in the distance behind me, I hear the sound of rattling wheels. I listen closely—it's the quick, shallow chatter of a light-running *drozhky*. I turn and see that someone's gaining on me. Someone's drawing closer by the second—already his horse is clearly visible as it flies with all its strength down the road, and then the figure of a man emerges from behind: in brief snatches I see him covering the horse's back with blows from his whip and his reins. . . . Even as I wonder at this sight, he gains on me, draws level to my mount. Over the rattling wheels, I hear his horse's powerful breathing, and then a desperate cry: "To the side, sir! To the side!" Startled and amazed, I turn sharply from the road, and a beautiful bay mare flashes by: I see her eye, her nostril, new reins the color of sealing wax, a shiny new harness lathered with sweat from inside her thighs, and then a handsome, dark-haired *mouzhik*, who looks half-crazed from the reckless speed of his driving and some mindless, all-consuming mania. He gives me a furious glance as he passes, and I am struck by his brilliant red mouth; his fresh, tar-black beard; his new cap and the yellow silk shirt which he wears under an open black coat—I know him, I think to myself, it's that well-off miller from near Livny—and already he's gone like the wind. He runs another *verst* down the road, then stops and jumps down from his *drozhky*. I race after him, and drawing close, I see the horse standing in the middle of the road with her sides heaving, the sealing-wax reins hanging loose from the shaft, the driver face-down on the ground, the long flaps of his coat flung open.

"Sir," he shouts into the dirt. "Sir, the cranes!" He waves his arms in despair. "It's so sad! The cranes have flown away!" And shaking his head, he chokes on drunken tears.

[1930]

Chang's Dreams

Isn't it all the same of whom we speak? Everyone who lives on earth is worthy of attention.

There was a time when Chang first grew familiar with the world, first came to know the captain—his owner, that man to whom his earthly existence was bound. Six years have passed since then, slipped away like sand in a ship's clock.

And one more night has come and gone—reality or dream? And one more morning has begun—reality or dream? Chang's old. Chang's a drunk. All he does is sleep.

Outside it's winter in the city of Odessa. Spiteful, gloomy weather—worse even than that Chinese day when Chang and the captain first met. The small, sharp grains of a driving, horizontal snow stream along the slick and icy asphalt of the empty seaside boulevard and lash painfully at the face of every Jew who runs awkwardly there to the left or to the right, his hands thrust deep into his pockets, his body bent against the wind. Beyond the equally deserted harbor and the bay that lies beneath a fog of swirling snow, one can just make out bare steppe descending to the sea. A thick grey smoke surrounds the pier.

From morning until night waves come crashing over it like the foaming maw of the sea. The wind whistles sharply through the telephone wires.

On such days as these life starts late in town. Chang and the captain wake up late as well. Six years—is that a lot of time, or just a little? In six years Chang and the captain have turned old—though the captain is still not forty—and their fate has altered roughly. They no longer sail the oceans but live "on shore," as sailors say—and not in their first residence but rather on a fairly gloomy, narrow street, in the attic of a five-story house that smells of coal and is populated by those Jews who return to their families only toward evening and eat dinner with their hats pushed back on their heads. Their room is large and cold, the ceiling low. And the light is always dull: two windows cut into the sloping wall of the attic roof resemble portholes on a ship. Between them stands something resembling a dresser, and an old iron bed has been placed against the left-hand wall. These items alone comprise the furnishings of that dreary room, unless one counts the fireplace, from which a fresh wind always blows. Chang sleeps in a little corner behind the fireplace while the captain occupies the bed. Those who have lived in attics can easily imagine just the kind of mattress on which he sleeps, the dilapidated bed sagging almost to the floor. The grimy pillow is so flat the captain has put his coat beneath it. And still, the captain sleeps very peacefully on that bed. He lies on his back with his eyes closed and his face gone grey, lies motionless as a corpse. What a wonderful bed he had before! Tall and gracefully designed, with drawers built into its bottom, with deep, plush bedding and thin, slippery sheets, with pillows that were cold and white as snow! But even then, even with the rocking of the waves, the captain never slept as soundly as he does now. Each day leaves him spent. And what reason is there now for him to worry that he'll oversleep? What joy can the next day offer him? Once there were two truths on earth, constantly replacing one another. The first truth was that life is beautiful beyond words; the second truth was that life is comprehensible only to the insane. Now the captain insists that there is, was, and will be for all time only one truth—the last truth, the truth of the Hebrew Job, the truth of Ecclesiastes, sage of an unknown tribe. Often now, while sitting in a beer hall, the captain says, "Recall, man, those hard days and years from your youth, of which you will say, 'In them there is no pleasure for me.'" The days and nights keep coming as they did before. And now, again, a night has passed. Another morning has arrived. Chang and the captain begin to wake.

But the captain doesn't open his eyes. His thoughts at that moment are a mystery even to Chang, lying on the floor near the unused fireplace, through which streamed, all night, the sea's freshness. Only this is known to Chang: the captain will remain in bed for at least another hour. Chang glances at him from the corner of his eye, then drops back off to sleep. Chang too is a drunk. He too is weak and torpid in the morning, and he registers the world with that revulsion so well known to seasick travelers on ships. For this reason, Chang's dreams are dull and tedious when he dozes at that morning hour. . . .

He dreams:

An old Chinaman with a sour expression climbed onto a steamship's deck and squatted there on his haunches, pleading with everyone who passed to buy the basket of half-rotten fish that he'd brought. It was a cold and dusty day on the wide Chinese river. A puppy sat in the Chinaman's boat, under a sail of rushes, rocking on the river's murk. There was something of the fox and something of the wolf in him—a ginger-colored male with thick coarse hair around his neck. He held his ears straight up as he cast his black eyes with stern intelligence along the ship's high, steel side.

"Sell me the dog instead," the ship's young captain called out happily and loudly from the watchtower, where he was standing idle. He shouted as if calling down to someone who was deaf. The Chinaman—Chang's first owner—hurriedly looked up, froze for a moment from the shock of both the sudden shout and his resulting joy, then began to bow and chatter:

"Ve'y good dog, ve'y good!"

And so the puppy was sold for just a silver ruble and named Chang. That same day he set sail for Russia with his new owner, and at the start of his voyage, for three full weeks, Chang suffered from such violent seasickness, languished in such a druglike haze of nausea, that he saw nothing—not the ocean, not Singapore, not Colombo. . . .

Fall had begun in China, and the weather was difficult. Chang started to feel sick while the ship was still just entering the estuary, its engulfing gloom and rain. Whitecaps gleamed among the watery plains that lay ahead, while senseless ripples swelled and surged and scattered spray across the choppy grey-green surface; the last level strips of land gave way, disappeared into the fog, and more and more water—always more water—surrounded them. The captain wore a slicker with the hood raised while Chang's coat was silvered by the rain. The bridge seemed even higher than before as he stood there, trembling, and turned his face away from the wind, the captain shouting orders. The water's span grew only wider, enveloping the entire, inclement horizon, blending with the murky sky. The wind flew in from all directions, tearing sheets of spray from the roiling swell, whistling in the rigging, beating dully at the canvas awnings down below on deck, where sailors in streaming capes and steel-heeled boots struggled to untie them, roll them up before they flew away. The wind seemed to search for the best direction from which to aim its blows, and as the ship, bowing slowly to the gale's force, veered to the right, it unleashed a huge, boiling wave that raised the steamer high on its crest, where the vessel couldn't hold, and came crashing down, plunged into the foaming surf—and sent flying from the table in the navigator's room a coffee cup forgotten by a steward. It shattered on the floor with a sharp ringing—and from that moment on the music truly played in earnest!

The days that followed varied. Sometimes the sun was like a fire raging in the azure. Sometimes storm clouds rose like mountains, resonant and menacing with thunder. Sometimes violent downpours broke over the ship and the sea like a weight collapsing from the sky. But the rocking never ceased—always, even when it moored, the ship would rock and sway. Lying in a hot, half-dark corridor among deserted second-class compartments on the quarterdeck, Chang was tortured past all limits. For three entire weeks he never left his corner there, beside the high threshold of the door that led onto the deck—a door that opened only once each day, when the captain's orderly brought Chang his food. All that remained in Chang's memory of the entire journey to the Red Sea was the heavy scraping of the bulkhead; nausea and a stopped heart as the shuddering hull lurched skyward or flew into a precipice; the rush of prickly, mortal fear that came when that hull suddenly tipped to one side as it was raised into the air with its propeller roaring, and a mountain of water broke over it, booming like a cannon shot, blocking momentarily all daylight from the portals, and then pouring over their thick glass in dark streams. In his sickness Chang heard orders being shouted in the distance, the whistles of the boatswain's pipe, the heavy tread of sailors' boats somewhere overhead. He heard the splashing surf and the sea. Through half-opened eyes he discerned the gloomy corridor, packed tight with bass-mat bales of tea—and sank into delirium, utterly inebriated by his nausea, the heat, and the heavy scent of tea.

But now the dream breaks off. . . .

Chang flinches and opens his eyes. That banging wasn't a wave striking the stern. It was a door somewhere downstairs—someone slamming it shut with a flourish. And in the wake of its banging, the captain coughs loudly, slowly rises from his sagging bed. He pulls on broken shoes and laces them up, dons the black jacket with gold buttons that he's taken from beneath his pillow, and moves toward the dresser while Chang, dissatisfied, rises from the floor in his thinning coat of ginger fur and yawns with a little squeal. An open bottle of vodka stands on the dresser—the captain drinks straight from it, then struggles a little to catch his breath, blows heavily through his moustache as he walks to the fireplace and pours a little vodka into a saucer set specially there for Chang, who greedily begins to lap it up. The captain lights a cigarette and lies back down to wait for that hour when it's undeniably day. Already one can hear the distant rumbling of trams. The constant *ching* of horseshoes striking paving stones streams through the streets below— and still, it is too early to go out. The captain lies in bed and smokes. Done lapping at his dish, Chang too goes to rest—jumps up onto the captain's bed and rolls into a ball at his feet, slowly drifts into that blissful state that vodka always grants its drinker. His half-closed eyes begin to darken as he looks dimly at his owner, feels an ever-growing tenderness toward him, and thinks something that might be put in human words as, "Foolishness, what foolishness! There is only one truth on this earth, and if only you could know what a wonderful truth it is!" And again it comes to Chang—either as a dream or as a thought—that distant morning when a ship en route from China left the ocean's harrowing and ceaseless agitation, and sailed into the Red Sea.

He dreams:

Passing Perim the ship rocked ever more slowly, as if lulling Chang to sleep. He drifted in a sweet, deep slumber—then suddenly woke up. And as he woke, Chang was utterly astounded: everywhere it was quiet. The hull's trembling had grown deliberate and restrained. It wasn't falling anywhere. The water running past the walls was moving at a steady, easy pace. From under the door to the outer deck came the warm and inviting smell of food being prepared in the galley. Chang rose and looked into the empty lounge. There in the twilight softly shimmered something gold and lilac, something barely visible, something filled with rare exuberance. The rear portal had been opened onto the sunny, pale blue expanse—onto endless, empty space and air—and now the daylight's shimmering reflection flowed in winding, ceaseless streams along the low ceiling. And what had occurred many times with his owner, the captain, now took place with Chang: suddenly he understood that on this earth there exist not one, but two truths: the first being that it is terrible to live on earth and sail on the ocean, the second . . . But Chang did not have time to finish thinking of the second truth. Suddenly the door flew open and he saw the spar-deck ladder, the black, gleaming mass of the steamer's smokestack, the clear sky of that summer morning, and the captain quickly coming up the ladder from the engine room—the captain, washed and clean-shaven, smelling of fresh cologne, trim and spotless in his snow-white uniform, the corners of his light-brown moustache raised in German style, his light eyes shining and alert. And seeing this, Chang raced forward so joyfully that the captain caught him in midair, kissed him loudly on the head, turned back, bounded up the ladder to the spar-deck in three quick jumps, and with Chang still in his arms, proceeded even higher, to the bridge—the very place where Chang had been so terrified in the estuary of the great Chinese river.

There the captain went into the navigator's cabin while Chang, deposited on the floor, sat a little with his fox's tail stuck out straight behind him on the smooth boards. Behind him Chang could feel the heat and bright light of the low sun. It must have been hot in Arabia, passing nearby on the right, with its golden coastline; with its black and brown mountains, whose peaks were also dusted heavily in dry gold and resembled the crests of some dead planet; with all of that dusty, mountainous desert now so close and clearly visible it seemed that one could reach it in a single leap. But it still felt like morning high up on the bridge, where the air streamed with a light freshness and the captain's assistant cheerfully paced back and forth—the assistant who later would so often enrage Chang by blowing into his nose, a man dressed all in white, with a white helmet and terrifying dark glasses, who now glanced constantly at the sharp, lofty point of the forward mast, above which curled like a white ostrich feather the most delicate of clouds. . . . Then the captain shouted from the navigator's cabin, "Chang—time for coffee!" Chang immediately jumped to his feet, circled the cabin, and leapt gracefully across its bronze threshold. And on the other side of that threshold, things were even better than on the bridge: a wide leather couch had been built into the wall; above it hung something resembling a large clock with shining glass and pointers shaped like arrows. On the floor stood a slop basin with sweet milk and bread. Chang lapped greedily at the scraps while the captain went to work. Across from the couch, on a stand positioned beneath the window, he unrolled a large nautical map, placed a ruler on its surface, and firmly drew a long line in scarlet ink. Chang finished lapping and, with drops of milk still hanging in his whiskers, jumped onto the stand and sat down near the window, through which he could see the wide blue collar and ample shirt of a sailor standing at a pegged wheel. And then the captain, who would prove to be very fond of speaking to Chang when they were alone, started talking:

"You see this—brother—this is the Red Sea. And you and I have to use our heads to get across it carefully. See how it's all dotted with little islands and reefs? I have to get you to Odessa in mint condition, since they know now of your existence there. I let it slip already to a certain capricious little girl—boasted about you, kind sir, while I was talking to her. You see, there's a cable, a long cable that some very smart people put along the floor of the oceans and the seas, and I was using it to talk to her. I'm a terribly happy man, Chang, despite it all—you can't even imagine how happy—and for that reason I have absolutely no desire to run into one of those reefs, spatter myself with shame on my first major voyage. . . ."

As he spoke the captain suddenly looked at Chang sternly and slapped his muzzle. "Keep your paws off the map!" he shouted. "And don't you dare go climbing on government property!"

Chang shook his head, snarled, narrowed his eyes. This was the first slap he'd ever received, and once more it seemed repellant to live on earth and sail on the ocean. He turned away, his clear, bright eyes dimming as he narrowed them and bared his teeth with a quiet growl. But the captain paid no heed to Chang's offense and began to speak to him again in a friendly tone as he lit a cigarette and returned to the couch, took a watch from his side pocket, pried open its gold, stippled cover with his firm thumbnail, and looked at something glowing there, something of rare vibrancy that ran hurriedly inside the watch with a clear, brisk sound. He began once more to tell Chang that he was taking him to Odessa, to Yelisavetinskaya Street, where he, the captain, had first an apartment, second a beautiful wife, and third a wonderful daughter; and that he, the captain, was a very happy man, despite it all.

"Happy, Chang, happy all the same!" he said, and added: "That daughter of mine, Chang, she's a lively one—curious, persistent. It will be hard on you for a while—especially your tail. But if you only knew,

Chang, what a charming creature she is! I love her so much, brother, that it frightens me. For me the entire world is in her alone—well, almost the entire world. And is that the way it's supposed to be? As a general rule, should we love anyone so strongly?" he asked. "Could it be that all those Buddhas of yours were somehow bigger fools than you and I? Just listen to what they say about that kind of love for the world—and in general, for everything incarnate—from sunlight and waves and air to a woman, a child, the scent of white acacias! Or maybe you know something about the Tao—something you Chinese made up. I know it poorly, brother, and really—everyone understands it poorly. What's it supposed to mean? The great Mother-Abyss—she gives birth to everything, then swallows it, and in swallowing it, gives birth again to all that exists on earth. Or, to put it in other words, this is the Path of all things; nothing that exists should resist it. But we resist it constantly! We want constantly to turn aside from that Path not only, let's say, the soul of a beloved woman, but the entire world as we know it. It is terrifying to live on this earth, Chang," the captain said. "It is very good, but terrifying—especially for those like me! I am terribly greedy when it comes to happiness already, Chang, and I often go astray. Is that Path dark and evil—or is it something else, something just the opposite?"

He fell silent for a moment, then added:

"And what's the most important part of all this, Chang? *When you love someone, there's no one on earth with the power to make you believe that your beloved might not love you in return.* And that, Chang, is where the real crux of the matter lies—that is where the dog is buried, as we like to say. But life is glorious—my God, how glorious it is!"

Incandescent from the sun now hanging high above it, the ship trembled slightly with accelerated speed as it sliced tirelessly through the Red Sea, lying becalmed and still in the endless void of the burning air. The bright emptiness of the tropical sky filled the doorway of the navigator's cabin. Noon approached, and the threshold grew hot in the sun. The glassy waves grew more and more sluggish as they swelled and broke apart, scattering their brilliance in a blinding flash and casting still more light into the navigator's cabin. Chang sat on the couch and listened to the captain. The captain stroked his head, then pushed him down onto the floor, saying, "No, brother—it's too hot!"—but this time Chang took no offense: it was too good to live on earth during that joyful noon. And then . . .

But here again Chang's dream is broken off.

"We're going, Chang!" the captain says, dropping his feet from the bed. And again Chang is surprised to find himself not on a ship in the Red Sea but in an attic in Odessa. He's surprised too to discover that here it's noon as well—but this noon lacks all joy, is gloomy, dull, inimical. He growls quietly at the captain for startling him. But the captain pays him no attention, puts on the peaked cap and overcoat of his old uniform, thrusts his hands into his pockets, and stooping, starts toward the door. Against his utmost will, Chang is forced to jump down from the bed. The captain descends the staircase heavily, reluctantly, as if compelled by a tedious necessity, while Chang barrels ahead, spurred by that vexation into which the blessed state of vodka invariably dissolves. . . .

And it's been two years now—two full years that Chang and the captain have been going from one restaurant to the next. In all of them they drink, eat, look at the other drunks eating and drinking next to them amid the noise, the clouds of tobacco smoke, and the stench. Chang lies on the floor at the captain's feet. And the captain sits and smokes, his elbows propped firmly on the table—a habit he developed as a sailor. He waits for that hour when some law that he alone has invented will dictate that they migrate to some other restaurant or café. Chang and the captain have breakfast in one location, coffee in a second, lunch in a third, and dinner in a fourth. The captain rarely speaks. But occasionally he meets a former friend from the old times, and then he spends the entire day speaking incessantly about the nullity of life and pouring wine for himself, his interlocutor, and Chang, before whom always stands some kind of saucer on the floor. The captain is spending the current day in precisely this manner, for he has arranged to have breakfast with an old friend—an artist in a top hat. This means that they will sit first in a stinking beer hall, among red-faced Germans, dull and practical people who work from morning until night in order, obviously, to eat and drink and work again—and to one day spawn more human beings similar to them. Then they'll go to a café packed with Greeks and Jews, whose lives are also meaningless but overwrought, consumed with the ceaseless expectation of new rumors about stocks. And from the café they will go to a restaurant, where a wide range of human debris gathers in the tide, and sit there until late into the night. . . .

A winter day is short, and it grows even shorter with a bottle of wine and a conversation with an old acquaintance. Chang, the captain, and the artist have already patronized the beer hall and the café, and now they are sitting, drinking interminably in the restaurant. And again the captain, with his elbows propped firmly on the table, is asserting to the artist that only one truth—ignoble and malign—exists on earth. "You just look around," he says. "Just remember everything that you and I see every day in the streets, in the beer halls and the cafés! My friend, I've traveled the entire globe, and everywhere life is just the same! It's all lies and nonsense, these ideas people are supposed to live by. They have no god, no conscience, no rational purpose for existence, no love, no friendship, no honesty—not even simple pity. Life is just a boring winter day in a dirty tavern—nothing more. . . ."

And Chang, lying on the floor, listens to all of this in a drunken haze that lost all novelty long ago. Does he agree or disagree with the captain? It's impossible to say with certainty, and this itself, this lack of certainty, is a troubling sign. Chang doesn't know, doesn't understand if the captain's right—but surely it's only in sadness and sorrow that we speak this way: "I don't know; I don't understand." In joy, every living thing is certain that it knows all, understands everything. . . . Then, suddenly, it seems that sunlight's broken through the haze: a conductor's baton taps a music stand on a little raised platform in the restaurant, a violin begins to sing; followed by a second, then a third. . . . Their song grows more and more mellifluous and ardent, and in a moment Chang's soul is flooded with a completely different kind of sadness, a separate strain of sorrow. It trembles from an ecstasy it cannot understand, from some sweet agony, from thirst—and already it's impossible for Chang to say if he is dreaming or awake. He surrenders all his being to the music, humbly submits, and follows it to some other world—sees himself, once more, on the threshold of that beautiful world, a trusting, foolish puppy on a steamer in the Red Sea.

"What was it then? How did it go?" The words come from somewhere in between the realms of thoughts and dreams. "I remember, yes. It was good to be alive on that hot noon on the Red Sea!" Chang sat with the captain in the navigator's cabin; then they stood on the bridge. . . . Oh, there was so much light! What brilliant flashing! What azure and deep blues! How colorful those white and red and yellow sailors' shirts became against the backdrop of the sky as they hung with their sleeves spread wide on the rails above the prow! Then Chang and the captain and the other sailors—their faces brick red, their eyes glistening like oil paints, their white foreheads damp with sweat—ate breakfast in the hot, first-class lounge for passengers, an electric fan blowing and humming in the corner. After breakfast he dozed, after tea he had lunch, and after lunch he sat again on the top of the ship, before the navigator's cabin, where the steward had arranged a deck chair for the captain, and looked far out to sea, looked at the dusk turning a delicate green among the many shapes of multicolored clouds, looked at the wine-red sun, stripped of all its rays and suddenly stretching out, lengthening, as it touched the dim horizon and turned into a darkly flaming miter. As if in pursuit, the ship raced after the sun, and the smooth hummocks of water seemed to fly past its sides, each of them shot through with shagreen strips of lilac and dark blue. But the sun was setting quickly, quickly—as if drawn down by the sea—and it grew ever smaller and smaller, turned into a long, burning ember, began to tremble, and then died out. Precisely at that moment, the shadow of some great sadness fell across the earth, and the wind that had been strengthening steadily as night approached began to blow with even greater agitation. The captain's hair stirred in the wind as he sat without his hat and looked at the sunset's darkening flame, his expression thoughtful, proud, and sad. It was evident that he was nonetheless happy at that moment—and that within his power lay not only the entire steamship running by his will but all the world as well. He felt this way because the entire world was in his soul at that moment, and because, even then, he smelled of wine.

Terrifying and magnificent, restive, black—night came, and with it, a disordered wind and waves that leapt so fitfully around the ship, swelled with such a glowing light and sudden noise, that Chang on several occasions bolted, squealing, from the ship's side as he ran to keep up with the captain in his quick and tireless pacing around the deck. The captain took Chang in his arms again, and with his cheek held near Chang's beating heart—it beat exactly as the captain's beat—walked with him to the very end of the ship, to the quarterdeck, and stood there for a long time, enthralling Chang with sights both miraculous and terrible. A myriad of fire-white needles scattered in a dry, rustling stream from beneath the massive stern and the propeller in its muffled raging while huge cerulean stars and dense plumes of darkening blue broke loose and fell away into the road of snow and sparks now laid by the steamer, where they burst apart with vivid light and, dying out, smoldered with a secret, phosphorescent green among the boiling mounds of water. The wind varied its direction, blowing softly, firmly into Chang's face, spreading its chill as it ruffled the thick fur on his chest. With familial ease, Chang pressed himself against the captain and smelled what seemed to be cold sulfur, breathed the scent of the roiled womb of the ocean's depths. And as the stern trembled, as it rose and descended according to the will of some huge and ineffably free force, Chang rocked and peered excitedly at that abyss that was blind and dark and utterly alive in its muted rioting. And from time to time some particularly erratic, ponderous wave would come surging past the stern to bathe in eerie light the captain's arms and his silver uniform.

That night the captain took Chang to his cabin, which was large and comfortable and softly lit by a lamp under a red silk shade. A desk stood in the tight space beside the captain's bed, and on it, in the shadows and light cast by the lamp, were two photographs. In one, a pretty, querulous girl with her hair in ringlets sat willfully and capriciously in a deep armchair; in the other, a young lady appeared in almost full length, wearing a stylish spring dress and large white hat of lace, a lace umbrella resting on her shoulder. She was lovely and slender, with a graceful build and an air of sadness like that of a Georgian princess.

"She's not going to love us, Chang, that woman," the captain said amid the noise of the black waves outside his open window. *"There are certain female souls, brother, that languish forever with some kind of sad thirst for love, and which, because of that love, are never able themselves to love.* There are such souls. And how can one judge them for their heartlessness and falsity, their dreams of the stage, of their own personal automobiles, of picnics on yachts and some athlete or other, whose hair is so larded with fixative it tears when he tries to part it down the middle? Who can make sense of them? To each his own, Chang. And aren't they merely following the sacred commands of the Tao, just as a sea creature follows those commands in its willful roaming, here, beneath black waves that glint like armor?"

"Oh, oh," said the captain, as he sat on the chair, shaking his head and unlacing one white shoe. "What I went through, Chang, when I first sensed that she was no longer completely mine—that night when she went alone, for the first time, to the yacht club ball and returned near morning, looking like a faded rose, pale from both exhaustion and her lingering excitement, her eyes wide open and completely black—and utterly remote from me! If you only knew how perfectly, how peerlessly she sought to make a fool of me! With what simple surprise she said, 'Oh, you're still awake? Poor thing!' I couldn't speak a word; she understood me instantly and fell silent—just glanced at me for a moment—and silently began undressing. I wanted to kill her, but she spoke so dryly, so impassively: 'Help me, please, undo my dress'—and humbly

CALGARY
PUBLIC
LIBRARY

Central Library
Self Checkout

January,07,2020 10:30

39065003042908   2020-01-28
Restless nights --
39065128009501   2020-01-28
Midsummer passion & other tales of Main
e cussedness --

Total   2 item(s)

You have 0 item(s) ready for pickup

To check your card and renew items

go to www.calgarylibrary.ca

or call 403-262-2928

I went to her; with trembling hands I began to open those buttons and hooks—and the moment I saw her body, saw the space between her shoulder blades in that opened dress, her camisole slipping from her shoulders while still tucked inside her corset—the moment I smelled her black hair and glanced at the lit pier glass, the reflection there of her breasts raised high by that corset . . ."

Without finishing his words, the captain waved his hand.

He undressed and lay down, turned out the light. Chang too prepared to sleep, and as he turned in tightening circles on the Moroccan leather chair beside the table, he saw white streaks of flame furrowing the sea's black shroud as they flared and died out, saw what seemed to be sinister fires flashing along the black horizon, while at times a particularly animated wave would come hurtling forward from there and with a threatening noise shoot up higher than the ship's side, glance into the captain's cabin like some fantastic serpent, shot through with the light of countless eyes that shimmered like semi-precious stones, like emeralds and sapphires—only to be knocked aside by the ship as it ran steadily forward through the heavy, seething mass of that primordial essence, which for us, already, has grown inimical and alien, and which we call the ocean. . . .

The captain suddenly shouted something in the night and immediately woke up, startled by his own cry—an utterance of some mournful and degrading passion. He lay silent for a moment, then sighed and said with derision: "Yes, yes—as a golden ring in a pig's snout, so is a fine woman! You are right three times over, O Solomon the Wise!"

He found his cigarettes in the darkness, lit one, and twice drew on its smoke before dropping his arm and dozing off again, the red ember still glowing in his hand. And once more it was quiet—only the waves rocked and flashed and made their constant noise beyond the ship's side. From behind black clouds, the Southern Cross . . .

But suddenly a thundering crash deafens Chang and he leaps up in terror. What's happened? Has the ship again struck some submerged bed of stone at the fault of its drunken captain—just the way it did three years ago? Has the captain once again shot a pistol at his sad and lovely wife? No, he's not surrounded by night, or the sea, or a winter afternoon on Yelisavetinskaya Street. Instead he's in a restaurant—one that's very bright, filled with noise and smoke. It is the drunken captain pounding his fist on the table and shouting at the artist:

"Nonsense, nonsense! A golden ring in a pig's snout—that's who your woman is! 'I have made my bed with tapestries and many-colored clothes from Egypt. Come inside. We will make ourselves drunk with tenderness, for my husband is not home.' Ah, woman! Her household leads to death; hers is the way to the dead. But enough, already, my friend—enough. It's time to go—they're closing up."

A few minutes later Chang, the captain, and the artist are on the dark street, where the lamps' gas flames are barely burning in the wind and snow. The captain kisses the artist, and they go their separate ways. Dispirited and half asleep, his hind legs askew from his front, Chang trots after the captain as he hurries, swaying, down the street. . . . Another day has passed. Was it a dream or reality? In the world again there's darkness, cold, fatigue.

And so Chang's days and nights pass by, unvaried and unchanging, until suddenly, one morning, the world is like a ship that's run full tilt into a submerged reef—a reef concealed from inattentive eyes. As he wakes up one winter day, Chang is struck by a great silence that reigns inside the room. He jumps up from his place on the floor and rushes to the captain's bed—and sees the captain lying there, his head tossed back, his features pale and stiffened, his eyelids parted, the lashes still. And seeing those lashes, Chang lets out a howl of such despair it seems a speeding car has knocked him from his feet, split his body on the boulevard.

Later, when the door is taken from its hinges, when all the different people come and go in noisy conversation—the yardmen and police, the artist and his top hat, the other men who joined the captain in the restaurants—Chang is like an object made of stone. Oh, what terrible words the captain had once uttered: "On that day the keepers of the house will tremble and those who look out from the window will grow dark. The heights for them will be terrifying, and on the road there will be horrors. For a man is going out to his eternal home, and the mourners are prepared to surround him; for the pitcher is smashed at the spring, and the wheel is broken at the well." But now not even horror registers with Chang. He lies on the floor with his face in the corner, his eyes closed tight to keep from seeing the world—to forget it. And over him the world's noise is dim and distant, like the sea above one who's descending deeper and deeper into its abyss.

When he comes back to himself, he's already on a portico, near the doors to a church. He's sitting next to the doors with his head lowered, dull, half dead but for the slight shuddering that has spread through all his body. Suddenly the church doors open wide, and the scene inside fills Chang's heart and eyes with splendor and resounding song: before him is the half-dark hall of a Gothic church, little flames like red stars, a forest of tropical plants, a coffin of oak raised high on a black dais, and a dark throng of people. Two women are there; they resemble sisters of varying age, and both are stunning in their marble beauty and their grieving. And above it all—claps of thunder, a rumbling, a choir of angels loudly singing of some mournful joy, exaltations and commotion, grandeur—and a constant stream of celestial music that runs through everything, covers everything. Chang's fur stands on end from the pain and ecstasy he feels before this scene, and the artist, leaving the church at that moment with reddened eyes, stops in amazement:

"Chang," he says with alarm as he bends closer. "Chang, what's wrong?" Touching Chang's head with a trembling hand, the artist bends still lower, and their eyes meet, filled with tears and such mutual love that all of Chang's being cries out inaudibly to the world: "Oh no, no—there is some other truth on this earth—a third truth still invisible to me!"

That day, returning from the graveyard, Chang moved into the home of his third owner—once again high up, in an attic, but warm and fragrant with the scent of cigars, with antique furniture and carpets on the floor, huge canvases and brocade tapestries covering the walls. . . . It's growing dark. The fireplace is full of burning embers that glow like cloudy, scarlet mounds of heat. Chang's new owner is sitting in an armchair. He didn't even remove his top hat or his coat when he came home—just sat down with a cigar, and now he smokes and stares at the twilight in his studio while Chang lies on the carpet near the fireplace, his eyes closed, his head resting on his paws.

Someone else is lying motionless as well—past the darkening town, past the cemetery fence, there—inside what's called the crypt, the grave. But it is not the captain, no. If Chang loves him and still feels his presence, sees him still through the eye of memory—that divine vision that no one understands—then the captain stays, remains with him in a world that has no end and no beginning, and no entry point for death. In that world there can be only one truth—the third—but what it is—this knows only Chang's final Master, to whom, soon, he must return.

[1916]

Ballad

B EFORE the big winter holidays our country home was always as hot as a sauna. The house consisted of spacious rooms with low ceilings, and we left all the doors inside wide open. It made a strange picture: one could see right through the house, from the entrance hall to the den, and every room glowed with the flames of lamps and wax candles that stood before the icons in the holy corners.

In preparation for those holidays the smooth oak floors of the house were carefully washed; they dried quickly in the heat, and then they were covered with clean horse cloths. The furniture that had been moved during the washing was meticulously rearranged in the rooms; the candles and lamps were lit before the icons in their gold and silver frames, and all the other lights were extinguished. By then the winter sky outside would be turning dark blue, and when we went to our separate rooms, full silence settled in the house—a reverential hush that seemed, somehow, to be waiting for another kind of peace. Nothing could have been more fitting among those icons and the mournful, tender light that played upon them in the dark.

Sometimes in the winter a wanderer named Mashenka stayed at the estate. She was a skinny, grey-haired old woman, as small as a young girl. She alone never slept during those nights: coming from the servants' quarters into the hall after dinner, she would remove her felt boots and softly walk along the horse cloths in her stocking feet, go soundlessly to every one of those rooms, kneel down in the heat and the mysterious light, cross herself and bow before each icon. Then she'd go back to the entrance hall to read prayers and psalms or simply talk to herself quietly while sitting on an old, black chest we'd kept there for years. It was by overhearing Mashenka's prayers that I learned of that sacred beast, "God's wolf."

Late one night when I was unable to sleep, I got up and started down the hall toward the den, where I hoped to find a book to read among those on the shelves. Mashenka didn't hear me; she was sitting in the dark foyer, saying something to herself. I stopped in the hall to listen—she was reciting psalms from memory:

"Lord, hear my prayer, listen to my cry," she said without expression. "Do not be unmoved by my tears, for I am your pilgrim and a stranger to this earth, like my fathers before me. . . .

"Speak, God: How terrible you are in your works!

"He who lives under the Lord's high roof, under your all-powerful protection is at peace. . . . You tread upon the asp and the serpent, flout the dragon and the lion. . . ."

She raised her voice softly but emphatically as she recited the last words, pronouncing them with conviction: "flout the dragon and the lion." Then she fell silent for a moment, sighed, and said as if talking to someone else in the room: "For all the beasts in the forests and the cattle on the thousand hills are His."

I glanced into the foyer and saw her on the chest, her small feet in wool stockings held level above the floor, her arms crossed over her chest. She stared straight ahead without noticing me. Then she raised her eyes to the ceiling and said distinctly: "And you, sacred beast, God's wolf, pray for us to the heavenly mother."

I approached her and said softly, "Mashenka, don't be afraid, it's me."

She dropped her arms, stood, and made a low bow. "Hello, sir. I'm not afraid. What should I fear now? No, that was all childishness—being afraid. The dark-eyed devil confused me."

"Please, sit down," I said.

"No, sir, I'll stand, sir."

I laid my hand on her thin shoulder and her collarbone and made her sit beside me. "Please, if you won't sit down, I'll have to leave. Tell me, who were you praying to? Is there really such a saint—God's wolf?"

She tried to get up again; I held her down. "Wait, hold on. You say you aren't afraid of anything! I'm asking you—is there really a God's wolf?"

She paused, then answered solemnly. "There must be, sir. There is such a creature as the Tiger-Euphrates. And there was a picture of it in the church, so it must be so. I saw it myself, sir."

"How? Where did you see it? When?"

"A long time ago, sir—in a time older than memory. I can't even say where it was. All I remember is that we traveled there three days—a village called Krutye Gory. As you might know, sir, I myself come from far away—I was born in Ryazan. This place was even farther south, beyond the Don. Such a primitive place, sir—you can't find words for it. The prince had been exiled there, but it came to be his favorite village—probably a thousand clay huts on the bare side of a mountain. Above them stood the manor house, a three-story building all exposed on the mountain peak over Stone River. Beside the house was a church with yellow walls and columns, and that sacred wolf's inside. In the middle of the church there's an iron slab over the grave of the prince he killed, and to the right there's a pillar where the wolf's painted, exactly as he appeared. His coat's grey and full, and he's leaning back on his hind legs, with his thick tail tucked under him. His front paws are pushing against the ground so that all his body seems to stretch and strain upward. He has a big head with sharp, pointed ears and a mane of grey fur around his neck. He stares at you with glowing eyes. His fangs are bared, and a golden light shines around his head, like the halo of a saint. It's terrible even to remember it, sir. He looks so real you think he's going to throw himself on you."

"Wait, Mashenka," I said. "I don't understand any of this. Who painted that wolf in the church? You say he killed the prince—then how can he be holy? And why is he beside the prince's tomb? And how did you wind up there, in that terrible village? Tell me everything in order."

And Mashenka began to explain:

"I wound up there, sir, because I was a serf at the time—as a girl I served in the household of a young prince. I was an orphan—they said my father was some kind of drifter, a runaway probably who seduced my mother and disappeared God knows where. My mother died soon after I was born, but the masters pitied me. They brought me from the servants' quarters into the household when I turned thirteen, made me an errand girl for the young lady of the house. She grew very fond of me for some reason and never let me out of her sight. So I went too when the young prince decided they should see the estate his grandfather had left him — it was that manor house in Krutye Gory. The estate had been deserted for years; it stood all empty and forgotten, abandoned after the grandfather's death. We'd all heard legends about the terrible way he died, and the young prince wanted to see the house for himself."

In the hallway something sizzled, then softly struck the floor. Mashenka jumped down from the chest and ran toward the noise: a candle had fallen, and we could smell something burning. Mashenka quickly put the candle out, stepped on the nap of the smoldering horse cloth, and then climbed onto a chair to relight the taper from those that still burned before the icon. As the candle flared up, she tipped it over and dripped wax like warm honey into the hole from which it had fallen; then she carefully reinserted the candle, trimmed the snuff from the others, and jumped down to the floor.

"Look how nicely it's all lit up," she said, crossing herself and glancing at the golden flames of the candles she'd revived. "The house feels like a holy place."

The rooms had filled with the sweet smell of burning wicks and wax. A saint stared out from a round silver frame behind the trembling flames of the candles. The bottom halves of the windows were covered in grey rime, but in the clear spaces above the frost I could see the night and the trees in the front garden; matted with snow, their sagging branches looked like the white paws of some strange animal. Mashenka glanced at them, crossed herself again, and came back to the foyer.

"It's time for you to rest, sir," she said as she sat back down on the chest and suppressed a yawn, covering her mouth with her small, bony hand. "This is when the night grows strict and cruel."

"Why do you say that?"

"Because this is a secret time, when only the rooster and the owl can keep awake. This is when the Lord himself listens to the earth, and the most important stars begin to play, and the ice holes freeze in the rivers and the oceans."

"Then why don't you sleep at night?"

"I sleep as much as I need to, sir. What good is sleep for an old person? We're like birds on a branch."

"Well, you should go to bed soon, all the same. But finish the story about the wolf."

"That's an old, dark business, sir. Maybe it was all just a ballad someone made up."

"What did you say?"

"A ballad, sir. All the prince's family talked about ballads. They liked reading them out loud. Sometimes I hear them and shivers run down my spine—

'The forest howls beyond the hills,
Wind rages in the chalk-white fields—
A storm has come,
The road is lost . . .'

Ah, it's wonderful!"

"What's wonderful about it?"

"It's wonderful because you can't say why it's wonderful. Because there's awe in it. Because it's terrifying."

"Everything was terrifying in the old days, Mashenka."

"What can I say, sir? Maybe you're right—maybe everything was terrifying then, and I just remember wrong when it all seems dear and good. What was it really like? . . . So many tsars have passed, so many ancient trees have turned bare, so many graves grown level with the ground. . . . But here's how the story went—the serfs told it this way word for word—though who knows if it's true. It all took place during the reign of the Great Tsarina. She was actually the reason why he was in Krutye Gory—he'd angered her somehow, and she'd sent him as far away as possible from her. He grew savage in his exile—became a butcher of slaves and a rapist. He was still very strong and, as appearances go, very handsome. Apparently there wasn't a single girl among his household serfs or all his villagers he hadn't used—they had to spend a night with him before they married. And then he fell to the worst of sins: he began to lust for his own son's newlywed wife. The son had served in the army in Petersburg. When he found himself a bride, the father blessed the marriage and he, naturally, brought his new wife to meet his father in Krutye Gory. But the father soon wanted the girl himself. There's good reason, sir, for them to sing that love exists in every kingdom, that it warms all things on earth. And there's no sin in it, of course, if an old man just thinks about the girl he loves, and sighs. But this was not the same—the girl was like his own daughter, and he'd laid traps to get her in his bed."

"And what happened?"

"Well, the son, seeing what his father wanted, made plans to run away in secret. He bribed the stablemen, told them to harness a sleigh with three fast horses toward midnight. He came in secret from the house as soon as the old prince was asleep, called out his wife—and they fled. But the old prince wasn't asleep at all—he'd already heard everything from his spies and immediately tore off after his son.

"It was a dark, bitter night. The frost hung like a ring around the moon, and the snow was piled higher than a man could stand, but he doesn't feel a thing—he flies, flies on his horse with sabers and pistols in his belt, his favorite hounds-man galloping beside him. He sees the horses and the sleigh in the distance and shrieks like an eagle, 'Stop, or I'll shoot!' But they don't listen to him—they're driving as hard as they can. So the old prince starts to shoot. He kills the right trace horse in mid-stride, then he brings down the left trace. But as he takes aim at the shaft horse, he looks to his side and sees a great wolf in the moonlight, a wolf racing over the snow toward him: its eyes glow like red flames, and a golden light shines around its head! The old prince starts shooting at it, but the animal doesn't even blink. It rushes at him in a frenzy, leaps onto his chest, and in a flash tears out his throat with its fangs."

"Oh, how terrible, Mashenka," I said. "It really is like a ballad!"

"It's a sin to laugh, sir," she answered. "Everything is possible with God."

"I won't argue with you, Mashenka. But it's still strange that they painted that wolf right beside the prince's tomb after he killed the man."

"He was painted there, sir, at the prince's own request. He was still alive when they got him home. He had time to repent before death and receive communion. And in his last moment he ordered that the wolf be painted beside his tomb in the church: a warning to his descendants. And who could deny his last request? The church was his, after all. He'd built it himself."

[1938]

Mitya's Love

T HE NINTH of March was Mitya's last happy day in Moscow. So it seemed, at least, to him.

Katya and he were walking on Tverskoy Boulevard. Winter had suddenly given way to spring, and it was almost hot in the sun. One could almost believe the larks had returned, bringing warmth and joy. Everything was melting, glistening, wet. Water dripped from all the eaves while yardmen hacked ice from the sidewalks and flung damp, sticky snow from the roofs. All the streets were crowded and alive. The high clouds had dispersed, transformed into a delicate white smoke that drifted in the sky's damp blue. In the distance Pushkin's statue rose, pensive and benevolent; the domes of the Strastnoy Monastery gleamed in the sun. The fact that Katya was so winsome, so engaging—this was best of all that day: everything she did expressed a kind of easy, natural intimacy. Repeatedly she took his arm and peered up at him with childlike trust, studied the happy, slightly condescending look on Mitya's face as he continued walking, taking such long strides that she struggled to keep up.

"You're so funny," she said unexpectedly when they were near the Pushkin monument. "When you laugh with that big mouth of yours, there's a kind of awkward, almost boyish way you stretch your lips. It's terribly endearing. . . . Don't be hurt—I love you for that smile! . . . that smile and your Byzantine eyes. . . ."

Mitya tried not to smile as he overcame a feeling of both secret satisfaction and slightly wounded pride. "When it comes to looking like children," he answered amicably, looking at the statue that now towered above them, "I think it's safe to say that you and I haven't grown very far apart. And I resemble a Byzantine about as much as you look like the empress of China. It's just that you're all crazy about these so-called Byzantines, these children of the Renaissance. I really don't understand your mother!"

"What would you do in her place—lock me up in a tower?" Katya asked.

"Not a tower, no. But all of these supposedly artistic Bohemians, all of these future stars from studios and conservatories—I wouldn't let any of them through your door," Mitya said, trying to stay calm and keep a friendly, casual tone. "You told me yourself that Bukovetsky already asked you to dinner at the Strelna, and Yegorov asked to sculpt you naked in the form of some kind of dying sea-wave—an honor, of course, that you find terribly flattering."

"I won't turn away from art. Even for you, I won't do it," said Katya. "Maybe I am depraved, the way you often say I am," she continued, although Mitya had never said this. "Maybe I am ruined. But you'll have to take me as I am. I don't want to argue anymore. Stop being jealous over me—at least for now, on such a wonderful day. . . . How can you not understand that you—regardless of all else—you alone are best of all," she said with soft insistence as she looked into his eyes, her expression now deliberately composed to be alluring. "A drowsing secret lies between us," she recited, drawing out the words as if deep in thought. "A soul gave a soul a ring."

These last words, this verse, hurt Mitya deeply. In general, much was painful and unpleasant—even on that day. The joke about boyish awkwardness was unpleasant. He'd heard many such comments from Katya before, and they were far from accidental: she quite often revealed herself to be more adult than he in certain aspects of their intimacy, and quite often—unwittingly, which is to say completely naturally—she brandished this superiority above him while Mitya took it as a painful sign of her secret and depraved experiences. The phrase "regardless of all else" (regardless of all else, you alone are best of all) was unpleasant too, as was the fact that she suddenly lowered her voice to speak these words. And more than anything, that poem, its mannered reading—this was particularly unpleasant. But later, when he looked back at the ninth of March, it would seem that on that last happy day in Moscow he'd endured quite easily both the poem and its reading, despite the fact that this, most of all, reminded him of that artistic set that was robbing him of Katya and therefore sharply stirred his jealousy and his hatred.

Returning from Kuznetsky Most that day, they stopped at Zimmerman's so that Katya could buy several works by Scriabin, and there, in passing, she began to speak of Mitya's mother. "You can't imagine how afraid I am of her, even now, long before we meet," she said, laughing.

Throughout their affair, for some reason they'd never touched on the question of the future—had never asked where all of this would lead. And now, suddenly, Katya began to talk about his mother, began to talk as if there couldn't be the slightest doubt that they would join as one family.

II

After that day, nothing seemed to change: it all continued just as before. Mitya accompanied Katya to the actors' studio at the Moscow Art Theatre, to concerts, and to literary evenings; sometimes he visited her at home in Kislovka until two in the morning, taking advantage of the strange freedom granted her by her mother, a kind, appealing woman with bright red hair who never stopped smoking and always wore rouge. She had long ago separated from her husband, who now had a second family. Katya also stopped to visit Mitya in his student's rooms on Molchanovka, and these meetings almost always passed in the deep, narcotic haze of their kisses. But Mitya had a gnawing sense that something terrible had been set in motion, that some change had taken place—and now was taking hold of Katya.

It had passed quickly—that easy, carefree time when they'd just met, when they'd barely grown acquainted, and suddenly both felt that nothing could be better than to sit alone and talk (sometimes from morning until night), and Mitya found himself inside that made-up world of love that he'd been waiting for since his childhood and adolescence. It was December—frost and clear skies, each day decorating Moscow with heavy rime and the dim, red disk of the low sun. January and February seemed to spin Mitya's love in a whirlwind of happiness and small joys that had either come to life already or now, right now, would burst into the world. But even then, something had begun to cloud that happiness, to poison it—and this would be the case more and more often. Even then it often seemed as if two Katyas existed: one for whom he'd felt a stubborn and insistent need from the first minutes of their acquaintance, and another who was real, pedestrian, and painfully impossible to reconcile with the first. And still, what Mitya went through then was nothing like his current state.

It could all be explained. Spring had begun with all its feminine concerns, its purchases and orders, its endless alterations. Katya often had to go with her mother to the tailor's, and soon her exams would begin at the private drama school where she studied. Her preoccupied, distracted state of mind was therefore only natural. Mitya tried repeatedly to comfort himself with these thoughts, but they were little help; the utterances of his suspicious heart—its refutations of those equitable thoughts—were far more powerful than reason, and everywhere his doubts were confirmed with growing patency. Katya's inner disregard for him grew steadily, and with it rose his jealousy, his grim suspicions. The director of her school filled Katya's head with praise, and she couldn't keep from sharing this with Mitya. The director had told her, "You, my darling"—he called all his pupils "darling"—"are the pride of my school," and then, in addition to his regular classes, he began to work with her individually during the spring fast so that she could pass her final exams with particular distinction and add to his renown. It was a well-known fact that he debauched his students, taking one of them every summer to Finland, the Caucasus, or abroad. And now it entered Mitya's head that the director had his sights on Katya. Of course she was not to blame for this, but Katya likely felt and understood the director's intentions and thus already shared a secret, foul relationship with him. This idea tortured Mitya more and more as the apathy that Katya felt for him became too obvious to deny.

In general something seemed to be distracting her from Mitya. He couldn't think calmly about the director. But he was not the only problem! Something larger—some new set of interests now seemed to dominate her love. What was it? Who was it? Mitya didn't know, and thus he was jealous of everyone and everything, fearing above all else some secret life that he imagined she'd begun to lead without him, and which, he was convinced, she kept from him deliberately. It seemed that she was being pulled inexorably away from him—drawn, perhaps, to something he found too terrible to contemplate.

Once, when her mother was present, Katya said to him half jokingly, "You, in general, Mitya, think of women in keeping with the *Domostroy*. You'll become an absolute Othello! I wouldn't want to fall in love and marry you!"

"I can't imagine love without jealousy," her mother countered. "He who feels no jealousy, I think, also feels no love."

"No, mama," said Katya, with her habit of repeating other people's words. "Jealousy is disrespect for the person whom you love. . . . You could say, 'If I'm not trusted, then I'm not loved,'" she added, deliberately not looking toward Mitya.

"I'd say just the opposite," her mother responded. "In my opinion, jealousy is love. I even read about it somewhere—an article that proved this point very well. It even used examples from the Bible, showing God himself is jealous, vengeful. . . ."

As for Mitya's love, it now expressed itself almost entirely in jealousy alone. And Mitya believed it wasn't ordinary jealousy but some particular strain. Although he and Katya had not yet breached the final bounds of intimacy, they allowed themselves too much during those hours spent alone, and Katya at times grew even more passionate than she'd been before. And now this stirred suspicions, roused in him a horror. All the feelings that comprised his jealousy were terrible, but one among them was most terrible of all—and Mitya couldn't sort it from the rest, couldn't see it clearly, couldn't understand. It was rooted in those passionate displays: when he and Katya shared them, they were pure and sweet, blissful, almost divine. But when Mitya thought of Katya and another man, those same displays seemed foul beyond all words, seemed to violate the laws of nature. At those moments Katya aroused in him a sharp hatred. Everything he allowed himself with her was steeped in virtue and celestial pleasure, but the moment he imagined another man in his place, everything changed, became utterly indecent, and stirred in him a violent urge to strangle Katya—strangle *her* and not his phantom rival.

III

Katya's exams were finally conducted during the sixth week of the fast. And that day seemed to validate all of Mitya's suffering, all his agonizing doubts.

She didn't see him, didn't notice him in the least that day. She was completely alien to him, completely public.

She enjoyed great success. She was dressed all in white like a bride, and her nervousness made her charming. She received warm, affectionate applause, and the director, a self-satisfied actor with sad and shameless eyes, made only occasional comments in order to inflate his own pride. He spoke quietly from his seat in the front row, but in such a way that the unbearable sound of his every word was audible throughout the hall.

"Less reading," he told her, his voice calm and grave—and so authoritative that Katya seemed to be his personal possession. "Don't act, experience. Feel," he said distinctly.

It was unendurable. That performance which elicited such warm applause was simply unendurable. Katya flushed hotly, her small voice broke, her breathing faltered—and all of this was touching and charming. But she read in a meretricious, singsong voice, the false and stupid notes of which were taken for high art in that milieu that Mitya so despised and that Katya already occupied in all her thoughts. She didn't speak. She declaimed. With a kind of languid passion, she delivered every line like some objectless entreaty, a belabored, ardent plea on behalf of nothing. Mitya didn't know how to hide his eyes in his embarrassment for her. Worst of all was the mix of angelic purity and prurience that seemed so evident in her, in her small, flushed face; in her white shoes and white dress, which seemed shorter now, as everyone was looking up at her on the stage; in the white silk stockings stretched taut across her calves. "A girl sang in the church choir. . . ." With excessive and contrived naiveté Katya was reading about some other girl, supposedly as innocent as an angel. And listening, Mitya felt that keen sense of closeness that always comes when you see a loved one in a crowd. He felt bitter enmity. He felt proud of Katya when the thought passed through his mind that she was his, despite all else—and then he felt a tearing in his chest: "No, she isn't mine . . . no more. . . ."

There were good days again after the exam. But Mitya didn't trust them as he had before. "You're so silly," Katya said to him, remembering her performance. "Couldn't you feel it? Couldn't you tell that it was for you—just for you—that I read so well?"

But he couldn't forget what he'd felt during the exam, and he couldn't admit that those emotions hadn't left him. Katya seemed to sense his secret feelings and once shouted in the midst of an argument: "I don't understand why you love me if you find everything about me so repulsive! What do you want from me? What, really—what is it that you want?"

He himself didn't know why he loved her, but he felt that, rather than subsiding, his love was growing stronger with the incessant, jealous struggle he now fought against someone, something because of her, and this taxing love, which gathered greater strength each day, grew more and more severe in its demands.

"You love my body—only my body, and not my soul," Katya once told him bitterly. And again these were someone else's words, some bit of theatre. But trite and shallow as they were, they touched on something painfully insoluble. He didn't know what he loved her for. He couldn't say exactly what it was he wanted. . . . What in general does it mean to love? Answering such a question was made all the more impossible by the fact that Mitya hadn't come across a single word in everything he'd read and heard about love that could come close to offering a definition of the subject. Everything in books and life seemed bent on speaking only of an utterly discarnate love or something known as sensuality and passion. His love resembled neither. What was it that he felt for her? That abstract love, or passion? Was it Katya's body or her soul that almost made him faint, that stirred in him the bliss one feels before death as he undid the buttons on her blouse and kissed her breasts, that immaculate, exquisite flesh laid bare with a submissiveness that stunned his soul—laid bare with all the shamelessness of utter innocence?

IV

More and more she changed.

Her success on her exam explained a great deal. But there were other reasons too.

The arrival of spring seemed to transform Katya into a young woman of high society: an elegant girl in a constant hurry. Soon Mitya felt ashamed of his hallway whenever she arrived—she always came by coach instead of walking now—and hurried down its dark length with her silks rustling, her veil covering her face. She was invariably tender with him but also invariably late, and ever prone to cutting short their time together with the excuse that she had to see the tailor with her mother yet again.

"We're possessed when it comes to clothes!" she told him, her shining eyes round with happiness and surprise. She knew full well that Mitya didn't believe her, but there was nothing else to say, nothing more to talk about. She rarely removed her hat anymore, rarely let go of her umbrella as she sat on the edge of Mitya's bed and drove him almost mad with glimpses of her calves in tight silk stockings. And then, before she rode away again, before she told him once more that she would not be home that evening—she had to see someone with mother!—she always acted out the same small scene, obviously designed both to make a fool of him and to offer compensation for his "silly worrying," as Katya called it: glancing at the door with affected secrecy, she slipped down from the bed and brushed her hip against his leg, said to him in a hurried whisper, "Quickly—kiss me!"

V

Near the end of April Mitya finally decided to give himself a rest and leave Moscow for the countryside.

He'd tormented Katya and himself to the point of exhaustion. Its apparent lack of any cause or reason made their suffering all the more unbearable: what in fact had happened? What was Katya guilty of?

"Go, yes—go to the country! I don't have the strength for this anymore!" she told him once, with the finality that follows despair. "We need to be apart for a little while. We need some time to make sense of this relationship. . . . You've gotten so thin my mother actually believes you have consumption! I can't do this anymore!"

And so Mitya's departure was decided. But to his great amazement Mitya found himself almost happy as he prepared to leave, despite his overwhelming grief. Everything they'd had in better days came back the very moment they agreed on his departure. He still struggled to resist the dreadful thoughts that plagued him day and night, and the slightest change in Katya was sufficient to convince him that everything had changed for the worse between them once again. But her passion and her tenderness seemed to grow more genuine, seemed to lose all traces of affectation—he felt this with the flawless sensory perception that a jealous nature seems to spawn. Again he stayed in her room until two in the morning; again they had things to talk about. And the closer his departure drew, the more senseless their impending separation seemed, the more pointless any attempt to "clarify" their relationship. Once, Katya wept—she'd never cried before— and those tears seemed to make her part of Mitya's flesh and blood; seeing them, he was pierced with tenderness for her and vaguely troubled by a sense of blame.

Katya's mother was leaving in June to spend her summer in the Crimea; Katya was to join her in Miskhor. They decided that Mitya would join them there as well.

And Mitya continued to prepare for his departure. He walked around Moscow in that strange delirium that comes when a man continues cheerfully with all his ordinary duties while knowing that he's gravely ill. He was ill, drunk with grief and sorrow, yet at the same time he was filled with a sickly happiness, elated by Katya's renewed intimacy and her concern for him (she'd even gone with him to buy packing belts for his trip, as if she were his bride or wife), deeply moved in general by the return of almost everything he'd experienced when they first fell in love. And everything he encountered was charged with these emotions: houses and streets, the people walking past, the people riding in their coaches, the typically cloudy spring weather, the smell of dust and rain, the churchlike scent of poplars opening their buds behind the fences in the alleys: everything spoke of the bitterness of separation and the sweetness of his hopes for summer, their meeting in the Crimea, where nothing would hinder them, where everything would finally be realized (though he still didn't know what, exactly, "everything" entailed).

On the day of his departure, Protasov came to say goodbye. Among university students and older boys in grammar school, it's not unusual to find a few who've perfected a demeanor of endless, genial derision and subsequently act as if they're older and more experienced than anyone on earth. Such was Protasov, one of Mitya's closest friends and his only confidant: despite Mitya's general reticence, Protasov had learned all the secrets of his love for Katya. Watching Mitya strap his suitcase shut, he noticed that his hands were trembling, and he smiled with melancholy wisdom.

"You're just children, God help you," he said. "And yet, it's time for you to understand, my dear Werther from Tambov, that Katya is, above all else, an embodiment of the feminine—she's a feminine essence, and even the chief of police is powerless to change this fact. You are a male essence, and so you climb the walls, present to Katya all the high demands of instinct—all those stipulations that she propagate the species. Of course, all of this is in keeping with the law—to some degree it's even sacred. The body is superior to the intellect, as Herr Nietzsche rightly pointed out. But it's also in keeping with the law for some to break their necks when they set out along this sacred course. After all, there are certain individuals in the animal world who must pay for their first and final reproductive act with their very existence. But that requirement is probably not mandatory for you, so you ought to be careful. Use your eyes. Look both ways. Try not to hurry. 'Junker Schmidt, it's true—summer does return.' The world's not held together by a single thread, and it doesn't ride only on Katya's shoulders. . . . But I can see from your efforts to strangle that suitcase that you don't entirely agree—and those shoulders for you are all too dear. Well, forgive me for dispensing advice that you never asked to hear. May St. Nicholas and all his cohorts keep you safe!"

After Protasov pressed Mitya's hand and left, a student of singing who lived across from him—and practiced from morning until night—began to test his voice. Mitya had his window open to the courtyard, and as he bundled up his blankets and his pillows, the words to "The Asra" boomed into his room.

Then Mitya began to hurry with the packing belts. He fastened them haphazardly, grabbed his hat, and left for Kislovka to say goodbye to Katya's mother. The words and music of the student's song played so insistently inside his head that he walked without seeing the streets or passersby, feeling even more intoxicated than he had the weeks before. As a matter of fact, it did seem that the world rode only on those shoulders. And Junker Schmidt was quite prepared to shoot himself! Well, what can you do? If it rides on those shoulders, it rides on those shoulders, he thought to himself, and went back to the song again: how the sultan's daughter who is "radiant with beauty" wanders in the garden and meets a dark-skinned slave who stands "as pale as death" beside a fountain; how she asks him who he is and where he's from, and when he answers her, his voice is menacing but restrained, filled with sad simplicity: "My name is Magomet"; how his voice then builds toward a kind of howl, an exultant, tragic wail: "I'm descended from the wretched race of Asra: If we love, we die."

Katya was getting dressed in order to see him off at the station. She called out tenderly to him from her room—that room in which he'd spent so many unforgettable hours!—promising to find him on the platform before the first bell. Sitting alone and smoking, the kind sweet woman with bright red hair looked at Mitya very sadly: she'd probably understood everything long ago, had probably guessed it all. Flushed and trembling inside, he kissed the soft, slack flesh of her hand and bowed his head before her like a son. With maternal tenderness she kissed Mitya on the temple several times, then made the sign of the cross above him.

"Oh, darling, live and laugh," she said, quoting Griboyedov with a timid smile. "Well, Christ be with you. . . . Go now, go on. . . ."

VI

Mitya finished the last few chores at his lodgings and with the help of the house attendant loaded his possessions onto the crooked bed of the cart he'd ordered, then awkwardly climbed in among his things and started his ride down the street. The moment the cart began to move, he was struck by that sensation that so often comes with a departure: *forever, a chapter of your life has ended.* And together with this realization came an unexpected lightness, a hope for the beginning of something new. He grew calmer as he rode, began to watch the passing streets more cheerfully: at times it almost seemed he'd never looked at them before. It was over. Farewell to Moscow! Farewell to everything that happened here! A fine rain fell from the overcast sky, and all the alleys were deserted; the dark cobblestones shone like iron; a sadness hung around the dirty houses. The cabbie drove at a painfully slow pace and repeatedly forced Mitya to turn his face away and struggle not to breathe. They passed the Kremlin and Pokrovka Street, then started down the alleys once again, where a crow shouted hoarsely at the evening and the rain—and still it was spring, the scent of spring was in the air. Finally they arrived, and Mitya ran behind the porter through the crowded station, down the platform to track three, where the long, heavy train stood ready to depart for Kursk. And in the great, chaotic mass of people assaulting that train, among the countless porters shouting at the crowd to let them through as they wheeled their roaring carts of luggage to the platform's edge, instantly he picked her out—a being who was "radiant with beauty"—solitary, somehow, in the distance, as if something held her separate not just from the crowd but from all the world. The first bell had already rung—this time it was he instead of Katya who was late: she'd touchingly arrived before him at the station, waited there, and now rushed forward, again as caring and attentive as a wife or bride.

"Darling, hurry—find a place. The second bell's about to ring."

And after the second bell she even more touchingly stood on the platform, looking up at him as he stood in the doorway of a third-class car that was already jammed with people and beginning to stink. Everything about her was enchanting: her small, endearing face; her delicate figure; her freshness and her youth in which the childlike mingled with the feminine; her raised and shining eyes; her modest blue hat and the alluring, elegant curve of its brim; even her dark grey suit, the cloth and silk lining of which Mitya could almost feel as he looked at her admiringly. Skinny and ungainly, he stood there in an old coat with worn-out, tarnished buttons and a pair of heavy, clumsy boots he'd put on specially for the trip—and still Katya was looking at him with genuine love and sorrow. The third bell rang so unexpectedly and struck so hard at Mitya's heart that he leapt onto the platform like a madman. Terrified, Katya rushed toward him as if she too were mad. Mitya pressed his face to her gloved hand, jumped back onto the train, and began to wave his hat ecstatically, watching through his tears as Katya clutched her skirt in one hand and began to fall away with the platform, never lowering her eyes from him. Katya fell farther and farther back, the wind blew with growing force through Mitya's hair as he held his head out the window, and the engine gathered speed: relentless, ever more impervious, it demanded open track with a disdainful, menacing roar—and together with the platform, she was torn away.

VII

Dark with rain clouds, the slow dusk had fallen long ago; the conductor was passing through the corridor, collecting tickets, placing lit candles in their holders as the heavy car rumbled through cool, bare fields where spring had begun later than it did in Moscow—and still Mitya stood before the rattling window, the scent of Katya's glove still perceptible on his lips, the last moment of their separation still burning like a sharp flame. The long Moscow winter that had changed his life now stood before him with all its joys and agonies in a new light. And Katya—she too stood in a stark new light. Who is she?. . . Yes—what is she?. . . And love and passion, the body, the soul—what is it all? None of it exists. None of it is. There is something else. Something absolutely other. Here: the scent of her glove—is this not love, not Katya? Not body, not soul? And the *mouzhiki* on the train, the woman who now leads her ghastly child to the lavatory, the dim candles in their trembling stands, the twilight in these empty spring fields—all of it is love, is soul, torture, inexpressible joy.

Morning found him in Oryol. He changed to a local train on the far platform. And Mitya felt how simple this world was, how calm, how much more a part of him than Moscow, which now had drifted into some imaginary, distant kingdom with Katya at its center—Katya who seemed sad and lonely now, the object of mere tenderness. Even the sky, streaked here and there with pale blue clouds that promised rain, even the wind was calmer, simpler. . . . The train moved unhurriedly from Oryol, and Mitya slowly ate a Tulsky Pryanik while sitting in the almost empty car. Then the engine gathered speed and the car began to rock, lulling him to sleep.

He woke up only in Verkhovye. The train had stopped. The station was crowded and quite busy, but it felt remote. A pleasant smell of cooking smoke and charcoal rose from the kitchen. He ate a bowl of cabbage soup, drank a bottle of beer with pleasure. And then he dozed again: a heavy tiredness had taken hold of him. When he stirred, the train was already racing through a familiar forest of spring birches that stood before the final stop. Again there was a spring cloudiness to the dusk; the air that streamed through the open window seemed to smell of mushrooms and rain. Although they were still completely bare, the trees reverberated with the roaring of the train more distinctly than the fields, and the small, sad lights of the station blinking in the distance once more revealed the change of season. There it is—the signal light burning green! It is lovely in this kind of dusk, this twilight from the bare birches. . . . With a knock the train began to switch its track. . . . My God, how forlorn he looks on the platform, the worker waiting for the owner's son— for me, the *barchuk*—to arrive. . . . Poor. . . . Endearing and forlorn in that way only country people have.

The dusk and rain clouds thickened as they drove from the station through the big village, already grimy with spring. Everything sank into the remarkably soft twilight and that profound silence that comes when a warm night blends with the vague darkness of rain clouds hanging low in the sky. And again Mitya was seized by joy and wonder: how calm and simple it was, this wretched countryside, these small, chimneyless huts with their heavy scents, everyone gone to sleep long ago—good people who leave their lamps unlit after the Annunciation. . . . How good it is— the warm, dark world of the steppe! Their *tarantass* plunged up and down the muddy hummocks of the road. Beyond the courtyard of a rich *mouzhik* stood several massive oaks—completely bare, unwelcoming, rooks' nests blackening their branches. A strange man stood beside a hut and peered into the twilight: he looked like something from ancient history with his bare feet, his tattered, heavy coat, his long, straight hair beneath a sheepskin hat. . . . And then a warm, sweet-smelling rain began to fall. . . . Mitya thought of the girls, all the young women sleeping in those huts, thought about everything feminine to which he'd drawn so close with Katya in the winter—and all of it merged into one: Katya, the girls in the huts, the night, the spring, the smell of rain and turned earth ready for the planting, the smell of the horse's sweat, the scent of her kid glove.

VIII

Life in the country began with sweet and peaceful days.

During the night when he rode from the station, Katya seemed to dissipate, seemed to fade and dissolve into everything around him. But this sensation wouldn't last. It would seem this way for only a few days while Mitya caught up on his sleep and rested from his journey, grew accustomed to the stream of childhood impressions that now returned to him as if completely new—impressions of the house where he was born, the village, the countryside in spring, the bare and empty earth prepared to bloom again, ageless and pristine.

The estate was modest and the manor house was old, lacking ostentation, and as its maintenance required only a small staff, a quiet life began for Mitya. His sister Anya, a second-year high school student, and his brother Kostya, a teenage cadet, were both still studying in Oryol and would not come home before early June. His mother, Olga Petrovna, was always busy running the estate, assisted by a single steward. She was often in the fields all day and went to bed as soon as it was dark.

Having slept for twelve hours after his arrival, Mitya came scrubbed and spotlessly clean from his sunny room—it had windows on the garden and faced to the east—and roamed through all the other rooms of the house, feeling an acute calm within them, a kindred, peaceful simplicity that put his mind and body at ease. All the rooms had been cleaned, all the floors washed before his arrival, and now everything stood in its customary place, everything smelled as familiar and pleasant as it had so many years ago. Only the dining hall, which joined the foyer, remained to be washed. A girl covered in freckles—a day worker from the village—was standing on the windowsill near the balcony door, stretching to reach the upper squares of glass which she wiped clean with a whistling sound, her dark blue, seemingly distant reflection hanging in the lower panes. The maid Parasha pulled a large, steaming rag from a bucket and walked barefoot through the water that had been poured across the floor, her delicate heels and white calves exposed.

"Go and have tea," she said, running her rapid words together with friendly familiarity. "Your *mamasha* left before sunrise for the station with the steward. You didn't hear a thing, I'll bet."

At that moment Katya asserted herself powerfully in his memory. For a moment Mitya had found himself looking with desire at the girl on the windowsill, the freckled skin of her outstretched arm, the curve of her figure as she extended herself upward, her skirt and her full, sturdy legs—and suddenly with joy he felt Katya's power, her ownership of him, her secret presence in all the morning's impressions.

And that presence became more and more perceptible with each new day, grew ever more enchanting as Mitya returned to himself, settled down, forgot that ordinary Katya who had failed so often and so painfully in Moscow to correspond with the Katya created by his desires.

IX

For the first time he was living at home as an adult—an adult with whom even his mother acted differently than before. But most important, he lived now with a real love inside his soul. And it was giving life to everything he'd waited for, everything his core had sought since childhood, since adolescence.

Even during infancy something had stirred—secretly, transcendently—inside him, something inexpressible in words. . . . Somewhere . . . At some moment . . . It must have been in spring as well. . . . He was still a very small child, standing in a garden somewhere, near a lilac bush—he recalled the sharp scent of blister beetles. . . . A young woman was nearby. His nanny, probably. . . . Suddenly something before him seemed to fill with a celestial light—the woman's face, perhaps, or the *sarafan* covering her heavy breasts. And a surge of heat passed through him, seemed to stir inside him like an infant in its mother's womb. . . . But all of it was like a dream. . . . And everything that followed—his years of childhood, adolescence, school—this too was like a dream. There were moments of intense delight—each distinct and unrepeatable and utterly unique—brought on by some young girl or other who would come to visit on some children's holiday with her mother—a secret, all-consuming curiosity he felt for these small, intriguing creatures who resembled nothing else with their dresses, their small, delicate shoes, and the silk ribbons in their hair. He developed a much more conscious fascination with a girl from grammar school, later, in the major town of the province. It lasted almost the entire fall. She would periodically appear in the evenings in a tree beyond the fence of the neighboring yard: her exuberance, her taunting, the round comb she wore in her hair, her brown dress, and her dirty hands, her laughter, her pleasant shouts—all of this made Mitya think of her from morning until night, and suffer bouts of sadness, even weep from his relentless longing for something from her. Then it somehow finished on its own, faded from his memory—and there were new, secret fascinations that transported him—some brief, some more sustained. There was the knife-edged joy, the grief of falling suddenly in love at high school dances. And there was a languor to his body, a dim presentiment—a vague expectation in his heart.

He was born and grew up in the countryside, but during secondary school he was forced to spend the spring in town, with the exception of one year—the year before last—when he fell ill while home for *Maslenitsa* and had to stay there for all of March and half of April. It was unforgettable. For some two weeks he lay in bed and did nothing but look out the window, study the snow, the garden's trunks and branches as they changed each day with the earth's growing warmth and the sky's increasing light. He saw: now it's morning and the room's so bright, so warm from the sunlight that already flies have stirred, begun to crawl along the window panes. . . . One day later, in the hour after lunch: the sun's behind the far side of the house, its light is falling through the western windows. And here the spring snow's so pale it's almost blue. Big clouds are hanging in the treetops, drifting in the clear, deep sky. And after one more day: bright clearings have emerged in the cloudy sky. A glistening sheen on all the bark. A constant dripping from the roof above the window. One cannot see enough. One cannot feel enough joy. . . . And then began warm mists and rain. The snow was eaten away in a few days. Dissolved. The ice on the river broke. In the garden and the yard the earth began to bare itself, to show its joyous black. . . .

For a long time Mitya remembered a day at the end of March when for the first time he went for a ride in the fields. The sky wasn't bright, but it gleamed with freshness and vigor in the pale, flowerless trees in the garden. A cold wind blew across the fields; the stubble of the cut plots was rough and overgrown, a reddish brown like rust. They were planting oats, and as they plowed, a primeval force seemed to rise in the rich, clumped soil, the almost fatty blackness of the fields. He'd ridden right across those plots of stubble and turned earth toward the forest, which he could see far off in the clear air—small, bare, its entire length visible from start to finish. When he reached it, he rode down into the forest hollow, and his horse's hooves rustled loudly through the deep beds of last year's leaves, wet and brown in places, dry and pale as straw in others. He crossed ravines where leaves were scattered lightly over the rocks, and the snowmelt was still running in streams. And suddenly a woodcock rose with a sharp crack from the underbrush, its cloudy, dark gold body bursting into flight beneath the horse's legs. . . .

And what had it been for him, that spring—that day in particular when a fresh wind blew in his face and his horse breathed heavily, its nostrils flared as it strode hard through the boggy fields of cut stubble and black plowing, snorted from its depths, bellowed with the majesty and power of some wild, untrammeled force? It seemed then that the spring itself was his first real love—that spring and all its days of artless love for every girl in school, for every girl on earth. But how distant those days seemed to him now! What a boy he was then—so innocent and simplehearted, so limited in his joys, his hopes and sorrows! That aimless and incorporeal love now seemed to be a dream—or, more accurately, the memory of some lovely dream. Now there was Katya. Now there was a soul that embraced the world—reigned over it, and everyone.

X

Only once in those early days did Katya make him think of her through something sinister.

Late one evening Mitya went onto the back porch. It was dark and quiet, and the air smelled of damp earth from the fields; stars hung above the vague, black outlines of the garden, glistening like tears as the night clouds streamed across them. Something in the distance suddenly erupted into shouts, a wild and devilish shrieking followed by strange barks and squeals. Mitya flinched and froze, then carefully descended from the porch into the dark avenue of trees, which seemed to hold themselves inimically, as if on guard against him. There he stopped again and waited, listening. Where was it? What was it? What would fill the garden with those awful shrieks so suddenly at night? A *sych*. A screech owl with a mate — nothing more, he thought, going completely still, as if he could feel the devil's invisible presence in the darkness. And again it wailed from somewhere near him; Mitya's soul convulsed as the voice sent up another howl, followed by a rustling and cracking in the trees. Soundlessly the devil moved to some other perch in the garden, where he began to bark, then whine and cry in a child's beseeching, plaintive voice. He beat his wings and screamed with tortured pleasure, squealed, then broke into hysterical, mocking laughter like a lunatic being tickled violently. His entire body shaking, Mitya peered into the darkness, strained to hear the slightest movement. But the devil had suddenly stopped, choked off its jabbering. It split the garden's darkness with one final cry — a call containing all the lassitude of death — and vanished, as if swallowed by the earth. For several minutes Mitya waited in vain for that amatory horror to resume, then quietly returned to the house. And all night he was tormented by the same pernicious thoughts and poisonous emotions that had fouled his love in March in Moscow.

But his suffering quickly dissipated in the morning sun. He remembered how Katya had wept when they decided firmly that Mitya should leave Moscow; he remembered how ecstatically she'd seized upon the idea that he too would come to the Crimea at the start of June; how touchingly she'd helped in his preparations for the trip; how she'd seen him off at the station. . . . He took out her photograph and for a long time studied her elegant hair and delicate features, struck by her forthright, open expression and the clarity of her slightly rounded eyes. . . . He wrote her a particularly long, emotional letter expressing his faith in their love — and then, once more, he began to feel her radiant and loving presence, her unfaltering participation in everything that brought him life and pleasure.

He remembered what he went through when his father died eight years ago. That too was in the spring. Bewildered, horrified, Mitya had passed timidly through the hall where his father's body lay on a table the day after his death. He was elaborately dressed in a nobleman's full uniform, his large pale hands folded over his elevated chest. His nose was white; the blackness of his sparse beard seemed deeper than before. Mitya went onto the porch and glanced at the huge coffin lid wrapped in gold brocade that leaned near the door, and suddenly he felt it: death is in the world. It's in everything: the sunlight, the spring grass in the yard, the garden, the sky. . . . He went into the garden and down the avenue of lindens, where everything was mottled with bright sunlight and shade, then turned onto a side path where the sun was even stronger. He looked at the trees and the first white butterflies, listened to the first tender songs of the birds—and he recognized nothing: in everything there was death, that terrible table in the hall, that long lid wrapped in gold brocade, leaning on the porch. The sun shone differently now. The spring grass had changed. There was something else, something new in the way the butterflies settled and went still on the sunstruck tips of its blades. None of it was the same as it had been a day ago. It seemed that everything had been transformed by the close proximity of the world's end. Now the eternal youth of spring and all its charms seemed only pitiful and sad! This sensation lasted for a long time—lasted the entire spring, just as that terrifying, sweet smell seemed to linger in the house even after they had scrubbed the floors and aired the rooms repeatedly.

Now a spell held Mitya in its thrall again. But it was of a different order. This spring, the spring of his first love, was unlike any other. Once more the world had been recast; again it was filled with some new and unfamiliar element. But it was not a horror. Just the opposite: inexplicably, delightfully, it seemed to coalesce with all the youth and joy of spring. And this new element was Katya—or, more accurately, it was something Mitya sought from her—that sweetness, that loveliness to which nothing in the world compares. Now the intensity of his demands grew proportionally with each spring day that passed, and in her absence Katya was replaced by an image—an image of a woman who did not exist but who was earnestly desired—and thus she didn't stain the purity, didn't break the charming spell of what Mitya sought from her, and with every passing day he felt her presence more acutely in everything he saw.

XI

He was joyfully convinced of this during his first week at home, when spring seemed just about to break open. He would sit with a book near an open window in the living room, looking past the trunks of pines and firs in the front garden to the muddy river in the meadow and the village on the hillside beyond it. As they do only in early spring, rooks still shouted ardently in the bare branches of the ancient birches on the bordering estate, exhausting themselves in a ceaseless, cheerful commotion that lasted from morning until night. There on its hill, the village still looked grey and lifeless, its only color confined to a yellowish green spreading through the willows. . . . He would walk in the garden: it too was stunted, bare, transparent. Only the glades were going green, specked with small turquoise flowers, and the acacias near the avenue were coming into leaf; in the hollow that formed the garden's southernmost edge, the cherry trees alone had released their pale, thin blooms. . . . He would walk out to the fields, where all the land was still empty, damp, and raw; where the stubble of the cut wheat still bristled in the barren tracts; where the dried-out mud of the uneven roads among the plots was still a deep red-blue. . . . And it was all a rich display of stark anticipation—youth laid bare, exposed. . . . And all of it was Katya. He only seemed to be distracted by the girls who came to work during the day on the estate and the laborers who lived in the servants' quarters, by his reading and his visits to the *mouzhiki* he knew in the village, by his conversations with his mother and his trips in the fields on a *drozhky* with the steward—a hulking, crass, retired soldier.

Then began another week. One night there was a pounding rain, and in the morning the sun turned hot, came into its own. The spring lost its pallor and reserve; everything in sight began to change—not by the day but by the hour. They began to plow, turning the dry stalks and stubble of last year's cuttings into black velvet; the borders of the fields began to green; the grass turned succulent in the yard; the sky took on a brighter, fuller blue. A soft fresh verdure spread across the garden like a cloak; the lilac went from grey to a rich, reddish blue and began to scent the air while large black flies massed on its lustrous, deep-green leaves and in the spots of hot sun that dappled the small roads, their bodies glinting with a metallic, dark blue sheen. The limbs of pear and apple trees were still visible beneath the slightly grey, unusually soft small leaves that they'd just begun to release, but their nets of crooked branches wound beneath the other trees with a milky whiteness, a dusting of snow that grew lighter, thicker, sweeter-smelling every day. During that remarkable time Mitya observed with joy and close attention all the changes taking place around him. But Katya was not lost among them—just the opposite: rather than receding, she took part in everything he witnessed, added herself and her own flourishing beauty to the spring blooms, to the luxuriant white of the garden, to the darkening blue of the sky.

XII

And so it was that one day, as the late afternoon sun sloped into the dining hall, Mitya came to tea and was surprised to see the morning mail, which he'd been waiting for in vain, lying near the samovar. He went quickly to the table—Katya should have answered at least one of his letters long ago—and a tasteful envelope, its address written in a familiar, touching script, flashed before his eyes with terrifying irrefutability. He snatched it up, bolted from the house and down the avenue, then entered the garden and walked into the hollow that descended from its far side. There he stopped, looked around, and quickly tore the envelope open. The letter was short, only a few lines altogether, but Mitya's heart was pounding so violently that he had to read it several times before he could understand. "My beloved, my one and only" he read over and again, and the earth began to swim beneath his feet with those fervid exclamations. He raised his eyes: the sky seemed to shine with triumph and joy, and beneath it the garden's white petals were as bright as snow. Already sensing the approaching chill of dusk, a nightingale chirped sharply and distinctly among the fresh green leaves of the distant bushes, its notes filled with that sweet selflessness that drifts so often in the songs of nightingales. The blood drained from Mitya's face; a shivering swept through his body.

He walked home slowly. His love was like a cup filled to the brim. And for several days he continued to carry that cup carefully within him, quietly, happily expecting a new letter.

XIII

The garden varied its attire.

The huge old maple that towered over its southern corner, visible from all directions, seemed to grow even larger and more imposing in its coat of thick fresh leaves.

The trees of the central avenue also seemed to rise and grow more striking. Mitya studied them constantly from his room. He could still see through the tops of the old lindens, but their new leaves were thick enough to form a bed of pale green lace above the garden in the distance.

A leafy covering spread beneath the maples and the lindens. It smelled sweet; it curled like ivy; it was white as cream.

And all of it—the huge luxuriant maple, the pale green bed above the garden, the bridal-white blooms of the fruit trees, the sun, the deep blue sky, all the riotous growth in the garden hollow, all the bushes and burgeoning shrubs along the small roads and secondary avenues, all the sprouting plants at the base of the southernmost wall of the manor house—the lilac and black currant, the burdock and acacia, the worm-wood, the nettles—all of it was staggering in its vitality, its abundance, and its youth.

The green open space surrounding the house seemed to grow smaller as the blooms and new leaves pressed in from all sides; somehow this made the house too seem smaller, and more becoming. It seemed to be waiting for someone to arrive; for entire days all the windows and doors were left open in every room—in the white hall; in the old-fash-ioned parlor with its dark blue decor; in the small den where the walls were also dark blue and decorated with small pictures and lithographs in round frames; in the library, which formed one corner of the house—a large and sunny, often empty room with old icons in one corner and low bookshelves made of ash along the walls. Everywhere the encroaching trees glanced buoyantly before the windows with their pale or dark green leaves, the bright blue sky visible among their branches.

But there was no letter. Mitya knew that Katya had no faculty for writing, that she had trouble sitting down at a desk, finding a pen and paper and an envelope, buying a stamp. . . . But rational thought was lit-tle help once more. The happy certainty and unflagging pride with which he'd waited for several days for a second letter had vanished: now he was increasingly despondent and alarmed. It stood to reason that a letter like the first would soon be followed by something even more de-lightful and uplifting. But Katya had gone silent.

He went less often to the village and the fields. He sat in the library, leafing through journals that had dried and yellowed on the shelves for decades. They contained many fine works by old poets, their exquisite lines almost invariably consigned to the same subject—that subject which has driven almost every poem and song since the beginning of the world, that subject which now gave life to his soul, and which, no matter how a given work described it, he could always link, in some way or an-other, to Katya and himself. And so for hours on end he sat in an arm-chair near the open shelves and tortured himself, reading and rereading:

Find me, dearest, in the darkened garden
Now, while everyone's asleep
And only stars look down on us. . . .

It seemed that all of these affecting words, all of these appeals were his alone—and all of them were dedicated to just one listener, she whom Mitya found in everything, saw everywhere. Sometimes they seemed almost threatening:

> *The water's like a mirror*
> *Until the swans unfold their wings,*
> *Then the surface swells and trembles:*
> *Come now to me! While stars still shine,*
> *While leaves stir softly in this wind,*
> *And storms assemble in the night.*

Closing his eyes, growing cold, he repeated this plea, this entreaty from a heart unable to contain the force of its love, a heart driven by its need to triumph, to satiate its longing. Then he looked for a long time into space, listened to the deep silence of the countryside surrounding the house—and shook his head bitterly. No, she would not respond to any supplication. Somewhere far off in the distance she shone, somewhere in the foreign world of Moscow. And again tenderness welled up in his heart! Again that threatening call, that slightly sinister invocation, resounded in his mind:

> *Come now to me! While stars still shine,*
> *While leaves stir softly in this wind,*
> *And storms assemble in the night.*

XIV

Having dozed after lunch, which they ate at noon, Mitya left the house and walked unhurriedly to the garden. Girls often worked there, digging around the apple trees—and they were there today. It had already become a habit of sorts for Mitya to sit and talk with them.

It was a hot, quiet afternoon. He walked in the transparent shade of the avenue, surrounded by tendrilous white branches that in the distance resembled snow. The pear tree blossoms were particularly thick and full, and their pallor mixed with the bright sky to tinge the shadows violet. Together with the blooming apple trees, they scattered white petals on the upturned earth around them while their sweet, tender scent mixed with the smell of manure warmed by the sun in the cattle yard. Occasionally a small cloud drifted overhead, the sky turned a lighter blue, and those smells of growth and decay turned even sweeter and more delicate. All of the warm, fragrant air was filled with a contented, soporific buzzing as bees and bumblebees buried themselves in those curling leaves of snow laced with the scent of honey. The intermittent songs of nightingales drifted in the distance and nearby, their notes filled with the afternoon's blissful tedium.

The alley ended at the gate to the threshing barn; in the distance to the left, a black grove of fir trees rose from one corner of the garden. There two girls in bright clothes stood out sharply among the apple trees. Mitya turned when he was only halfway down the avenue, as he usually did, and began to make his way toward them through the trees. The low splayed limbs brushed against his face as gently as a girl's hand when he pushed past them, inhaling their scents of honey and lemon. One of the girls, a thin redhead named Sonka, began to laugh wildly and shout the moment she saw him.

"Oh, the owner's coming!" she yelled with mock alarm, jumping up from the bough of the pear tree on which she'd been resting, and hurrying toward her shovel.

The other girl, Glashka, acted as if she hadn't noticed Mitya in the least. Wearing short, black felt boots—the tops of which were filled with white petals—she planted one foot firmly on the iron blade of her shovel, calmly drove it down, and turned the fresh-cut turf. As she worked, she broke into a loud song, her voice strong and pleasant: "Ah my garden, my darling garden, whom are your blossoms for?" She was a strong, somewhat masculine, and always serious girl.

Mitya took Sonka's place on the thick pear bough that rested in the fork of another tree. Sonka looked at him conspicuously.

"Ah, just got out of bed? Be careful not to oversleep. You might miss something!" she said loudly, trying to sound casual and blithe.

Sonka liked Mitya. She tried hard to hide this but never knew how, and wound up holding herself awkwardly or saying the first thing that came into her head whenever he was near her. She often hinted at her vague but persistent suspicion that Mitya's constant lassitude had no innocent cause: she believed he was sleeping with Parasha—or at the very least aimed to do so. Jealous, at times she spoke tenderly and looked at him with a kind of languor, hinting at her feelings—while on other occasions her words and tone of voice turned sharp and cutting, and her stares expressed a cold hostility. All of this gave Mitya a strange kind of pleasure. There was no letter. There was no letter, and it seemed that he no longer lived, only passed from one day to the next in a state of constant expectation, feeling more and more oppressed by his desperate hope and his inability to speak with anyone about his secret love and his misery, about Katya and his hopes for the summer in the Crimea. It was pleasant therefore to hear Sonka hint at his involvement in a nonexistent love affair, for at least these conversations bore some connection to the hidden cause of his despondency. And her obvious affection excited him, in part because it meant that she now suffered some of the same emotions that tormented him and thus shared secretly in the afflictions of his heart. Indeed, he even felt, at times, a strange hope that he might find a confidante in Sonka, or even, somehow, a replacement for Katya.

Now, unknowingly, Sonka once again touched on Mitya's secret. "Don't oversleep! You might miss something!" He looked around. The solid, dark green grove of firs seemed almost black in the brilliant afternoon, and the sky that hung between the sharp tops of the trees was a rich, magnificent blue. Shot through with sun, the fresh leaves of the lindens, the maples, and the elms spread a cheerful, lambent canopy over the entire garden, flecked the grass and small paths with spots of shade and brilliant light. The hot, sweet-smelling blossoms turned even whiter beneath that canopy, flashing and gleaming like porcelain where the sun fell unencumbered through the leaves. Mitya smiled against his will.

"What could I sleep through?" he asked Sonka. "That's what's so regrettable—I have no affairs to oversleep!"

"Fine, fine—I'll take your word for it. Just don't cross yourself or take God's name to make me think it's true. I'll believe you as it is," Sonka shouted in a crude, happy voice, pleasing Mitya with her skepticism about his lack of love affairs. Then she began to shout again. A red calf with a few white curls on its head had wandered out from the firs and slowly approached her from behind to begin chewing on the flounce of her blue calico dress.

"A fainting fit for you!" she shouted, waving it away. "Go find a mother somewhere else!"

"Is it true—what I heard?" said Mitya, not knowing how to continue the conversation but not wanting it to end. "Are there plans for your wedding? They say his family's rich, and the groom himself is handsome. But you keep refusing him, won't listen to your father."

"Rich, but not too bright. Dusk starts early in his head," Sonka answered playfully, slightly flattered. "Besides, I might have someone else in mind."

Glashka, taciturn and unamused as ever, shook her head. "Words run out of you like water from the Don," she said softly without pausing in her work. "You bark out anything that comes into your head. But just wait until they hear your barking in the village—you'll be famous then!"

"Oh, stop clucking," Sonka shouted. "I've been weaned already."

"Who do you have in mind, then?" Mitya asked.

"You think I'd tell you?. . . All right—I'll go ahead and confess it all, just because you ask: I've fallen in love with your old shepherd! I see him and my thighs get hot—my legs burn right down to my heels. I'm just like you—I like a good ride on an old horse," she said provocatively, hinting at the twenty-two-year-old Parasha, who was widely considered an old maid in the village. As if her secret feelings for the *barchuk* entitled her to such bold behavior, Sonka suddenly tossed her shovel aside, sat down on the ground, and stretched out her legs, displaying a pair of mottled wool tights and coarse boots. Sitting with her legs slightly parted, she helplessly dropped her arms to her sides.

"Oh, I haven't gotten anything done—but I'm all worn out," she shouted, laughing. She began to sing in a piercing voice, "My leather boots are worn and broken," then broke off, laughing again. "Come and rest with me in the hunters' shed," she called out. "I'll do anything you like."

Her laughter enticed him. With a large, awkward smile, Mitya got up from the tree limb, lay down on the ground beside Sonka, and put his head in her lap. She pushed him away, but he rested his head against her thigh again, thinking of a poem that he had read again and again during the last few days:

Oh rose,
The potency of joy's made manifest
When you unfurl this tiny scroll
That has no end,
When you unfold the folded petals
Folded past all reckoning,
When you expose these whorls
Rich and redolent beyond all reason,
And they turn damp with dew. . . .

"Don't touch me," Sonka shouted with genuine fear, trying to lift his head and move it away. "I'll shout so loud the wolves come out of the woods! I don't have anything to give you now. That little fire's all burned out!"

Mitya closed his eyes and didn't speak. Broken up by the pear trees' leaves and branches, the sun fell in narrow shafts, warmed his face in little specks of prickling light. Sonka pulled at his coarse black hair with both tenderness and scorn. "Like a horse's hide," she shouted, and covered his eyes with his hat. The back of his head touched her legs—that most frightening thing in the world, a woman's legs!—then brushed against her stomach; he inhaled the scent of her cotton skirt and blouse—and all of this mixed with the blooming garden and with Katya, mingled with the near and distant chirping of the listless nightingales, the steady buzzing—the voluptuous and drowsy hum—of countless bees, the warm and honey-scented air. Even the sensation of earth behind his back created in him an acute and overwhelming desire, a painful longing for a strain of joy that lay beyond all ordinary human experience.

Suddenly something rustled in the grove of firs, chuckled as if gloating, then rang out: Ku-ku, ku-ku. . . . It was so close, its call was so distinct, so sharp and startling, that Mitya even heard the wheezing and trembling of its small, sharp tongue as the cuckoo began to wail. He was seized again by a longing for Katya, seized by an almost violent demand that she provide him with the superhuman joy he craved. And this longing took hold of him so violently that Mitya suddenly got up and strode off through the trees, to Sonka's absolute astonishment.

Together with a wrenching, furious demand for joy, that voice that sailed out of the fir grove and resounded with such terrifying clarity above his head—that voice that cleaved the spring calm to its core—also stirred in Mitya a stark and absolute conviction that nothing more would come from Moscow: not another letter. Something had happened there—or would at any moment. And he was lost. Destroyed.

XV

Entering the house, he paused for a moment before the mirror. "She's right," he thought. "They're Byzantine eyes. Or just the eyes of a lunatic. . . . Gloomy eyebrows. Like something drawn with charcoal on a sack of bones. Black hair. A horse's hide—isn't that what Sonka said?"

He heard the quick, light padding of bare feet and turned, embarrassed.

"You must be in love—looking at yourself so much," Parasha said, gently teasing him as she hurried past, carrying a heated samovar toward the balcony. "Your mother wants to see you," she added as she placed the samovar with a flourish on the table set for tea, then turned and looked at him intently.

"They've all caught on. They know everything," Mitya thought. "Where is she?" he forced himself to ask.

"In her room. . . ."

Slowly descending into the western sky, the sun sloped across the roof and flashed as if reflected by a mirror beneath the needled branches of the pines and firs shading the balcony. The shrubs and staff trees beneath them also gleamed with a summer glassiness. Covered with a limpid shade and patches of hot, bright light, the tablecloth seemed to shine while wasps hung over the basket of white bread, the cups, and the cut-glass dish of jam. All of it spoke to the joys of summer in the country, the countless possibilities for happiness and contentment. Hoping to convince her that no great weight was burdening his soul, Mitya decided to approach his mother before she came to him.

He left the hall and walked down a corridor that led to his room and his mother's as well as those in which Anya and Kostya lived during the summer. Dusk already filled the corridor, and a dark blue shade had gathered in Olga Petrovna's room, which was comfortably crowded with all the most antique furniture in the house: old wardrobes and chiffoniers, a large bed, and an icon stand, before which, as always, a lamp was burning, though his mother had never demonstrated any particular religiosity. Beyond the open windows a wide shadow lay across a neglected flower bed before the entrance to the main avenue; beyond it the green and white garden blazed cheerfully in the last full light of the sun. Paying no attention to this familiar view, Olga Petrovna sat in an armchair in the corner, wearing eyeglasses and crocheting rapidly. A tall, thin woman in her forties, she had dark hair and a serious, slightly dry disposition.

"You asked for me, mama?" Mitya said, standing in the doorway to her room.

"No, no—nothing important, really. I just wanted to see you. It seems I hardly ever do anymore, other than at lunch," answered Olga Petrovna without interrupting her work. Her manner seemed inordinately nonchalant.

Mitya remembered how Katya had said on March 9 that she for some reason feared his mother—remembered the delightful, secret hint she meant to deliver with those words.

"Well, perhaps there was something you wanted to tell me?" he muttered awkwardly.

"No, nothing really. Just that, lately you've seemed a little sad. A little at loose ends," said Olga Petrovna. "Maybe it would be good for you to take a little trip. Maybe visit the Meshcherskys, for example. There's a crowd of young ladies in that house," she added, smiling. "And they really are a very nice family."

"I'll be very glad to visit them one of these days," Mitya answered with difficulty. "But come and have some tea. It's lovely on the balcony. We'll talk more there," he said, knowing that his mother's sensitivity and tact would keep her from returning to this pointless conversation.

They sat on the balcony almost until sunset. After tea his mother continued crocheting as they talked about the neighbors, the farmland, Anya and Kostya. Again Anya had to retake an exam in August! Although he listened and responded periodically, Mitya felt intoxicated, delirious from some grave illness throughout the conversation, just as he had before departing Moscow.

In the evening he paced ceaselessly for some two hours, walking back and forth through the hall, the living room, the den, and the library, where he marched right up to the southern windows, which opened on the garden. Through the windows in the living room and the hall he saw the sunset's soft red glow between the branches of the firs and pines, heard the laughter and the voices of the laborers gathering to eat their dinner near the servants' quarters. Looking down the row of adjoining rooms, he could see the library windows and a pink, motionless star suspended in the evening sky, which was such a constant shade of blue it seemed to have no color at all. Against that backdrop, the landscape seemed particularly picturesque, with the massive green crown of the ancient maple and all the blossoms in the garden, so white they made one think of winter. And still he marched back and forth, no longer caring in the least how everyone would talk about him in the house. He clenched his teeth so hard his head began to ache.

XVI

From that day on he stopped observing all the changes brought on by the approaching summer. He saw them everywhere he looked, even felt them, but they had lost all independent meaning. He could enjoy them only as a source of torment: the lovelier they were, the more suffering they caused him. Katya occupied his mind to an absurd degree; she haunted him like a phantom: anywhere he looked, he saw her—she was in everything, behind everything. And as each new day confirmed even more terribly than its predecessor that Katya no longer existed for him—that she was already in someone else's power, that she was already giving herself and her love to someone else, despite the fact that both were meant exclusively for him—as each day proved these facts more cruelly than the last, everything in the world seemed to grow increasingly useless: all the earth's beauty, all its charm only made more savage its gratuity.

He hardly slept at night. And nothing could compare to the beauty of those hours when the moon was out and the silence of the milky garden seemed deliberate, as if every leaf and stalk were intent on keeping still. The nightingales could barely stir in their exquisite languor; they sang cautiously, deliberately—each trying to produce a note that had no equal in its delicate precision, its intricate and absolute sonority. Reticent and tender, the pallid moon hung low over the garden, invariably accompanied by a bluish strand of clouds that spread below it like a ripple on the surface of a lake, its charm beyond all words. Mitya slept without any curtains on his windows; the garden and the moon peered constantly into his room, and the moment he opened his eyes on that white disk, Mitya uttered in his thoughts the word "Katya," like a man possessed—uttered it with a degree of ecstasy and agony that he himself found frightening: why should the moon bring her to mind? What possible connection could there be? But it was something visible. How strange! He saw something in the moon that made him think of her. At other moments he saw nothing at all. Memories of Katya and everything they had shared in Moscow would sometimes seize him with such force that he trembled as if consumed with fever and begged God—alas, always to no avail—to let him see her, now, here in bed with him—if only in a dream. Once he'd gone with her to the Bolshoi Theatre to see Sobinov and Chaliapin sing in *Faust*. Everything sent him into raptures that night—the vast, bright hall that opened like a brilliant chasm below them, already crowded and warm and richly scented with perfume; the gold and red-velvet tiers of box seats that could barely hold their scores of stylish occupants; the soft, nacreous glow of the gigantic chandelier that hung above it all; and then, from far below them, as the conductor waved his arms, the overture rising, streaming up into the air—at times roaring and demonic, at others sad and tender beyond words: "*There was a King of Thule. . . .*" Afterward he walked her home to Kislovka through the night's heavy frost and bright moonlight, and then stayed especially late, her kisses more than ever like a drug. When he finally left, he took with him the silk ribbon that she used to tie her hair at night, and now, during these torturous nights, he couldn't think of that ribbon, which lay on his writing table, without shuddering.

During the day he slept, then rode on horseback to the village with a railway station, where there was a post office. The weather stayed fine. Rain fell, thunderstorms passed through, and again the hot sun beat down, continuing without a pause its rapid work in the gardens, woods, and fields. The garden bloomed, dispersed its petals, then continued to grow, turning a luxurious dark green as its leaves thickened. The forests seemed to be sinking beneath countless flowers and tall grasses; the calls of nightingales and cuckoos never stopped rising from their green, sonorous depths. Rich and varied shoots of wheat now covered the fields that once seemed so barren and exposed. For entire days he disappeared into those fields and forests.

It was too embarrassing to linger all morning on the balcony or in the courtyard, waiting in vain for the steward or a worker to come with the mail. And neither the steward nor the workers necessarily had time to travel eight *versts* for such trivialities. And so he started to make the trip himself. But he invariably came home with nothing but an issue of the local paper or a letter from Anya or Kostya. His torments grew extreme. The beauty of the forests and the fields through which he rode weighed on him so heavily that Mitya felt a physical pain in his chest.

Once, just before evening, he was riding home through the empty estate next to his mother's. It stood in an old park that merged with a surrounding forest of birches. He was riding down the main avenue, known by the local *mouzhiki* as Table Road. Its broad surface lay between two rows of huge black firs that led all the way to the old house. The avenue was covered with a slick layer of pine needles the color of rust, and a magnificent gloom hung between the trees. The sun was setting to Mitya's left; its reddening light sloped peacefully between the trunks of the firs and flashed like gold among the thick covering of needles. Stirred only by the intermittent, solitary songs of nightingales rising from the far ends of the park, the silence that reigned over the land seemed so spellbound and transfixed, the scent of firs and jasmine bushes surrounding the house hung so sweetly in the air, and the happiness that others must have shared there, long ago on that estate, returned to Mitya now with such intensity, and Katya suddenly appeared so vividly before him—appeared in the image of his wife on the huge, decaying balcony among the jasmine—that Mitya felt his face go tight, felt the morbid pallor that spread across his cheeks.

"One week," he said aloud, his voice carrying through the woods. "I'll wait one week. And if no letter comes, I'll put a bullet in my head."

XVII

He got up very late the next day. After lunch he sat on the balcony with a book on his lap, looking at the pages covered with print and stupidly asking himself, "Should I ride to the post office or not?"

It was hot. White butterflies drifted in pairs over the warm grass and the staff shrubs, which shimmered like glass in the sun. "Ride to the post office or finally stop—finally break this ridiculous habit?"

The steward came over the hill on horseback, paused at the gate, and glanced at the balcony, then rode straight toward it.

"Good morning," he said, stopping his horse before Mitya. "Still reading?" He grinned and looked around, then lowered his voice. "Your mama still asleep?"

"I think so," Mitya answered. "Why?"

The steward was silent for a moment, then spoke in a serious tone. "Well, *barchuk*, what can I say? Books are good. Fine things, books. But everything has its time. Why live like a monk? No girls, no ladies for you?"

Mitya lowered his eyes to his book without responding. "Where were you?" he asked, not looking up.

"I was at the post office," said the steward. "And of course there wasn't a single letter. Just a newspaper."

"Why do you say 'of course'?"

"Because they're still writing you a letter—a long, long letter that's not quite done yet," the steward answered with crude derision, insulted by Mitya's refusal to maintain the conversation. "Take it please, here," he said, extending the newspaper to Mitya. Then he spurred his horse and rode off.

"I'll put a bullet in my head," Mitya told himself with conviction, looking at his book and seeing nothing.

XVIII

Mitya knew that nothing more insane than this could be imagined: to shatter your own skull; to stop the beating of a young, strong heart; to eradicate all thought and feeling; to extinguish every sight and sound; to vanish from a world that had only recently revealed itself to him in all its glory and now defied all human language with its beauty; to reject—instantly, inexorably—this life that contained Katya and the approaching summer, sky and clouds, sun, warm wind, wheat in the fields, villages and towns, girls, mama, the estate, Anya, Kostya, poems in old journals, and somewhere in the future—Sevastopol, the Baidar Gates, those lilac-colored mountains with their forests of pine and beech in the blazing heat, the still and heavy air of the blinding white highway, the gardens of Alupka and Livadiya, scorching sand by the brilliant sea, children and bathers tan from the sun—and again Katya, in a white dress beneath a white umbrella, sitting on the pebbled beach, sitting right among the waves that blind you with their glare and make you smile reflexively from a happiness without cause. . . .

He understood all of this. But what was there to do? How else could he break free from this vicious cycle in which the better anything became, the more savage and unbearable he found it. It was this that he had no more strength to endure—this happiness with which the world crushed him, and which lacked some vital element at its core.

When he woke up in the morning, the first thing he saw was the cheerful light of the sun; the first thing he heard was the cheerful ringing of chapel bells in the village, a sound he'd known since childhood, rising there, beyond the garden with its dew and deep shade, its birds and flowers and flashes of sun; even the yellow wallpaper in his room— that wallpaper that had been fading since his childhood—even it was cheerful and close to his heart. But momentarily another thought cut into his soul with ecstasy and horror: Katya! The morning sun was shining with her youth; the freshness of the garden came from her; everything lighthearted and buoyant in the pealing of the bells played with her beauty, her image, and its elegance; the old wallpaper became a stark demand that she share in the rural life that was so much a part of Mitya, that life his father and his grandfathers had lived and died on this estate, inside this house. And so it was that Mitya—young and thin, long-legged, strong, still warm from sleep—threw off his covers and leapt to his feet in just a nightshirt with the collar unbuttoned, yanked open his desk drawer and pulled out his cherished photograph of her, then fell into a stupor, staring at her with greed and wonder. Everything that was alluring and graceful in a woman, all the mysteries, radiance, and charm that a girl could possess now appeared in her small, slightly serpentine head, in the arrangement of her hair, in her inviting yet completely innocent expression. But it was impenetrable, that look. It answered him with an enigmatic, cheerful silence that nothing could disturb—and where was he to find the strength to endure it now, that expression which was so close to him and yet so distant, that look which once revealed to him the ineffable happiness of life and which now, after deceiving him with such a terrifying lack of shame, might be forever alien?

That evening, when he rode back from the post office through Shakhovskoe—that old empty estate with an avenue of black firs—he'd let out an unexpected cry that almost perfectly expressed the exhausted state of mind to which he'd been reduced. Earlier, waiting at the post office window, watching from the saddle as the postmaster vainly dug through a pile of newspapers and letters, he'd heard a train approaching the platform behind him, and that sound, together with the engine's steam, made him think of Kursk Station and Moscow in general: he was stunned by the happiness those memories entailed. Later, as he rode through the village, he was startled to discover something of Katya in the swaying hips of every petite young woman who walked before him. In the fields he met three horses pulling a *tarantass*, and as it shot by, Mitya glimpsed two hats inside the carriage, one of which was worn by a young girl: this nearly made him scream out Katya's name. The white flowers blooming along the roads suddenly merged with her white gloves in his mind; the dark blue mullein took on the color of her veil. . . . The sun was setting when he started down the avenue at Shakhovskoe; the sweet, dry smell of the firs and the luxuriant scent of jasmine produced such a sharp sensation of summer, so strongly brought to mind the antiquated summer-life of that rich and wonderful estate, that when he glanced through the red and gold light of the evening sun that had filled the avenue, and looked toward the house that stood in the deepening shadows beyond those rows of black firs, Mitya suddenly found Katya there, saw her descending from the balcony toward the garden with all her female charm in force, her image as distinct as the jasmine and the house itself. He had long ago lost any recollection of how she actually appeared in life, and now she came to him almost every day in some new and more remarkable transfiguration. Her image that evening possessed such power, exuded such an air of utter triumph, that Mitya found it even more terrifying than that moment at midday when the cuckoo's song had begun to pulse above him.

XIX

He stopped riding to the post office, forced himself through a drastic, desperate act of self-will to end those daily trips. He stopped himself from writing too. After all, everything had been written: frenzied avowals of love that had no equals on this earth; degrading pleas for her affection — or at least her "friendship"; shameless hints that he was ill — that he was writing while he lay in bed — in the hopes this might elicit some small expression of pity, some slight attention; even threatening suggestions that it was time to make life simpler for Katya and his "more fortunate" rivals by ending his existence on earth. No longer writing, no longer seeking a response from her, he used his strength to eradicate all vestiges of expectation, to force himself to wait for nothing (while secretly hoping that a letter would arrive at that moment when he'd somehow reached a state of true indifference or had managed to deceive fate by pretending so convincingly that he no longer cared). He did everything he could to keep Katya from his mind, searched everywhere for some salvation from her terrifying presence. And to that end he started once again to read whatever he happened to pick up, began to go on errands with the steward to the neighboring villages, ceaselessly repeating to himself, "It's all the same — whatever happens, happens."

And so it was that they were returning one day from a nearby farm. The cart horse was cantering hard, as usual. They were sitting high on the upper bench — the steward, who held the horse's reins, was perched in front while Mitya sat behind him. Both men bounced violently in their seats from the blows of potholes in the road, particularly Mitya, who clutched the bench's padding as he rode, studying the back of the steward's red neck and the fields that jumped before his eyes. As they approached the house, the steward let go of the reins; the horse slowed to a walk, and he began to roll a cigarette.

"Well now, *barchuk*," he said, grinning down at his tobacco pouch. "You were angry with me a little while ago. But really, didn't I tell you the truth? A book's a fine thing. Why not read when you want a little rest? But your books won't go away without you. You have to know the proper time for things."

Mitya blushed and surprised himself by answering with contrived simplicity and an awkward smile: "There's nothing else to do, really. . . . And no one's caught my eye. . . ."

"What do you mean?" said the steward. "With so many girls? So many women?"

"Girls just like to play games," Mitya answered, trying to speak in the same tone as the steward. "You can't hope for anything from them."

"They'll do more than play games. You just don't know how to approach them," the steward said admonishingly. "And you can't be stingy. A dry spoon scrapes the mouth."

"I wouldn't be stingy at all if there were some real chance of something," Mitya suddenly answered shamelessly.

"If you can be a little generous, then everything will work out fine," the steward said, lighting a cigarette. He still sounded slightly offended. "You don't even have to give me a whole ruble. It's not a present from you that matters to me. I want to do something nice for you. Every time I look around, I see the *barchuk*'s feeling gloomy. No, I think to myself, this can't be! We can't just leave this as it is! I always take my masters into account. This is already my second year living here with you—and I've never heard a bad word, thank God, not a single bad word from you or your mother. What do the others say, for example, about the owner's cattle? If they're fed, fine, if not, to hell with it. But not me. I'm not like that. The cattle's dearest of all for me. And I say to the boys: Do what you want with me, but the cattle must be fed!"

Mitya had begun to wonder if the steward was drunk, but he suddenly dropped the intimate, slightly injured tone he'd adopted and shot an inquisitive look over his shoulder. "What could be better than Alyonka?" he asked. "She's a saucy girl! Young. Husband's in the mines. . . . Only, you'll have to stick some kind of little present in her hand. . . . Spend, let's say, five rubles on the whole business. . . . One ruble on entertaining her and two in her hand. And something for a little tobacco for me. . . ."

"That won't hold things up," Mitya answered, again against his will. "Only, which Alyonka do you mean?"

"You know—the forestkeeper's Alyonka," said the steward. "Don't you know her? She's married to the forestkeeper's son. It seems to me you saw her in church last Sunday. . . . Right then I thought—she's just what our *barchuk* needs! Only married two years. Keeps herself clean. . . ."

"Well then," Mitya answered, smiling, "set it up."

"I'll do my best," said the steward, picking up the reins. "I'll sound her out the next few days. And in the meantime you should keep awake. Tomorrow she'll be working with the other girls on the garden wall—on the embankment. You come too. . . . That book of yours won't go anywhere at all. . . . Besides, you can always read your fill in Moscow. . . ."

He flicked the reins; the *drozhky* began to jump and shudder again. Mitya held firmly to the seat padding, and, trying to avoid the steward's fat, red neck, looked past the trees of his garden and the willows in the village, looked toward the valleys lying far beyond the houses nestled in the sloping river bed. Something absurd and wildly unexpected was already halfway to completion, and it now produced a chill in him, a cold languor that slowly spread through his body. Already the bell tower that he'd known since childhood seemed to have changed; already there was something different about the way it rose before him now, its cross glinting in the evening sun above the garden trees.

XX

Mitya was so thin that the girls on the estate called him "the Borzoi." He belonged to that breed of people who always seem to hold their large, black eyes wide open, and who can grow only a few curly hairs instead of a full beard or moustache, even as adults. Nevertheless Mitya shaved on the morning after his conversation with the steward and put on a yellow silk shirt, which cast a strange and pleasant light on his exhausted yet somehow animated face.

Sometime after ten he started walking slowly toward the garden, trying to look aimless and bored.

He came out onto the main porch. It faced north, where an overcast sky the color of slate hung above the roof of the carriage house, the cattle barn, and that part of the garden where the bell tower showed behind the trees. Everything was dull. The air was heavy and damp; it smelled from the chimney of the servants' quarters. Mitya went around the house and started down the avenue of lindens, looking at the sky and the tops of the trees. A hot, weak wind rose from the southeast, where a clotted mass of rain clouds hung above the garden. The birds were not singing; even the nightingales were silent. Countless bees sailed noise-lessly across the garden, carrying their nectar home.

The girls were working near the grove of firs again, repairing a low embankment that ran along the garden's edge. They were closing up gaps the cattle had trodden into the wall, using dirt and fresh, pleasant-smelling manure that workers delivered periodically from the livestock barn, driving it across the avenue, which was now thickly strewn with the damp and shining droppings. There were six girls there. Sonka was not among them; despite all, her father had finally committed her to be married, and she was at home, preparing something for the wedding. The group consisted of three weak and feeble-looking girls, the chubby and appealing Anyutka, Glashka—who seemed to grow ever more severe and masculine—and Alyonka. Mitya picked her out immediately among the trees and understood exactly who she was, though he'd never seen her before. And some essential similarity between her and Katya—some likeness that perhaps he alone could see—struck him with such force that he was stunned, like the victim of a lightning bolt. He stopped in his tracks, went dumb, then walked decisively toward her, never lowering his eyes.

She too was small and full of life. Despite the grimy work she'd come to do, she was dressed in a good cotton blouse (white, with red polka dots), and a matching skirt, a black patent-leather belt, a pink silk headscarf, and red wool tights. Some feature of Katya seemed particularly pronounced in the black felt boots she wore (or, perhaps it was her small, delicate feet), for they combined something childlike with the feminine. Her head was small, and both the setting and the shine of her dark eyes were almost identical to Katya's. When Mitya arrived, she alone was not working. As if sensing her somewhat privileged position among the others, she stood on the broad embankment with one foot resting on her pitchfork and talked with the steward, who was reclining under an apple tree on his coat with its tattered lining, smoking and leaning back on one arm. As Mitya approached them, the steward deferentially moved onto the grass in order to make room for him on the coat.

"Please, sit down, Mitry Palych," he said in a polite and friendly voice. "Have a cigarette."

Mitya glanced furtively at Alyonka and noticed the pleasant light that her pink headscarf cast on her face. Then he sat down, lowered his eyes, and lit a cigarette (he'd quit several times during the winter and summer, and now found himself starting once again). Alyonka offered him no greeting—it was as if she hadn't noticed his arrival. The steward continued telling her something that Mitya didn't fully understand, not knowing where the conversation had begun. Alyonka laughed, but she did so in a way that made her laughter seem cut off, utterly divorced from both her mind and heart. The steward's tone was insultingly familiar, and he dropped obscene little innuendos into almost every phrase he spoke. She answered him with easy, sharp derision, mocking his designs on some young woman and showing him to be both a crass and stupid lecher and a gutless coward frightened by his wife.

"Ah well, I can't yelp as loud as you," the steward said, interrupting their exchange as if he'd grown tired of the pointless argument. "You'd do better to come sit here with us. The *barin* wants a word with you."

Alyonka looked aside, tucked a few curls of her dark hair back inside her headscarf, and didn't move.

"Come here, I said, you fool!" the steward insisted.

Alyonka paused to think for another moment, then gracefully jumped down from the embankment and ran toward Mitya. A few steps from where he lay on the steward's coat, she squatted on her heels and looked into his dark, wide-open eyes with playful curiosity.

"Is it true you live without girls, *barchuk*?" she asked. "Like a deacon or something?"

"How would you know if he lives without them?" asked the steward.

"I just know. I heard about it," Alyonka answered. "But the *barchuk's* not allowed. . . . He has someone in Moscow," she said, suddenly directing a flirtatious glance at Mitya.

"There's no one suitable for the gentleman here, so he does without," the steward answered. "You don't know a thing about their ways."

"What do you mean not suitable? With so many girls?" Alyonka answered laughing. "There's Anyutka—what could be better? Anyutka, come here. We need to talk!" she shouted, her voice ringing out.

Anyutka's back was wide and soft, and her arms were short. She turned—her face was appealing, her smile kind and pleasant—and shouted something back in a melodic voice, then set to work with even greater energy.

"They say for you to come here," Alyonka repeated, even more resoundingly.

"You don't need me there. I don't know the least about those things," Anyutka sang out joyfully.

"We don't want Anyutka. We need someone cleaner. With more breeding," the steward said in a cultivated tone of voice. "We know who we need." He looked deliberately at Alyonka, who grew flustered, lightly blushed.

"No, no, no," she answered, concealing her embarrassment with a smile. "You won't find better than Anyutka. And if you don't like her, there's Nastka. She keeps clean too. She used to live in town. . . ."

"Enough, already. Close your mouth," said the steward with sudden sharpness. "Stop nattering and go back to work. Enough already. The mistress yells at me as it is, says you all just misbehave with me."

Again with surprising lightness, Alyonka jumped to her feet and picked up her pitchfork. But at that moment a worker who'd just emptied the last wagonload of manure shouted "Lunch," flicked his reins, and went rattling down the avenue in his empty cart.

"Lunch, time for lunch," the girls called out in varied tones as they dropped their shovels and pitchforks, leapt over the embankment or skipped down from its top, their bare legs and different-colored tights flashing as they hurried toward the edge of the fir grove where their bundles lay.

The steward shot a sidelong look at Mitya and winked, as if to say, "We're on our way."

"Well, if it's time for lunch, it's time for lunch," he said in an authoritative voice as he sat up.

The girls stood out brightly against the dark backdrop of the fir grove as they spread out on the grass in random groups. They untied their bundles and took out loaves of unleavened bread, set them carefully on the hems of their skirts, between their outstretched legs—and then began to chew, washing down their bread with milk or *kvass* they swigged from bottles while talking raucously, bursting into laughter with every word and glancing constantly at Mitya with curious, inviting eyes. Alyonka leaned toward Anyutka and whispered something in her ear. Unable to hold back a charming smile, Anyutka firmly pushed her away (Alyonka toppled over with her head bent toward her knees, choking on her laughter) and began to shout with mock indignation, her pleasant voice carrying through the grove.

"You fool! What's so funny? Why do you keep giggling?"

"Let's leave this sinful scene, Mitry Palych," said the steward. "The devil's in them all!"

XXI

The next day was Sunday, so no one worked in the garden.

A heavy rain had fallen the night before, streaming loudly over the roof while again and again the garden filled with a pale light that spread far into its depths and made it look like something from a story told to a child. By morning, however, the weather had cleared, and once again everything seemed simple and benign when Mitya woke to the cheerful, sun-filled pealing of the church bells in the tower.

He washed and dressed unhurriedly, drank a cup of tea, then left for church. "Your mother already left. . . . Anyone would think that you're a Tatar," Parasha said with gentle chiding.

There were two ways to reach the church. One could walk along the pasture, pass through the estate's main gate, and then turn right; or, alternatively, one could follow the main avenue away from the house, take the road between the garden and the threshing barn, and then turn left. Mitya set off through the garden.

Summer was in full force. He walked directly in the sun, which fell hard between the trees of the avenue and shone with a crisp light on the fields and the threshing barn. The pealing of the church bells streamed gently, peacefully into that brilliant light, coalesced with all the details of that morning in the country—with the simple fact that Mitya had just washed and combed his glistening black hair, had just put on his student's hat—and suddenly everything seemed so good that Mitya, having passed another sleepless night in the grip of his wildly ranging and erratic thoughts, was suddenly seized by hope, momentarily believed that his torture might be ended, that he might one day be released, saved from further agony. The bells continued ringing, calling playfully, and the threshing barn gleamed hotly in the sun before him. A woodpecker paused on one of the lindens, raised its crested head, then scampered up the knotted bark until it reached the tree's pale green, sunny top. Black and red bumblebees climbed into the flowers in the glades, inserting their velvet bodies with solicitude into the sun-shot blooms while everywhere in the garden birds poured out their sweet, untroubled songs. . . . It was all as it had been many, many times before in childhood, in adolescence. And those carefree, captivating years returned to him with such lucidity that he was suddenly convinced that God would pity him, that even without Katya he might find a way to live his life on earth.

"I really should go to see the Meshcherskys," he thought to himself.

But then he raised his eyes and saw Alyonka passing by the gate some twenty feet before him. Her hair was again covered by a headscarf of pink silk. She wore a light blue, stylish dress with frill, and new half-boots, their heels lined with steel strips. Her haunches swayed seductively as she hurried past, not seeing Mitya, who bolted from the avenue and hid behind a tree. He waited until she'd passed from sight, then started back, hurrying toward the house while his heart pounded. Suddenly he understood that he had left for church with a hidden motive: to see Alyonka there. And it was wrong to look for her in church. Wrong.

XXII

During lunch a courier from the station brought a telegram: Anya and Kostya sent word that they'd arrive tomorrow evening. Mitya was utterly indifferent to this news.

After lunch he went out to the balcony, lay on his back on a wicker couch, closed his eyes. He could feel the hot sun that reached the balcony's edge, could hear the summer drone of flies. His heart seemed to tremble. His head was filled with questions that he couldn't answer. How will these plans with Alyonka be made? When will it be settled once and for all? Why didn't the steward ask her yesterday if she agrees—and if she does, when and where? And together with these thoughts, another line of questions troubled him: Should he make another trip to the post office despite his resolution to end those excursions? Why not go there one last time? Would he wind up making a fresh mockery of his pride for no real reason? Would he just be torturing himself once more with pathetic hopes? But how could the trip really deepen his misery? After all, it's really just a reason to get out of the house. Isn't it completely obvious that everything in Moscow's finished for him now? What's he supposed to do?

"*Barchuk*," a quiet voice sounded sharply near the balcony. "*Barchuk*, are you asleep?"

He opened his eyes: the steward was standing in front of him, festively dressed in a new cotton shirt and a new cap. He looked self-satisfied, slightly sleepy, and half drunk.

"*Barchuk*, let's go quickly to the forest," he whispered. "I told your mother that I need to see Trifon to talk about bees. Let's go before she wakes up from her nap, rethinks it all, says no. We'll get a little something for Trifon along the way. He'll have a bit to drink, get a little tipsy, and you'll chat with him while I find a way to slip Alyonka a few little words. Let's go quickly, now. I'm already harnessed. . . ."

Mitya jumped up and ran through the servants' hall, grabbed his cap, and headed quickly to the carriage house, where a spirited young stallion was harnessed to a *drozhky*.

XXIII

The stallion went from standing still to flying like the wind: they barreled through the gate at a full gallop, stopped at a shop across from the church to buy a bottle of vodka and a pound of *salo*, then set off flying once again.

As they drove out of the village, a hut flashed by where Anyutka stood, dressed up and looking lost, as if she couldn't think of anywhere to go. The steward shouted something crude and unpleasant that he intended as a joke, then lashed the horse's rump, snapping his reins with senseless, cruel, and drunken showmanship. The stallion ran even harder.

Mitya held on with all his strength as he bounced wildly in his seat. The sun's warmth felt pleasant on the back of his head; a hot wind blew into his face from the fields. It smelled of the flowering rye, axle grease, dust from the road. Small currents of wind rippled through the rye, which flashed its grey and silver lining like some miraculous fur while countless larks shot up from its waves, sailed slantwise in the breeze and sang, then dove back down. The forest was a soft dark blue in the distance.

Fifteen minutes later they were already in those woods, their wheels knocking over roots and stumps as they sailed down the shady road, made cheerful now by brilliant spots of sunlight and countless flowers in the tall grass on the sidings. Still wearing her blue dress and short boots, Alyonka sat embroidering in a little grove of young oaks, her legs stretched straight and evenly before her. The steward brandished his whip at her as they flew by, then deftly reined in his horse at the front door. Mitya was astounded by the fresh, bitter scent of the forest and the young oaks—and deafened by the dogs that quickly surrounded the *drozhky*, filled the woods with their barking. They stood there yelping furiously in almost every tone imaginable, but their shaggy faces were friendly, and their tails were wagging.

Mitya and the steward climbed down from the *drozhky* and tied the stallion to a withered tree, evidently struck by lightning, that stood before the windows. Then they passed through a small, dark anteroom and entered the hut.

It was clean and comfortable inside, crowded and hot from the sun, which slanted through the forest and shone in both windows, and from the stove, which had been lit that morning to bake bread. Alyonka's mother-in-law, a clean and pleasant-looking woman named Fedosya, was sitting at the table, her back to one of the small windows, which was filled with sunlight and gnats. Seeing the *barchuk*, she stood and made a low bow. Mitya and the steward greeted her, sat down, and began to smoke.

"And where is Trifon?" asked the steward.

"He's resting in the shed," Fedosya said. "I'll go and call him."

"Things are moving now!" the steward whispered, winking with both eyes the moment she left.

But Mitya saw no movement at all. So far the visit had produced nothing but excruciating awkwardness, for it seemed Fedosya understood precisely why they'd come. For the third straight day a horrifying thought flitted through his mind: *What am I doing? I'm going insane!* He felt as if he were a sleepwalker who'd fallen under the control of some external force that now led him with increasing speed toward a terrible but irresistible abyss. All the same, he still tried to appear forthright and relaxed as he sat and smoked, looked around the hut. He was particularly ashamed to think that Trifon would soon come into the room: he was said to be both smart and ill-tempered, a calculating *mouzhik* who'd see the reasons for this visit right away, understand it still more clearly than Fedosya. But another thought accompanied this one: Where does she sleep? On that plank bed? Or in the shed? The shed, of course, he thought. The windows have no frames, no glass. All night the drowsy whispering of the forest. And she lies there, sleeping. . . .

XXIV

Trifon made a low bow to Mitya as he entered the room but did not speak or look him in the eye. He sat down on a bench before the table and began to talk with the steward. His tone was dry, unwelcoming: What had happened? Why had they come? The steward hurriedly explained that the mistress had sent him to ask that Trifon come to examine their beehives. The estate's beekeeper, he said, was a deaf old fool, whereas Trifon's knowledge and understanding of bees was unequalled in the entire region. Here he quickly pulled the bottle of vodka from one pocket of his pants, the pound of *salo*—its wrapping of grey paper already soaked through with grease—from the other. Trifon looked askance at him with cold derision but rose nevertheless to get a teacup from the shelf. The steward poured for Mitya first, then Trifon, followed by Fedosya—who drained her cupful slowly, as if savoring the taste—and finally himself. As soon as he had drunk, he started pouring seconds, chewing on a piece of bread, his nostrils flaring.

Trifon showed signs of being drunk quite quickly, but he remained unfriendly, speaking with thinly veiled derision to the steward, who had fallen into a complete stupor after his second drink. Although their conversation appeared reasonably amicable on the surface, both men's eyes displayed hostility and distrust. Fedosya sat without speaking, looking at them politely but obviously not happy they were there. Alyonka did not appear. Having given up all hope that she might come into the house, and seeing clearly now that this had been an absurd plan—how would the steward "slip her a few little words" if she wasn't even there?—Mitya rose and said sternly that it was time to go.

"In a minute. We've got a little time," the steward replied sullenly. "I need to say a little word or two to you in private."

"You can tell me on the way home," Mitya said, his voice restrained, but even sterner. "We're going."

But the steward slapped his palm on the table. "I told you—I can't say this on the way home. Come outside with me for a minute," he said with besotted stealth. He rose heavily from the table and threw open the door to the little front room. Mitya followed him.

"Well, what is it?"

"Quiet," the steward whispered conspiratorially, swaying as he closed the door behind him.

"Be quiet about what?"

"Be quiet."

"I can't understand you."

"Be quiet. She's ours. On my word!"

Mitya pushed past him and went outside. He paused on the front step, not knowing what to do. Wait a little longer? Drive home alone? Walk?

Ten feet from him stood the thick green forest, already filled with an evening shade that made it seem cleaner, fresher, even lovelier than before. The sun had already slipped behind the tops of the trees; its unclouded light fell through the branches in beams of reddish gold. Suddenly a female voice rang out in the forest's depths, echoing among the trees beyond the ravine. It carried with it all the alluring charm that a voice acquires only in a forest when the sun is setting.

"Aaa-ooo"—the voice produced another drawn-out call, its owner evidently playing with the forest echo. "Aaa-ooo."

Mitya bolted from the step, ran through the tall grass and the flowers into the forest, which sloped toward a rocky ravine. Alyonka stood at its bottom, chewing on a cowslip stem. She looked up with a startled expression as Mitya ran to the ravine's edge and stopped.

"What are you doing here?" he asked quietly.

"Looking for Maruska and our cow," she answered, lowering her voice as well. "What's it to you?"

"Well, will you come or not?"

"Why should I just for free?" she said.

"Who said it was for free?" asked Mitya, almost whispering. "Don't worry about that."

"When?" Alyonka asked.

"Tomorrow. . . . Can you come tomorrow?"

Alyonka paused to think. "I'm going to my mother's to shear her sheep," she said, looking carefully around the forest on the slope behind Mitya. "I'll come after that. In the evening, when it gets dark. But where? The threshing barn's no good—someone might come in. We could go to the hunter's hut, if you want. The one in your garden, in the dip. Only don't play games with me. . . . I'm not doing it for free. This isn't Moscow, after all," she said, glancing up at him with laughter in her eyes, "I hear women pay to get it there. . . ."

XXV

The trip home was disgraceful.

Trifon had not remained in debt for long. He opened a second bottle, and the steward drank himself into such a state that when they finally went to leave, he fell against the *drozhky* and the startled horse almost ran away without them. But Mitya said nothing, watched the steward indifferently, waited patiently for him to climb into his seat. Once again the steward drove with senseless fury. Mitya remained silent, holding firmly to the seat, looking at the evening sky, at the fields that jumped before him. The larks were finishing their short songs above the rye as the dusk deepened in the west; to the east it had already taken on the dark blue shade of night, flickering occasionally with those peaceful sheets of summer lightning that presage nothing but fair weather. Mitya understood all the beauty of the evening that surrounded him, but it was foreign now, completely alien. His mind and soul were occupied by one idea: tomorrow night!

At home he was greeted by the news that Anya and Kostya would arrive tomorrow on the evening train. He was horrified: they'll arrive and go running to the garden, blunder into the hunter's hut in the hollow! But then he remembered that they would not arrive from the station before ten that night, and then they would eat, have tea. . . .

"Are you going to meet them at the station?" Olga Petrovna asked.

He could feel himself blanching. "No, I don't think so. I don't really feel like it for some reason. And there's no room for me."

"Well, you could go on horseback."

"Yes, of course. I don't know . . . I mean, what for, really?. . . I don't feel like it right now."

Olga Petrovna stared at him. "Are you all right?"

"Absolutely," Mitya answered almost rudely. "I just need to sleep."

Without another word he went into his room, lay down on the couch in the dark, and fell asleep without undressing.

During the night he heard the slow, muted strains of distant music and saw himself suspended over a huge, dimly lit abyss. It grew steadily brighter, more and more brilliant with gold, more and more crowded with people. Its bottom continued to recede from view until it seemed there was no end to the abyss, and the music grew completely clear, its every note distinct: with sorrow and a tenderness too delicate for words, the melody and singing came to him: "There was a king of Thule. . . ." He quavered with emotion, rolled over, fell back to sleep.

XXVI

The day seemed endless.

Lifeless as a mannequin, Mitya left his room for tea and lunch, then lay back down, picked up a book by Pisemsky that had been lying on his desk for weeks, and read without comprehending a single word. Sometimes he just stared at length at the ceiling, listening to the even, satinlike sounds of the garden filled with sun beyond his window. . . . He rose once and went to the library to change his book, but with its peaceful views—one window opening on his cherished maple, the others taking in the brilliant western sky—that room, which once felt charmingly old-fashioned, now seemed so much a part of Katya, and reminded him so sharply of those spring days (now as distant as the Earth's creation) when he would sit among its shelves and read old journals filled with poetry, that he abruptly turned away. To hell with it, he thought with irritation. To hell with love's poetic little tragedies!

With indignation he recalled his sincere intentions to shoot himself if no letter came from Katya within a week, then again took up his book by Pisemsky. But he understood no more than he had before, and from time to time a trembling began in the pit of his stomach, then spread through his entire body as he stared at the book and thought about Alyonka. The closer evening came, the more frequently those fits of shuddering passed through him. Footsteps, voices in the house, people talking in the courtyard, where a *tarantass* had already been harnessed for the trip to the station—these sounds came to him the way they do when you are sick in bed and ordinary life continues all around you— utterly indifferent to your condition and therefore alien, almost hostile. At last Parasha shouted somewhere, "The horses are ready, Madame!"— and he heard the dry prattling of little harness bells, then the tread of hooves, the rustling of the *tarantass* as it rolled toward the front porch. "For God's sake, when will it end!" Mitya muttered to himself with impatience. But he didn't move, just listened anxiously as Olga Petrovna called out final instructions in the servants' hall and the harness bells began to prattle once again. As the *tarantass* rolled downhill, their noise blended with the larger racket of the carriage wheels, then died away entirely. . . .

Mitya stood up quickly and went into the hall, which was empty and full of light from the clear, yellowish dusk. The entire house was empty; something in that emptiness felt strange and sinister. With the odd sensation that he was leaving for a long time, Mitya looked down the line of silent rooms adjoining one another—the den, the drawing room, and the library, where through one window he could see the dark blue light of the evening sky and the maple's green, magnificent top, above which hung the pink star of Antares. Then he glanced into the servants' hall to make sure Parasha wasn't there. Convinced that it too was empty, he snatched his hat from the coatrack, ran back into his room, and climbed out the window, stretching his long legs down to the flower bed. Once down, he froze for a moment, then ran hunched over through the garden and plunged into an overgrown, silent avenue, thickly hedged by lilac and acacia.

XXVII

Since there was no dew, the garden's scents could not have been especially strong. But even though he acted that evening like a man who'd lost all conscious contact with the world around him, Mitya couldn't think of any time in his life—other than perhaps his childhood—when he'd encountered such diverse and heady smells as he did now. Everything was pungent: the bushes of acacia, the leaves of lilac and black currant, the wormwood and the burdock, the flowers and the dirt and the grass. . . .

He took several quick steps with a new and terrifying thought: What if she doesn't come? Suddenly it seemed that his entire life depended on her meeting him. Among the scent of blooming shrubs and flowers, he caught the smell of smoke from the village and stopped again, looking back. A beetle hummed and slowly drifted through the air beside him; the twilight and the evening's peaceful calm seemed to spread out from its tiny wings as it rose. The sky was still light, its western half firmly occupied by the level, slow-burning rays of the first summer sunset. High above the house, visible in snatches through the trees, a sliver of the nascent moon hung like the severe, sharp blade of a scythe in the sky's blue, transparent void. Mitya glanced at it, quickly crossed himself with shallow strokes below the center of his chest, and stepped into the bushes of acacia: the avenue he'd started following would lead him down into the hollow, but he had to veer off to the left now to reach the hunter's hut. As soon as he was out of the acacia, Mitya began to run through the trees, pushing past or crouching to avoid their splayed, low branches. He reached the agreed-upon meeting place in no more than a minute.

He was afraid when he stepped into the hut, its darkness smelling heavily of dry and musty straw. He peered into the gloom and almost joyfully assured himself that he was still alone. But the fateful moment was drawing near; he stayed beside the hut, straining for a sign that someone was approaching, all his senses focused on the woods. An intense physical excitement had left him for no more than a few minutes during the entire day. Now it seemed to reach its apex. But just as it had been all day, this sensation remained oddly disconnected, isolated: it absorbed his body but left his soul unmoved. Still, the beating of his heart was terrible, and the silence that surrounded him was so astonishingly complete that he heard nothing but that violent pounding in his chest. Colorless moths hovered soundlessly among the branches of the apple trees, fluttering their soft, tireless wings among the intricate and varied patterns of the grey foliage silhouetted against the evening sky. And because of them, the silence seemed to deepen, as if those moths were practicing some kind of magic, as if they'd cast a spell. Startled by the sound of something crackling behind him, Mitya turned abruptly and looked through the trees toward the garden wall: something black seemed to be rolling toward him beneath the branches. Before he'd had a chance to understand what it was, the black shape approached him, rose up in a sweeping motion, and revealed itself to be Alyonka. She'd covered her head with her skirt, and now threw off its short, black hem of homemade wool, revealing her face, a bright and frightened smile. She was barefoot, wearing just a simple, unbleached blouse she'd tucked into the skirt, taut across her girlish breasts. The wide cut of its collar revealed her neck and part of her shoulders; the sleeves were rolled up past her elbows, exposing her full arms. Everything about her—from her small head and the yellow silk kerchief that covered it to her petite bare feet, feminine and childlike—everything was so good, so graceful and alluring that Mitya gasped to himself. She'd always worn somewhat stylish clothes whenever he encountered her before; the simple charm of her appearance now was startling.

"Don't take all night, okay?" she said in a cheerful, furtive whisper, and plunged into the musty twilight of the hut.

There she stopped, and Mitya, clenching his teeth to stop their chattering inside his head, quickly stuck his hand into his pocket—his legs were so tense they felt like something made of iron—then thrust a crumpled five-ruble note into her palm. She quickly hid it in her blouse and sat down on the ground. Mitya sat beside her and put his arms around her neck, not knowing what to do. Should he kiss her now, or not? The smell of her kerchief and her hair, the slight scent of onions mixed with smoke and all the other smells of a peasant hut that seemed to come from her—it was enough to make him giddy with desire. And

Mitya felt this, recorded it with all his senses. But at the same time nothing had changed: he felt a physical desire of terrifying potency, but it bore no link to the longings of the soul, to bliss or ecstasy; it couldn't bring that joyful lassitude that washes over one's entire being. She leaned back, stretched out on the ground. He lay down as well, pressed against her side, stretched his hand toward her. She caught it, pulled it down with an awkward, nervous laugh.

"None of that's allowed," she said, her voice half serious, half joking.

She drew his hand away and held it firmly in her small grip, aimed her stare at the triangular window of the hut, the branches of the apple trees outside, the darkening blue of the sky beyond those limbs, and the fixed, red point of Antares, which still hung there, alone. What did those eyes express? What was he supposed to do? Kiss her neck, her lips?

"Don't take all night, okay?" she said abruptly, reaching for her short black skirt. . . .

When they rose—when Mitya rose completely stunned by the depth of his disillusionment—she straightened her hair and retied her kerchief, speaking in an animated whisper, as if she'd now become an intimate, as if she were his lover.

"They say you went to Subbotino. The priest there's supposed to be selling pigs for cheap," she said. "Did you hear about that?"

XXVIII

The rain began on Wednesday and continued through the week without a pause; on Saturday it grew into a torrent, pouring from the cheerless sky in heavy gusts.

And all day Mitya walked in the garden. All day he wept so terribly that he himself was sometimes startled by the violence and abundance of his tears.

Parasha looked for him, shouted his name in the avenue of lindens and the courtyard; she called him to lunch and to tea—he didn't answer.

It was cold. The rain and damp bore into everything. Black clouds clotted the sky: against their dark mass the greenery of the garden stood out brightly, looked especially full and fresh. The wind would sometimes race through the trees and bring down another shower, a stream of drops shaken from the leaves. But Mitya saw nothing, took no account of anything around him. His once white hat was so completely sopped that it had turned dark grey and lost its shape; his student's coat was black; his boots were spattered with mud up to his knees. It was terrible to see him—his clothing drenched, soaked through; his face devoid of blood and color; his half-mad eyes worn out and swollen from his weeping.

He smoked one cigarette after another as he strode through the mud in the avenue or at random moments set off where there was no path, wading through the high, wet grass among the pear and apple trees, stumbling among their crooked, gnarled branches, flecked with grey-green lichens sodden from the rain. He sat on benches that were black and swollen, walked into the hollow in the garden, went into the hunter's hut, lay down in the wet straw precisely where he'd lain not long ago with Alyonka. His big hands had turned blue from the cold and the raw damp; his lips were purpling; the deathly pallor of his face and sunken cheeks now took on a violet tinge. Lying on his back with one foot resting on the other and his hands behind his head, Mitya stared uncomprehendingly at the blackened thatch of the roof, which dripped large beads of water the color of rust. Then his eyebrows began to twitch, his jaw clamped shut. He leapt convulsively to his feet and pulled a letter from his pocket—a letter he'd received late last evening, delivered by a land surveyor who'd come to the estate for several days on business. Mitya had already read the smudged and tattered letter a hundred times, but now he greedily consumed it once again:

Dear Mitya,
Don't think ill of me! Forget everything, forget all of it! I am rotten, fallen, foul.
I'm not worthy of you in the least. But I madly love my art. And now I've decided.
The die is cast: I'm leaving—you know with whom. . . . You're so sensitive and smart, I know you'll understand me. I beg you not to torture yourself, or me. You mustn't write—it's useless. . . .

When he reached that sentence, Mitya balled the letter up and buried his face in the wet straw, violently clenching his teeth and choking on sobs, for there she had addressed him inadvertently with the informal form of "you" in Russian—ty. And with all the intimacy it invoked, that accidental ty was more than he could bear: it reminded him of everything he'd lost and at the same time established all their closeness once again. Reading it, a lacerating tenderness welled up inside his heart. It was beyond all human strength! And together with that *ty* came a strict assertion that even writing was no use. But yes—he knew that now. Useless! Absolutely useless! And everything was finished, finished for eternity!

The intensity of the crashing rain seemed to grow tenfold toward evening, and this, combined with unexpected claps of thunder, finally drove him home. Soaked from head to foot, his teeth chattering wildly from the bitter chill and the violent shuddering of his entire body, Mitya peered out from the trees. Convinced that he would not be seen, he ran up to the window of his room, raised it, and climbed inside. He locked the door and threw himself on the bed.

It began to grow dark quickly. He heard the rain everywhere—on the roof, around the house, in the garden. But it made two distinct and separate sets of sounds. One came from the garden, the other from the house, where water splashed and murmured ceaselessly as it streamed from gutters into puddles. For Mitya, who had momentarily gone blank and rigid, this phenomenon produced an inexplicable alarm and virtual narcosis: while a sudden heat raged inside his head, blazed within his mouth and nostrils as he breathed, those dual sounds of the falling rain brought forth some other world, some other moment just before the evening's onset in some other house—one filled with terrible presentiments.

He knew he was in his room, where it was almost dark from the rain and the approaching night; he knew he could hear the voices of his mother, Anya, Kostya, and the land surveyor as they had tea nearby in the hall. But at the same time he was moving through some unfamiliar house, following a young nursemaid as she walked away from him. A mysterious and ever-growing fear held him in its grip, but it was mixed with desire, a premonition that someone would soon draw close to someone else, that they would share an intimacy that was unnatural and repulsive—an intimacy in which he too was bound, somehow, to participate. These feelings were triggered in him by a child with a large white face whom the nursemaid carried and rocked in her arms, leaning back to support the extra weight as she walked. Believing that she might be Alyonka, Mitya hurried to pass the nursemaid in order to see her face, but suddenly he found himself in a gloomy classroom with chalk smeared on the windows. She who stood in the front of the room before a chest of drawers and a mirror could not see him—he had suddenly become invisible. She wore a yellow silk slip that clung tightly to her rounded hips, high-heeled shoes, and fine, black fishnet stockings that revealed her flesh: She was sweetly bashful and ashamed; she knew what was about to happen. She had already had time to hide the baby in one of the dresser drawers. She tossed her braid over one shoulder and began to redo it, hurrying as she glanced sidelong at the door or looked directly in the mirror, where her small, slightly powdered face, her bare shoulders, her milky blue breasts and pink nipples were reflected.

The door flew open, and a gentleman dressed in a tuxedo looked around the room with horrifying joviality. He had short, black, curly hair and a clean-shaven face completely drained of color. Once inside the room, he took out a thin, gold cigarette case and casually began to smoke. She finished with her braid and looked at him timidly, evidently understanding his intentions, then swung her braid behind her shoulder, raised her bare arms. . . . He held her condescendingly around the waist as she clung to his neck, revealing her dark underarms. She pressed herself to him. She nestled her face against his chest.

XXIX

Mitya came to himself in a sweat with the shockingly clear realization that he was destroyed, that nothing in the underworld or in the grave could be as hopeless, as monstrously gloomy as the world that now surrounded him. It was dark in his room; the rain tapped and splashed outside his window, and that sound, those glinting drops (even the sound alone) were more than his body, trembling with fever, could endure. But even more horrific and unbearable was that perversion, that hideously unnatural act of human copulation, which it seemed he'd shared with that clean-shaven gentleman. He could hear voices, laughter in the hall. And those sounds also seemed to him both terrible and perverse, for they were full of life's vulgarity; they were absolutely alien to him, merciless, indifferent.

"Katya," he said, sitting up, swinging his legs to the floor. "Katya, what is happening?" he said out loud, absolutely certain that she could hear him, that she was there but didn't speak, didn't call to him because she too was completely despondent, grasping the utter, irrevocable horror of everything she'd done. "Ah, it's all the same, Katya," he whispered bitterly, tenderly—wanting to say that he'd forgive her for everything she'd done if she would only once more rush toward him so that they could save themselves, save their love in this beautiful spring world, which had so recently resembled paradise. But as soon as he had whispered, "Ah, it's all the same, Katya," he understood that no, it wasn't all the same: there was no salvation, no going back to that marvelous vision once granted him in Shakhovskoe, on a balcony overgrown with jasmine. There was no return, and there never could be. Realizing this, he began quietly to weep from the tearing pain inside his chest.

And that pain grew so strong, so unbearable, that he did not consider what would come of it, did not contemplate his actions, but rather, wished for just one thing—to save himself for a moment from that agony, not to fall back into the awful world where he had spent the day, where he had plunged into the most horrific and repulsive of all dreams possible on earth—as he groped for the nightstand drawer and pulled it open, as he felt the cold and heavy mass of the revolver and deeply, gladly sighed, then opened his mouth and pulled the trigger hard, pulled it with delight.

[*Maritime Alps, 1924*]

Calf's Head

A FRECKLED five-year-old boy in a sailor's suit stands speechless at a butcher's stall, as if entranced. Father had to go to work at the post office, so mother took him with her to the market.

"We'll have calf's head with parsley today," she'd said to him, and he'd imagined something small and delicate sprinkled with bright green leaves.

So here he stands and looks, surrounded on all sides by something huge and red that hangs from rusty hooks to the floor, little stumps protruding from the joints where legs have been lopped off, and headless necks stretching to the ceiling. Among opalescent layers of fat, an empty stomach yawns at the front of each slab, and thin strips of rich meat shine with a pellucid film at the hip and shoulder bones. But the transfixed child stares only at the head, which happens to be lying on the marble counter directly in front of him. Mother is looking at the head as well, and arguing heatedly with the stall's owner. He too is huge and fleshy. His coarse white apron displays a sickening, rust-colored stain above his belly. A heavy, greasy scabbard dangles from his wide and low-slung belt. Mother's arguing about the head—just it, and nothing else.

The owner shouts something angrily and pokes it with his soft finger. They are arguing about the head, but it lies motionless, indifferent. Its flat, bullish forehead is smooth and relaxed, the turbid blue eyes are half closed, the thick lashes look heavy with sleep. The nostrils, however, are distended, and the lips are so swollen that the head has a haughty, displeased expression. All of it's laid bare—the color of flesh going grey, resilient as rubber.

Then the butcher splits it down the middle with a terrifying blow from his axe and shoves one-half toward mother—one eye, one ear, one nostril flared on cotton-fiber paper.

[1930]

Sunstroke

T HEY CAME from the hot, brightly lit dining room onto the ship's deck after dinner and stood by the handrail. She closed her eyes, pressed the back of her hand against her cheek, and laughed. Her laughter was simple and pleasant, as was everything about this small, attractive woman.

"I think I'm drunk," she said. "Where did you come from? Three hours ago I didn't even know you existed. I don't even know where you got on this boat. Samara? Well, I guess it doesn't matter. . . . Is my head spinning, or are we turning?"

Darkness and distant lights hung before them. But now the lights fell away; a strong, soft breeze rose from the darkness and blew into their faces as the steamer veered to one side—describing an expansive, slightly grandiose arc, it seemed to flaunt the Volga's breadth—and then approached a small pier.

The lieutenant brought her hand to his lips: small and tan, it smelled of the sun. He imagined that all the skin beneath her gingham dress was equally as strong and tan, for she had said that she was coming from Anapa, where she'd spent a solid month lying under the hot southern sun on the sand by the sea—and this thought made his heart go still with fear and joy.

"Let's get off," he mumbled.

"Where?" she asked, surprised.

"On that pier."

"Why?"

He didn't answer. She laid the back of her hand against her warm cheek again.

"Insanity. . . ."

"Let's get off," the lieutenant repeated stupidly. "I'm begging you."

"Oh, all right. As you wish . . . ," she said, turning away.

They almost fell over each other when the steamer bumped with a soft thud against the dimly lit pier. A mooring line flew over their heads; the water seemed to boil as the engines reversed and pushed the ship back toward the dock, and then the gangplanks dropped with a bang— the lieutenant rushed to get their bags.

A moment later they emerged from a drowsy little office on the dock, crossed a stretch of sand in which a carriage wheel would sink up to the center of its spokes, and climbed into a dusty cab without exchanging words. Soft with dust and lit by only a few crooked lamps, the road seemed endless as they traveled its gradual slope up the mountainside. But at last they reached the top and began to rattle down a paved carriageway past little offices, the local watchtower, a public square. It was warm, and the air was heavy with all the smells of a provincial town on a summer night. The driver stopped before the lighted entrance to an inn, the open doors of which displayed a worn, steep wooden staircase. An old, unshaven porter with big, wide feet, a pink shirt, and a frock coat sullenly took their bags and lugged them up the steps. They entered a large room that was terribly stuffy and still sweltering from the day's sun; white curtains were closed over the windows and two unused candles stood on the mantelpiece. As soon as the porter left and shut the door, the lieutenant rushed to her with such ardent desire, and they both gasped with such ecstasy as they kissed, that each would remember that moment for many years to come: they had never experienced anything similar in all their separate lives.

The next morning was cheerful, sunny, and hot, and at ten o'clock—while church bells rang, while people shopped at a market near the inn, while the warm air was filled with the smell of hay and tar and all the other complex, pungent odors of a provincial Russian town—

that small, anonymous woman, who refused to say her name and jokingly referred to herself as "the beautiful stranger," went away. They had slept very little, but after washing and dressing for five minutes, she looked as fresh as a seventeen-year-old girl when she came out from behind the screen near the bed. Was she awkward or ashamed? Not very, no. Instead she was as happy and as open as she'd been the day before, and her mind was clear.

"No, no, darling," she'd said in answer to his request that they continue traveling together. "You should stay here and wait for the next boat. If we go together, everything will be ruined. It would be very unpleasant for me. I give you my honest word that I'm nothing like the person you might imagine me to be. Nothing even remotely similar to this has ever happened to me—and it never will again. I must have lost my mind. Or we've both suffered some kind of sunstroke."

For some reason the lieutenant easily agreed, and he rode with her to the pier in a lighthearted mood. They arrived just before the pink steamer *Samolyot* left the dock, and he kissed her openly on deck, despite the crowd, then jumped back onto the gangplank as it was being pulled away.

He returned to the inn feeling equally happy and carefree. But something had changed. The room seemed completely different from the room where she had been. It was still full of her, and yet, it was completely empty. How strange! The air still smelled of her English perfume, the cup from which she'd drunk her tea still stood half empty on the tray—and already she was gone. Overwhelmed by a sudden wave of tenderness and longing, the lieutenant hurriedly lit a cigarette and began to pace the room.

"What a strange adventure," he said out loud, laughing as he felt tears well up in his eyes. *I give you my honest word that I'm nothing like the person you might imagine me to be.* And then she's gone.

The screen had been moved aside; he put it back before the unmade bed, knowing that he couldn't bare to look at those sheets and pillows now. He shut the windows in order to escape the sound of carriage wheels creaking in the street and voices rising from the market, then he closed the filmy white curtains and sat down on the couch. Yes, this is it—the end of the "traveler's adventure." She's already gone, already far away, riding in a ship's salon that's all windows and white paint, or sitting on the deck, looking at the huge, gleaming surface of the river in the sun, looking at the yellow sandbars and the rafts drifting downstream, looking at the endless open space of the Volga and a horizon where shimmering water meets the sky. . . . Goodbye—say goodbye and that's it, always and forever. . . . For where could they possibly meet again? "I could never turn up in the town where she leads a normal life, has a husband and a three-year-old daughter, all her family," he thought to himself. Indeed, that town seemed to be an utterly forbidden place, and the thought that she would live out her lonely life there, often, perhaps, remembering their fleeting, chance encounter, while he would never see her again—this thought stunned him like a sharp, sudden blow. No, it couldn't be! It was too cruel, impossible, insane. The prospect of his life—all the painful, senseless years he'd spend without her—plunged him into horror and despair. "For God's sake!" he thought, struggling to keep his eyes from the bed behind the screen as he began to pace the room again. "What's wrong with me? What is it about her? What exactly happened yesterday? It must be some kind of sunstroke! And now I'm stuck in this backwater without her. How the hell will I get through the day?"

He still remembered everything about her, remembered all the small, fine details of her presence—the smell of her suntanned skin and her gingham dress, her supple body, the simple, uplifting sound of her voice. Traces of the exquisite pleasure that she'd given him with all her feminine charm remained extraordinarily acute within him, but those sensations were now eclipsed by a strange new feeling that he couldn't comprehend. He could never have imagined such a feeling taking hold of him when he pursued her yesterday, seeking what he thought would be a casual acquaintance; when they were together, there'd been no hint of it—and now it was impossible to tell her what he felt! "I'll never have the chance," he thought. "That's the worst of all—I'll never get to speak to her again! And what now? . . . Memories I can't dispel. . . . Pain I can't relieve. . . . An interminable day stuck in this godforsaken town. And the Volga shining in the sun while it carries her away on a pink steamer!"

He had to save himself somehow—occupy his mind with something, go somewhere, find some kind of diversion. He put his hat on decisively, picked up his riding crop, and quickly passed through the empty corridor, his spurs chinking. "But where am I going?" he wondered as he bolted down the steep wooden stairs. A young driver waited near the hotel entrance, wearing a trim, sleeveless coat and placidly smoking a cigarette. The lieutenant looked at him uncomprehendingly. "How can he just sit there on his coach, smoke a cigarette, and be perfectly content, carefree, resigned? I must be the only person in this town who feels so miserable," he thought, heading toward the market.

The market was closing down, and many of the merchants had already driven off. But for some reason he walked among the fresh droppings left by the horses, walked among the wagons and carts loaded with cucumbers, the displays of new pots and bowls. And all of it—the men who overwhelmed him with their shouts of *Here's a first-class cucumber, your lordship*, and the women sitting on the ground who vied for his attention, urging him to come closer as they lifted up their pots and rapped them with their knuckles to prove they had no cracks—all of it seemed so stupid and absurd that he quickly ran away and went inside a church, where the choristers were singing with emphatic joy and confidence, and a keen awareness of the duty they were carrying out. Then he wandered into a small, neglected garden on the mountain's edge and slowly walked around in circles, the river's measureless expanse shining like bright steel beneath him. . . . The shoulder straps and buttons of his uniform grew too hot to touch. The inside of his cap turned wet with sweat. His face began to burn. . . . When he returned to the inn he felt a certain pleasure as he entered the spacious, cool, and empty dining room on the lower floor. He felt pleasure as he removed his hat and sat down at a small table by an open window that let a little air into the room despite the heat. He ordered cold fish soup with ice. . . . Everything was good. There was enormous happiness in everything. Even the heat; even the smells of the marketplace and this unfamiliar, little town; even this old, provincial inn contained great joy: and in its midst his heart was being torn to shreds. . . . He ate half-sour pickles with dill and downed four shots of vodka, thinking he'd die willingly tomorrow if some miracle would let him bring her back, let him spend one more day with her just so he could tell her everything. That was all he wanted now—to convince her, to show her how ecstatically and miserably he loved her. . . . What for? Why try to convince her? Why show her anything? He didn't know, but this was more essential than his life.

"I'm falling completely apart," he said out loud, and poured another drink.

He pushed his bowl of soup away, ordered black coffee, and began to smoke, wondering desperately what he could do to save himself from this sudden, completely unexpected love. But even as he sought some means of escape, he felt all too clearly that escaping was impossible. And suddenly he got up again, grabbed his hat and riding crop, asked directions to the post office, and hurried off—a telegram already written in his head: "My entire life is yours from this day on—completely yours, forever, until I die." But he stopped in horror as he approached the old, squat building that housed the postal center: he knew the town where she lived, knew she had a husband and a three-year-old daughter, but he didn't know her name! He'd asked her several times at dinner and at the hotel, but she had only laughed. *Why do you need to know my name, or who I am?*

A shop window on the corner near the post office was filled with photographs. He looked for a long time at the portrait of some military type with bulging eyes, a low forehead, and a stunning pair of lavish sideburns. He wore thick epaulets, and his exceedingly broad chest was completely covered with medals. . . . How terrible and savage everything mundane and ordinary becomes when the heart's been destroyed—yes, he understood that now—destroyed by sunstroke, destroyed by too much happiness and love. He glanced at a photograph of two newlyweds—a young man with a crew cut stood at attention in a long frock coat and a white tie, his bride in a gauzy wedding dress on his arm—then moved his eyes to the portrait of an attractive, upper-class girl with an ardent expression and a student's cap cocked to one side on her head. And then, overwhelmed with envy for all these unknown people who were free of suffering, he began to study the street, looking desperately for something.

Where to? What now?

The street was completely empty and all the buildings looked identical: white, two-story merchant-class homes with big gardens and not a soul inside. A thick white dust lay on the paving stones; and all of it was blinding, all of it was flooded with hot, joyful, flaming sunlight which now seemed useless beyond words. The street rose in the distance, then dipped down, as if stooping under the cloudless sky. The glare reflected from its surface turned the horizon slightly grey, which reminded him of the south—of Sevastopol, Kerch, Anapa. And that was more than he could bare: stumbling and tripping on his spurs, squinting in the light, struggling to see the ground beneath his feet, the lieutenant staggered back the way he'd come.

When he reached the inn, he was as exhausted as a man who'd marched for miles in Turkestan or the Sahara. Gathering the last of his strength, he re-entered his large and empty room: it had been cleaned—

every trace of her was gone except for a forgotten hairpin that now lay on the nightstand. He removed his jacket and glanced at his reflection in the mirror: his moustache had been bleached white and his face looked grey from the sun; the whites of his eyes—slightly tinged with blue— stood out sharply against his darkened skin. It was an ordinary officer's face, but it now looked haggard and deranged, and there was something both youthful and profoundly sad about his thin white shirt and its small starched collar. He lay down on his back on the bed and propped his dusty boots up on the footboard. The curtains hung loose before the open windows, rustling occasionally as a small breeze blew into the room, laden with more heat from the scorching metal roofs—more heat from all the silent, glaring, lifeless world around him. He put his hands behind his head and stared fixedly in front of him, then clenched his teeth and closed his eyes, feeling tears spill down his cheeks—and finally, he dozed off. It was evening when he awoke: a red and yellow sun hung behind the curtains, the breeze had died away, the room felt as hot and dry as an oven. When the morning and the day before resurfaced in his memory, it seemed they'd taken place ten years ago.

He rose unhurriedly and washed, opened the curtains, asked for his bill and a samovar, slowly drank a cup of tea with lemon. Then he ordered a driver, had his bags brought out, climbed into the coach's rusty, sun-scorched seat, and handed five whole rubles to the porter.

"I think it was me who brought you here last night," the driver said cheerfully, picking up his reins.

The summer evening sky had already turned dark blue above the Volga by the time they reached the dock. Different colored lights were scattered in profusion along the river; other, larger lights hung in the masts of an approaching steamer.

"Right on time," the driver said ingratiatingly.

The lieutenant tipped him five rubles as well, bought his ticket, walked out onto the landing. Everything was like the day before: a soft blow to the pier and a slight giddiness as it rocks underfoot, a glimpse of the mooring line flying through the air; and then the engine's thrown into reverse, the river surges forward from the paddle wheel, and the water seems to boil as the steamer's driven back toward the dock. . . . This time the ship seemed unusually welcoming: its brightly lit deck was crowded with people, and the air smelled of cooking smoke from the galley.

A moment later they were being carried up the river, just as she'd been carried off so recently.

The summer dusk was dying out in the distance ahead: it glowed in drowsy, muted colors on the water, while trembling ripples flashed sporadically beneath the last, spent traces of the setting sun—and all the lights scattered in the surrounding dark kept on drifting, drifting off.

The lieutenant sat under an awning on deck, feeling like he'd aged ten years.

[1925]

Sky Above a Wall

I'M LEAVING Rome on a sunny winter morning.

The old cabby driving me to the train station is excited and drunk. Dressed lightly in a jacket and a cap, he sits high on the coach box, his elbows jabbing the air as he drives his skinny nag at a hard run through the shadows and the fresh damp of the narrow streets. Suddenly the road turns sharply to the right and drops down to a large square, flooded by the warm, blinding sun. The horse's hind legs buckle beneath her, and the old man, falling to the side, pulls hard on the brake. The wheels scrape and whine, the nag's hooves clatter loudly on the stones. In the damp and brilliant light still wavering before us, a huge fountain throws out thick grey columns of water, its spray hanging in the air like dust and smoke, while a long, crude wall—some ancient ruin resembling a rampart—slides slowly past us on the left, its stones resplendent in the sun, its top bordered by the thick, bright azure of the sky. As he brakes, the old man lifts his eyes to that astounding and divine expanse of color, shouts, cries out:

"Madonna! Madonna!"

[1930]

The Elagin Affair

I T WAS a strange and terrible affair. Inexplicable. Confounding. . . . At first, perhaps, it seems simple—like the plot of a cheap paperback (everyone in town referred to it this way). But a slight shift in perspective—and suddenly it turns elusive, recondite—resists all easy answers. Lends itself, almost, to the writing of real literature. . . .

The defense attorney put it well in court:

"There seems to be no room for me to argue with the prosecution in this case," he said in his opening statement. "For the defendant has already admitted his guilt, and almost everyone in this hall finds his crime and his character—like that of his supposedly unwilling victim—far too common and too shallow to warrant careful examination or serious debate. But such opinions are completely wrong, for they take into account only outward appearances. There is a great deal to argue about here. There are many, many reasons why we ought to pause, reflect, debate. . . ."

And he continued:

"Let us suppose that my sole purpose is to gain leniency for the accused. Were this the case, there would be relatively little I could say.

Our legal system offers no guidelines for a judge to follow in a case like this. Instead it grants that judge great leeway in his rulings. It assumes that his conscience, his informed opinion, and his intelligence will lead him to identify the proper legal code by which to treat the crime at hand. . . . Obviously, then, if my goal were simple leniency, I would appeal to the court's reason and its conscience; I would try to sway its opinion by focusing all attention on the defendant's most positive qualities. I would emphasize those circumstances that mitigate his guilt. With great persistence I would cultivate among the judges a positive disposition toward my client—a task made relatively easy by the fact that he denies only one component of the charges brought against him: that of conscious, premeditated evil. But could I even then avoid an argument with the prosecutor, who has labeled my client as nothing more and nothing less than a 'predatory criminal'? Everything is subject to interpretation. All events may be shaded one way or another, all statements set in a different key, all facts presented in a different light. And what do we find in this case? We find that the prosecutor and I look differently upon its every feature. We find there's not a single detail he and I can describe or elucidate without drastic disagreement. Every minute I must say to him, 'It wasn't so,' and that phrase—'it wasn't so, it wasn't so'—is more important than anything else in this case: it is the heart of the matter before us."

It had a terrible beginning, this strange affair.

It was the nineteenth of June of last year. Early morning, sometime after five. The dining room of Hussar Captain Likharyov had grown stuffy, hot and dry in the strong summer sun that already blanketed the city, but it was still quiet, for the captain's quarters were part of a hussar barracks in the suburbs. The captain, taking full advantage of his youth amid this quietude, was sound asleep. On a nearby table stood various bottles of liquor and cups of cold, unfinished coffee. A staff captain, Count Koshits, was sleeping in the adjoining guest room, and farther on, in the study, dozed Cornet Sevsky. All in all, it was a very simple scene, an altogether ordinary morning. But as is so often the case when something extraordinary occurs amid the everyday, this quotidian scene would make even more terrible, fantastic, and surprising those events that were about to unfold in the early morning of June 19 in the apartment of Hussar Captain Likharyov. In the midst of the sheer morning silence, a bell suddenly rang in the foyer, and the captain's orderly ran to open the front door, his bare feet padding lightly, cautiously across the floor. A deliberately loud voice rang out:

"Is he home?"

The arriving visitor came inside with the same deliberate racket. There was a particular recklessness in the way he flung open the dining room door, a marked audacity to the chinking of his spurs, the scraping of his boot heels. Astounded and still half asleep, the captain raised his head from his pillow: before him stood a colleague from the regiment, Cornet Elagin—a small, frail man with red hair and freckles. His legs were bowed and unusually thin, and his boots revealed a certain foppishness, which Elagin himself often called his "most essential" weakness. He quickly removed his officer's coat and threw it on a chair.

"Here, take my stripes," he said loudly as he crossed the room and collapsed onto a couch that stood against the wall, then put his hands behind his head.

"Wait, hold on," muttered the captain as he watched Elagin, his eyes wide with surprise. "Where did you come from? What's wrong?"

"I killed Manya," said Elagin.

"Are you drunk? Who's Manya?" asked the captain.

"Mariya Iosifovna Sosnovskaya, the actress."

The captain lowered his feet to the floor. "What? You're joking, right?"

"Alas, no. Sadly, I'm not joking in the least. But then, that might be for the best."

"Who's there? What's going on?" shouted the count from the living room.

Elagin stretched out one foot and lightly kicked the door open. "Don't shout," he said. "It's me—Elagin. I shot Manya."

"What?" said the count. He fell silent for a moment, then burst into laughter. "Of course—yes, that's good. Very funny! You had me for a second," he called out happily. "We'll forgive you this time, as we needed to be woken up. Otherwise I'm sure we would have overslept—we were up until three again last night, fooling around."

"I give you my word that I killed her," Elagin said again insistently.

"You're lying, brother—lying!" shouted the captain, picking up his socks. "You had me worried for a moment. I thought that something really happened. . . . Yefrem—tea!"

Elagin thrust his hand into his pocket, pulled out a small key, and deftly tossed it over his shoulder onto the table. "Go and see for yourselves."

In court the prosecutor revisited this scene many times, speaking at length of the horror and cynicism it revealed, like many other moments in Elagin's drama. He forgot, however, that on the morning in question, only a few more moments would pass before the captain was stunned by Elagin's appearance—the "supernatural" pallor of his skin, something "inhuman," as he later put it, in the cornet's eyes.

II

Here, then, are the events as they unfolded on the morning of June 19 last year.

Half an hour after Elagin's declaration, Count Koshits and Cornet Sevsky were already standing at the entrance to Sosnovskaya's house. There was no joking anymore.

They'd made their driver race through the streets and had leapt headlong from the cab as it stopped, then tried to jam Elagin's key into the lock while frantically ringing the front bell. But the key did not fit, and everything beyond the door was silent. Losing patience, they hurried to the courtyard where they found the yardman; he ran from the servants' entrance to the kitchen, then returned and reported that, according to the maid, Sosnovskaya did not sleep at home last night, having left earlier in the evening with some sort of package in her hands. The count and the cornet were at a loss: what to do in light of such news? They paused to think; they shrugged their shoulders; and then they took a cab to the police station, insisting that the yardman come as well. From the station they called Captain Likharyov.

"Soon I'll be a raving lunatic because of this fool!" he shouted into the receiver. "He forgot to mention that you shouldn't go to Sosnovskaya's at all. There's another place—an apartment where they had their trysts. Fourteen Starogradskaya. Do you hear me?—house fourteen, Starogradskaya. It looks like some kind of Parisian call girl's house. The door to their rooms opens right onto the street."

They galloped off to Starogradskaya.

The yardman rode beside the cabby on the driver's box while a policeman joined the officers inside the carriage, sitting across from them with an air of quiet independence. The day was already hot, the streets crowded and noisy. It seemed unimaginable that on such a sunny, lively day someone could be lying dead somewhere. And it boggled the mind to think that twenty-two-year-old Sashka Elagin had done this. How could he have brought himself to murder? Why did he kill her? How? None of it made the slightest sense, and all of these questions were impossible to answer.

When they finally stopped before an old, unpleasant-looking, two-story house on Starogradskaya, the count and the cornet, in their words, "fell into complete despair." Was *that* really here? Was it really necessary that they go to see it—though, of course, it pulled inexorably; it urged one to look. . . . The policeman's mood, on the other hand, immediately improved as he assumed the role of a strict and self-assured professional. "The key, please," he said in a cold, firm voice. The officers hurried to relinquish it, deferential as the yardman would have been. The front of the house was divided by a gate, beyond which they could see a small courtyard where a sapling grew. Its green leaves seemed unnaturally bright, perhaps because of the dark grey walls of stone surrounding it. To the right of the gate stood the door about which they'd been told—that secret door onto the street, that door they had to open. The policeman frowned and inserted the key: the door swung back, and the count and the cornet saw what seemed to be a pitch black corridor. As if guided by some sixth sense, the policeman swept his hand along the wall and threw a switch: the lights came on in a narrow room, in the depths of which they found a small table between two chairs, a few plates of un-eaten fruit and wildfowl. But something even gloomier appeared before them as they walked into those quarters: on the right-hand side of the corridor they discovered a small entranceway into a neighboring room. It too was dark, illuminated only by a small lamp that hung from the ceiling and cast a morbid, opalescent light beneath a huge umbrella of black silk. Every wall of that windowless and muffled room was also draped in black from top to bottom. In its farthest recess stood a wide, low, Turkish couch—and there a woman of rare beauty lay, wearing nothing but a camisole, her lips and eyes half open, her head drooping to her chest, her arms stretched along her sides and her legs slightly parted, her body white.

They stopped and froze before her.

III

The dead woman's beauty was extraordinary in the degree to which it satisfied all those demands a fashionable artist might contrive for a portrait of feminine perfection. She had all the attributes such a picture would require: a well-proportioned figure and clear, light skin; graceful legs; thick, full hair; a refined nose and delicate cheeks; a tender mouth expressing innocence and artless charm. And now, all of it was dead; all of it was turning blank and dull as stone: her beauty only made the dead woman more terrible. Her hair was perfectly arranged, as if she'd soon be going to a ball. Her head was raised by a pillow resting on the couch's arm, and her chin lightly touched her chest, giving her face and her vacant, half-closed eyes a slightly puzzled, preoccupied expression. Everything in the room was strangely lit by the opal lamp that hung from the ceiling, set far into the depths of that huge, black umbrella which spread above the corpse like some strange bird of prey with outstretched, membranous wings.

Even the policeman was shaken by this scene, but he and his companions soon began a tentative investigation of the crime scene.

The dead woman's beautiful and naked arms were extended straight along her sides. Two of Elagin's calling cards lay on her chest, which was covered only by a lacy shirt; a cavalry sword had been placed next to her legs, and now it seemed exceedingly crude beside that bare and tender feminine flesh. The count wanted to pick it up in order to remove the scabbard and check the blade for blood, but the policeman held him back.

"Oh yes, of course, of course," the count whispered. "We can't touch anything yet. But I'm surprised that I don't see any blood—indeed, I don't see any traces of the crime at all. Poisoning apparently?"

"Be patient," the policeman said reprovingly. "We will have to wait for the doctor and the investigator. But it does look like poisoning. . . ."

This was certainly the case. There was no blood to be seen anywhere—none on the floor or the couch, and none on the victim's body or her camisole. In an armchair near the couch, a pair of women's underwear and a peignoir lay on top of a light blue shirt with a pearly sheen, a skirt of very fine, dark grey material, and a woman's grey silk coat. All these items had been cast off carelessly, but none was soiled with a single drop of blood. The idea of poisoning was further confirmed by evidence discovered on a small ledge that jutted out from the wall above the couch: there, among champagne bottles and corks, candle stubs and hairpins, among scraps of paper that had been covered with words and torn to shreds—there they discovered a glass of unfinished porter and a small vial with a white label, where the menacing words "Op. Pulv." were written in black ink.

But just as the policeman, the count, and the cornet had each finished reading these Latin abbreviations, a carriage with the doctor and the investigator could be heard arriving at the house, and a few minutes later it turned out that Elagin had spoken the truth: Sosnovskaya had in fact been killed with a revolver. There were no specks of blood on the camisole, but underneath it, near the victim's heart, they uncovered a crimson spot, in the middle of which thin dark blood oozed from a circular wound with burnt edges. A wadded handkerchief had been used to cover the wound and stanch the flow of blood.

What more did the medical examination bring to light? Not much: the right lung of the deceased showed traces of tuberculosis; the gun was fired at point-blank range, and death was instantaneous, although the victim might have managed to utter a short phrase after the trigger had been pulled; there had been no struggle between the killer and his victim; she had drunk champagne and ingested a small quantity (not sufficient to cause poisoning) of opium mixed with porter; and, finally, she had engaged in sexual relations on the fateful night of her death.

But why had that man murdered her? In answer to this question, Elagin stubbornly insisted that both he and Sosnovskaya had "fallen into tragedy," that they could see no escape other than death, and that he had only been fulfilling her command when he took his victim's life. But notes written by the deceased shortly before her death flatly contradicted this statement. After all, on Sosnovskaya's chest lay two of Elagin's calling cards—and both of them bore messages written by her hand in Polish (almost illiterate Polish, it must be noted). One read:

"To General Konovnitsyn, chair of the theatre board of directors: My friend! I thank you for your noble friendship of the past several years and send you my final greetings. I ask that all proceeds from my last performances be sent to my mother."

The other:

"In killing me, this man has acted justly. Mother—my poor, unhappy mother! I will not ask for your forgiveness as I did not choose to die. Mother, we will see each other there, above. I can feel it—this is my last moment."

Before her death, Sosnovskaya wrote several other notes on Elagin's cards—they were scattered on the ledge above the couch, painstakingly torn into pieces. Later reassembled, they revealed the following messages:

"This man demands my death and his. . . . I will not leave alive."

"My final hour has come. . . . Dear God, do not leave me. . . . My last thought—my mother, the sanctity of art."

"The abyss! The abyss! This man is my fate. God save me, God help me."

And finally, most puzzling of all:

"*Quand même pour toujours.*"

All these notes—both those found lying intact on Sosnovskaya's chest and those discovered in shreds on the ledge above her—seemed to contradict Elagin's claims. But they only *seemed* to do so. For why were the two notes that lay on Sosnovskaya's chest not also torn to pieces, particularly as they bore such phrases as "I did not choose to die," words clearly fatal for Elagin? Not only did Elagin fail to destroy or remove these cards, he actually placed them in the most prominent place possible, for who else could have set them on Sosnovskaya's chest? It's certainly possible that his haste might have caused him to forget to destroy the cards. But how could his haste cause him to place those cards with all their damning statements upon his victim's chest? And was he truly in a hurry? Evidently not, for he stanched the bullet hole with a handkerchief, carefully arranged the body, and covered it with a camisole—then dressed and washed. No, here the prosecutor was correct—this act was not performed in haste.

IV

"There are two basic categories of criminal," the prosecutor told the court. "In the first we find those whom science terms as 'temporarily insane': they are ultimately criminals by accident; their evil acts are the end result of a tragic confluence of events and random irritants. The second category includes those who commit their crimes deliberately, following a malicious, premeditated plan: these are natural-born enemies of social order and society. They are predatory criminals. In which category should we place the man who sits before us now? He belongs, of course, to the second. There can be no doubt that he's a predator. He's led an idle, reckless life, and it's destroyed his sense of right and wrong, led him to commit this crime."

This tirade was quite peculiar (though it reflected the opinion of almost everyone in town), particularly because Elagin sat with his hand over his face throughout the trial, as if trying to conceal himself from the public while answering the questions put to him in a quiet but agitated voice so filled with sorrow and temerity that one's soul ached from the sound. On one point, though, the prosecutor was utterly correct: the defendant was no ordinary criminal, and he'd never come close to a state of "temporary insanity."

The prosecutor posed two questions: first, was the crime committed in a fit of passion, and, second, could it possibly be viewed as some form of accidental manslaughter? He answered both questions with absolute certainty: no.

"No," he said in answer to the first, "there could be no talk about a fit of passion, first and foremost for the simple reason that such fits last for only a few minutes—never hours. And what could have triggered such a fit in Elagin?"

To answer the second question the prosecutor posed several smaller questions to himself, each of which he immediately rejected, sometimes in a mocking tone:

"Did Elagin drink more than usual on that fateful day? No, he drank a great deal every day, and this particular day was no exception.

"Was the defendant then, and is he now, in good health? I subscribe to the opinion of those doctors who examined him: the defendant is perfectly healthy but completely unable to exercise even a modicum of self-restraint.

"Allowing that the defendant truly loved the victim, could it be that the impossibility of marriage produced in him a state of temporary insanity? No, for we know precisely that the defendant never concerned himself with marriage and never took the slightest step toward arranging such a union."

And further:

"Could not Sosnovskaya's plan to go abroad have brought him to a state of madness? No, for he'd learned long ago of her planned departure.

"Then perhaps the fear that her departure would bring an end to their relationship? Again no, for they had talked of a permanent separation many times before that night. What then could have made him lose his senses? The conversations about death? The strange milieu of the room—its, how shall I put it, hallucinatory effects? The overall oppressive atmosphere that filled that room and pervaded the entire, morbid night? But talk about death could not have been new for Elagin—he had such conversations with his lover constantly, and they, of course, had long ago grown dull for him. And it's quite comical to speak of hallucinations. For they must have passed quite quickly, given way to far more prosaic matters—dinner, the leftovers on the table, bottles, and, forgive me, chamber pots. . . .

"Elagin ate, drank, satisfied his bodily demands, went into the next room for a glass of wine, a knife to sharpen a pencil. . . ."

And the prosecutor concluded:

"We need not deliberate long in order to determine whether the murder Elagin committed was in fact the fulfillment of his victim's wishes. For, in order to decide that question, we must only weigh Elagin's groundless assertions that Sosnovskaya asked him to kill her against the note that Sosnovskaya herself wrote—a note containing words that are disastrous for Elagin: 'I did not choose to die.'"

V

One could take issue with many of the details of the prosecutor's speech. "The defendant is completely healthy." But where lies the border between illness and health, normality and abnormality? "The defendant never concerned himself with marriage, and never took the slightest step toward arranging such a union." But clearly he never took such a step because he was so utterly convinced of its futility. And further, is it really true that love and marriage are so closely linked? Would Elagin have found peace in marriage with Sosnovskaya? Would all the tragedy inherent to their love have ended if they'd married? And isn't it well known that a tendency to avoid marriage runs through every strong, uncommon kind of love?

But all this, I repeat, is a matter of details. The prosecutor was essentially correct: there was no fit of passion.

He continued: "Expert medical opinion has concluded that Elagin was 'in all likelihood' calm rather than agitated or insane at the time of the crime. I would maintain that he was not merely calm but surprisingly so. This becomes quite obvious when one considers the carefully cleaned room where the crime was committed, and where Elagin remained long after Sosnovskaya's murder. And then there is the testimony of the witness Yaroshenko, who saw how calmly Elagin left the apartment, how carefully, how unhurriedly he locked it with his key. And finally let us remember Elagin's behavior during his visit to Captain Likharyov's quarters. His response, for example, to Cornet Sevsky, who urged him to 'come to his senses' and remember if perhaps Sosnovskaya had shot herself. 'No, brother,' Elagin said to him. 'I remember everything *perfectly*'—and then he proceeded to describe in detail how he himself fired the shot. The witness Budberg stated that Elagin 'gave him a disturbing shock' by 'calmly drinking tea after his confession.' The witness Fokht was even more astounded. 'Sir Staff Captain,' Elagin said to him sarcastically, 'I hope you'll let me skip our drills today.' 'It was so shocking,' said Fokht, 'that Cornet Sevsky could not contain himself and began to weep.'

"True, there was a moment when Elagin also wept. The captain had gone to the regiment commander to receive orders concerning the defendant's fate. When he returned, the captain glanced at Fokht, and seeing their expressions Elagin understood that he was no longer an officer. Then he wept," the prosecutor concluded, "only then!"

Of course this statement too is quite strange, for who is not familiar with the way a random detail can shake a person out of semi-consciousness, plunge him from a stupor into grief? Something wholly insignificant and accidental falls into your field of vision, and suddenly you realize all the happiness of your previous life, all the hopelessness and horror of your present situation. And in Elagin's case it was no small fact that brought this realization: for ten generations his family had served. He was practically born an officer. And now, *voilà*—it's over. Moreover this loss occurred because the one person whom he truly loved more than his own life no longer existed. And he himself had committed this monstrous act!

But this too is a matter of mere details. The central fact remains: there was no period of "temporary insanity." What then led to the murder? The prosecutor himself recognized that "in order to make sense of this dark business, we must first examine Sosnovskaya and Elagin as individuals, then attempt to clarify their relationship." He proceeded to declare with great conviction that "these individuals were intimate despite the fact that they had not the slightest thing in common."

Is that true? Here lies the real heart of the matter.

VI

In describing Elagin I would first mention his age—twenty-two, a frightening and fateful age that determines one's entire future. Usually at this time one experiences what science calls "sexual maturity," and which in life is known as "first love." This first love is often viewed as poetic but insignificant. It's known to foster tragedies and upheaval, but no one ever thinks that such distress is linked to something deeper, something more complex than the anxiety and pain we call devotion to another. But in fact people at these moments live through something they cannot understand. A terrible blooming. A savage opening and laying bare, a solemn reckoning of all that lies between the sexes. If I were the defense attorney, I would ask the judge to note Elagin's age with precisely that point in mind, and I would urge him to recognize that the young man sitting before him was a striking illustration of the dynamic I'd described. "A young hussar gone mad from fast living," the prosecutor said, repeating a widely held view of Elagin. To support this claim he cited the testimony of an actor named Lisovsky, who described how Elagin came to the theatre as the cast was assembling for rehearsal, and Sosnovskaya, seeing Elagin, quickly stepped behind Lisovsky with the hurried words "Hide me from him, friend!" "I stood there so she could keep out of sight," Lisovsky testified, "and that little hussar, who was full of wine, he just stops and spreads his legs apart, stands there like a man who's stunned or half crazy, dumbfounded: 'Where'd Sosnovskaya go?!'"

It's true of course, he was out of his mind. But what brought him to this state? Was it really idle, reckless living?

Elagin came from a wealthy, high-born family. He lost his mother (who, it should be noted, was highly prone to states of exaltation) while still very young, and the fear that pervaded all his youth and adolescence had long ago estranged him from his father, a severe, strict man. The prosecutor described not only Elagin's moral character but also his physical appearance with cruel abandon:

"Our hero might have cut an impressive figure when he had a uniform to wear. But look at him now, with no adornments to dress him up. He certainly does not bring Othello to mind, sitting here in a black frock coat. Indeed, we have before us just a short young man with sloped shoulders, a pallid moustache, and an utterly vacant expression on his face. We have before us a man whose physical appearance is marked by atrophy and listlessness, a weakling who is paralyzed by fear in one set of circumstances—when, for instance, he must interact with his father—and filled with bravado in another, when, freed from his father's gaze, he loses all sense of restraint, counts on never being caught or punished."

What can one say to this? There is some truth of course in the prosecutor's crude characterization of Elagin. But listening to it, I wondered at the fact that one could speak with such offhandedness about those terribly complex and tragic forces of heredity that so sharply mark some people's lives and personalities. And as I listened further, I realized that the truth contained in the prosecutor's words was actually quite small. Yes, Elagin did grow up in trepidation of his father. But when it's experienced before one's parents, such trepidation should never be confused with cowardice, especially if the man suffering this fear is one who feels acutely all the weight of those hereditary ties that bind him to his father, his grandfather, and all his other ancestors. To be sure, Elagin lacked the classic physical appearance of a hussar, but it is in this deficiency that I find evidence of his extraordinary character. And so I would say to the prosecutor, "Look more carefully at this red-haired man with skinny legs and sloped shoulders, look more carefully and you'll be startled to discover the seriousness of this freckled face, the depth of these small, green eyes that so carefully avoid our own. And then, consider once again his atrophied physique, his weakness: on the day of the murder he drilled with his regiment from early morning. At breakfast he drank six shots of vodka, a bottle of champagne, and two cognacs—and he stayed almost completely sober!"

VII

The testimony of Elagin's fellow officers contrasted sharply with the general public's poor opinion of the defendant. Indeed, these officers portrayed Elagin in only the most positive light. Here for example is the squadron commander's opinion:

"Elagin gained the respect of his fellow officers soon after joining the regiment, and he was always extremely kind, considerate, and fair with the lower ranks. His character in my opinion had only one peculiarity—a certain unevenness that never expressed itself in any unpleasant way but often caused his moods to shift sharply and abruptly from happiness to melancholy, from loquaciousness to silence, from great self-confidence to despair about his worth and fate."

And then there is the view of Captain Likharyov:

"Elagin was always a kind and good fellow officer, but he had some eccentricities. At one moment he might be modest and withdrawn, and then, suddenly, a kind of bravado would seize him. After confessing his crime, Elagin stayed in my quarters while Sevsky and Koshits went to check on Sosnovskaya. While we waited, he either wept inconsolably or laughed with bitter raucousness. When they led him away to detainment, Elagin looked at us with a savage smile and asked what tailor he should go to for civilian clothes."

Then there is the testimony of Count Koshits:

"Elagin's disposition was generally happy and affectionate. He was a sensitive young man, high strung and impressionable, even prone to fits of exaltation. Music and the theatre had a particularly strong effect on him, often moving him to tears. He himself had an unusual talent for music. He could play almost any instrument. . . ."

All the other witnesses said relatively the same things:

"A man who was consumed by his passions while at the same time always searching for some other, still more meaningful, unique experience."

"On drinking bouts with his comrades, he was usually cheerful and upbeat, a little tedious at times, but always amiable. He drank more champagne than anyone in the regiment and shared it with whoever was at hand. . . . He did everything he could to conceal his feelings for Sosnovskaya, but once his relationship with her began, Elagin changed markedly, often appearing sad and preoccupied. On several occasions he spoke of his resolve to end his life in suicide."

Such was the testimony of those who lived most closely to Elagin. Where then, I wondered as I sat in the courthouse, has the prosecutor found so much black paint for his portrait? Does he have other witnesses to call? But no, there were no other witnesses. One had to conclude, therefore, that all the prosecutor's sinister impressions stemmed from his understanding of "golden youth" in general and his reading of a letter that Elagin wrote to a friend in Kishinyov. It was the only letter in the court's possession, and in it Elagin spoke of his life with casual disregard:

"I have come, brother, to a state of complete indifference: everything, absolutely everything's the same. All's fine today—so give your thanks to God. And what will tomorrow bring? Forget about it while you can. After all, we're always wiser in the morning than at night. I've earned myself a stellar reputation here—first-class drunk and village fool. Almost everyone in town has heard of me."

The prosecutor linked this critical self-assessment to his own, more elegantly phrased argument that "in pursuit of animal pleasures, Elagin took from Sosnovskaya everything she possessed, then abandoned her to society's opprobrium. Not only did he take her life, he even robbed her of her final honor—the right to a Christian burial." But does Elagin's letter truly lead to this conclusion? It does not. The prosecutor quoted only a few lines from a longer text. This is how it reads in full:

"Dear Sergey, I received your letter and am finally writing back. I know it's late, but what can I say at this point? As you read this note, you're bound to think, 'What penmanship—it looks as if a fly fell into the inkwell, then crawled around the paper!' Well, you know what they say: if handwriting isn't a perfect mirror of the inner self, it's certainly a clear expression of the author's character. I'm just as lazy as I used to be—in fact, if you really want the truth, I'm even worse. After all, two years of independent living and *something* else must have put their stamp on me. Brother, there are certain things that even Solomon the Wise could not express! And so, please don't be surprised if one fine day you learn that I've done myself in. I have come, brother, to a state of complete indifference: everything, absolutely everything's the same. All's fine today—so give your thanks to God. And what will tomorrow bring? Forget about it while you can. After all, we're always wiser in the morning than at night. I've earned myself a stellar reputation here—first-class drunk and village fool. Almost everyone in town has heard of me. And along with that—can you believe it?—my soul seems to be filled with such agony and strength, it seems to strain and pull so hard toward the good and the sublime—toward the devil knows what!—that I fear my chest will burst. You will say that this is simply youth. If so, then why do my comrades feel nothing similar? I've grown irritable and ill-at-ease. Sometimes at night, in a freezing winter blizzard, I'll get out of bed and ride hard through the town, fly along the streets, astounding even the night patrolman who's so used to taking everything in stride. Keep in mind, I do this when I'm sober, when I haven't had a drink. It's as if I heard some fleeting, delicate refrain somewhere, and now all I want to do is hear it long enough to learn the notes. But those notes have disappeared. No matter what I do, they're gone! I'll confess one fact to you: I've fallen in love with a woman who is absolutely, utterly unlike all the other girls who fill this town. . . . But enough about that. Write to me again, please. You know the address. Remember how you said it? 'Cornet Elagin, Russia.'"

It's astounding—how could anyone who read this letter claim that Elagin and Sosnovskaya were lovers without "the slightest thing in common"!

VIII

A pure-blooded Pole, Sosnovskaya was twenty-eight—older than Elagin. Her father had worked as a petty bureaucrat until taking his own life when she was only three. Her mother lived as a widow for many years, then married another petty bureaucrat who once more left her a widow.

As you can see, Sosnovskaya's background was quite conventional. What, then, produced in her those strange spiritual qualities that made her so unusual? What gave her that passion for the stage that appeared so early in her life? I am quite sure it was neither the home where she was raised nor the private boarding school where she was educated. They say, however, that she studied well and read a great deal in her free time. In the course of that reading, Sosnovskaya periodically wrote down maxims and ideas that she found appealing—always, of course, connecting them somehow to her own life, as almost every reader does when moved to save an excerpt from a book. These notes, together with her own observations, might be called a diary if such a formal title can be applied to those scraps of paper that sometimes lay untouched for months and where, in addition to her scattered dreams and thoughts about the world, she recorded bills for laundry and new dresses. What, exactly, did she write?

"'To remain unborn—the greatest happiness. The second—a quick return to oblivion.' What a charming thought!"

"How dull the world seems. Fatally dull. My soul strains to rise above the ordinary."

"'People understand only that suffering from which they die'—de Musset."

"No, I'll never marry. Everyone says this—but I swear to it before God. I swear to it on my life."

"If not love, then death. But where in the universe can I find such a person—someone I can love? There is no one! But how does one die while loving life the way I do—like a woman raving in delirium?"

"There's nothing on earth or in heaven more terrible, more alluring, more mysterious than love."

"Mama, for example, says that I should marry for money. Me—for money! How unearthly it is, this word 'love.' What hell it holds, what charm—although I've never loved."

"The world looks at me with predatory eyes—like those animals at the menagerie when I was a girl. . . . Millions of those eyes."

" 'It's not worthwhile to be a man. Nor an angel. For the angels cried out in protest and rebelled against God. To be God or to be nothing—this alone has value.' — Krasinski."

" 'Who can claim to penetrate so far that he has tapped into her soul when everything she does in life is meant to bury those deep veins?' — de Musset."

As soon as she finished her studies, Sosnovskaya told her mother that she'd decided to devote herself to art. An upright Catholic, her mother, of course, wished to hear nothing of Sosnovskaya's plans to become an actress. But her daughter was not one to abide the will of others, and she'd already begun to convince her mother that her life — the life of Mariya Sosnovskaya — could never be inglorious and ordinary.

At eighteen she left for Lvov, and there she realized her dreams, reaching the stage with little difficulty and quickly making her mark in the local theatres. Her following among stage professionals and the general public grew so substantial that at the end of her third year on the circuit she received an invitation to our city. Even in Lvov, however, the observations she recorded were much the same as those she wrote in school:

" 'Everyone is talking about her. On her account they laugh or cry. But who among them knows her?' — de Musset."

"If not for mother, I would kill myself. It's my constant wish."

"I don't know what happens to me when I go somewhere outside the city. When I see the sky, so beautiful and limitless, I want to shout, sing, declaim, weep . . . love and die. . . ."

"I will compose a beautiful death for myself. I'll rent a small room and have it shrouded in black. Music will play from some other room while I lie in a simple white dress, surrounded by countless flowers, whose heavy scents will suffocate me. How wonderful it will be!"

And further:

"Everyone, everyone demands my body, never my soul. . . ."

"If I were rich, I'd travel the world, sampling love wherever I went. . . ."

" 'Does a man know what he wants? Can he be sure he knows his thoughts?' — Krasinski."

And finally:

"Villain!"

Who was this villain whose transgressions are not hard to imagine? We know only that he appeared in her life — and that this appearance was inevitable. "Already in Lvov," testified the witness Zauze, a colleague from the theatre, "she didn't dress so much as she undressed for the stage. At home she received admirers and acquaintances while wearing a transparent peignoir without stockings. The beauty of her bare legs plunged them all into a kind of dazed ecstasy—especially the newcomers. And she would say, 'Don't be surprised—they're all mine, nothing artificial here,' as she raised her gown above her knees. At the same time she never stopped insisting—sometimes tearfully—that no one was worthy of her love, and that her only hope was death."

And so appeared the so-called villain, whom she accompanied to Constantinople, Venice, and Paris, and later visited in Krakow and Berlin. He was some kind of Galician landowner with extraordinary sums of money. The witness Volsky, who'd known Sosnovskaya since childhood, gave this testimony in reference to him:

"I always considered Sosnovskaya a woman of very little virtue. She didn't know how to conduct herself either on or off the stage. She loved only money—money and men. She was still a girl, almost, when she sold herself to that old boar from Galicia. The cynicism was quite astounding."

Sosnovskaya talked precisely about this boar to Elagin during their last conversation before her death. No longer guarding her words, she complained openly about him:

"I grew up completely alone—no one ever looked after me. In my own family—in the entire world!—I was always a stranger. . . . A woman—may all of her descendants go to hell—corrupted me when I was still a trusting, innocent girl. . . . In Lvov I sincerely loved a man—loved him like a father—and he turned out to be a villain, such a villain that I can't remember him without horror! He got me used to wine and hash, took me to Constantinople. He had a whole harem there! He'd lie there in his harem, looking at his naked slaves. And then he'd make me undress. A sick, vile man. . . ."

IX

Sosnovskaya became the talk of our town.

"While still in Lvov," said the witness Meshkov, "she proposed to many men that they agree to die in exchange for one night with her, while at the same time insisting that she sought a heart capable of real love. She searched for that heart very stubbornly while saying all along:

'My goal's to live—to live and use life. After all, a connoisseur must sample many different wines without getting drunk on one in particular. So too should a woman behave with men.' And she was true to her word," Meshkov continued. "I can't possibly say if she sampled all the wines, but she certainly surrounded herself with a huge quantity of them. Of course, she might have done this just in order to create a stir and gather *claqueurs* for her shows. 'Money,' she'd say, 'doesn't interest me. I'm tightfisted, sometimes stingy as a banker's wife—but somehow I don't really think about money. It's fame that counts. Everything else will follow.' I think she constantly brought up death for the same reason—to keep everyone talking about her. . . ."

Everything that had begun in Lvov continued in our town. And Sosnovskaya's notes remained much the same:

"My God, what loneliness! What misery! An earthquake, an eclipse—some relief!"

"One evening I was at the graveyard. And it was lovely there! It seemed that . . . No, I can't describe the feeling. I wanted to stay there all night, declaiming over the graves until I died of exhaustion. My performance the next day was better than anything I've done before. . . ."

And again:

"I was at the graveyard at ten o'clock last night. What a somber sight! Shafts of moonlight fell across the headstones and the crosses. It seemed I was surrounded by thousands of the dead. And I was happy, filled with joy. It was wonderful there. . . ."

Soon after meeting Elagin and learning from him that a cavalry sergeant had recently died in the regiment, she demanded that the cornet drive her to the chapel where the deceased lay. Later she wrote that the chapel and the body in the moonlight had made on her a "shockingly ecstatic impression."

The thirst for fame, for human attention, brought her to a kind of frenzy during this time. She was certainly attractive. Although her beauty was not particularly original, it possessed something uniquely its own—a rare charm that stemmed from a combination of childlike innocence and predatory cunning, a mix of constant play and absolute sincerity. You can see this in her portraits: look closely at her expression—that expression so uniquely hers—as she looks up at you with her head slightly lowered, her eyes raised to meet yours, her lips ever so slightly parted. It's both a winsome, melancholy look and an almost lurid invitation—as if she has consented to perform some secret, shocking act. She knew how to use her beauty. On stage she won admirers not only with a skillful demonstration of her charms—the sound of her voice, the taut energy of her gestures, her laughter and her tears—but also with a readiness to take on roles that usually required the baring of her flesh. At home she wore seductive Greek and Eastern clothes even as she entertained her numerous guests. Among her rooms, one was set aside, as she said, for suicide: it contained daggers and revolvers, swords with blades shaped like sickles and corkscrews, glass jars containing every possible poison. Death was her favorite topic of conversation and, moreover, while discussing the various ways to rid oneself of life, she was known at times to suddenly seize a loaded pistol from the wall, pull the trigger back, and raise it to her temple, saying, "Kiss me or I'll shoot"—or, on other occasions, to take a capsule filled with strychnine into her mouth and announce that she would swallow it if her visitor did not immediately fall to his knees and begin kissing her bare feet. The guest inevitably blanched with fear, left for home feeling doubly charmed, and soon spread all over town precisely the enticing stories she wanted to be heard.

"In general, she was never just herself," testified the witness Zalessky, who for many years was close to Sosnovskaya. "It was her constant occupation to play with people, to tease them. She was a master in the art of driving someone to the brink of madness with a tender, enigmatic glance, a suggestive smile, the sad sighs of a defenseless child. And she practiced this art with Elagin—bringing him to a white-hot pitch, then dousing him with cold water. Did she want to die? She loved life with a physical passion—and she feared death with a rare intensity. All in all, her personality was actually quite happy and lighthearted; she appreciated life and often showed it. I remember, for example, how Elagin once gave her a polar bearskin rug. She had many visitors at the time, but that bearskin made her so ecstatic that she forgot them all immediately. She spread it on the floor and, paying no attention to the other people in the room, started doing somersaults across the rug, started doing tricks that any acrobat would envy. . . . She was a captivating woman!"

But the same Zalessky also testified that the victim suffered attacks of depression and despair. Dr. Seroshevsky, who had known Sosnovskaya for ten years and was still treating her when she left for Lvov (her consumption began at that time), also testified that near the end of his acquaintance with her, the victim was plagued with such severe hallucinations, memory loss, and general nervous disorder that he feared for her mental faculties. Dr. Schumacher (from whom Sosnovskaya borrowed two volumes of Schopenhauer, which she "read very carefully and, most surprisingly of all, understood perfectly") subsequently treated her for the same nervous disorder and was repeatedly assured by his patient that she would not die a natural death. Finally, Dr. Nedzelsky gave this testimony:

"She was a strange woman. When entertaining guests she was usually very happy and flirtatious. But sometimes it would happen that, for no apparent reason, she'd suddenly go silent, roll her eyes, and lower her head to the tabletop. . . . Or she'd start to throw things, smash glasses on the floor. At such moments one had to demand quickly that she continue this activity—'Go on, go on, smash another one!'—and she would stop immediately."

It was with this "strange and charming woman" that the young cornet, Aleksandr Mikhailovich Elagin, would soon become acquainted.

X

How did that meeting occur? What drew them together? What were their feelings for each other? What was their relationship? Elagin spoke only twice about these matters: once—briefly and disjointedly—a few hours after the murder, and a second time during his interrogation three weeks later.

"Yes," he said, "I'm guilty in the taking of Sosnovskaya's life—but I did so *by her will.*

"I met her a year and a half ago through Lieutenant Budberg—we ran into her at the box office in the theatre. I loved her passionately and believed she shared my feelings. But I was not always sure of this. At times it seemed that she loved me even more than I did her, and at other times just the opposite. She was constantly surrounded by admirers, with whom she flirted, and I was tormented by intense feelings of jealousy. But ultimately it was not this that led to our tragic situation; it was something else—something I can't express. . . . Regardless of all else, I swear I didn't kill her out of jealousy.

"As I said, I became acquainted with her in February of last year at the theatre, near the box office. I soon began visiting her at home, but even by late October I had called on her no more than twice a month, and always during the day. In October I confessed my love for her, and she allowed me to kiss her. A week later we went with an acquaintance of mine, Voloshin, to a restaurant outside town. The two of us returned alone. Slightly tipsy, she grew playful and affectionate in the cab—but I felt so timid in her presence that I didn't even dare to kiss her hand. Later she asked to borrow a volume of Pushkin's poems; while reading *Egyptian Nights* she asked: "Would you give up your life for one night with your lover?" I did not hesitate to tell her that I would, and hearing this, she smiled enigmatically. I was already deeply in love with her, and I saw clearly—felt clearly—that this love would prove fateful for me. As we became more intimate, I grew bolder and began to speak more freely of my love for her. I also told her of my presentiment that I'd perish . . . if only for the reason that my father would never allow me to marry her, and that she—an actress whom Polish society would never forgive for an open, illicit affair with a Russian officer—could not possibly live with me outside of marriage. She too lamented her fate and her ill-fitted soul. And although she never answered my unspoken questions about her feelings for me, the intimacy of these discussions gave me hope that she shared my love.

"And then, in January of this year, I began to visit her every day at home. I sent her bouquets at the theatre, sent her flowers at home, bought her gifts. . . . I gave her two mandolins, a polar bearskin rug, a ring, and a jeweled bracelet. And I decided to give her a brooch in the shape of a skull, for she adored all emblems of death and often told me that she'd like to own precisely such a brooch, engraved with the words, '*Quand même pour toujours!*'

"On March 26 I received from her an invitation to dinner. After dinner she gave herself for the first time to me. . . . We were in the 'Japanese room,' as she called it, and all our future encounters took place there, after the maid had been dismissed. Then she gave me a key to her bedroom, the outer door of which opened directly onto the stairwell. . . . To commemorate March 26, we ordered wedding bands and, in keeping with her wishes, had our initials and the date of our first intimacy engraved inside them.

"During one of our trips outside the city we visited a small village where a cross stood before the local Catholic church. I swore my eternal love to her before that cross, swore that before God she was my wife, to whom I would be true until the grave. . . . She stood there sadly, silently, lost in contemplation. And then she said simply, firmly: 'And I love you. *Quand même pour toujours!*'

"In early May when I was dining at her house, she produced a vial of powdered opium and said, 'How easy it is to die! Just drop a little in your glass—and it's done.' Then she poured the powder into her champagne and raised the glass to her mouth. I tore it from her hand, flung the wine into the fireplace, and smashed the glass against my spur. She said to me the next day, 'Instead of tragedy, we wound up playing in a farce yesterday. But what can be done?' she added. 'I lack resolve—and you're incapable. What a disgrace!'

"After that we saw each other less. She said she could no longer receive me in the evenings. Why? I was in hell; I nearly lost my mind. But she had changed toward me—grown cold and mocking. Sometimes she treated me as if we hardly knew each other, and she constantly derided what she called my lack of character. . . . And then, suddenly, everything changed again. She began driving to my quarters in order to go for walks, began to flirt with me—perhaps because I'd finally forced myself to act with cold restraint whenever she was near. Finally she told me to rent a separate apartment for our rendezvous. But it had to meet her specifications: an apartment in some gloomy old house on an empty and deserted street, with dark rooms decorated precisely as she ordered. . . . You've seen those rooms—you know how she wanted them.

"And so, on June 16, at 4 P.M., I stopped at her house, told her the apartment was ready, and handed her a key. She smiled, said, 'We'll talk about this later,' and returned the key to me. At that moment the bell rang and a certain Shklyarevich entered the room. I quickly hid the key in my pocket and started making small talk. As I prepared to leave together with Shklyarevich, she said to him loudly in the hallway, 'Come back to visit me on Monday,' while whispering to me, 'Come tomorrow at four.' The way she whispered made my head spin.

"I returned the next day promptly at four. And how surprised I was when the cook who opened the door handed me a letter and explained that Sosnovskaya could not receive me. She wrote that she felt unwell, that she was going to visit her mother at her dacha, that it was 'already late.' Beside myself, I went inside the first café I saw and wrote an angry letter in response, asking her to explain what she meant by the word 'late.' But the messenger I sent to her home returned almost immediately with my note: she wasn't there to receive it. I returned to my quarters and wrote another letter. In it I reproached her sharply for the games she'd played with me and requested that she return my wedding band, which, I wrote, I intended to take to my grave, for it was the one object I valued most in life, despite the fact that she almost certainly considered it a joke. With these words I wanted to show her that everything between us was finished, and that death alone remained for me. Together with the note I sent back her portrait, all her previous letters, and all the things she'd left with me — gloves, a hat, hairpins. . . . When the orderly returned, he informed me that he'd left my package and my letter with the yardman at Sosnovskaya's building, for she still was not at home.

"That evening I went to the circus, where I ran into Shklyarevich. I don't know him well, but we wound up drinking champagne together, for I was afraid to be alone. Suddenly he said, 'Listen, I can see you're hurt, and I know the cause of your suffering. Believe me, she isn't worth it. We've all been through this. She's led us all around by the nose.' I had the urge to draw my sword and split his head down the middle, but I was such a ruin that I did nothing. I didn't even break the conversation off; indeed, I was secretly glad to be talking with someone, to have found some source of empathy. I don't know what got into me then. . . . Of course I offered no response to his statements, didn't say a word about Sosnovskaya. But I took him to Starogradskaya and showed him the apartment I'd so carefully selected for our rendezvous. What a fool she'd made of me with that apartment! I felt so bitter, so ashamed. . . .

"From there we took a cab to the Nevyarovskoy Restaurant. A light rain was falling as the cab flew along the streets, and even the lights that hung before us, even that soft rain filled me with terror and pain. I returned with Shklyarevich to my house at about one in the morning; I was already getting ready for bed when the orderly brought me a note: she was waiting outside and asked that I come out immediately. She had driven there with her maid, she said, because she'd been so alarmed by my note that she couldn't stand to make the trip alone. I told the orderly to take the maid home and went with her in the cab to Starogradskaya. On the way there I reproached her, said that she was merely playing games with me again. She sat silently, staring ahead and occasionally wiping tears from her eyes. But she seemed quite calm, and as her frame of mind invariably influenced mine, I too grew quiet as we rode. When we arrived, her spirits rose dramatically; indeed, she became quite cheerful, for she liked the apartment very much. I took her hand, asked her forgiveness for my reproaches, and requested that she return the portrait that I'd had delivered to her house in all my anger earlier that day. We often fought, and it was always I who felt to blame and wound up asking for forgiveness. . . . At three in the morning I left to take her home. Again our conversation grew strained as we rode in the cab. She sat looking straight ahead; I couldn't see her face, only smelled her perfume, heard her cold and angry voice: 'You're not a man,' she said. 'You have no character at all. I can do whatever I want with you—enrage you one minute, pacify you the next. If I were a man, I'd cut a woman like that to pieces.' 'In that case, take back your ring!' I shouted, and violently thrust my wedding band onto her finger. She turned to me, smiling uncertainly. 'Come to see me tomorrow,' she said. I answered that I would not, under any circumstances. She began to plead, awkwardly, timidly, saying, 'No, no—you'll come, you'll come . . . to Starogradskaya.' And then she added with finality, 'No, I'm begging you to come. I'm going abroad soon, and I want to see you for the last time. I need to tell you something very important.' Then she began to cry again, saying, 'I'm just surprised—you say you love me, say you can't live without me, that you'll shoot yourself—and yet you don't want to see me for the last time.' Trying to sound distant and reserved, I said that if this was in fact the case, I would inform her of a time when I'd be free. My heart seemed to be bursting with love and tenderness for her when we parted in the rain outside her apartment. Then I went home, where I was appalled to find Shklyarevich sound asleep in my room.

"On the morning of Monday, June 18, I sent her a note, stating that I would be free after twelve o'clock that day. She answered: 'Six o'clock. Starogradskaya.'"

XI

Sosnovskaya's maid, Antonina Kovanko, and her cook, Vanda Linevich, both testified that on Saturday the sixteenth, after lighting a spirit lamp to curl her bangs, Sosnovskaya distractedly dropped a lit match on the hem of her peignoir, which quickly began to burn. Sosnovskaya shrieked and frantically tore the garment from her body, and later, still profoundly shaken by the incident, took to her bed and summoned a doctor. "It's a sign," she insisted. "Something terrible is going to happen."

Poor, unhappy woman! For me the story of that peignoir and her childlike horror is strikingly sad and moving. For me, that triviality casts a new light on Sosnovskaya; it ties together all those fragmented, contradictory stories we heard when she was alive and which, after her death, grew slightly passé from their constant retelling in both the courtroom and polite society. Above all else, it stirs in me a vivid sense of the genuine woman—the real Sosnovskaya—whom no one truly understood, just as no one understood Elagin—despite the intense interest in her daily life, the desire to decipher her, and the endless gossip of the past year.

I will say it once again: the poverty of human reason is astounding! It is always the same when people try to make sense of even the smallest events: we discover, once more, that they look without seeing, listen without hearing. To so thoroughly distort Elagin and Sosnovskaya and everything that occurred between them, one must disregard countless obvious facts—dismiss them all, as if deliberately. But it seems that everyone agreed to speak of nothing but vulgarities. There's nothing complicated here, they say. He's just a hussar—jealous, drunk, and reckless. And she's an actress who's become entangled in her own disordered and amoral way of life. . . .

Private rooms in restaurants, courtesans and wine, debauchery— this is how they saw Elagin. The rowdy excess of military life, they said, obliterated all his refinement, eradicated any higher feelings he might have had. . . .

They talk of wine and higher feelings! What was wine for someone like Elagin? "My soul seems to be filled with such agony and strength, it seems to strain and pull so hard toward the good and the sublime— toward the devil knows what!—that I fear my chest will burst. . . . I want to catch some delicate and fleeting melody which it seems I heard somewhere but can never hear again!" Drinking helps one breathe a little easier, a little deeper—makes that soundless melody seem clearer, closer. And what does it matter if music, drunkenness, and love are all the same deceptions, if they serve only to increase the strength of those impressions that the world and life create in us—those impressions that no human word can match in their abundance and intensity?

"She didn't love him," everybody said of her. "She was just afraid. After all, he constantly threatened to kill himself, and not only would his suicide have weighed down her soul, it would have put her at the center of a massive scandal." There was testimony that she even felt "a certain revulsion" toward the cornet. But didn't she willingly give herself to him? Suppose she did—does that really change anything? Who didn't possess her? It just happened that Elagin felt the urge to make a tragedy from that romantic farce in which she so enjoyed performing. . . .

And further:

"She was terrified by the pathological jealousy that he exhibited with growing frequency. Once the actor Strakun came to visit her while Elagin was there. At first he sat calmly and only blanched with jealousy.

But then he stood and abruptly strode into the next room. She raced after him and, seeing a revolver in his hand, dropped to her knees before him, begging him to pity both himself and her. Such scenes were probably quite commonplace for the two of them. Is it surprising, then, that she would finally decide to try to get away from him—take a trip abroad, just as she'd prepared to do on the evening of her death? He brought her a key to the apartment on Starogradskaya—the apartment she'd arranged in order to avoid receiving him at home—and she refused to take it. When he insisted, she told him: 'There's no point—I'm leaving town. It's too late.' But then he sent her such a desperate letter that she drove off to see him in the middle of the night, terrified she'd find him dead."

Let's assume that all of this is true (though Elagin's confession completely contradicts such reasoning). Why, then, was Elagin so "pathologically" jealous? Why did he want to turn that comedy into a tragedy? Why didn't he just kill her in one of his fits of jealous rage? Why was there "no struggle between the victim and his killer"? And then there's the claim that she at times found him repellent: "She'd belittle him in front of people, make up insulting names for him. 'My bowlegged puppy,' she'd call him sometimes." But my God, this is absolutely typical behavior for Sosnovskaya. Even in her Lvov notes, she writes about feelings of revulsion: "He's still in love with me. . . . And what do I feel for him? Both love and revulsion. . . ." She insulted Elagin? No doubt. Indeed, in the midst of one of their many fights she called for her maid, then threw her wedding band on the floor, saying, "You can keep this bit of garbage for yourself." But what had she done before this scene? She'd run into the kitchen and said: "I'm going to call you in a moment and throw this ring on the floor. I'm going to tell you to keep it, but remember—this is only a little farce. Later you must give it back, because this ring makes me his wife—makes me the wife of that fool. And it matters more to me than anything on earth. . . ."

They were not at all mistaken in calling her an "easy woman," and the Catholic church had good reason to deny her Christian burial as a person of "corrupt morals and depraved behavior." Her character had much in common with that of prostitutes and devotees of "free love." What kind of character is that? One shaped by a sharp and irrepressible, indeed insatiable, sexuality. What produces such a character? This I cannot answer. But note what always seems to happen: unusual and complex men, men whose characters are somewhat atavistic, and whose sensitivities to both women and the world are unusually refined—these men are drawn by body and soul to such women as Sosnovskaya, and consequently they wind up heroes in a great number of romantic tragedies and dramas. Why? Are they impelled by their basest desires, driven by some sordid urge? Or is the mere awareness that these women are available sufficient to entice them? Of course not, no—a thousand times no: it is nothing like this. For these men know full well—they see, they sense—exactly what will come from their involvement with these women. They know the pain that these relationships will inevitably inflict on them, they know the genuine terror, the ruin they can bring. All of this they see, know, sense—and yet this awareness only adds to the attraction, only draws them more inexorably toward such women, toward their pain, and even ruin. Why?

Of course she was only playing a role in some farce when she wrote those little notes before death, trying to convince herself that her final hour had truly come. There's simply nothing to suggest otherwise—certainly not her banal and childish diaries or her visits to the graveyard. . . .

No one denies the theatricality of those walks among the graves or the naiveté of the notes she kept. And everyone recalls the way she liked to hint at similarities between herself and Mariya Bashkirtseva or Mariya Vechyora. But why did she decide to write such a diary? Why did she decide to emulate those women in particular? She had everything: beauty, youth, money, fame, hundreds of admirers—and she found all of this intoxicating, she reveled in it. And yet her life was one long, enervating search for something else, an incessant wish to leave behind this dull, repulsive world where nothing is the way it ought to be. Why? Because she liked this image. And why this image over all the other possibilities? It's a common choice among women who describe themselves as devotees of art. But why? What makes it so widespread?

XII

She woke up and summoned her maid much earlier than usual on Sunday: the little hand-bell that she kept beside her bed began to ring sometime near eight o'clock. The maid brought cocoa on a tray and drew open the curtains in her room. She sat up in bed and watched distractedly. As was her habit, she sat with her head slightly lowered and her eyes raised, her lips half parted.

"You know, Tonya, I fell asleep yesterday as soon as the doctor left," she said. "Dear Mother of God, what a shock! I was terrified! But as soon as he arrived I started to calm down, started feeling better. I woke up in the middle of the night and knelt in bed, prayed for an entire hour. Just imagine how I'd look all burned! My eyes would have burst. The flames would have scorched my lips. It would be horrible to look at me. . . . They would have wrapped my face in gauze. . . ."

She left her cup untouched on the tray and sat thinking for a long time. Then she drank her cocoa, bathed, put on a bathrobe, and, with her hair still undone, sat at a small desk, writing letters on stationery edged in black, like the paper used for funeral announcements: she'd ordered such stationery long ago. She then dressed, ate breakfast, and left to spend the day visiting her mother at her dacha. She returned near midnight with the actor Strakun, whom she always considered "one of my people."

"They were both in good moods when they arrived," the maid said. "When I met them in the entranceway, I immediately called her aside and gave her the note and those things that Elagin had returned while she was gone. 'Hide them quickly. Don't let Strakun see!' she whispered, hurrying to open the letter. She blanched as she read, then grew hysterical. 'For the love of God, run this second to get a cab,' she shouted, no longer paying attention to the fact that her guest was sitting in the living room. I did as she requested and, returning in a carriage, found her on the steps to the house. The horses ran at a full gallop all the way to Elagin's while she sat crossing herself, repeating 'Dear Mother of God, please—just let me find him alive.' "

On Monday morning she visited the bathing houses on the river outside town. Later she was joined for lunch at home by Strakun and an Englishwoman (who came almost every day to teach Sosnovskaya her native language but practically never conducted an actual lesson). After lunch the Englishwoman left; Strakun stayed for another hour and a half. He lay on the couch and smoked, his head on Sosnovskaya's lap, despite the fact that she was dressed "in nothing but a house coat and Japanese slippers." When Strakun finally began to leave, Sosnovskaya asked him "to come again at ten o'clock tonight."

"Aren't you getting tired of me?" he said, laughing as he looked for his walking stick in the hall.

"Oh no, not at all, you're very welcome," she said. "But if I'm not here, Lyusya, don't be angry. . . ."

Once her guest was gone, she spent a long time burning various papers and letters in the fireplace. She hummed to herself and joked with the maid: "I'll burn everything now," she laughed, "since I wasn't burned. . . . And really, it wouldn't be so bad to burn—but all of it, everything to ash at once!"

And then:

"Tell Vanda to have dinner ready at ten. . . . I'm going out."

She left after five, carrying "something wrapped in paper that resembled a revolver."

She was going to Starogradskaya, but she stopped en route at the seamstress Leshchinskaya's shop, where the peignoir that had begun to burn while she wore it on Saturday had been shortened so that she could wear it again. According to Leshchinskaya, she was in a "warm, happy mood." She looked at the altered peignoir, then wrapped it up with the package she'd taken from home and proceeded to sit for a long time with the girls who sewed in the shop, saying all the while, "Dear Mother of God, I'm so late. I have to leave right now!" but never rising from her seat. At last she stood up, sighed, and said in a cheerful voice: "Goodbye, Pani Leshchinskaya. Goodbye, sisters, my little angels. Thank you for letting me sit with you. It's such a pleasure to join this little circle of women after being surrounded by men for so long!"

She smiled once more from the doorway, nodded, and left. . . .

Why had she taken a revolver with her? It actually belonged to Elagin, but she kept it at her house, fearing he would shoot himself. "She intended at that time to return all his possessions to Elagin," the prosecutor said, "because she was leaving in a few days for an extended trip abroad. . . ." He continued:

"And so she headed off to that meeting which, unknown to her, would prove so fateful. By seven o'clock she was already inside house number 14 on Starogradskaya—had already entered the apartment. And the door that was closed behind her would remain locked until the morning of June 19. What took place in those rooms during the night? Only Elagin can tell us. Let's listen, once more, to him. . . ."

XIII

And so each of us listened once more in the hushed and crowded courtroom to those pages of the indictment that concluded Elagin's story—pages that the prosecutor wanted most to keep alive within our memories.

"On Monday, June 18, I sent her a note, telling her that I would be available after twelve noon. She wrote back: 'Six o'clock. Starogradskaya.'

"I was already there at a quarter til. I'd brought hors d'oeuvres as well as two bottles of champagne, two bottles of porter, glasses, and a bottle of perfume. But I wound up waiting for a long time. She didn't arrive until seven.

"She kissed me distractedly as she entered the apartment, then walked into the back room where she tossed the package she was carrying on the couch. 'Leave me,' she said in French. 'I want to get undressed.' I went into the next room and sat there alone for a long time. I was perfectly sober and utterly despondent, sensing, somehow, that everything was over—that everything was coming to an end. . . . It was a strange scene. I sat with the lamps lit, as if it were night, but I knew full well that a lovely summer evening was just beginning beyond the walls of those dark, windowless rooms. She didn't speak to me for a long time. I have no idea what she was doing—it was completely silent behind the door. Finally she called out, 'You can come in now.'

"She was lying on the couch in just a peignoir—no stockings, no slippers, nothing covering her legs. . . . She was looking up at the ceiling—at the lamp. Her head was slightly lowered, her eyes raised. She didn't speak. The package that she'd brought was opened: I saw my revolver. 'Why did you bring that?' I asked. She paused before answering. 'You know I'm leaving . . . it will be better if you keep it here. . . .' A terrible thought flashed through my head: 'No, it's nothing so simple! . . .' But I didn't question her. . . .

"We talked for quite a long time after that, but our conversation was cold and forced. In secret I was agitated: I wanted desperately to formulate and express some idea to her, and I thought, 'Now, now my thoughts will come together and I'll tell her something important, something vital,' for I knew that this could be our last meeting, or at least our farewell before a long separation—and still I said nothing, felt nothing but my lack of strength. 'Have a cigarette if you want,' she told me at some point. 'You don't like it when I smoke,' I said. 'It doesn't matter *now*,' she answered. 'And you can pour me a glass of champagne, too. . . .' This simple request made me wildly happy—you would have thought it was my personal salvation. In a few minutes we drank an entire bottle of champagne. I moved closer to her, began to kiss her hands, tell her how I couldn't bear our separation. She played with my hair and said distractedly, "Yes . . . what a tragedy that I can't be your wife. . . . Everyone's against us. Everyone and everything. . . . Only God, perhaps, is with us. . . . I love your soul, your *imagination*. . . .' I don't know what she wanted to express with those last words. I looked up at the umbrella above us. 'It's as if we're in a tomb,' I said. 'So quiet. . . .' She only smiled sadly in response.

"At about ten o'clock she said she was hungry, and we moved into the front room. But she ate very little—as did I. We drank more than anything. Suddenly she looked at the food I'd brought: 'Oh, you brought so much! You're such a schoolboy,' she exclaimed. 'Don't buy so much next time!' 'But when would I have the chance? When could I do this again?' I asked. She gave me a strange look, then lowered her head. 'Dear Jesus. Dear Mary,' she whispered, looking at me with raised eyes. 'What are we to do?. . . I want you, now. . . . Hurry. . . . Now. . . .'

"When I looked at the clock again it was already after one in the morning. 'Oh, it's so late,' she said. 'I have to go home right away.' But she made no effort to rise. 'You know—I realize that I have to go. Right away,' she said. 'But I can't move. I feel as if I'll never leave. You're my destiny, my fate—God's will.' I couldn't understand what she meant by those words, but I believe she wanted to express something similar to the message that she later wrote: 'I didn't choose to die.' You believe she wrote these words in order to express her helplessness before me. But I think she wanted to say something else—namely, that our unhappy meeting was destiny, was divine will—and she was dying not by her own choice but by God's. At the time, however, I didn't attach such importance to her words—I'd grown used to her eccentricities long ago. Then she asked, abruptly, if I had a pencil. This too surprised me: 'Why now?' But I hurried all the same to give her the pencil that I carried in my address book. Then she asked for my calling card. 'But wait, listen—you shouldn't write on it,' I said when she began to use it for her notes. 'No, it's all right. . . . This is just for me,' she answered. 'Give me some time alone, now, to think and take a little nap.' She laid the calling card on her chest and closed her eyes. It grew so quiet in the room that I too slipped into some kind of semi-conscious state. . . .

"At least half an hour passed. Then, suddenly, she opened her eyes. 'I forgot,' she said in a cold voice. 'I came here to return your ring. You yourself wanted to end everything yesterday.' She tossed her ring onto the ledge above the couch. 'Do you really love me?' she almost shouted. 'I can't understand it, then—how can you just calmly let me go on living? I'm a woman. I don't have the will to end it! It's not that I'm afraid of death—I'm afraid of suffering. But you could end my life with one shot. End my life—and then your own.' As she spoke, I understood with terrifying clarity all the horror, all the hopelessness of our situation. And I knew it had to be resolved, finally, somehow. But to kill her? No, this was more than I could bear. Something else had taken place: some other, equally decisive moment had arrived for me. I picked up the revolver and cocked it. 'What? Just you? No,' she shouted as she leapt up. 'I swear to God, never!' and she snatched the gun from my hand.

"Again that brutal silence filled the room. I sat while she lay motionless on the couch. She muttered something indistinctly to herself in Polish, then asked me to return the ring she'd earlier discarded. I gave it to her. 'Yours too,' she said. I gave her mine as well. She slipped her ring back onto her finger and told me to do the same. 'I always loved you and I love you now. I know that I've tormented you. I've brought you to the verge of madness. But that's my character. That's our fate. . . . Give me my skirt, please, and bring us some porter.' I did as she asked and left to get the porter. Coming back into the room, I saw that she'd taken out a little vial of opium. 'Listen,' she said firmly, 'we've reached the end of our little farce. Can you live without me?' I told her that I couldn't. 'Yes,' she said, 'I've taken all your soul. All your thoughts. You won't hesitate to kill yourself? If that's true, then take me with you. I can't live without you either. Kill me first, and then you'll know that I'm completely yours—for all eternity. And now, listen to my life. . . .' She lay down again in silence, and grew calmer. And then, unhurriedly, she began to tell me her entire life, beginning with her childhood. . . . I remember almost nothing of that story."

XIV

"I don't remember which of us started writing first. . . . I broke the pencil in two and we wrote, wrote without talking. I believe my first note was to my father. . . . You wonder why I reproached him—why I wrote that he 'didn't want me to be happy' when I never even asked him to accept her as my bride. . . . I don't know. . . . But it's all the same. . . . He wouldn't have allowed our marriage. Then I wrote to my friends in the regiment, wrote to say goodbye. And then—who else? The commander—I asked him to arrange a proper burial for me. You ask if this means that I was absolutely certain I would kill myself. Of course I was. Then how could I have failed to do so? I don't know. . . .

"I remember that she wrote very slowly, pausing, contemplating every phrase. She writes a word, stops, looks at the wall with raised eyes. . . . It was she who tore up the notes, not me. She did it herself: wrote them, tore them up, scattered the pieces. . . . I think the grave itself will be less terrifying than that hour we spent writing those superfluous notes in the silence beneath that lamp. . . . All of it was her idea. I did everything she asked that night. I did everything she wanted and I never questioned her, right up to the end.

"'That's enough,' she said abruptly. 'If we're going to do this, we have to do it now. Give me some porter. . . . Mother of God, bless me.' I poured it for her. She sat up, dropped a few grams of powder into her glass, and drank more than half. The rest she gave to me, saying I should finish it. I did. Then she became disturbed and agitated, started pulling at my arm, begging me. 'Kill me,' she said. 'Kill me now. For our love. Do it—kill me.'

"How exactly did I do it? I think I held her with my left arm—yes, of course it was my left—and I brought her mouth close to mine. 'Farewell, farewell,' she said. 'But no—it should be hello. Hello—this time forever. If we didn't make it here—then there, above. . . .' I pressed myself to her and held my finger on the trigger. I remember how my body was trembling—it seemed to jerk and twitch as I held her there, and then my finger twitched—as if it had its own will. . . . She managed to say three words in Polish: 'Aleksandr, my beloved. . . .'

"What time was it then? I think it was three. What did I do for the two hours that followed? It took me an hour to walk to Likharyov's quarters. The rest of the time I spent sitting next to her. And then I decided to clean up for some reason.

"Why didn't I shoot myself? Somehow I forgot about it. When I saw her dead, I forgot everything in the world. I just sat and looked at her. And then, in the same delirium, I started cleaning her, started straightening the room, putting everything in order. . . . I couldn't fail to keep my word, couldn't fail to follow through on that promise to kill myself after killing her. But I was seized by absolute indifference. . . . I feel the same indifference now toward the fact that I'm alive. . . . But I can't stand to think that you believe I'm a murderer—a butcher. No, no! I might be guilty according to the laws of man and God, but I'm innocent—innocent before her."

[*Maritime Alps, 1925*]

Old and Young

L OVELY summer days and the Black Sea's calm.

A steamer overloaded with people and goods; its deck packed solid from forecastle to stern.

And a long, circular route from the Crimea to the Caucasus, the shores of Anatolia, Constantinople.

Hot sun and blue sky, a lilac-colored sea. Endless stops in crowded ports where the winches crash like thunder and the deckhands shout and curse. *Heave to! Lift!* And then the calm again. A slow and peaceful passage along the base of distant mountains, their peaks melting in the sun's haze.

A cool breeze blows through the spacious, clean, and empty lounge for first-class passengers. But it's dirty and crowded on deck, where throngs of passengers ride in the galley's stench and the engine's heat, sleeping on plank beds under the ship's awnings, or nestled among anchor chains and hawsers on the forecastle. Here there is always a pungent odor: sometimes it's hot and pleasant, sometimes it's warm and disgusting, but always it is stirring—the unmistakable smell of a steamer mixed with the sea's freshness. And here there are hordes of every nationality—Russians and Ukrainians, Athonian Monks, Georgians, Kurds, and Greeks. . . . The Kurds sleep from morning until night, a completely savage race, while the Georgians either sing or dance in pairs: tossing their wide sleeves back with coquettish nonchalance, jumping lightly, and floating into the parting crowd as they clap their hands in rhythm: *tash-tash, tash-tash*. . . . Meanwhile, the Russian pilgrims bound for Palestine never stop drinking tea, and a woman camped near the kitchen watches intently as a slope-shouldered *mouzhik* with straight hair and a narrow yellow beard reads out loud from the Holy Scripture: alone and unabashed, she wears a red jacket and a gauzy green scarf in her lusterless black hair—and her defiant eyes are always fixed on this man as he reads.

I went ashore at Trabzon, where we were docked for a long time. Returning to the ship, I saw a new band of armed and ragged Kurds walking up the gangway—a retinue escorting an elder. Big and broad-chested, he wore an astrakhan and a grey Circassian coat snugly fastened around his narrow waist by a silver-plated belt. All the Kurds already camped on deck—they had gathered there en masse—got up and cleared a space for the newcomer. His retinue put down many rugs and pillows, and then the old man lay down majestically. His beard was white as steam; his face was dark and worn from the sun, and his brown eyes shone with an unusual brilliance.

I walked over to him, crouched, and said, "*Salaam.*" Then I asked in Russian if he was coming from the Caucasus.

"From farther away than that, sir," he answered amicably in Russian. "We are Kurds."

"And where are you traveling to?"

"To Istanbul, sir," he answered with modest pride. "To the Padishah himself. I am taking him a gift—seven whips. The Padishah took seven sons from me in the war—all I had. And all seven were killed. Seven times the Padishah brought glory to my name."

"Tsk, tsk, tsk," muttered a young Kerchen Greek with offhanded pity. He was standing above us holding a cigarette—a portly, handsome fop in a cherry-red fez, a grey frock coat and a white vest, stylish slacks, shiny boots that buttoned down the side. "Such an old man to wind up all alone," he said, shaking his head.

The Kurd looked at his fez. "How foolish you are," he answered simply. "It is you who will be old. I'm not old now, and never will be. Do you know about the ape?"

"What ape?" the fop answered uneasily.

"Listen, God made heaven and earth—you know that, right?"

"Well, yes."

"Then God made man. And he said, 'You, man, will live thirty years on the earth. It will be a good life. You will be happy. You will think that everything on earth was made for you alone by God. Are you satisfied with that?' And man thought, 'It's good—but only thirty years to live? That's not enough!' Are you listening?" the old man asked with a sardonic smile.

"I can hear you," the fop responded.

"Then God made a mule and said, 'You, mule, will live thirty years on this earth. You will carry wine sacks and heavy loads. People will ride on your back and beat you over the head with a stick. Are you satisfied with thirty years?' The mule cried out and wept and said to God: 'Why must I live so long? Let me live only fifteen years.' 'And give me fifteen more,' man said to God. 'Please, take fifteen years from his share and give them to me.' And God did as he was asked: Man received forty-five years of life. Things worked out well for man, didn't they?" the old man asked, glancing at the fop.

"Not bad," he answered tentatively, unsure of where all this would lead.

"Then God made a dog and gave him thirty years as well. 'You,' God said to the dog, 'will be angry all your life. You will guard your owner's riches, distrust strangers, stand barking in a doorway. You will not sleep at night for worrying.' And the dog began to howl: 'Please, please—give me only half of such a life.' And again man begged from God: 'Give me his half-life as well!' And again God did as he was asked. How many years does man have now?"

"That would make sixty," the fop answered more happily.

"Well, then God made an ape. He gave him thirty years to live, and said: 'You will live without labor and without concerns. But your face will be unpleasant. It will be bald and wrinkled, and you'll have no eyebrows. You will ask people to look at you, and they will only laugh at your face.'"

"So the ape refused—asked for half as many years as well?" asked the fop.

"That's right, the ape also refused half of his life," the old man answered, sitting up to take the mouthpiece of a water pipe from the Kurd next to him. "And man asked for that half-life as well," he said, lying down again and drawing on the pipe. He fell silent then, and stared straight ahead, as if he had forgotten us. When he began to talk again, he seemed to be addressing no one in particular:

"Man lived his own thirty years like a man—he ate, drank, fought wars, danced at weddings. Loved young women and girls. And for fifteen years he worked like a mule, gathering his riches. For fifteen years he guarded those riches like a dog, barking and being angry, and not sleeping at night. Then he became as old and foul as the ape. And everyone shook their heads and laughed at his old age. And it will all be the same with you," the old man said derisively, rolling the pipe's mouthpiece on his teeth.

"Why hasn't that happened to you?" asked the fop.

"It isn't that way with me."

"But *why?*"

"There are not many people like me," the old man said firmly. "I didn't live like a donkey or a dog. Why now should I live like an ape? Why should I be old?"

[1936]

Styopa

J UST BEFORE evening, the young merchant Krasilshchikov was
caught in a thunderstorm on the road to Chern.

He drove hard in the downpour, sitting high over the front axle of
his light-running *drozhky*, the collar turned up on his long, cloth coat,
his feet in big boots planted firmly over the mudguard. Water streamed
from the peaked cap he wore low over his eyes, and his hands grew cold
as he held the slick leather reins and needlessly urged on the already excited horse. Its tongue lolling from its mouth, a brown pointer ran in a
fountain of mud that sprayed from the left front wheel.

At first Krasilshchikov followed a black dirt lane near the highway,
but the lane soon turned into a grey, bubbling stream, and he moved
onto the main road, clattering over its surface of crushed stone. For
some time it had been impossible to see the surrounding fields and the
sky in the showering rain, which smelled of phosphorous and fresh cucumbers. Like a banner repeatedly unfurled to announce the end of the
world, lightning burst with a blinding, ruby flash across the entire length
of the great cloud wall before him, branching out and twisting into
sharp strands as the tail of each bolt sizzled overhead, then exploded in a

stunning clap of thunder. The horse flattened its ears and lunged forward with each blast; the dog broke into a leaping stride.... Krasilshchikov had grown up and studied in Moscow, but during summers at his Tula estate, which resembled an expensive dacha, he enjoyed his position as a merchant-landowner, a *mouzhik* who'd risen from the peasantry. So he drank Lafitte and carried his cigarettes in a gold-plated case while wearing tarred boots, shirts with collars that button on the side, and the snug-fitting jackets popular among simple country people. He was proud of his healthy Russian build and now, in the thundering downpour, with cold rain streaming from his nose and hat, he felt flush with the energetic joy of country living. That summer he often remembered the previous one, which he'd spent being miserable in Moscow because of an affair he was having with a well-known actress. He'd lingered in the city until July, waiting for her to leave for Kislovodsk: idle days and heat; the stench of green smoke from boiling tar in metal tubs along the dug-up streets; breakfast at the Troitsky café with actors from the Maly Theatre who were also going south to Kislovodsk, empty hours over coffee at Trambler's—and those nights he waited for her in his apartment with the furniture already covered in dust cloths, the chandeliers and the pictures wrapped in muslin, the smell of naphthalene in every room. Moscow evenings are endless in the summer—darkness comes only around eleven; and so he sits and sits—and for hours she isn't there. Then, finally, the bell—she appears in all her summer elegance, says all at once in her breathless voice, "I'm sorry I'm so late. I've been in bed all day with an absolutely brutal headache—yes, your tea rose is terribly faded today. I took the fastest cab I could. I haven't eaten all day—I'm starving."

As the rain and thunderclaps receded, the fields came back into view, and to the left of the highway he saw a familiar two-room hut built from unplaned logs: it was owned by the old widower Pronin, who used one of the rooms as lodging for travelers. Krasilshchikov was still twenty *versts* from town, his horse was already in a lather, and lightning continued to flash across the black sky ahead. "I'll have to stop and wait a little," he decided. At the crossing he turned sharply and pulled up to the inn's small wooden porch.

"Hello! Hey!" he shouted. "You have a guest, old man."

But all the windows under the rusty tin roof were dark; no one answered his call. He wrapped the reins around the *drozhky*'s front panel and followed his dripping, grimy dog onto the porch. Its eyes shining with a bright, senseless light, the animal looked almost rabid. Krasil-shchikov's forehead was damp with sweat; he took off his cap and tossed his waterlogged coat over the porch rail, revealing a tight-fitting jacket and a silver-plated belt. Then he wiped his mud-spattered face and began scraping the muck from his boots with his whip handle. The front door stood open to a small corridor that joined the owner's quarters with the guest room, but the entire building seemed to be deserted. "Must have gone to get the cattle in," he thought as he turned and looked at the field, wondering if he shouldn't drive farther. The evening air was damp and still; in the distance he could hear quail calling cheerfully from the sopped rye. The rain had stopped, but night was coming on; the sky and the land were turning dark and gloomy, and beyond the highway, be-yond the ink-black ridge of the forest, the clouds looked even thicker than before, and the lightning still flickered like a red, menacing flame. Krasilshchikov stepped into the narrow entrance hall and groped through the darkness to the guest room—it too was dark and silent: a cheap clock ticked on the wall. He slammed the door and turned to the left, groping again in the blackness until he found the door that led into the owner's private room: again, there was no one; flies droned on the ceiling as if dissatisfied and half asleep in the hot dark.

"Like they're dead and gone!" Krasilshchikov said out loud, and im-mediately he heard a soft, hurried voice. Styopa, the innkeeper's daugh-ter, had climbed down from the plank bed in the dark.

"Is that you, Vasil Likseich? I'm here all alone. The cook had a big fight with papa and went home, and now papa's taken his helper to town on an errand. They probably won't get back till tomorrow. The storm scared me to death, and all of a sudden I hear someone drive up: it scared me even more. . . . Excuse me, please—hello."

Krasilshchikov struck a match and held it toward her, revealing her small, dark-skinned face and black eyes.

"Hello, my little fool," he said. "I was going to town too, but I decided to wait out the storm. . . . And you thought it was thieves pulling in?"

The match began to burn down, but he could still see her smile and her startled expression, the coral necklace she wore, her small breasts under a yellow chintz dress. Slightly more than half his height, she looked exactly like a little girl.

"We need some light," she said hurriedly. Flustered by Krasil-shchikov's impertinent stare, she rushed toward the lamp that hung over the table. "God himself must have sent you. What would I do all alone?"

she said in her sweet-sounding voice as she stood on her toes and awk-wardly lifted the lamp's glass cylinder from its serrated tin base.

Krasilshchikov lit another match and stared at her body as she stretched and leaned away from him. "It's fine like this," he said sud-denly, throwing down the match and reaching around her waist. "Wait a minute. Turn around."

She looked at him over her shoulder with frightened eyes, dropped her hands by her sides and turned. He pulled her toward him; she threw her head back in alarm but didn't try to wrench free.

Looking down through the darkness, he fixed his eyes on hers and laughed. "Are you even more frightened now?"

"Vasil Likseich . . . ," she said imploringly as she pulled against his arms.

"Wait, don't you like me? You're always glad when I stop by."

"There's no one on earth better than you," she whispered ardently.

"There—you see." He kissed her lips slowly and his hands slipped farther down.

"Vasil Likseich . . . in the name of Christ. . . . You forgot your horse, it's still by the porch. . . . Papa will come back. . . . No. . . . No, you shouldn't."

Half an hour later he came outside, tied his horse under an awning in the courtyard, took off its bridle, gave it some wet, fresh-cut grass from a hayrack that stood nearby. Then he walked back to the hut, looking up at the peaceful stars and the rain-washed sky. Distant summer lightning still flickered in the hot, dark, and silent room. She was curled up tightly on the plank bed with her chin pressed to her chest, wrung out from cry-ing in ecstasy, shock, and horror at everything that had taken place. He kissed her wet, salty cheek, lay down on his back, and drew her head to his shoulder with his left hand while holding a cigarette in the other. She lay peaceful and silent beside him, her hair lightly touching his chin as he gently stroked it and smoked, his mind wandering. Soon she was fast asleep. He stared up at the darkness and grinned with satisfac-tion. "Papa went to town." There he goes, and—*voilà*—here we are! It's too bad, though—one look at her and he'll know everything. That with-ered old man with a little grey coat is shrewd. You can tell by just look-ing at him—that beard that's white as snow, those black eyebrows of his. He talks nonstop when he's drunk, but his eyes are sharp, and he sees through everyone. . . .

He lay without sleeping until the hut's darkness diminished and the room began to reappear. Turning his head, he saw the greenish hue of the eastern sky turning white outside the window, and in a gloomy corner of the room he noticed a large icon hanging over a table: a saint in holy vestments raised his hand in blessing, an adamant and stern expression on his face. Krasilshchikov looked at the girl: she was still curled up, her knees drawn to her chest, everything forgotten in sleep! A sweet and pitiful girl. . . .

When the sky was completely light and the rooster began to crow in changing tones beyond the wall, he made a move to get out of bed, and she immediately sat up. With her dress unbuttoned and her hair disheveled, she leaned to one side and stared at him with uncomprehending eyes.

"Styopa," he said cautiously. "It's time—I have to go."

"You're already leaving?" she whispered without understanding.

But then she suddenly came to her senses: her fists struck her shoulders as she clasped her arms to her chest. "Where are you going? What will I do without you? What am I supposed to do now?"

"Styopa, I'll come back soon."

"You know papa will be here! How will I see you? I'd come through the woods, but how will I get out of the house?"

He clenched his teeth and pushed her down on her back. She threw out her arms and gasped, as if despairing before death: "Ah!"

And then he was standing in front of the plank bed, already in his tight-fitting jacket and his peaked cap, already holding his whip in his hand. His back was turned to the heavy, brilliant light of the rising sun as she kneeled on the bed, sobbing like a child and contorting her mouth as she struggled to speak:

"Vasil Likseich . . . in the name of Christ. . . . In the name of the heavenly father himself, marry me! I'll be like your slave! I'll sleep by your door! I'd run away with you now if I could, but they'll never let me go. Vasil Likseich. . . ."

"Be quiet," Krasilshchikov said sternly. "In a few days I'll go to your father and tell him that I'm marrying you. Hear?"

She sat back and stopped sobbing, lifted her wet, radiant eyes with a trusting expression. "Really?"

"Of course—really."

"I turned fifteen at Epiphany," she said hurriedly.

"Well, there—you see. Six months and we can marry. . . ."

As soon as he got home he began packing his things; toward evening he drove in his troika to the railway station. Two days later he was already in Kislovodsk.

[1938]

Muza

ALTHOUGH I was well past my youth, I'd gotten it into my head to
learn how to paint—I'd loved painting all my life. So I left my estate
near Tambov to spend the winter studying in Moscow, where I took
lessons from a fairly well-known and utterly talentless artist. A fat,
slovenly man, he'd mastered all the requisite artifices: a condescending
air, an offhand manner with everyone he met, a velvet coat the color of a
pomegranate, and a pair of dirty grey gaiters, which I especially hated.
With a pipe in his teeth and his hair combed back in long, greasy curls,
he would glance at a student's work, screw up his eyes, and say, as if to
himself, "Amusing, most amusing. . . . A sure success."

During those days I lived on the Arbat—in the Capital Hotel, right
next to the Prague Restaurant. I worked with the artist or painted in my
room during the day, and spent most of my evenings with new bo-
hemian friends—some of them were young, others were old and seedy,
but they all had the same affection for billiards, crawfish, and beer. How
sad and dull it was! The gloomy Capital, that girlish artist and his grimy
clothes, his "creatively" neglected studio with dusty props strewn around
the floor. Mostly I remember the constant blur of falling snow outside

my window, the muffled ring of harness bells and the scrape of horse-drawn trams on the Arbat, the sour smell of beer and gaslights in a hazy restaurant. I don't know why I lived so miserably—I was far from poor.

One day in March I was working in my room. The air drifting through the open *fortochka* was damp from the rain and the wet snow outside, but it was no longer winter air; the sharp clattering of the horses' hooves sounded of spring, and the jingling harness bells seemed almost musical. I was sketching with pastels when someone knocked on the door. "Who is it?" I shouted, but no answer followed. I waited, shouted again, and again heard nothing—then, another knock. I went into the hall and opened the door: on the threshold stood a tall young woman in a grey winter hat, grey overshoes, and a grey coat. She stared straight at me with eyes the color of acorns. Drops of rain and melting snow glistened on her face, her long eyelashes, the hair under the brim of her hat. She looked at me and said:

"I'm Muza Graf—I study in the conservatory. I heard that you're an interesting man, so I came to meet you. Is that all right with you?"

"I'm very flattered," I said, surprised but trying to be polite. "You're welcome anytime. But I should warn you—the rumors that you've heard aren't true: there's nothing interesting about me."

"All the same, why don't you ask me in?" she said, still staring straight into my eyes. "Since I've flattered you, you shouldn't keep me in the hall."

She came inside as if entering her own home, removed her hat, and patted down her chestnut hair before my chipped and greying mirror. Then she slipped off her coat, tossed it over a chair, and sat down on the couch in a checkered flannel dress.

Her nose was wet from the rain and snow. She sniffled. "There's a handkerchief in my coat pocket, bring it to me please," she said commandingly. "And help me with these overshoes."

I brought the handkerchief; she wiped her nose and stretched her legs toward me. "I saw you at Shor's concert yesterday," she said indifferently.

Suppressing a stupid smile of pleasure and surprise—what an eccentric guest!—I timidly removed her overshoes. She smelled of fresh, cold air; the smell excited me. And the boldness that was somehow fused with youth and femininity in her features—in her forthright eyes, in her large and pretty hands—all of it excited me as I removed those overshoes while she sat with her round full knees beneath her dress, and I glimpsed the thin grey stockings stretched across her calves, her narrow feet in patent leather shoes.

Then she settled into the couch, obviously content to stay awhile. Not knowing what to talk about, I started asking questions. Who told her about me? What had she heard? Who was she? Where did she live?

"It doesn't matter where I heard about you. I really came because I saw you at the concert—you're quite handsome. And I live not far from here, on Prechistensky Boulevard; my father's a doctor."

She spoke abruptly, almost sharply.

"Would you like some tea?" I asked, again not knowing what to say.

"I would. And if you have some money, send the bellhop for some apples," she said. "Belov's has Rennets—it's right on the Arbat. But tell him to hurry—I don't like waiting."

"And you seem so easygoing."

"Things are rarely how they seem."

When the bellhop brought the samovar and a bag of apples, she made us tea and wiped the cups and spoons, despite the fact that they were clean. And after eating a Rennet with her tea, she nestled farther into the couch, patted the place beside her, and said, "Now, come sit next to me."

I went to her and she embraced me, kissed my lips unhurriedly, then pulled away and briefly studied my face. As if she'd reassured herself that I was worthy, she closed her eyes and began again—she kissed me for a long time, with a kind of studied, slow precision.

"Well then," she said, as if relieved. "That's all for now. Day after tomorrow."

It had grown completely dark; only the street lamps cast a sad, dim light into the room. You can imagine how I felt. Why this sudden happiness? Why this young, strong woman? The unusual taste . . . the rare shape of her lips. . . . I heard the steady monotone of harness bells and clattering hooves like something from a dream.

"I'd like to have lunch with you at the Prague day after tomorrow," she said. "I've never eaten there—I'm really very inexperienced. I can imagine what you're thinking, but the truth is, you're my first love."

"Love?"

"What would you call this?"

Soon after that I quit my lessons, although she continued taking classes now and then at the conservatory. And instead of parting ways, we lived like newlyweds. We went to galleries and concerts, even sat through public lectures. . . . At her suggestion, I moved in May to an old estate near Moscow—the owners had built dachas on their land and put them up for rent. She took the train to visit me, returning to the city after midnight. I would never have expected such a life—a little summer house near Moscow and days without a thing to do, an estate so different from the one I owned in the steppe, a climate so unlike the one at home.

Evergreens and constant rain. . . . Again and again, white clouds gather in the blue above the trees, the thunder starts to roll, and then a shimmering rain falls through the sunlight, steams in the heat, becomes a mist that smells of pine. And everything's damp; everything's lush, rinsed to a sheen. . . . The pond on the estate resembled a huge black mirror half-buried in the weeds, and the trees were so massive that our dachas looked like little shacks scattered around a forest in the tropics. I lived in a log cabin at the edge of the park. It was still in need of work— they hadn't caulked the walls or planed the floor; the stove didn't have a screen, and most of the rooms lacked furniture. I left a pair of boots under the bed, and soon they were covered in a mold as thick as velvet from the constant damp.

It never grew dark before midnight: among hushed trees the twilight of the west hung on and on. When the moon came out, its still and spellbound light mixed strangely with that lingering dusk. The silence of the forest, the calm air, and the peaceful sky promised an end to the rain as I dozed off in my cabin after walking her to the station, but later I'd be woken by another downpour pelting the roof, more thunderclaps as lightning plumbed the dark. In the morning, the lilac-colored earth was speckled with shade and blinding spots of light; thrushes made a reedy, churring sound, and small birds called flycatchers ticked like metal tapping stone among the leaves. The air turned hot and heavy by midday; clouds bunched up, and soon more rain was coming down. The sky would clear again in the evening, and as the sun set, its rays streamed through the leaves, sloped into my room, formed a golden grid that flashed and wavered on the rough, log-cabin walls like light refracted by a crystal. Then I'd leave to meet her at the station. The arriving train would unload throngs of people headed for their dachas, the smell of burning coal would mix with the damp, fresh air of the forest, and she'd appear among the crowd, holding a string bag, her arms weighed down with fruit and packages of food, a bottle of Madeira. . . . We always dined alone, enjoying each other's company. . . . Before her train back to Moscow, we'd wander in the park, and she'd lean her head on my shoulder like a woman walking in her sleep beside a black pond where ancient trees reach into the stars, where the pale night sky stuns us with its infinite silence, and the shadows of the evergreens fall endlessly across fields that look like silver lakes in the distance.

In June we moved to my estate near Tambov; we didn't marry, but she lived with me and ran the household as if she were my wife. During the long fall she was content to occupy her time with reading and everyday chores. Our most regular visitor from among the neighbors was a lonely, impoverished landowner named Zavistovsky. He lived only two *versts* away, and during the winter he began coming to our house almost every night. I'd known him since childhood, and I soon grew so used to his presence that it seemed strange to be at home without him. He was a red-haired, frail, timid, and slow-witted man, but he was a fairly good musician. The two of us would play checkers, or Muza and he would play duets on the piano.

Just before Christmas I made a trip into town. The moon was already up when I returned. Entering the house, I failed to find her anywhere.

"Where is your ladyship, Dunya?" I asked the maid while drinking tea alone. "Did she go for a walk?"

"I don't know, sir. She's been gone since breakfast."

"She dressed and left," my old nurse said gloomily as she passed through the dining room without looking up.

"Must have gone to Zavistovsky's," I thought to myself. "They're probably on their way back here, it's already seven." Still chilled from my journey, I lay down in the study and unexpectedly dozed off. And just as suddenly, I snapped out of my sleep an hour later with a clear and savage thought: "She's left me! She's hired a *mouzhik* to take her to the station—gone back to Moscow! She could do anything! But maybe she's here now. . . . Maybe she's come back. . . ." I walked through the house again. "No, not here. . . . And the servants see me searching for her. . . . Humiliating."

At about ten, not knowing what else to do, I put on my coat, picked up my gun for some reason, and left on the main road for Zavistovsky's. "It's as if he didn't come on purpose today—and I have the whole damn night ahead of me! Has she really left me? It's impossible, no!" I walk and my boots squeal in the packed snow of the road. White fields shine to my left under a low, pitiful moon. . . . I turn off the main road and approach the sorry-looking estate: a row of barren trees leading across a field, the entrance to the courtyard, the run-down house standing to the left, all of it in darkness. . . . The porch is covered with ice. I climb the steps and wrench open the door with its tattered padding and upholstery: the foyer glows from the flames of an open stove. It's warm and dark. . . . Even in the living room it's dark. . . .

"Vikenty Vikentich!"

Wearing felt boots, he appeared without a sound at the threshold of his study. There too it was dark, except for the moonlight falling through a three-pane window.

"Oh, it's you. Come in, come in," he said. "I was just sitting here in the twilight, enjoying a night without lamps."

I entered and sat down on his battered couch.

"Can you believe it—Muza's disappeared."

He was silent for a moment. And then, in a voice I could barely hear: "Yes, I understand you."

"You 'understand'? What do you mean?"

Immediately Muza entered the study from the adjoining bedroom. Like him, she wore felt boots; like him, she moved without a sound, a shawl around her shoulders.

"I see you've brought a gun," she said, sitting down on the couch opposite me. "If you want to shoot, shoot me, not him."

Everything was visible in the golden moonlight coming through the window. I looked at her felt boots and her knees under her grey skirt. I wanted to scream, "I can't live without you—I would die for those knees and that skirt, those boots!"

"Everything's finished," she said. "It's over. There's no point in making a scene."

"You're a monster," I said, choking on the words.

"Could you give me a cigarette, darling?" she said to Zavistovsky. He timidly leaned toward her, extended his cigarette case, and began digging in his pockets for a match.

"You already speak to me like a stranger," I gasped. "Couldn't you wait to call him 'darling'?"

"Why?" she asked, raising her eyebrows while the cigarette dangled from her fingers.

My heart hammered in my throat. Blood throbbed in my temples . . . I got up and staggered out.

[1938]

Old Woman

THE OLD WOMAN came from far away to Moscow. She calls her northern region Rus. She's big, round-hipped—wears felt boots and a bulky, quilted vest. Her face is large; her eyes are yellow; her thick grey hair's unkempt—an eighteenth-century character.

Once I asked how old she is.

"I am seventy-seven, sir."

"And god willing, you'll long continue on this earth."

"Why not? Those aren't so many years. My father lived to be a hundred."

She drinks hot water, eats black bread with herring or pickles, never touches tea or sugar.

"You've been healthy all those years, I'm sure."

"No, I had the shaking sickness once. Someone cast a spell on me. I was terrified of my husband. If he came to me for love, I'd shake and writhe. I'd burn her alive—the one who cast that spell."

The phrase "to burn alive" is among her favorites. She has harsh words for atheists:

"How dare they say such things. God's ours, not theirs. I'd burn them all alive."

Her stories of her homeland are magnificent. The forests there are dark and overgrown. Sometimes the snow piles higher than the tops of the hundred-year-old pines. People sail along the roads in bast sleds towed by shaggy, stocky horses. They wear sheepskin coats dyed sky-blue with tall stiff collars that are made of dog fur, like their hats. The cold burns right through your chest. At dusk the setting sun's like something from a fairy tale, playing on the land with lilac-colored light and bursts of brilliant red, or cloaking everything in green and gold. Stars at night the size of swans' eggs. . . .

[1930]

Late Hour

So LONG since I was there, so long, I told myself. Not since my nineteenth year. I lived in Russia once, felt it was my own, had the full freedom to go where I wanted. And traveling was no great labor; I could have gone three hundred *versts* quite easily. But always I delayed. The years moved on, decades passed, and now there's no more time for waiting. Go now, or never go. This is the last and final chance, for the hour is late, and no one will meet me.

So I crossed the bridge over the river, seeing far into the distance in the July moonlight.

The bridge was so familiar that I felt I'd seen it only yesterday: humpbacked and crudely aged, as if instead of being built with stone, it was formed from something else that slowly petrified, turned hard and indestructible with time. As a boy, I used to think it was already bending over the water when Batu reigned. But in this town the bridge and the ruined walls on the cliff below the cathedral are all that speak of ancient days. The rest is simply old, provincial, nothing more. There was only one oddity for me, only one sign that things had changed on earth since I was just a child: earlier you couldn't sail the river. But now, apparently, they'd deepened it and cleared the rocks and snags. The moon was to my left, quite high above the river. In its unsteady light and the trembling sheen of the water, I could see a white paddle-wheel steamer with all its lamps burning: the portals glowed like unmoving, golden eyes, and the lights' reflections formed long columns as they stretched across the water: the ship stood silently on them, as if abandoned. I've seen the same on the Suez Canal, in Yaroslavl, and on the Nile. But in Paris the nights are thick and damp. A pinkish haze spreads across the impenetrable sky, the Seine flows black as tar beneath the bridges, and all the big columns of light falling from their lamps turn into tricolors on the water's surface: white, blue, and red—the colors of the Russian flag. Here there are no lamps, and the bridge is dry and dusty. A fire tower rises over the town and the black gardens on the hill ahead. My God, what happiness it was! During the night of the wildfire I kissed your hand for the first time, and you squeezed my fingers in response. I will never forget that secret gesture of consent. In the eerie light of the flames, all the street was black with crowds. I'd been at your house when the alarm bell rang, and everyone rushed to the windows, then hurried to the gate. The fire was far beyond the river, but it burned with terrifying greed and urgency. Smoke poured into thick clouds of blackened, purple fleece, and the flames billowed in the air like huge red sails of calico, their reflections forming copper waves in the nearby dome of Michael the Archangel's Church. In the confusion of a frightened crowd, pressed by simple people speaking with concern, excitement, and alarm, I smelled your hair, your neck, your gingham dress, and suddenly it was decided: everything went still inside me and I took your hand. . . .

I climbed the hill beyond the bridge, walked the pavement into town.

There was no one there, and not one light was burning in the houses. The wide, mute streets were full of that peaceful sadness that comes to every Russian town sleeping in the steppe. Only the gardens could be heard—a cautious rustling of leaves in a weak and even wind that began somewhere in the fields, trailed through town, passed softly over me. I walked, and the big moon followed like a brilliant disk rocking its way through the black branches. Shade covered most of the streets, but houses on the right stood out sharp and clear with their white walls in the moonlight, a black luster spilling from their darkened windowpanes. I stepped on shadows that lay like black silk lace across the dappled pavement. She had a long and narrow evening dress of lace. It fit perfectly her narrow waist; it matched her young, black eyes. When she wore it she was so mysterious, so unaware of me, that I was hurt. Whose house were we visiting? Where were we when she wore that dress?

I'd planned to visit Old Street, and I could have gone there by another, shorter route. But instead I followed the wide streets through the gardens and went to see my school. I was surprised again when I reached it. Everything had stayed the same for half a century: a stone wall and a stone courtyard, a big stone building in the center of it all—everything as colorless and dull as it had been when I was there. I lingered by the gate and tried to feel the self-indulgent sadness of remembrance, and couldn't. Yes, a first-grade boy with his hair cropped short walked through this gate. He wore a blue cadet's cap with little silver palms above the brim, a new overcoat with silver buttons. And then he turned into a thin young man wearing a grey jacket and stylish pants with stirrups. But was that really me?

Old Street seemed only to have narrowed. Nothing else had changed: dusty merchant houses still lined both its sides, there were still no trees, and the road was still full of potholes. The sidewalk was riddled with holes as well, so I kept to the middle of the street, where I could see my feet in the moonlight. . . . And the night was like another night—that one at the end of August, when I wore a narrow belt around a long shirt with a collar that buttoned on the side, and apples lay in mounds in the markets, and we could smell them everywhere in the warm, dark air. Are you able to remember such a night in the place that you inhabit now?

I couldn't bring myself to visit your old house. It too was probably unchanged—but that would make it all the more unbearable to see. New and unfamiliar people live there now. Your mother and your father, your brother—they all outlived you, but they died in turn. And all those close to me have died—not only relatives but friends and mere acquaintances who started life with me. How long ago we all began to live. They were sure there would be no end: but it all began, it all flowed on and reached its end, passed before my eyes—so quickly before my eyes! Sitting on a curbstone before the tall, locked gate of some impregnable merchant house, I imagined her in that distant time when we were together: her dark hair tied back, her clear eyes and her youthful, suntanned face; the strength and purity, the freedom of a young body under a light summer dress. That was the start of our love, our closeness, and our joy. A time when happiness was clouded by nothing, when trust was transparent and tenderness a kind of ecstasy.

There's something in the warm, light nights of provincial Russian towns at the end of summer—a kind of peace, a certainty that you are safe. An old night watchman with a *kolotushka* wanders around the dark town, but only for his own pleasure: there's nothing to guard. Sleep well, good people—like providence, this boundless, glowing night is watching over you. And the old man who rattles his *kolotushka* to the rhythms of some dance inside his head as he walks on roads still warm from the day—he looks at the sky without a care. On a night like that, at that late hour when only he was awake, you waited for me among the dry leaves of late summer. I slipped through the gate you'd unlocked, quietly ran through the courtyard. And on the other side of the barn, at the far edge of that courtyard, I entered the mottled twilight of the garden, where faintly I could see your white dress in the distance: you were sitting on a bench under an apple tree. I hurried there, and when you raised your hopeful, shining eyes to me, I was filled with joy and fear.

We sat stupefied with happiness. I put my arm around you and could hear your beating heart; I held your hand and all of you was there. It grew so late that even the *kolotushka* fell silent—the old man had lain down on a bench somewhere and dozed off, warming himself in the moonlight, a pipe still clamped between his teeth. When I looked to my right, I saw the moon hanging high and pure above the courtyard, the house's roof shining like fish scales in its light. When I looked to my left, I saw a little path overgrown with dry weeds that trailed off into an apple orchard, and from behind the orchard trees I glimpsed a single green star. Suspended somewhere over another garden, it burned calmly but expectantly; it was saying something without words. But I looked only briefly at the courtyard and that star: all that mattered in the world was the twilight and your glistening eyes.

You walked me to the gate, and I said: "If there is a future life, and we meet in it, I will kneel down and kiss your feet for everything you've given me on earth." Then I stepped into the middle of the moonlit road and started walking to my house. And when I turned, I saw a whiteness still there, still lingering at your gate.

I got up from the curbstone and started down the road the way I'd come. Old Street wasn't all I'd planned to see. I had another aim in mind—one I'd hidden from myself while knowing all along it was inevitable. And so I started out in that direction—I would visit one more place, and leave for good.

Once again, I knew the way: straight ahead, straight ahead, then left at the bazaar, and out from town on Monastery Road.

The bazaar is like another town within the town. Each row has its own distinctive smell. Awnings cast a gloom over the long tables and benches where people eat. In the middle of the hardware aisle, an icon hangs on a chain: the Savior stares with his eyes wide open from a rusty frame. In the morning fat pigeons flock around the bakers' stalls, run and peck at crumbs. You walk to school and you're amazed, somehow, by all these pigeons—how rainbows shine around their necks, how they bob their heads in rhythm, rock from side to side, mince as if they're trying to be coquettes. They act as if you don't exist until the last possible moment, then burst into flight from under your feet, rise on their whistling wings. At night, big rats come out and scurry through the stalls, intent on something, terrifying, dark and foul.

Monastery Road's a quick and easy route into the fields. Some travel it to their houses in the countryside; others to the city of the dead. In Paris the entrance to some nondescript house will suddenly take on the trappings of a play about the plague, and for two days these morbid decorations will set the house apart from all the others on its street. The front door is draped in black and silver crepe, and a piece of paper edged in black is set neatly on a table under a black cloth in the entranceway. For forty-eight hours polite visitors write their names here as a sign of sympathy, and then, at some last, appointed hour, a huge hearse with a black canopy rolls up. The rounded edges of the canopy are decorated with big white stars in order to preserve our dreams of heaven, but the wooden carriage frame itself is pitch black, like a plague coffin, and black plumes flutter from the corners of the roof like ostrich feathers from the underworld. The massive creatures pulling it are draped in coal-black studded cloths with little eyelets rimmed in white. Waiting for the body to be carried out, an old drunk sits on the towering driver's box. He too must be attired for the occasion, so he wears a somber tricorn and a mourning coat to play his role, even though he's prone to smirking at those solemn words: *Requiem aeternam dona eis, Domine, et lux perpetua luceat eis.* . . . Here it's all done differently. An open coffin's carried on linen cloths into the breeze that blows down Monastery Road. A rice-white face rocks from side to side with its heavy eyelids shut, a bright paper band around the forehead. This is how they carried her away.

Built in the time of Tsar Aleksey Mikhaylovich, the monastery stands like a fortress at the edge of town, just left of the highway. Its gates are always locked, and forbidding walls surround the cathedral's golden domes. But farther on, already in the open countryside, low walls enclose a wide grove of birches, elms, and limes. Long, intersecting avenues run through the grove; monuments and crosses are spread among the trees beside them. There the gate was open wide, and I could see the main avenue—smooth and endless. Timidly I took off my hat and went into the grove. Such a late and silent hour! The moon was hanging low behind the trees, but everything was clear: I could see the full expanse of that forest of the dead, the pattern of its monuments and crosses in the limpid shade. The wind had settled; patches of darkness and light that had trembled under the trees now lay motionless in the hour before dawn. Suddenly something stirred at the far end of the grove. From behind the graveyard church it flashed with terrible speed, flew at me like a black ball: outside myself, I jumped aside, my head turning to ice and tightening, my heart lurching, going still. . . . What was it? It raced away and disappeared. But my heart stayed motionless. And so, carrying my heart like a heavy cup inside my chest, I walked straight on, knowing where I had to go. At the end of the path I came to a patch of level ground that was overgrown with dry grass. There an isolated, narrow slab of stone lay facing out from the back wall of the cemetery. And from behind the wall, a green star hung like a brilliant gem. It glowed like that earlier star, but it was mute and still.

[1938]

Zoyka and Valeriya

IN THE WINTER Levitsky spent all of his free time at the Danilevskys'
Moscow apartment, and in the summer he began to visit their dacha in
the pine forest along the Kazan railway line.

He was in his fifth year at the university and was twenty-four years
old, but at the Danilevskys' only the doctor referred to him as "colleague"; everyone else called him "Zhorzh" or "Zhorzhik." Lonely and
prone to falling in love, he often attached himself to some familiar
household and soon became a member of the family, visiting for days
on end, sometimes from morning until night if his lessons allowed —
and so it was with the Danilevskys. Not only the hostess but even the
children — the plump Zoyka and the big-eared Grishka — treated him
like some kind of distant, homeless relative. Outwardly he was simple
and kind, quiet but obliging, always ready to respond if a word was di-
rected toward him.

When patients came to see Danilevsky, an old woman in a nurse's
uniform opened the door and ushered them into a big parlor furnished
with rugs and imposing antique furniture; there she put on her glasses,
picked up a pencil, and looked sternly at her appointment book. Some

of the patients were then told the hour and the day of their future appointments; others were led through the tall doors of the reception room. Here they waited a long time to be called into yet another room, where a young assistant in a smock as white as sugar questioned and examined them. It was only after all of this that the patients finally reached Danilevsky himself in his big office where, along the back wall, there was a high bed on which some of the patients were made to lie in the most pitiful, awkward, and frightening positions: all of it confused and embarrassed the patients—the assistant and the woman in the hall, the shiny copper disk at the end of the pendulum that swung so gravely in the grandfather clock, the general air of importance that permeated the spacious, rich apartment, and the expectant silence of the waiting room, where no one dared to take an extra breath. All of the patients therefore believed that this was an eternally lifeless place, and they were sure that Danilevsky, who was tall, thick-set, and rather rude, must smile no more than once a year. But they were wrong: to the right of the entrance, a set of double doors led to the living quarters, and here there was almost constant noise from the guests. The samovar was never taken from the table, and the maid never stopped running, bringing more glasses and cups, a jar of jam, biscuits and white bread. Even during his receiving hours, Danilevsky would often sneak down the hall to drink tea with his visitors and talk about the patients, saying, "Ah, they can wait a bit—may the devil have their mothers," while the patients themselves sat quietly, convinced the doctor was busy with some critical case.

Once, while sitting this way, Danilevsky looked with a smile at Levitsky's stooped and skinny frame, his sunken stomach and his slightly crooked legs. "Tell the truth, colleague," he said, studying the young man's taut, freckled skin, his hawkish eyes and wiry red hair, "surely you have some Eastern blood—Jewish maybe, or Caucasian?"

"None at all, Nikolay Grigoryevich, no Jewish blood," Levitsky answered with his unflagging eagerness to speak when spoken to. "There are some Ukrainian Levitskys, so, like you, I might have a little Ukrainian blood. And some Polish. And I hear from my grandfather there might be some Turkish. . . . But really, Allah only knows."

Danilevsky roared with laughter. "Ah, you see, I was right! Be careful ladies and girls—he's a Turk! Not at all the humble fellow you might take him for! And as we know, he loves like a Turk. Whose turn is it now, colleague? Who is the woman of your generous heart these days?"

"Dariya Tadiyevna," Levitsky answered with a simplehearted smile, turning red as if a small flame were passing over his body. He often smiled and blushed this way.

Dariya Tadiyevna was a good-looking woman with a bluish down on her upper lip and along her cheeks. Still recovering from typhus, she wore a little cap of black silk as she half sat and half lay in an armchair nearby. Overhearing Levitsky, she was so charmingly embarrassed that her black-currant eyes seemed to disappear completely for a moment.

"Well?" she said. "That's not a secret to anyone. It's completely natural, since I have Eastern blood as well."

Then Grishka began to shout lustily, "They've been caught, they've been caught!" while Zoyka, screwing up her eyes, bolted into the next room and fell across the armrest of the couch.

That winter Levitsky really was secretly in love with Dariya Tadiyevna, and before her, he had felt something for Zoyka. She was only fourteen, but she was physically mature, especially when seen from behind, although the slightly blue knees below her short, plaid skirt were still as round and tender as a child's. A year ago they'd taken Zoyka out of school after Danilevsky diagnosed her with the early signs of some sort of brain disease, and since no one taught her anything at home, Zoyka lived in a state of carefree idleness without ever being bored. She felt such tenderness for people that she licked her lips whenever they came close. Her forehead was high and domed, her mouth was always damp, and her oily blue eyes expressed a naive joy, as if the world were a constant, delightful surprise. For all her corpulence, Zoyka moved with a seductive grace, and the red ribbon tied in her shimmering, nut-brown hair made her only more appealing. She often sat in Levitsky's lap, and although she acted like an innocent child at such moments, she probably understood quite well what he was suffering in secret as he held her plump body and tried to keep from looking at those bare knees below her checkered skirt. Sometimes he couldn't control himself and kissed her on the cheek as if joking, and she closed her eyes and smiled in a languid, teasing way. Once she secretly told Levitsky what she alone in the world knew about her mother—she was in love with the young doctor Titov! Mama's forty, but she looks very young, and she's so thin—just like a girl with noble blood, and both of them—she and the doctor— they're so beautiful and tall! Then Levitsky became inattentive to her, for Dariya Tadiyevna had begun to appear in the house. Zoyka pretended to be even happier, even more carefree, and sometimes she would throw herself on Dariya Tadiyevna with a shout, kissing her and hating her so intensely that when the woman later fell ill, Zoyka daily awaited the joyous news of her death. Then she waited for her to leave — and for summer, knowing Levitsky would be freed from his studies to visit the dacha her family had kept for three years in the forest near the Kazan railway line: in secret she was hunting him.

Then summer came, and he began to visit for two or three days at a time each week. But soon another guest arrived — papa's niece from Kharkov, Valeriya Ostrogradskaya, whom neither Grishka nor Zoyka had ever seen. Levitsky was sent to Moscow early one morning to meet her at Kursk station, and he returned from the dacha train stop not on his bicycle but with her in a cart, looking tired, hollow-eyed, and joyously excited. It was obvious he'd fallen in love with her before the train even left Moscow, and she treated him like her subject as he carried her bags to the house. As soon as she ran onto the porch to meet mother, however, she forgot all about Levitsky and didn't notice him again for the rest of the day. To Zoyka she was completely incomprehensible — while sorting her things in her room, and later, while having breakfast on the balcony, she would talk a great deal, then suddenly fall silent, as if lost in her own thoughts. But she was a true Ukrainian beauty! And Zoyka stuck to her with unshakable determination.

"Did you bring leather boots? And a brocade kerchief? Will you put them on? May I call you Valechka?"

Even without her Ukrainian apparel, she was very attractive indeed: shapely and strong, with thick dark hair and velvety eyebrows that almost joined in the middle. Her unnerving eyes were the color of black blood and her face had a dark, warm glow from the sun. She had shiny white teeth and lips like ripe cherries. Her hands were small but strong and evenly tanned, like meat that had been delicately smoked. And what shoulders! And how easy it was to see the pink, silk straps of the camisole that touched those shoulders under her thin white blouse! Her skirt was short and simple, but it fit her to perfection! Zoyka was too carried away to be jealous of Levitsky, who had stopped going to Moscow altogether, and now never left Valeriya's side, happy because she'd grown more friendly, called him by his first name, and constantly ordered him to do something. Then the full, hot days of summer began, and more and more guests came from Moscow. Zoyka noticed that Levitsky had been dismissed: he often sat with mother now, helping her clean raspberries, while Valeriya had fallen in love with Dr. Titov, the same man whom mother secretly loved. Something strange had happened to Valeriya in general—when the guests were gone, she no longer changed from one elegant blouse into another, and sometimes she walked around from morning until night wearing mother's peignoir and looking mildly disgusted. Zoyka was terribly curious—did she kiss Levitsky before falling in love with Titov? Grishka swore that he had seen her walking once in the alley of spruces with Levitsky after swimming. She wore a towel on her head like a turban, and Levitsky stumbled along behind her, carrying a wet bath sheet and saying something over and over until she stopped, and he suddenly grabbed her by the shoulders and kissed her lips.

"I hid behind the trees so they couldn't see me," Grishka said excitedly, his eyes bulging out. "I saw everything. She looked very pretty—only red all over—it was still hot and she swam too much—you know how she always stays in the water for at least two hours a day—I spied on her then too—she looked like a Naiad when she was nude in the water! And he kept talking and talking—he really is like a Turk."

Grishka swore it was true, but he loved to make up stupid stories, and Zoyka believed and didn't believe.

On Saturdays and Sundays even the morning trains from Moscow were crowded with people coming to visit dachas. Sometimes a pleasant rain fell through the sunlight, and the green railroad cars were washed clean and shone as if new, and the white puffs of smoke from the engine became especially soft, and the rounded tops of the graceful pines that stood at closely measured intervals along the tracks seemed to extend even farther into the bright air above the passing trains. The arriving passengers competed for carts on hot, packed sand near the station, then rode happily down lanes that had been cut into the woods, the sky like streamers over their heads. Soon a mood of pure country bliss took over the forest that spread in all directions and sheltered the dry, undulating earth. When the hosts took their Moscow guests for walks, they'd boast that bears were the only thing missing in the forest; they'd recite, "*The dark woods smell of pitch and wild berries*" and shout out "hello" to one another, enjoying their idle summer days and their free-spirited clothes—their long peasant shirts with embroidered hems and colorful braided belts, their canvas caps. Indeed, it was not easy to recognize a Moscow acquaintance—a professor or the bearded, bespectacled editor of some journal—as he wandered in such clothes.

In this festive mood of summer living, Levitsky was doubly miserable, feeling pitiful, deceived, and extraneous from dawn until dusk. He wondered the same thing constantly: Why, why did she take him in so quickly and so ruthlessly, why did she make him a friend, and then a slave, and then a lover to be satisfied with the always rare and unexpected joy of mere kisses? Why did she call him "thou" one day and "you" the next? And how could she have the cruelty to so simply, so casually forget him after the first day of her acquaintance with Titov? He burned with shame over his ridiculous lingering at the house and planned to disappear in a day's time—run to Moscow, hide his disgraced and idiotic dacha love, which had grown obvious even to the servants.

But as soon as he began to think this way, he wound up paralyzed by the mere memory of her mouth. If she happened to pass by while he was sitting alone on the balcony, she would casually say something meaningless—"Where is my aunt? Have you seen her?"—and he would hurry to answer in the same tone while ready to scream from the pain. One day she saw Zoyka sitting in his lap—what did it matter to her? But she narrowed her eyes in rage and shouted, "You disgusting girl! Don't you dare climb into men's laps!"—and he was ecstatic. Jealousy! That was jealousy! Meanwhile, Zoyka sensed every moment it was possible to throw her arms around his neck in some empty room, stare at him with her shining eyes, lick her lips and whisper, "Dear, dear, dear." Once she caught his lips so neatly with her wet mouth that he couldn't think of Zoyka for the rest of the day without shudders of desire, and horror. "What's wrong with me! How can I face Nikolay Grigoryevich and Klavdiya Aleksandrovna!"

The dacha grounds were large, like those of a country estate. To the right of the courtyard entrance stood an empty stable with a hayloft, next to it the servants' wing extended to the kitchen. Birch trees and lindens glimmered in the background. To the left, old pines grew luxuriantly in firm, uneven soil; swing sets and giants' steps stood in a patch of grass below them. A smooth lawn for croquet lay farther on, already at the wood's edge. The house was large as well; it stood right at the end of the driveway with a disorienting mixture of garden and forest spreading out behind it. An elegant avenue of old spruces ran through this confusion from the back porch to the bathing house on the pond. With or without their guests, the hosts always sat on the front balcony, which was set back into the house and shaded from the sun. One hot Sunday morning only Levitsky was there with mother. Many guests had come, and, as always when guests were present, the day seemed especially festive. Their new dresses shining in the sun, maids trotted back and forth across the courtyard between the house and the kitchen, where hurried preparations were under way for breakfast. Five people had come to visit: a dark-faced, bilious writer who was both excessively serious and passionately devoted to games; a fifty-year-old professor with little legs and a face like Socrates'; his newly wedded wife and former student, who was thin, blond, and twenty years old; a small, chic woman whom everyone called "the wasp" because of her lean figure, her touchiness, and her vicious temper; and Titov, whom Danilevsky referred to as "the insolent gentleman." All of the guests, as well as Valeriya and Danilevsky himself, were under the pines near the forest. Danilevsky sat smoking a cigar in an armchair in the limpid shade. The children, the professor's wife, and the writer were riding the giants' steps while the professor, the wasp, Titov, and Valeriya ran around the croquet lawn, hitting balls with their mallets, shouting back and forth, arguing about the game. Levitsky and mother were listening to them. Earlier, Levitsky had tried to join the group, but as soon as he'd approached, Valeriya had driven him off—"My aunt is pitting the cherries all alone; why don't you go and help her?" He'd stood for a moment, smiling awkwardly and looking at her, the way she held a mallet in her hand and bent over a wooden ball, the way her tussore skirt hung over her taut calves in stockings of pale yellow silk, the way her breasts pulled heavily at her light blouse while its fabric revealed her round shoulders—dark from the sun and tinged slightly pink by the rose-colored straps of her camisole.

He'd looked, and then he'd plodded back to the balcony. He was especially pitiful that morning, and mother—who was always calm and even-tempered, with her young, serene face, her clear gaze, and her own secret pain from the voices under the trees—watched him from the corner of her eye.

"We'll never get our hands clean now," she said, sticking a little gilded fork into a cherry with her bloodied fingers. "And you, Zhorzhik, always manage to spill all over yourself. Dearest, why are you still wearing a jacket? It's so hot you could easily wear just a belted shirt. And you haven't shaved in ten days. . . ."

He knew that a reddish stubble had grown over his hollow cheeks, that his only white coat was grimy from continuous wear, that his student's pants had developed an unsightly sheen, and that his shoes were cloudy with dust. He knew that he slouched as he sat there with his sunken stomach and his scrawny chest.

"You're right, Klavdiya Aleksandrovna," he said, blushing. "You are absolutely right. I've let myself go terribly—I look like an escaped convict. I've exploited your kindness despicably. Forgive me, please, if you can. I'll pull myself together today. I should have left for Moscow long ago: I've already overstayed my welcome here, plaguing everyone. I've decided to leave tomorrow. A friend has invited me to Mogilev—he says it's a beautiful place."

Hearing Titov shouting at Valeriya, he bent lower over the table. "No, no, my lady, that's against the rules! It's your fault if you don't know how to hold one ball with your foot and hit with your mallet. You don't get to try twice. . . ."

At breakfast he felt as if everyone at the table had somehow crawled inside his body. They were eating, talking, making witty jokes, and bursting out with laughter inside him. Afterward they all went to rest in the avenue of spruces, where the maids had put pillows and rugs in the shade among beds of slippery pine needles. He walked through the courtyard's hot sunlight to the stable, climbed the wall ladder to the loft, and flopped down into the old hay and the semi-dark. Trying to decide something, he lay on his stomach and stared intently at a fly that had landed on a piece of straw near his face. At first the fly moved its front legs together in a quick, crisscross motion as if washing. But then it started struggling in some unnatural way to pull its hind legs forward. Suddenly someone ran inside and slammed the door: turning, he saw Zoyka in the light of the dormer window. She jumped toward him and sank into the hay on her stomach. Panting, she stared at him with somehow frightened eyes. "Zhorzhik dear, I have to tell you something," she whispered, "something exciting for you—something wonderful."

"What is it, Zoyechka?" he said, sitting up.

"You'll see, but first you have to kiss me. Right away," and she kicked her legs in the hay, exposing her full thighs.

He was too worn out by misery to suppress an unhealthy feeling of tenderness. "Zoyechka," he said, "you alone love me, and I love you too. But you shouldn't do this, please. . . ."

She kicked even harder. "You have to—right now!"

She put her head on his chest. He saw her shiny, fresh brown hair under the red ribbon, smelled its fragrance, and nestled his face in it. Suddenly she screamed, "Ah!" and grabbed the back of her skirt.

He jumped to his feet. "What is it?"

"Something bit me!" She dropped her head in the hay and began to wail. "What was it! Look, quickly!"

She flung her skirt up her back and tugged down her underwear. "What is it? Am I bleeding?"

"No, I don't see anything, Zoyechka."

"What do you mean!" She sobbed. "Blow on it! It hurts!"

He blew, and then he kissed the soft, cool flesh of her buttocks. He kissed her greedily until she jumped up, teary-eyed and almost insane from the pleasure.

"I fooled you!" she shouted. "I fooled you! And for that, I'll tell you my secret: Titov dumped her. Grishka and I heard everything. They were walking on the balcony while we were sitting on the floor in the living room, behind the armchairs. And he was very insulting. He says to her, 'My lady, I'm not one of those you can lead around by the nose. I don't even love you. I'll start to if you earn my affection, but for now, there won't be any declarations.' Isn't that great? It's just what she deserves!"

Then she rushed to the ladder and scurried down. He stared after her. "I'm sick! Hanging is too good for me!" he said loudly, still feeling her flesh on his lips.

Evening was quiet at the estate. The guests had left at six, and now the warm dusk, the cooking smoke from the kitchen where dinner was being prepared, and the soothing scent of lindens blooming in the yard brought a mood of peace and quiet domesticity to the house. But even in that peaceful happiness—in the dusk, among the smells—it remained: the ever-promising torture of her presence, her existence near him . . . the soul-wrenching pain of his love and her merciless indifference, her absence. . . . Where is she? He came down from the balcony and, hearing the steady squeak of a swing, walked toward the pines. Yes, it's her. He stopped, watching the way she sailed up and down, always stretching the cords to their limit, always trying to reach the last height, and pretending not to notice him. The rings squeal and she flies up, disappears among the branches, and shoots back down, her hem fluttering as she pumps with her legs. Oh, if only he could catch her! Grab her, strangle, rape her!

"Valeriya Andreyevna, be careful!"

She only swings harder, as if she hasn't heard.

During dinner on the balcony they laughed and argued about the guests while sitting under hot, bright lamps. Her laughter was bitter and unnatural; she ate *tvorog* with sour cream greedily, again never glancing in his direction. Only Zoyka was silent, her eyes shining as she looked at him with the knowledge that they alone shared.

Everyone went to bed early. Not a single light was left burning, and everything around turned dark and lifeless. He slipped into his room after supper and began stuffing his clothes into a shoulder bag, thinking, "I'll take the bicycle out quietly, ride straight to the station. I'll sleep somewhere in the woods until the first morning train. . . . But no, I can't do that. . . . God knows what they'd make of it. They'd say he ran off like a little boy, didn't say goodbye to anyone. I'll have to wait until tomorrow and leave casually, as if nothing had happened. 'Goodbye my dear Nikolay Grigoryevich, goodbye dear Klavdiya Aleksandrovna! Thank you, thanks for everything. Yes, yes, they say Mogilev is a beautiful city. . . . Zoyechka, take care. Grow and be happy! Grisha, let me shake your hand like a gentleman. Valeriya Andreyevna, all the best. Try to remember me kindly' . . . No, 'try to remember me kindly' is stupid, tactless — like some kind of hint about something. . . .'"

Certain that he couldn't fall asleep if he tried, Levitsky came down from the balcony to walk on the station road, hoping to wear himself out. But in the courtyard he stopped: warm dusk, sweet silence, a whiteness in the sky from small, innumerable stars. . . . He started again and stopped again, lifting his head: the stars go farther and farther into the sky, and then there's terror, blue-black dark, a bottomless gorge. . . . Then there's silence, peace, a vast wilderness that no one understands, and all the lifeless, pointless beauty of the world — all the mute, eternal psalms of night. . . . And he, alone, face to face with it — somewhere in the chasm between sky and earth. He began to pray without words for some small act of pity, some sign of heavenly compassion, and with bitter joy he felt himself freed from his body, felt himself linked to the sky. Then he looked back at the house. Trying to stay as he was, he looked at the starlight hanging in the black glass of the windows — hanging in her window. . . . Is she asleep, or lying in a daze, thinking about Titov? Yes, it's her turn now. . . .

The house loomed large and indistinct among the shadows. He walked around it to a small field between the rear balcony and two rows of ink-black, motionless spruces: they seemed menacing now, with their sharp tips so close to the stars. In the darkness below them hung the greenish, yellow flares of fireflies. Something white was lying on the balcony: he stopped and peered into the darkness, then started with surprise as a voice free of all emotion said, "Why are you wandering around in the night?" Dumbfounded, he moved forward and saw that she was sitting in a rocking chair, wearing the old silver shawl that all of Danilevsky's female guests put on when they stayed the night.

"Why aren't you asleep?" he stammered in confusion.

She sat without answering for a moment, then rose and came soundlessly down from the balcony, sliding the shawl up her shoulders as she moved.

"Take a walk with me."

He walked behind and then beside her in the hushed, still darkness of that avenue between the trees, where now, more than ever, it seemed something had been hidden. And how could it be? How was he walking alone with her again in this avenue at this hour? And that shawl again, always slipping from her shoulders, always pricking his fingers slightly with its silk fibers as he pulls it around her.

"Why do you torture me this way?" he said, struggling to overcome a spasm in his throat.

She shook her head. "I don't know. Be quiet."

He grew slightly bolder and raised his voice. "Yes, why—what for? Why did you . . ."

She caught his hand and pressed it. "Be quiet."

"Valya, I don't understand anything. . . ."

She let go of his hand and glanced at one of the spruces at the end of the avenue. The outline of its limbs formed a wide black triangle.

"Do you remember this place? I kissed you for the first time here. Now I want you to kiss me here for the last time. . . ."

Then she ducked under the branches and flung her shawl on the ground. "Come here."

As soon as it was over, she pushed him away with sharp revulsion, lowered her knees, and lay with her legs still spread, her hands stretched along her hips. He sprawled beside her, his face against the ground, pine needles turning damp with his warm tears. The forest had grown completely silent and still, and, like a slice of red melon suspended in the dead of night, the late moon hung motionless above the darkened fields.

When he returned to his room, he glanced at the clock with blood-shot, swollen eyes and panicked at the time: twenty minutes to two! He carried the bicycle down from the balcony as quickly and quietly as he could, then wheeled it hurriedly across the yard. Past the gate, he jumped on and leaned low over the handlebars, pedaling wildly and bouncing

[267]

over potholes in the sandy soil. The pines that lined the lane seemed to run toward him as he rode, their black trunks flickering against the predawn sky. "I'll miss it!" He wiped the sweat from his forehead with the crook of his arm and began to pedal even harder: an express from Moscow rolls past the station without stopping at 2:15—only a few minutes left! At the end of the lane, he suddenly caught sight of the station's silhouette in the early morning light, which still resembled dusk. There it is! He turned left onto a road that ran parallel to the tracks, then veered right to the crossing. There he ducked under the signal arm without stopping, swerved hard onto the tracks, started to roll down the incline: rattling over the crossties between the rails, he headed straight for the blinding lamp of the oncoming engine as it roared up the hill.

[1940]

The Eve

R IDING through town to the train station: the cabby drives with terrible zeal, and we tear downhill, onto the bridge over the river. On the sandbar below, a vagrant stands with his back to the traffic, hurriedly eating some kind of filling from a dirty rag like a dog, his shoulders hunched as if braced against an oncoming blow. Draft carts rumble close behind the cab: as if trying to catch us, they shudder and roar, fly down the road, *mouzhiki* dangling their terrible boots from the sides. And all the *mouzhiki* riding there are giants: hatless and red-haired, covered in flour dust from the milling, their long red shirts hanging loose.

And then the train—a second-class compartment where some rotund gentleman in his forties sits across from me, his hair cropped short, gold-rimmed glasses on his flat nose, his nostrils flared and impudent. Too superior to look at me, he gets up constantly to adjust his luggage in the rack—good cases with hard exteriors. A neat and well-kept gentleman, he's relaxed and easy with his privilege, his daunting arrogance.

But already it was passing, the fall of 1916.

[1930]

In Paris

His short, auburn hair was shot with grey, but if he wore a hat while walking down the street or riding on the subway, his fresh, clean-shaven face and his tall, thin frame—held straight and upright in a long raincoat—made him seem no more than forty. Still, his light eyes contained a kind of dry sadness, and he spoke and carried himself like a man who'd lived through much. Once he'd rented a farm in Provence, and now, while living in Paris, he liked to repeat the caustic aphorisms he'd heard so often in the countryside, smiling wryly as he inserted them into his always concise speech. Many people knew that his wife had left him when they were still in Constantinople, and that his soul had not healed since then. He never revealed that secret wound to anyone, but sometimes he couldn't help hinting at it, and if the conversation turned to women, he would joke unpleasantly: *"Rien n'est plus difficile que de reconnaître un bon melon et une femme de bien."*

One damp evening in late fall he stopped for supper at a small Russian restaurant in one of the dark alleys on Passy. At the front of the restaurant was a kind of delicatessen, and he paused instinctively before its window, where pink, cone-shaped bottles of Rowanberry vodka and rectangular yellow flasks of *zubrovka* had been arranged on the sill beside a dish of dried-out little pies, a dish of greying mincemeat cutlets, a box of halvah, and a can of sprats; farther on he could see a counter set with appetizers, behind which frowned the unappealing face of the Russian owner. It was light inside the shop, and something drew him from the dark alley and its cold, oily-looking stones toward that light. He entered, bowed to the hostess, and walked into the empty, dimly lit dining room, where tables were covered with white paper. There he slowly hung his grey hat and his long coat on the pegs of a standing rack, sat down at a table in the farthest corner, and began to read an endless list of appetizers and main courses while absentmindedly stroking the soft red hair that covered the backs of his hands. Part of the menu was typed, and part was written in a violet-colored ink that had begun to smudge on the greasy paper. Suddenly the lights were turned on in his corner, and he saw a woman approaching the table with detached complaisance. Wearing a white, lacy apron over a black dress, she looked about thirty; her eyes and hair were also black.

"Bonsoir, monsieur," she said in a pleasant voice.

As he looked at her, he realized she was beautiful, and her beauty flustered him. "Bonsoir. . . . But you're Russian, aren't you?" he answered awkwardly.

"Oh, yes. I'm sorry—speaking French to the customers has become a habit."

"Do you really get a lot of French customers here?"

"Quite a lot. And they always ask about *zubrovka, blinis*—even borscht. Have you decided?"

"No. . . . There's so much here. . . . What do you recommend?"

She began to recite. "Today we have sailor's shchi and Cossack rissole. . . . If you'd like, you could also have veal chops or Karski shashlik."

"Excellent. I'll have the shchi and rissole."

She lifted up a little notebook that hung from her belt and began to write with a pencil stub. Her hands looked very white and delicate, and although the dress was old, it obviously came from a good shop.

"Would you care for vodka?"

"Please—it's awfully damp out there."

"And what appetizers would you like? The Danube herring is excellent. And the red caviar is fresh. We have *korkunovsky* half-sour pickles as well."

He looked at her again—a very pretty white apron with lace over a black dress, the graceful outline of a young, strong woman's breasts beneath it. . . . She wore no lipstick, but her mouth looked full and fresh. Her hair was parted in the middle and wrapped around her head in just a simple braid, but the flesh of her white hands was sleek, and her glistening, slightly pink nails revealed a recent manicure.

"What appetizers would I like?" he said with a smile, slightly flustered by her courteous attention. "I'll just have the herring and hot potatoes, if that's all right."

"And what wine shall I bring?"

"Red. The house wine."

She wrote in her notebook and brought a carafe of water from the neighboring table. "No, merci," he said, shaking his head. "I don't drink water, especially with wine. *L'eau gâte le vin comme la charrette le chemin et la femme—l'âme.*"

"What a nice opinion you have of us!" she said indifferently as she left for his vodka and herring. He watched her walk gracefully away, watched her black dress swaying as she moved. . . . Yes, her good manners and her indifference, all her modest gestures are suited to a waitress. . . . But how does she afford those expensive shoes? Probably some well-to-do elderly "*ami.*" . . . Because of her he was more animated that night than he had been in years—and this realization annoyed him. Yes, from day to day, from year to year, you wait in secret for only one thing—that moment when you'll stumble onto happy love. Ultimately it is this hope alone that enables you to live, and all of it's in vain.

He returned the next day and sat down at the same table. She was busy at first, taking an order from two Frenchmen, repeating as she wrote in her notebook: "Caviar rouge, salad russe. . . . Deaux shashliks. . . ."

She went into the kitchen, then returned and approached him with a slight smile, as if he were an old acquaintance.

"Good evening. I'm glad you liked it here."

He rose up in his seat happily. "Hello, yes, I liked it very much. . . . Can I ask your name?"

"Olga Aleksandrovna. And yours, if I may ask?"

"Nikolay Platonych."

They shook hands, and she raised her little notebook.

"Today we have a wonderful rassolnik. Our cook's remarkable— you know, he served on Prince Aleksandr Mikhaylovich's yacht. . . ."

"Well then, the rassolnik must be good—I'll have that. . . . Have you worked here long?"

"About two months."

"And where did you work before?"

"Before this I was a sales clerk at Printemps."

"They must have laid you off—when they cut back on staff?"

"Yes, I would have stayed there if I'd had the chance."

Then the money doesn't come from an "*ami*," he thought happily. "Are you married?"

"Yes."

"What does your husband do?"

"He works in Yugoslavia now. He fought for the White Army—like you, I imagine."

"Yes, I fought in the civil war—and in the Great War before it as well."

"I could tell right away. You're probably a general," she said, smiling.

"I was. Now I'm writing a history of the wars for some foreign publishers. . . . But how did you wind up alone?"

"I just wound up that way—alone."

On his third night in the restaurant, he asked: "Do you like the cinema?"

"Sometimes it's interesting," she said, setting a bowl of borscht in front of him.

"They say there's an excellent film showing at the Étoile. Would you like to see it? You don't work every day, do you?"

"Merci. I'm free on Mondays."

"Well, let's go on Monday. What's today? Saturday? Day after tomorrow then. Does that sound possible?"

"Yes, that sounds good. But tomorrow—you won't be coming in?"

"No, I'm going out of town to see some people. Why do you ask?"

"I don't know. . . . It's strange—I guess I've gotten used to you somehow."

He looked at her with gratitude and blushed. "I've grown used to you as well. . . . It's so rare in this world—that you meet someone. . . ."

Hurriedly he changed the topic. "Well then, day after tomorrow. Where should we meet? Where do you live?"

"Near the Motte-Picquet stop."

"Well, that's perfect—the Étoile is on the same line. I'll be waiting for you at the subway exit at 8:30 sharp."

"Merci."

He bowed lightheartedly. "*C'est moi qui vous remercie*. Put the kids to bed and have an evening out," he added, to see if she had children.

"I haven't experienced the joy of children yet, thank God," she said, and smoothly whisked away his dirty plates.

Touched by her words, he walked home frowning. *I guess I've gotten used to you somehow*. Yes, maybe this is it—that long-awaited meeting, that happiness. But it is late, late. *Le bon Dieu envoie toujours des culottes à ceux qui n'ont pas de derrière. . . .*

It was raining Monday evening, and the Paris sky was filled with a turbid, reddish haze. He stopped at a café on Chaussée de la Muette and ate just a sandwich with a glass of beer, hoping she would dine with him later on Montparnasse. Then he hailed a cab, lit a cigarette, and rode toward the subway stop Étoile.

Near the station exit he got out and started down the sidewalk in the rain; his taxi driver—a chubby fellow with purple cheeks—waited trustingly with the car. A hot, damp breeze was streaming from the station doors; throngs of people in dark coats climbed the stairs, opening umbrellas as they walked. Behind him, a street vendor called out the names of the evening newspapers in a low, raspy voice that sounded like a duck quacking in the drizzle. Suddenly she appeared in the crowd; he felt elated as he rushed to meet her.

"Olga Aleksandrovna . . ."

She looked elegant and stylish in her long, black evening dress; and her dark, painted eyes expressed a kind of easy self-assurance that he hadn't seen before in the restaurant. She held the gown's hem as she approached, and then gracefully extended her free hand, a small umbrella dangling from her arm. He folded back her glove and kissed the back of her pale wrist. "She's in evening wear," he thought, feeling even happier. "She's planning on us dining out."

"Poor thing, have you been waiting long?"

"No, I just arrived. I have a taxi waiting. . . ."

And he climbed into that half-dark, damp-smelling cab with a feeling of excitement that had left his life long ago. The driver took a sharp turn hard, and light from a street lamp suddenly flooded the interior as the cab swayed; instinctively he held her steady by the waist, smelling the powder on her cheek, glimpsing the outline of her full knees beneath the evening dress, her shining eyes and damp, red lips: the woman next to him was nothing like the one who waited tables.

They spoke quietly in the darkened theatre while looking at a brilliant white screen where airplanes flew at angles through the sky and descended with a noisy drone toward the clouds.

"Do you live alone, or with a girlfriend?" he asked.

"Alone. It's awful, really. The hotel's quite clean and warm, but—
you know, it's one of those places men bring girls for a night, or for an
hour. I live on the sixth floor, and there's no elevator, of course. The carpet in the stairwell stops two stories down from me. . . . On rainy nights
it's terribly depressing. You open a window and there's not a soul to see,
the entire town seems dead. Somewhere below you, God knows where,
there's one streetlight in the rain. . . . But you're a bachelor—you must
live in a hotel too."

"I have a little apartment on Passy—I live alone there, a long-term
Parisian. I lived in Provence once, years ago—rented a farm there. I
wanted to get away from everything—and everyone. And I wanted to live
by my own labor. But the labor was unbearable. I hired a Cossack to
help me, and he turned out to be a drunk—a gloomy, frightening drunk.
I tried to raise poultry and rabbits, but they all died off, and my mule—a
very cunning, very nasty animal—practically ate me alive. . . . But
mostly it was the utter loneliness. . . . My wife left me when we were still
in Constantinople."

"You're joking?"

"Not at all. It's a very ordinary story. *Qui se marie par amour a
bonnes nuits et mauvais jours.* And I didn't have many days or nights—
we'd only been married for a year before she left."

"Where is she now?"

"I don't know. . . ."

She didn't speak for a long time. On the screen some kind of Char-
lie Chaplin imitator was running with his feet splayed like an idiot; he
wore ridiculous, battered shoes and a bowler hat cocked to the side.

"Yes, it must be awfully lonely," she said.

"It is. But what can you do? Just endure. *Patience—médecine des
pauvres.*"

"A very sad medicine."

"So sad, in fact," he said with a slight smile, "that I'd even started
looking at *Russia Illustrated*—it has a kind of dating section, you
know—announcements from people looking for companions: 'A Russian girl from Latvia is bored and wishes to correspond with a sensitive
Russian gentleman in Paris—photograph requested.' Or: 'A serious lady

seeks serious correspondence with a sober gentleman over forty who likes the comforts of family life. He should be financially secure, gainfully employed as a chauffeur or some similar, reliable profession. She's an old-fashioned but attractive brunette, a widow with a nine-year-old son. Will answer all inquiries. . . .' All inquiries. . . . I know exactly how she feels."

"But don't you have friends, people you know?"

"No friends—and acquaintances are poor comfort."

"Who keeps house for you?"

"My household's very modest. I make my own coffee and lunch. In the evenings a *femme de ménage* comes."

She squeezed his hand. "Poor thing."

They sat this way a long time, drawn together by the gloom and the cramped seats, holding hands and pretending to look at the screen while a beam of light from the projectionist's booth hung like a chalky, bluish stripe above their heads. The Chaplin imitator was driving a broken-down car with a little chimney that smoked like a samovar; his battered hat rose and hovered above his head—a sign of shock and horror—as the jalopy sailed toward a telegraph pole and music blared over the loudspeaker. They were sitting in the balcony, and the floor below them— dark and hazy with the smoke of countless cigarettes—was like a pit resounding with raucous laughter and applause. He leaned toward her. "This film is quite tedious, isn't it? And there's so much smoke in here it's hard to breathe. Maybe we should go to dine somewhere on Montparnasse?" She nodded and began putting on her gloves.

Once more they sat in the half-dark cab. He watched the rain shimmer on the windows—and having seen it flash like uncut diamonds as it caught the streetlights' glare, having seen it fill with the neon that streamed like blood and mercury from electric billboards perched in the blackness overhead, he folded back her glove again and slowly kissed her hand. The same strange light seemed to glitter from behind her thick, coal-black lashes as she looked at him—and then, with love and sadness, leaned closer, brought her rich, sweet-tasting mouth to his.

At the Café Coupole they started with oysters and Anjou, then partridge and a red claret. Over coffee and yellow chartreuse they began to feel light-headed, and both smoked heavily; filters stained blood-red with lipstick quickly filled the ashtray. While she talked, he studied her slightly flushed face, feeling more and more enamored of her beauty.

"Tell the truth," she said, lightly pinching a tobacco crumb from the tip of her tongue. "You must have had a few rendezvous in Paris."

"I did—but you know the kind. Hotels at night, nothing more. And you?"

She paused. "There was one very unhappy episode. . . . But I don't want to talk about that. Just a boy, a little womanizer, really. . . . But how did you and your wife split up?"

"Shamefully. She met a boy of her own, a handsome Greek who was extraordinarily rich. Two months later not a trace remained of that touching, innocent girl who'd idolized the White Army and everyone who served it. She began to dine with him in the most expensive pigsty in Pera, and he began to send huge baskets of flowers to her at home. 'I don't believe it,' she'd say. 'Are you really jealous of him? You're busy all day, and I have fun with him, that's all. He's just a sweet little boy for me, nothing more.' A sweet little boy! She was only twenty herself. . . . It wasn't easy to forget her—the girl I'd known before, in Ekaterinodar."

When the bill came, she looked it over carefully and refused to let him leave more than 10 percent for the waiter—and somehow this made it seem even stranger for them to say good night and separate in half an hour.

"Let's go to my apartment," he said with a certain wistfulness. "We can sit and talk a little more."

"Yes, let's go." She took his hand as she got up and drew it close to her.

A Russian cabby drove them down a deserted little side street to his apartment building. The rain looked hard as it fell through the metallic light of a gas lamp and pelted a garbage bin near the entrance. They entered the bright vestibule and took the elevator to his floor, kissing quietly as they rose in the narrow, slow-moving compartment. He had just enough time to unlock his door before the corridor light clicked off. She followed him through the apartment foyer to a little dining room, where just one bulb burned dully in a chandelier. They both looked tired; he offered her a glass of wine.

"No, darling," she said. "I can't drink any more."

He began to press. "Just one glass of white wine. I have a nice bottle of Pouilly chilling on the windowsill."

"You go ahead, love. I'm going to wash and get undressed. And sleep—sleep. You and I aren't children. I'm sure you knew that when I agreed to come here with you. . . . And really, why should we be apart?"

Too flustered to answer, he led her silently through the bedroom and turned on the lights in the bathroom. It was warm there from the furnace, and the lamps burned brightly while the rain continued drumming on the roof. She began to pull her dress over her head without closing the door.

He left and quickly drank two glasses of icy, bitter wine—and still unable to calm himself, went back into the bedroom. A mirror hung on the wall opposite the bathroom door, and he could see her there—could see all her strong, light-skinned body as she stood with her back to him and leaned over the sink to wash her neck and breasts.

"You can't come in!"—she threw on his dressing gown and left it hanging loose, walked toward him with her glistening breasts, her white hips and her taut, white stomach exposed. As if she were his wife, she embraced him. As if she were his wife, he embraced her—touched her cool skin, kissed her damp and lightly scented breasts, kissed the mouth and eyes from which she'd rinsed her makeup. . . .

Two days later she left her job and moved into his apartment.

In the winter he convinced her to put all of his earnings into a safe-deposit box in her name at the Bank Lyonnais. "It can't hurt us to be careful," he said. *"L'amour fait danser les ânes*—and I feel like I'm twenty—but anything could happen. . . ."

Three days after Easter he died on the subway—while reading a newspaper he suddenly tossed his head back against the seat, rolled his eyes. . . .

It was a lovely spring afternoon when she walked home from the graveyard in her mourning clothes. Soft clouds were drifting over Paris, and everything spoke of a life that was young and eternal—spoke of her life, which was finished.

At home she started cleaning the apartment. An old, grey officer's coat with a red lining was hanging in a closet in the corridor—for years he'd worn it in warm weather. She took it from the rack and pressed it to her face. She sat down on the floor, still clutching the coat, crying out and shuddering with sobs, begging someone for mercy.

[1940]

The Hunchback's Affair

THE HUNCHBACK received an anonymous love letter, an invitation to a rendezvous:

Come to the public garden on Cathedral Square on Saturday, April 5th, at seven in the evening. I am young, well off, and unencumbered, and—why hide it!—I have long known and loved you; your melancholy, proud expression; your intelligent and noble features; your loneliness. I would like to hope that in me you will find a soul kindred to your own. . . . I will be wearing a grey English suit; in my left hand I will carry a silk lavender umbrella; in my right a bouquet of violets.

How amazed he was! How he waited for the day! The first love letter of his life! On Saturday he went to the barber, bought a pair of lilac-colored gloves and a grey tie with a dash of red to match his suit. At home he dressed before a mirror, endlessly reknotting that tie while his long, delicate fingers trembled and turned cold. An attractive flush had begun to spread across his cheeks, and his handsome eyes seemed to grow darker. . . . Then he sat down in an armchair, and like an impeccably dressed guest—like a stranger in his own house—he waited for the fateful hour. At last the dining room clock ominously chimed 6:30. He shuddered, then rose with composure, calmly put on his spring hat in the hallway, picked up his walking stick, slowly left the house. Once outside he could no longer restrain himself, however, and although his steps retained the proud solemnity that misshapen backs invariably produce, he moved his long, delicate legs more quickly than usual, seized by that blissful fear with which we all anticipate happiness. Hurrying into the garden by the cathedral, he suddenly froze: a woman was coming toward him in the pink light of the spring sunset. She walked with a certain stateliness, taking long, measured strides. She wore a grey suit and an attractive hat that slightly resembled a man's. She carried an umbrella in her left hand; in her right a bouquet of violets. And she too was a hunchback.

Someone has no mercy for man!

[1930]

Caucasus

AFTER ARRIVING in Moscow, I furtively took a room in an inconspicuous guest house in an alley near the Arbat, and between our meetings, I lived like an anchorite, hungering for her. She came to me only three times during those days, saying, "I'm here for just a moment" as she darted into the room. The exquisite pallor of a woman filled with love and apprehension had blanched her skin. Her voice cracked when she spoke, and I was overwhelmed with tenderness and joy as she flung her umbrella on the floor, fumbled with her veil, hurried to embrace me.

"I think he suspects something," she said. "I think he knows something—he might have found the key to my desk and read one of your letters. You know how proud and cruel he can be. He's capable of anything when he's angry. He told me once straight out, 'I'll stop at nothing to defend my honor, the honor of a husband and an officer.' For some reason now he's begun to watch my every step—literally. I've got to be careful—extremely careful—for our plan to work. He's agreed to let me go—I convinced him I would die if I didn't see the south and the sea. But you, for God's sake—you must be patient."

It was a daring plan: take the same train together to the coast of the Caucasus and stay for three or four weeks in some utterly remote place. I knew that coast—I had lived a little while near Sochi when I was young and alone, and all my life I'd remembered autumn evenings among black cypresses and cold, grey waves. . . . She grew pale whenever I reminded her of this, and said, "But this time you'll be with me in that mountain jungle near the sea." We didn't believe our plan would come to life until the very last—it seemed too great a happiness.

Moscow was all mud and gloom. A cold rain fell as if summer had already ended and would not return; the streets glistened with the black umbrellas of pedestrians and the raised, trembling tops of horse-drawn cabs. As I drove through the dark, foul night to the train, everything inside me froze from fear and cold. I ran through the station with my hat pulled low over my eyes, my face buried in the collar of my coat.

The rain was pouring loudly over the roof of the small, first-class compartment that I'd reserved. I closed the window curtain; the porter wiped his hand on his white apron, took the tip I offered him, and went away. I locked the door behind him, parted the curtain, and sat completely still, my eyes fixed on the crowd flitting through the dim light of the station lamps as they hurried with their bags along the length of the train. To avoid a meeting on the platform, we'd agreed that I would come as early as I could and she as late as possible, but now it was time for her to arrive. I grew more and more alarmed—there was no sign of her. The second bell rang, and I shivered with fear: she'd missed the train, or he'd suddenly refused to let her go! But then I started at the sight of his tall figure, his officer's cap, his narrow overcoat, and the gloved hand with which he held her arm as he strode down the platform. I shrank into a corner of the berth and began to imagine how he would enter the second-class car behind mine, how he would inspect it all with an air of authority, how he would check whether the porter had arranged her well, how he would take off his hat, remove one suede glove, kiss her, make the sign of the cross. . . . I was stunned by the final bell, dazed by the first forward jerk of the train. It rocked and swayed from side to side as it pulled away; then the engine picked up speed and we were gliding smoothly down the rails. My hands were cold as ice when I gave ten rubles to the conductor who led her to me and carried in her bags.

She did not kiss me when she entered the compartment. Her hat had become tangled in her hair, and she smiled piteously as she sat down and struggled to remove it. "I couldn't eat," she said. "I was sure I wouldn't make it—sure I couldn't carry off this lie. . . . I'm desperately thirsty. Can you give me some Narzan?" she asked, addressing me for the first time with the familiar form of "you." "I know he'll come after me. I gave him two addresses—Gelendzhik and Gagry. And *voila*—he'll be in Gelendzhik in three or four days. But God be with him—death is better than this hell."

In the morning I went into the corridor, and it was full of sunlight. The stale air smelled of soap and cologne and all the other ordinary odors of daybreak on a crowded train. Through the hot, dusty windows I watched the steppe flow by. I saw the scorched stubble of the plains, oxen dragging carts down wide, dusty roads, and the metallic flash of the crossing-keepers' sheds, their gardens thick with scarlet mallow and sunflowers bright as canaries. The plain went on and on in all its emptiness: burial mounds and native graves under the dry, killing sun; the sky itself like a cloud of dust, and then, the rising ghosts of mountains.

She sent postcards from Gelendzhik and Gagry, telling him she didn't know where she would stay.
Then we started down the coast.

We found a pristine spot surrounded by plane trees and blooming shrubs, pomegranates, mahoganies and magnolias, black cypresses, palms with fan-shaped fronds.
I liked to get up early and follow the low hills far into the forest while she slept until seven, when we usually drank tea. The sun was already strong when I went out—clear, and full of joy. A fresh-smelling mist would slowly rise and burn in a blue radiance while I walked, the timeless white of mountain snow shining above the steep, wooded slopes. Returning home, I passed through the village bazaar, where the heat was already heavy, the air smelled of burning dung, and the crowd seethed around the merchants with their saddle horses and their mules. In the morning, different mountain tribes came down to the bazaar, and the Circassian women seemed to float along the ground in their long dark robes and red slippers, their heads wrapped in black fabric. Occasionally

I'd see their eyes—fleeting, birdlike glances darting out from folds of mournful cloth.

Later we went to the beach, which was always empty, and swam and lay in the sun until lunch—fish cooked on a skewer over an open fire, white wine, fresh fruit and nuts. In the afternoons we closed the window shutters; joyful strips of light sloped through their cracks into the warm twilight that gathered under the tiled roof.

When the heat lifted and we opened our window, we could see a portion of the sea between the cypresses that stood below us. It was violet, and it lay so still that one could believe there would be no end to this beauty, this peace.

At dusk, stunning clouds often drifted in from the sea, and they burned so beautifully that she would lie on the ottoman with a scarf of gauze across her face and weep: two weeks, maybe three—then Moscow once again.

The nights were warm and thick. Fireflies drifted like topaz in the murky dark; the songs of tree toads rang like small glass bells. When our eyes adjusted, we could see stars and the mountain crest; trees we'd overlooked in daylight stood out sharply above the village. All night the muffled beating of a drum rose from the *dukhan*, mingling with howls of joy and hopelessness, as if there were nothing but a single, endless song.

Near our house a clear, shallow stream flowed briskly down a rocky ravine from the forest to the sea. How wonderfully the falling water flashed, scattering itself like glass among the stones at that secret hour when the late moon comes from behind the mountains and the woods like a divinity, and looks down watchfully.

Sometimes at night terrible clouds moved down from the mountains, and vicious storms began: again and again, a fantastic green abyss would suddenly appear and gape before us, then vanish into the raging, mortal blackness of the forest, as thunder split apart the sky like some primeval force. . . . Baby eagles awoke in the rain and cried like cats, snow leopards roared, and jackals yelped. Once an entire pack of jackals came to our lighted window—they were always drawn to buildings in the storms. We opened the window and looked down at them, and they stood in the shimmering downpour, yelping—as if they wanted us to let them in. She wept with joy as she watched.

He searched for her in Gelendzhik, Gagry, and Sochi. On the morning after his arrival in Sochi, he swam in the sea, shaved, put on a clean shirt and an officer's jacket that was white as snow. He had breakfast on the restaurant terrace at his hotel, drank a bottle of champagne and coffee with Chartreuse, slowly smoked a cigar. Then he went back to his room, lay down on the couch, put a pistol to each of his temples, and fired.

[1937]

Calling Cards

I T WAS THE beginning of fall, and the steamship *Goncharov* was running the deserted Volga. Cold weather had come early. A fast, freezing
wind blew from the river's reddening eastern bank and streamed across
the Asiatic expanse of its grey floodwaters to meet the ship head on,
snapping the flag that flew above its stern, lashing skirts and sleeves, bat-
tering hats and creasing the faces of those men and women who walked
along the steamer's deck. A solitary seagull accompanied the ship without purpose or conviction, at times appearing in distinct relief against
the sky as it listed on sharp wings behind the stern, only to slant away to
the side, trail off as if not knowing what to do with itself in the vast
emptiness of that great river and the grey, autumnal air.

The ship was all but empty—just an artel of peasant laborers on the
lower deck, while up above three passengers strolled back and forth,
meeting periodically and parting ways. Two of them were inseparable;
traveling in second class and bound for the same destination, they
walked together constantly, discussing something all the while in dry,
pragmatic tones, and resembling one another in their utter lack of nota-
bility. The other passenger was traveling first class. A writer near the age

of thirty who had recently become quite famous, he stood out for a certain gravity that was either angry or lugubrious, and, to some degree, for his appearance: he was tall and powerfully built—even slightly stooped in that manner of very strong men, well dressed, and, in his own way, handsome, with dark hair and those Eastern features one encounters in Moscow among the city's ancient merchant classes. He had in fact descended from such people, though he had nothing in common with them now.

Alone, he strode firmly up and down the deck in durable, expensive shoes, a black cheviot overcoat, and a checkered English cap, breathing in the strong air of autumn and the Volga, the wind either in his face or at his back. Reaching the stern, he would pause for a moment to look at the river spreading out and streaming with grey ripples behind the ship, then turn sharply once again and start toward the prow, bowing his head against the wind as it filled his cap and listening to the steady drumming of the paddle-wheel blades, from which the churning water sprayed in glassy sheets. Finally he came to an abrupt halt and smiled gloomily: a cheap black hat seemed to be making its way up the ladder from the lower deck, from third class—and beneath the hat was the haggard but endearing face of a woman he had met by accident the night before. He moved toward her with long strides. Having raised herself entirely onto the deck, she started awkwardly toward him too, smiling but completely harried by the wind, her thin hand clutching at her hat as she stumbled sideways in the gale, dressed in just a sad, light overcoat that revealed her slender legs.

"Permit me to ask how you slept," he said, his voice loud and resolute.

"Wonderfully," she answered with unwarranted exuberance. "I always sleep like a sloth. . . ."

He held her small hand in his large one and looked into her eyes. She forced herself to meet his glance with euphoric effort.

"Why have you slept so late, my angel?" he asked with familiarity. "Good people are already eating breakfast."

"I've been lost in daydreams," she answered. Her appearance lacked all correspondence to her buoyant voice and words.

"Daydreams about what?"

"That's for me to know."

"Oh, watch out! 'That's how little children die, swimming in the summer months, near riverbanks where Chechens hide.'"

"A Chechen's what I'm waiting for," she answered with the same ebullience.

"Let's go and have some fish soup and vodka instead," he said, thinking, "She probably has no money to buy herself a decent breakfast."

She began to stamp her feet coyly. "Yes, yes—vodka, vodka. This cold's the devil's work!"

They went with hurried steps to the restaurant in first class, she leading the way and he behind, already studying her body with a certain greediness.

He'd remembered her during the night. Yesterday they'd met by sheer accident and wound up introducing themselves while standing at the ship's side as it approached some kind of tall, black bank, beneath which lights were already scattered. And then he'd sat with her on deck, on a long bench that ran along the outer wall of the first-class cabins, below their windows with white Venetian blinds. But they had not stayed together long, and later in the night he'd regretted this. To his surprise he even realized then that he desired her. Why? From that habitual desire he always felt for random, anonymous, female fellow passengers when he was traveling? Now, sitting with her in the restaurant, making toasts and lightly tapping glasses before each shot of vodka while they ate chilled and large-grained caviar with hot *kalach*, he understood already what it was that so attracted him to her, and he waited impatiently for that moment when everything would be brought to its conclusion. The fact that all of it—the vodka and her free-and-easy manner—so sharply contradicted everything about her looks and disposition only made him more excited.

"One more for each of us, and then we've hit our limit," he says.

"Oh yes, we're at our limit," she answers him in precisely the same tone. "But this vodka's just remarkable!"

Yesterday she had touched him, of course, with the obvious excitement and confusion that she felt upon learning his name. She was stunned by this completely unexpected encounter with a famous author—and it was pleasant, as always, for him to witness such bewilderment. It always drew him to a woman—provided she was neither hideous nor stupid—created an air of intimacy between them, granted him a new degree of self-assurance in his manner of address, gave him, even, a certain right to her. But it wasn't this alone that so excited him. He evidently fascinated her as a man, while it was precisely all her artlessness and poverty that he found deeply touching. He had already mastered a certain familiarity with his female admirers, a quick and light transition from the first few minutes of acquaintance to a discourse that permitted him wide latitude, an ostensibly artistic manner of address, and a contrived simplicity in his questioning. Who are you, exactly? Where are you from? Are you married? Yesterday he'd questioned her in precisely this manner while looking at the evening twilight, the different colored lights drifting on the buoys and their elongated reflections on the darkening water near the steamer, the red fires on the rafts. From there he'd caught the scent of smoke and thought to himself, "I must remember this—that smoke smells exactly like fish soup," as he delivered all his questions.

"May I ask your name?"

She told him both her first name and her patronymic quickly.

"Are you on your way home from somewhere?"

"I was at my sister's in Sviyazhsk. Her husband died unexpectedly and she's been left in an awful situation."

At first she was so flustered that she could only look into the distance. But later she began to answer him more boldly.

"Are you married too?"

She began to smirk strangely. "Married. And for more than one year, alas."

"Why 'alas'?"

"I jumped into it too early by stupidity. Far too early. You don't have time to look around, and your life's already passed."

"Well, it's still a long way to that point."

"No, not long, alas. And I've experienced nothing, nothing in this life so far."

"It's not too late to experience something new."

Here she shook her head and smirked again. "I am," she said.

"And what does your husband do? A bureaucrat?"

She waved her hand. "Oh, he's a very good and kind person, but, unfortunately, completely uninteresting. . . . He's the secretary of the district land authority."

"'So winsome and forlorn,'" he thought, taking out his cigarette case. "Would you like a cigarette?"

"Oh, yes—very much!"

She began to smoke clumsily, but with great enthusiasm, drawing on her cigarette in quick, short puffs the way most women do. Within him

stirred once more a certain pity for her and her contrived insouciance—
and together with that pity, tenderness, as well as a voluptuous desire to ex-
ploit her naiveté and her belated lack of experience, which he already
sensed would invariably lead to extremes of bold behavior. Sitting with her
now in the restaurant, he looked impatiently at her gaunt hands, at those
wan and faded features that only made her more endearing, at the abun-
dant dark hair she'd arranged haphazardly and now shook constantly, having removed her cheap black hat and slipped her sad grey overcoat from
the shoulders of her fustian dress. The openness with which she'd spoken
yesterday about her family life and her advancing age both aroused and
moved him—as did the sudden, growing boldness that she now displayed
along with an unflinching readiness to speak and act in ways that suited
her so very poorly. She was lightly flushed from the vodka—even her pale
lips had turned pink, and a drowsy, mocking light now filled her eyes.

"You know," she said, "we were just talking about dreams. Do you
know what I dreamt about when I was a schoolgirl? Ordering myself a set
of calling cards! We'd grown completely poor—sold off the last of our
property and moved into town. There was absolutely no one I could give
them to. But how I dreamed about those calling cards! Terribly stupid . . ."

He clenched his teeth and firmly grasped her hand, feeling all the
small bones beneath her thin skin. But she completely failed to understand his meaning, and with a languid look, brought the hand he'd
grasped toward his lips, like some experienced seductress.

"Let's go to my cabin. . . ."

"Yes, let's go. . . . It's really rather stuffy here from all the cigarettes."
She shook her hair once more and took her hat.

He embraced her in the corridor. She looked at him across her
shoulder with a prideful sultriness. He almost bit into her cheek with
that hatred spawned by love and passion. She turned her head and offered him her mouth across her shoulder like a priestess in some Bac-
chanalia.

She was eager to anticipate him and to boldly maximize in every
manner possible the happiness that had so suddenly fallen to her lot
with this handsome, strong, and famous man, and thus, the moment
that they entered the half-light of the cabin, where the window blinds
were down, she unbuttoned her dress and shook it to the floor, appeared
before him thin and graceful as a boy in her light camisole and white
underpants, her arms and shoulders bare. The sheer innocence of it all
pierced him like a blade.

"Take everything off?" she asked in a whisper, exactly like a school-girl.

"All of it, everything," he said, growing still more sullen.

She stepped quickly and obediently away from the pile of under-clothes discarded on the floor, wearing nothing but grey stockings, a simple garter belt, and cheap black shoes. Her flesh looked lilac-grey in the twilight, and in that way unique to a woman's body it was chilled with nervousness, taut and cool, goose bumps spreading all across its surface. She glanced at him with an air of drunken triumph, gathered her hair in her hands, and began taking out its pins while he observed her every movement, growing cold. Her body was better, younger than he ever would have thought. Her thin collarbone and sharp ribs accorded with her gaunt face and her delicate shins. But her hips were wide and gener-ous. With its small, deep belly button, her stomach curved inward past the ribs; the prominent triangle of dark, pretty hair rising from beneath it was in keeping with the hair that grew in rich abundance on her head. She removed the last pins and that mane spilled thickly down her back, where each vertebra appeared in sharp relief. She stooped to raise her fallen stockings, and her small breasts, their brown nipples wrinkled from the cold, drooped like thin pears, utterly enchanting in their poverty. And he did indeed force her to experience those extremes of shamelessness that suited her so poorly and therefore stirred in him such pity, tender-ness, and passion. . . . The window blinds were pointed up, and nothing could be seen through their slats, but she glanced at them with exultant terror, heard the footsteps and the idle talk of people walking on the deck, passing just below that very window – and all of this increased still more terribly the transports of her dissipation. Oh, how close they are! How nearby they walk and talk—and no one has an inkling of what's being done in here, just a step away from them, in this white cabin!

Then he laid her on the bed like a dead woman. She clenched her teeth and lay with her eyes closed, a mournful calm spreading across her face, now pale and filled with youth.

Toward evening the ship docked at that town where she was sched-uled to depart. She stood beside him quietly, her eyes cast down. He kissed her cold hand with that love that remains in the heart for all of one's life. Without looking around, she ran down the gangplank to the rough crowd waiting on the dock.

[October 5, 1940]

Rusya

S OMETIME after 10 P.M. the Moscow-Sevastopol express made an unscheduled stop at a small station past Podolsk and stood waiting for something on the other track. A couple riding in first class leaned toward an open window: outside a conductor was crossing the rails with a red lantern swinging from his hand.

"Why have we stopped?" the lady asked abruptly.

The conductor explained that another train that crossed their line was running late: they had to let it pass.

It was already dark and lonely at the station. The sun had set long ago, but in the west, beyond the station and the black, wooded fields, the ghostly light of Moscow's summer dusk remained. Moist air from the marshes drifted through the open windows, and in the silence one could hear the steady, monotonous screech of a corncrake—somehow the sound seemed as damp as the air.

The man propped his elbows up on the window; the woman leaned against his shoulder.

"I stayed here once during summer vacation when I was a student," he said. "I was a tutor at an estate about five *versts* from here. It's a boring place—a sparse forest and a lot of magpies. Mosquitoes. Dragonflies. And no good view of the land. If you really wanted to look at the horizon, you had to go to the house, up to the mezzanine. The house had been built in the fashion of most summer estates, but the family had fallen on hard times, and it was badly run down. Behind it there was something you could call a garden, and beyond that there was something you couldn't call a lake, but couldn't call a swamp either—just a mass of weeds and water lilies, and, of course, a flat-bottomed boat near a marshy shore."

"And, of course, a girl who's dying from boredom at her dacha until you start paddling her around the swamp."

"Yes, everything according to plan. Only the girl wasn't bored at all. And I took her out in the boat at night most of the time. It was really rather poetic. The sky in the west stayed a strange, transparent green all night, and something always seemed to be smoldering on the horizon, just like it is now. . . . I could only find one oar, and it was like a shovel, so I had to paddle like a savage—first on the right side, then on the left. On the other bank it was dark from a forest of brush and small trees, but that strange half-light glowed all night beyond the woods. And everywhere it's unbelievably quiet—only the mosquitoes whine and the dragonflies buzz past. I never thought they flew at night, but it turns out they do for some reason. The noise they make is downright frightening."

They finally heard the other train rumbling toward them. A breeze rose as it flew by, and the lights in the passing cars blended into a long, golden streak. Then the express lurched forward; an attendant entered the couple's compartment, turned on the lights, and began making their beds.

"So what happened with you and that girl? A full-scale affair? For some reason you've never mentioned her before. What was she like?"

"Skinny. Tall. She wore a yellow *sarafan*. It was made of cotton, sleeveless. And peasant shoes that had been woven from different colored wools."

"One of those girls who likes a very 'Russian' style. . . ."

"I think it was more a poor woman's style. She never had much to wear other than that dress. She was an artist—studied painting at the Stroganov School for fine arts. And she looked like something from a painting, from an icon even—a braid of black hair down her back; a dark face with a few freckles; a straight, thin nose. Her eyes and eyebrows were black. . . . And her hair was thick and dry, slightly curly. Her features and her skin looked very beautiful against the yellow cotton of that *sarafan* and the white muslin sleeves of the shirt she wore beneath it. I remember how her ankles and the tops of her feet always seemed very fragile. The skin over them was so delicate you could see her bones."

"I know that type. I had a girlfriend at the university like that. Very prone to hysterics, right?"

"Maybe. Her face was a lot like her mother's, and her mother suffered from terrible depression. She was some kind of princess by birth, had Eastern blood. She'd only come out of her room for meals. She'd come out, sit down—and dead silence. Maybe she'd cough, but she'd never look up from her plate—just shift her knife and fork around from one place to another. And if she did suddenly say something, she'd shout out her words and we'd all jump."

"And the father?"

"He was pretty silent too. Very tall and very removed—a retired military man. But their son was sweet—he's who I tutored."

The attendant said their beds were ready, wished them good night, and left the compartment.

"And what was her name?"

"Rusya."

"What kind of name is that?"

"Very simple—short for Marusya."

"And so, you were really in love with her?"

"Terribly in love. At least that's how it seemed at the time."

"And she?"

He fell silent for a moment, then answered dryly: "She probably thought the same thing. But let's go to bed—I'm exhausted."

"Oh, very nice! You've just gotten me interested! Come on—tell me in two words how the romance ended."

"It ended in nothing. I left and it was over."

"And why didn't you marry her?"

"Evidently I had a premonition that I'd meet you."

"No, really?"

"No. Actually, I shot myself, and she stabbed herself with a dagger."

Having washed their faces and brushed their teeth, the man and the woman locked themselves into the compartment, which seemed to grow more cluttered in the dark, and lay down on their beds, feeling that joy all travelers experience when they finally touch fresh linen sheets and rest their heads on those lustrous pillows that always slip down from the slightly raised end of the berth.

A blue night-light glowed above the door, as if quietly watching over the cabin. She quickly dozed off, but he was unable to sleep and lay smoking in bed, returning to that summer in his thoughts.

She had small, dark freckles on her stomach and her back as well — and they delighted him. Because she wore soft shoes without heels, her whole body seemed to sway under the yellow *sarafan* when she walked. The *sarafan* was light and loose-fitting, and her tall, girlish body moved freely under it. Once, her feet soaked by the rain, she ran from the garden into the living room: he hurried to remove her shoes, kissed the narrow, wet soles of her feet — and there had never been such happiness in his life. Everyone had gone to sleep in the darkened house after lunch; more and more fresh-smelling rain was pouring over the patio beyond the open doors — and how terribly that rooster frightened them as he too ran from the garden into the living room, his black feathers shot with a strange, metallic green, his crown as brilliant as a flame, his claws clicking on the floor at the very moment when they'd lost themselves and let all caution go. Seeing how they jumped up from the couch, he ducked his head, as if embarrassed, and politely trotted back into the rain with his shimmering tail drawn down.

In the beginning she'd scrutinized him constantly; if he spoke, she'd blush darkly and mutter something droll. At meals she liked to tease him, saying loudly to her father: "Don't give him any, papa. It's useless. He doesn't like *vareniki*. He doesn't like *okroshka* or noodles, either. He despises yogurt too, and he hates cottage cheese."

He was busy with his pupil in the mornings, and she had chores to do — the entire household depended on her. They'd have lunch at one, and then she'd go to her room on the mezzanine or, if it wasn't raining, to the garden, where she'd paint the landscape, waving off mosquitoes as she stood before her easel under the birches. Then she began to come out on the balcony, where he usually sat reading in a wicker chair after lunch. She'd stand with her hands behind her back and look at him with a derisive smile.

"Can I ask what subtleties you're absorbed in today?"

"The history of the French Revolution."

"Oh my! I didn't realize that we have a revolutionary in the house!"

"Why aren't you painting?"

"My lack of talent is becoming too obvious. I'm about to quit for good."

"Why don't you show me one of your pictures?"

"Why? Do you think you know something about painting?"

"You're awfully proud, you know."

"Yes, that is a flaw of mine."

One day she finally suggested that they take the boat out on the lake. "It looks like the rainy season has ended in this little jungle of ours," she said decisively. "Let's play while we have the chance. Of course, our boat is rotting and it's full of holes, but Petya and I have stopped the floor with marsh weeds."

It was a stifling afternoon. Hot, damp air had settled like a sheet on the grass flecked with buttercups along the shore; pale green moths hovered lazily above the flowers. As they walked to the boat, he began to speak in the same mocking tone that she'd adopted so consistently with him:

"You've finally come down from your pedestal to visit me!"

"And you've finally figured out a way to talk to me," she answered happily as she jumped into the bow, and startled frogs splashed into the water all around them. Suddenly she screamed, pulled the *sarafan* above her knees, and started stamping: "A snake! A snake!"

He glimpsed the wet, dark skin of her calves as he grabbed the oar from the bow; then he struck the grass snake coiled in the bottom of the boat and flung it far out into the lake.

She had turned pale with a kind of Indian pallor, and the contrast made her freckles seem darker, her hair and eyes even blacker.

"How disgusting!" she said, sighing with relief. "It's no wonder the devil took the form of a snake. They're everywhere around here—in the garden, under the house. And Petya picks them up with his hands! Can you believe it!"

It was the first time she'd spoken to him openly; the first time they'd looked straight into each other's eyes.

"But you were quick! You hit him perfectly!"

Relaxed again, she smiled as she scampered from the bow and sat down in the stern. The beauty she'd revealed in her terror stunned him. "She's still a little girl," he thought with tenderness. But he tried to appear nonchalant as he stepped carefully into the boat, stuck his oar into the gelatinous bottom of the lake, swung the bow forward, and began to

pole through the tangled weeds, the tufts of marsh grass, and the blooming lilies that layered the surface with their broad, flat leaves. When they
finally reached open water, he sat down on the seat in the middle of the
boat and began rowing—first on the right, then on the left.

"This is nice, isn't it?" she shouted.

"Yes, very nice!" he answered, taking off his cap and turning toward
her. "Could you keep this up there with you? Just toss it anywhere. I'm
afraid I'll knock it into the bottom of this wreck—it's full of leeches, you
know, and it still leaks."

She put the cap on her knees.

"Don't worry about it—just put it somewhere dry up there."

She hugged the hat against her chest: "No—I'm going to guard it!"

Tenderness welled up in his heart again, but he turned away and
started rowing harder in the water that shimmered between the lilies
and the weeds.

Mosquitoes stuck to his hands and face, and the silver glare of the
lake turned blinding. . . . Humid air and a shifting band of sunlight. . . .
Thin white strands of clouds shining softly in the sky and on the water
glades among islands of lilies and sedge. . . . It was shallow everywhere,
and he could see marsh grass growing on the bottom of the lake, but the
water's depth seemed endless when the sky and the clouds' reflections
stretched across it. Suddenly she screamed again, and they began to tip:
she had reached down from the stern toward a lily, grabbed its stem, and
pulled so hard that the boat heaved to one side and she began to fall—
he barely had time to catch her under her arms. She burst out laughing,
fell into the bow, and flicked the water from her hand into his eyes.
Then he grabbed her again and suddenly, without knowing what he was
doing, he kissed her lips as she laughed. She put her arms around his
neck and clumsily kissed his cheek.

From that time on, they started boating on the lake at night.

The next day she called him into the garden after lunch.

"Do you love me?" she asked.

Remembering the way they'd kissed in the boat, he answered
earnestly: "From the first day we met."

"And I," she said, "—no, I hated you at first because you never
seemed to notice me. But that's over now, thank God. When everyone
goes to bed tonight, go down to the lake and wait for me. Only be
careful—sneak out quietly. Mama watches everything I do—she's in-
sanely jealous."

That night she came to the shore carrying a blanket.

"What's that for?" he asked, flustered by the joy he felt at seeing her.

"You're so silly—we're bound to get cold. Let's hurry—get in and row us over to the other shore."

They crossed the lake without speaking.

"Okay, that's good," she said as the boat neared the forest on the other bank. "Now come here. Where's the blanket? Oh, I'm sitting on it. Wrap it around me—I'm freezing. And sit here. No, you see, we didn't kiss right yesterday. Now I'll kiss you first, only very, very softly. And you put your arms around me. . . . Everywhere. . . ."

Under the *sarafan* she was wearing only a blouse. Tenderly, barely touching him, she kissed the edges of his lips. He felt as if his head were spinning as he pushed her back into the stern, and she pressed herself against him. . . .

Afterward she lay resting quietly in the boat, then sat up and smiled in a way that expressed both happy exhaustion and lingering pain.

"Now we're husband and wife," she said. "Mama says she won't survive it if I get married, but I don't want to think about that now. . . . You know what? I'm going swimming. I love to at night."

Her long, thin body looked pale in the gloom when she pulled off her dress and began to wrap her braid around her head, exposing her dark underarms and making her breasts rise as she reached up: she was not at all embarrassed by her nakedness or the dark mound below her belly. Finished with her braid, she kissed him lightly, jumped onto her feet, and splashed into the lake. Holding her head out of the water, she kicked loudly as she swam.

Then he hurriedly helped her dress and wrapped her up in the blanket. Her eyes and her black hair, still tied in a braid, stood out sharply in the dim light. He didn't dare to touch her anymore; he only kissed her hands and sat without talking, seized by an almost unbearable joy. Sometimes they heard a light rustling in the leaves, and it seemed that someone was standing among the black trees and the scattered lights of the fireflies on the bank—standing and listening to them. She raised her head: "Wait, what was that?"

"Don't worry, it's probably a frog going up the bank. Or a hedgehog in the woods."

"But what if it's a goat."

"What goat?"

"I don't know. But just imagine it: a goat comes out of the forest and stands there and watches us. . . . Oh, I'm so happy I just feel like saying stupid things!"

He pressed her hands to his lips again, then solemnly kissed her cold breast. How suddenly she'd changed, become a wholly different creature in his eyes! The green summer twilight had not gone out; it was still glowing beyond the darkened forest, still hanging on the calm, pale surface of the lake. A sharp scent like the smell of celery rose from the dew-soaked weeds along the bank; the whining sound of the mosquitoes turned tentative, almost pleading—and terrifying, sleepless dragonflies darted over the water and the boat with their delicate, crackling wings. And still, still something rustled in the leaves, crawled, picked its way along the ground.

A week later he was disgraced, thrown out of the house, and forbidden to see her again. The scandal and their sudden, violent separation left him stunned.

They had been sitting in the living room after lunch, their heads lightly touching as they looked at the pictures in an old issue of *Niva*.

"Do you still love me?" he asked, pretending to study the drawings.

"Silly, you're so silly," she whispered.

Suddenly they heard someone running lightly toward the room, and her half-mad mother appeared at the threshold in a tattered black silk dressing gown and worn-out leather slippers. She rushed at them like an actress making her entrance on stage, her black eyes flashing with a tragic light.

"I know everything! I felt it! I've been watching you! I won't let you take her, you bastard!"

She flung up her hand and fired a deafening shot from the ancient pistol that Petya used to frighten sparrows—there was only powder in the gun. He jumped at her through the smoke and grabbed her arm, but she wrenched free and struck his forehead with the pistol; blood began to trickle from a gash above his eye. She threw the gun at him and, hearing others in the house running toward the noise, began to shout—even more theatrically.

"She'll have to step over my dead body to leave this house with you!" she screamed, her grey-blue lips flecked with foam. "I'll hang myself the day she runs away with you! Do you hear—I'll hang myself! I'll throw myself off the roof! Get out, you bastard—get out of my house! You choose, Marya Viktorovna—choose! Him or your mother!"

"You, mama," she whispered, "you. . . ."

He came back to himself and opened his eyes—the blue night-light above the door was still staring at him with morbid curiosity in the darkness, and the car was still rocking gently on its springs as the train flew inexorably forward. Already that sad little stop was far away, far back in the distance. And twenty years had passed since he first saw those thickets of trees, those magpies and the swamp, the lilies and the grass snakes and the cranes. . . . Yes, there were cranes—how could he have forgotten them! Like so much of that summer, they were a mystery, that pair that appeared occasionally on the banks of the swamp and allowed only her to approach them, bending their long, delicate necks and watching with curiosity and suspicion as softly she moved closer in her woven shoes, and finally sat before them, her yellow *sarafan* spreading out over the wet, warm grass: with childlike wonder she would study their eyes, look into the menacing and beautiful blackness of those pupils ringed by dark grey irises. Watching her and the cranes through binoculars, he could clearly see the birds' small, brilliant heads, the delicate slits of their nares, and the bony, powerful beaks with which they killed grass snakes in one blow. The feathers that thickly covered their torsos and their airy tails glinted like steel, and their legs—one pair black, the other green—resembled long, scaly reeds. Sometimes each bird would stand on just one leg, remaining inexplicably still for hours; then, for no apparent reason, they'd begin to hop and stretch their massive wings, or bob their heads and take slow, measured steps with an air of self-importance, clutching their feet into tight balls as they lifted them, then spreading them apart like a raptor's talons in the air. But still, when she ran toward those cranes, he thought of nothing—saw nothing—but her yellow *sarafan* spreading out over the grass; and the thought of her dark body—the dark freckles on her skin beneath that *sarafan*—filled him with such mortal longing that he shuddered. On that last day, during the last moments in which they sat together on the living room couch with an old copy of *Niva*, she was holding his cap again, and she hugged it against her chest, just as she had in the boat. Her black eyes were shining with joy when she said, "I love you so much that nothing's dearer to me now than the smell of this hat—the smell of your hair and your hideous cologne!"

He was drinking coffee and cognac in the dining car after breakfast as the train rolled on somewhere past Kursk.

"Why are you drinking so much?" his wife asked. "That's already your fifth, isn't it? Are you still sad? Still pining for your dacha girl with bony feet?"

"Still sad, still sad," he answered with an unpleasant smile. "The dacha girl. . . . *Amata nobis quantum amabitur nulla!*"

"Is that Latin? What does it mean?"

"You don't need to know."

"You're so rude," she said as she sighed and began staring out the sunlit window.

[1940]

Wolves

T HE DARKNESS of a warm August night. Dim stars you can barely see, gleaming here and there among the clouds. A road turned soft and soundless with deep dust; a wagon traveling it now toward the fields. Two passengers: a high school boy and the teenage daughter of some petty nobleman. Sometimes the summer lightning spills its muted glow across the simple harness and the tangled manes of two workhorses running at a level gait; sometimes it catches the peaked cap and the shoulders of the young driver perched on the coachman's box in a simple, linen shirt; sometimes it opens up the bare fields that lie ahead, deserted now, with the workday's end—or, farther on, reveals a small, sad forest rising from the plain. There was a great commotion in the village yesterday—shouts, squeals, and desperate whining from the dogs. Everyone had settled down to dinner when a wolf entered one of the yards with startling audacity, attacked a sheep, and almost carried it off. The men ran from their huts toward the frantic hounds and drove the wolf away with their clubs—but the sheep was already dead, its side torn open. Now the young girl bursts into loud and nervous laughter, lighting matches and casting them into the dark.

"I'm afraid of wolves!" she shouts out happily.

The match light falls across the boy's elongated and slightly crude countenance, the girl's small face, her high cheekbones and excited expression. She wears a red headscarf tied Ukrainian style, and a red chintz dress cut loosely around her firm, round neck. Swaying with the cart, she lights the matches and tosses them into the dark as if not noticing that the high school boy has her in his arms, is planting kisses on her neck and cheek, searching for her mouth. She nudges him away with her elbow, and he raises his voice for the driver to hear, says with deliberate simplicity:

"Give those matches back. I'll have no way to smoke!"

"Okay, okay," she shouts. Another match flame sputters up, another sheet of lightning trembles in the air, and then the darkness blinds them even more, the warm black—in which it seems the cart's forever rolling backward—turns even thicker than before. At last she gives her mouth to him in a long, slow kiss when suddenly the driver brings the horses to a violent halt—it seems the wagon's slammed into some obstacle—and both passengers pitch forward as if shoved.

"Wolves!" the driver screams.

To the right they see a fire glowing in the distance, its light so sharp it stuns their eyes. The wagon stands opposite that small forest that earlier the lightning had revealed. The fire's glow has turned it black, and everywhere it trembles, just as all the field before it trembles in the murky, red, shivering light of the flames, which rise voraciously into the sky, and despite the actual distance, seem less than a *verst* from the cart as they swell with the shadows of smoke that streams from inside them, and with mounting fury spread ever wider, reach ever higher and hotter and more menacingly across the horizon—it seems their heat even reaches the hands and faces of the onlookers, and already the red transom of some incinerated roof is visible now above the black earth. Beneath the forest wall stand three large wolves; their coats are crimson-grey, and their eyes are filled with a transparent light that flashes green, then red—vitreous and bright as hot syrup made from red currant jam. The horses snort, then bolt to the left, gallop wildly into the field. The driver falls back with the reins in his hands, and the wagon goes lurching over the rows of turned earth, rattles and knocks through the plowing. Somewhere near the ravine's edge, the horses are about to leap once more, but she jumps up, seizes the reins from the stupefied driver, and pulls so hard she's thrown headlong into the coachman's box, where she cuts her cheek on something metal. For all her life a light scar remained in the corner of her mouth, and whenever they asked her where it came from, she smiled with pleasure.

"Events of days long passed," she'd say, remembering that distant summer, the dry days and dark nights of August, the threshing in the barn, the stacks of new and fragrant straw—and that unshaven boy with whom she lay among them in the evening, studying the arcs of falling stars in all their stunning transience. "Wolves set our horses running," she would say. "But I was wild then, no fear at all. I went flying when I reined them in."

Many of those whom she loved in her life used to say there was nothing more endearing than that scar, which so resembled a delicate and constant smile.

[*October 3, 1940*]

Antigone

I N JUNE a student left his mother's estate to visit his aunt and uncle, a general who'd lost his legs. It was important to see how they were getting along and to check on his uncle's health. The student carried out this obligation every summer, and now he felt peacefully resigned to the trip as he sat with one muscular thigh draped over the armrest of the seat in a second-class compartment and read a few pages of a new book by Averchenko, or idly watched the telegraph poles rise and dip down, their white ceramic housings shaped like lilies of the valley. Although he wore a student's white hat with a blue band, he resembled a young officer, for all his clothes and finery had a military style—a white, high-collared jacket, greenish riding pants and shiny leather boots, a cigarette case with a brilliant orange braid.

His aunt and uncle were rich. When he came home from Moscow, his parents always sent a worker with two draft horses and a heavy *tarantass* instead of a driver with a carriage to meet him, but at the station near his aunt and uncle's house, the student seemed to enter a wealthy stranger's life. He immediately felt strong and happy, handsome, highly refined. And so it was this trip: three spirited bays pulled the light, rubber-wheeled carriage that came to meet him. The young driver wore a sleeveless, dark blue coat over a shirt of yellow silk, and the student took his seat with unwitting, foppish affectation.

Fifteen minutes later the carriage breezed into the driveway of an imposing estate. Its wheels hissed over the sand near a flower bed, and the harness bells rang playfully as the horses rounded the courtyard, then stopped before a new, two-story house. A brawny servant in sideburns came outside to unload the luggage; he wore low-cut boots and a red waistcoat with black stripes. The student made an improbably long and graceful leap from the carriage as his aunt came smiling and swaying to the vestibule door, a big silk chemise draped over her formless body. The flesh sagged on her large face, her nose was shaped like an anchor, and little pouches of yellowing skin hung under her brown eyes. She pecked his cheeks, and he pretended he was glad to see her as he bowed to kiss her warm, dark hand, thinking *three whole days of boredom and lies!* Answering with feigned respect the questions that she asked with feigned concern about his mother, the student followed his aunt into the vestibule and looked with gleeful contempt at the stuffed, slightly hunchbacked bear that stood awkwardly on its hind legs near the stairs, its glass eyes polished to a sheen, a bronze tray for visitors' cards gently cradled in its huge clawed paws. But suddenly he stopped, surprised and overjoyed: the fleshy, pale and blue-eyed general was being wheeled toward him by a beautiful woman in a grey gingham dress with a white apron, a white kerchief covering her hair. Her large grey eyes were radiant with youth and vigor, her delicate hands seemed to shine, and her face was suffused with a fresh, clear light. As he bent to kiss his uncle's hand, the student glanced at her legs and the long, graceful lines of her figure.

"This is my Antigone," the general joked. "Although I'm not as blind as Oedipus—especially when it comes to beautiful women. Say hello to each other."

She bowed in answer to his bow, smiled briefly, and said nothing.

The brawny servant with sideburns and a red waistcoat led him past the bear and up the staircase, its gleaming yellow wood covered by red carpets, then down an equally well-kept corridor to a large bedroom with a marble bath and windows looking out onto the park—a change from his room during previous visits, which had faced the courtyard. But the student didn't see a thing as he was led along. When he rode into the courtyard, a line from *Onegin* had been running through his head—*My uncle is a man of utmost principles*—but now another phrase eclipsed those words: *Christ, what a beautiful woman!*

He sang to himself while he shaved, washed, and changed, put on stirruped trousers—thinking all the while: What one would give for the love of a woman like that! How can there be such beautiful creatures pushing old people around in wheelchairs!

And soon his thoughts grew wild: I'll stay for a month, maybe two, and secretly befriend her. We'll grow intimate, I'll gain her love—and then, *Be my wife—I'm yours forever!* Mother, aunt, and uncle—they're all amazed when I announce our love and our plans to join our lives. They try to dissuade me, argue, shout, break down in tears. They curse and damn us, write me out of the will—and it's nothing. *I'll do anything for you. . . .*

But later, as he ran downstairs to his aunt and uncle—their rooms were on the first floor—the student thought: What nonsense gets into your head! You could come up with a reason to stay, you could start courting her secretly, even pretend you were madly in love, but would anything come of it? And if anything did come of it, what then? How would you get out of it? Would you marry—actually marry her?

He sat for an hour with his aunt and uncle in the latter's huge study, which contained a huge desk, a huge ottoman covered with fabrics from Turkestan, and little tables with inlaid ashtrays. The wall behind the ottoman was decorated with a rug and a pair of crossed swords from the east; above the fireplace, in a rosewood frame with a little golden crown, stood a large photograph of the tsar, which he'd signed with his own, free hand: Aleksandr.

"I'm so glad to see you again," said the student, thinking of the nurse. "It's so wonderful here, and I'll be so sorry to leave."

"Who's hurrying you? Stay as long as you like—where do you need to go?" his uncle answered.

"Of course, of course," his aunt said distractedly.

As he sat and chatted, the student waited impatiently: Now, now she'll come in—the maid will announce that tea is ready in the dining room, and she'll come to wheel uncle away. . . . But the servants rolled a table into the study with a silver teapot and a spirit lamp, and his aunt filled their cups herself. Then he clung to the hope that she would bring the general some odd dose of medicine. . . . But the nurse never appeared.

"To hell with her then," the student thought as he left the study and wandered into the dining room, where a servant was closing the blinds on the tall, sun-filled windows. In the hallway to the right, the glassy tips of a piano's legs caught the evening light and made it lie like little candle flames on the hardwood floor. He glanced in that direction, then aimlessly headed to the left, through the living room into the den. From there he went onto the porch, descended to the yard, walked around the brilliant, variegated flower beds, and started down a shady path between two rows of trees. . . . It was still hot in the sun. He had two hours to wait until dinner.

At seven-thirty a gong rang out in the vestibule. The dining room was festively lit with a chandelier. He arrived alone to find a fat, clean-shaven cook in a starched white uniform; a butler with sunken cheeks, white gloves, and tails; and a little maid who looked as dainty and refined as a Frenchwoman standing near a table by the wall. A moment later his aunt came swaying into the room: grey and powdered as a queen, she wore a dress of pale yellow silk with creamy lace and a pair of tight silk shoes that displayed her bulging ankles. Finally the nurse appeared—but she glided from the room as soon as the general had been arranged at the table. He had time only to notice a peculiarity about her eyes: she never blinked. With quick, shallow little strokes, the general made the sign of the cross over his light grey, double-breasted uniform; the student and his aunt ardently crossed themselves while still standing, then solemnly took their seats and spread their brilliant napkins on their laps. The general's damp, sparse, carefully combed hair and his pale, well-scrubbed skin made the hopelessness of his condition more obvious than ever, but he ate a great deal and talked tirelessly about the current war against Japan, shrugging his shoulders and muttering, *Why the hell did we start it anyway?* They drank red and white wine from Prince Golitsyn—an old friend of the general's—and ate scalding eelpout soup, rare roast beef, new potatoes seasoned with dill. The cook unveiled each new dish with the self-importance of a deity; the butler served them with insulting indifference, and the maid took mincing little steps around the room as she assisted him. The student talked, answered questions, nodded with a smile—but the same ridiculous ideas he'd entertained while dressing for dinner continued to play inside his head, like nonsense ceaselessly repeated by a parrot: Where does she eat? With the servants? Again he waited for the moment she'd appear, roll uncle away, then meet him somewhere, let him say a few words. . . . But after wheeling the general from the dining room, she disappeared for good.

During the night he could hear the careful, precise songs of nightingales in the park; the flower beds were wet with dew, and he could smell their dampness in the fresh, cold air that drifted through the windows and cooled the sheets of good Dutch linen on his bed. Lying in the dark, the student decided it was time to sleep and rolled onto his side—but suddenly he lifted his head from the pillow. While undressing he had noticed a small door near his bed; curious, he'd opened it and discovered a second door, which was locked on the other side. Now someone was walking quietly, doing something secretive behind that door. Holding his breath, he slipped out of bed, opened the first door, and listened: something clinked softly on the floor. The student went cold. Could it be her room? Peering through the keyhole, he saw a light and the edge of a woman's dressing table—then his view was blocked by something white. It must be her room! Whose else could it be? The maid didn't live upstairs, and Marya Ilinishna, his aunt's old helper, slept near the main bedroom on the first floor. This discovery hit him like an illness: she was just beyond the wall—just a few feet away, and still he couldn't reach her! The student slept badly and woke up late, his mind already feverish with images of her transparent nightshirt, her slippers, and her naked feet. "I should leave right now," he thought to himself, lighting up a cigarette.

They all had coffee in their separate rooms the next morning. He drank his while wearing a big nightshirt and a silk bathrobe that belonged to his uncle. He left the robe open and sat staring at his body, dismayed by its futility.

The dining room was gloomy and dull when he had breakfast with his aunt. The weather was bad. A strong wind shook the trees outside, and dark clouds clotted the sky.

"Well, darling, I'm leaving you," his aunt announced, getting up and crossing herself. "Try to entertain yourself as best you can, and forgive your uncle and me—we keep to ourselves until teatime. What a shame it's going to rain—you could have gone for a ride."

"Don't worry, aunt, I'll do some reading," he answered cheerfully, and headed for the den, where all the walls were lined with bookshelves.

Passing through the living room, he glanced out the window, wondering if he should order a horse to be saddled despite the weather. But a variety of rain clouds hung on the horizon, and the sky above the swaying trees had turned an unpleasant metallic blue among lilac-colored thunderheads. The den smelled of sweet cigar smoke; he glanced at a few superbly bound spines, then sat down, sinking helplessly into the plush leather of one of the couches that lined three walls of the room: *Truly hellish boredom.* If only he could see her, talk to her, find out what her voice was like, what kind of personality she had. Was she stupid? Or just the opposite—very in control, playing the role of a modest girl until just the right moment. Probably very guarded, and very aware of her worth. And probably stupid all the same. . . . But what a beauty! And again I'll have to sleep right next to her! He got up and opened the glass door, stepped outside toward the stone stairs that led to the garden. For a moment he could hear the trilling of the nightingales above the rustling leaves, but then a cold wind surged through a stand of young trees to his left, and he scrambled back inside. The room grew dark and the wind tore at the trees, bending their fresh, green branches. Sharp bursts of rain began to streak and flash across the windows and the glass door.

"They aren't bothered at all!" he said out loud, still listening to the trilling of the nightingales, whose songs seemed to gather in the wind and sail into the room. And immediately he heard a calm, impassive voice.

"Good day."

The nurse was standing before him. "I've come for a book," she said with friendly nonchalance as he gaped at her. "Reading's my only pleasure," she added with a smile, and walked toward the shelves.

"Hello—I didn't hear you come in," he mumbled.

"Very soft rugs." She turned around as she spoke and looked at him for a long time with her grey, unblinking eyes.

"And what do you like to read?" he asked, meeting her glance a little more boldly.

"Right now I'm reading Maupassant, Octave Mirbeau . . ."

"Of course—all women like Maupassant. He writes only about love."

"And what could be better than that?" Her voice was unassuming; a quiet smile played in her eyes.

"Love, love," he said, sighing. "There are surprising encounters, but . . . What is your full name, nurse?"

"Katerina Nikolayevna. And yours?"

"You can call me Pavlik," he answered, growing even more bold.

"You want me to use pet names for you—just like your aunt?"

"I'd be very happy to have an aunt like you. But for now I'm just your unlucky neighbor."

"Is it really such bad luck?"

"I heard you last night. Your room, it turns out, is right next to mine."

She laughed indifferently. "I heard you too. It's bad manners, you know, to peep through keyholes and listen at a woman's door."

"But you're so excessively beautiful!" he said, staring stubbornly at her grey eyes, her light complexion, and the dark, glossy hair under her white kerchief.

"Do you think so? And you'd forbid such excess?"

"I would. Your arms alone could make me lose my mind."

He caught her hand with playful daring as he spoke. Standing with her back to the shelves, she glanced over his shoulder into the living room, then looked at him with a strange, slightly mocking expression, as if to say: *Well—what now?* He tightened his grip on her hand, pulled down on it, and grabbed her by the waist. She glanced over his shoulder again, tossed back her head as if protecting her face from his kisses—and pressed her arcing waist against his body. Struggling to breathe, he brought his mouth to her half-parted lips, then moved toward the couch. The nurse frowned and shook her head. "No, no—if we lie down, we won't be able to see, or hear," she whispered, and then, her eyes growing dim, she slowly spread her legs apart. . . . A minute later he dropped his head against her shoulder. She remained standing, her teeth still clenched, then quietly freed herself from him and walked into the next room, projecting her indifferent voice over the pelting rain. "Oh, it's pouring—and all the windows are open upstairs."

The next morning he woke up in her bed. The sheets were still warm and disheveled from the night; she lay on her back with one hand behind her head and all her naked arm exposed. He looked happily into her unblinking eyes. The sharp scent that rose from her armpit made him almost giddy with desire.

Someone knocked hurriedly at the door.

"Who is it?" she asked calmly, without pushing him away. "Marya Ilinishna?"

"Yes, Katerina Nikolayevna, it's me."

"What's wrong?"

"Let me in, please—I'm afraid someone will hear me and run off to frighten the general's wife."

When he had slipped into his room, she unhurriedly turned the key in the lock.

"There's something wrong with his excellency. I think he needs an injection," Marya Ilinishna whispered as she entered. "Thank goodness the general's wife is still asleep—you must come right away. . . ."

Marya Ilinishna's eyes turned beady as a snake's while she spoke, for she'd caught sight of a man's slippers near the bed—the student had run away barefoot. Katerina Nikolayevna also saw the slippers—as well as Marya Ilinishna's eyes.

Before breakfast she went to the general's wife and said she had to leave for home right away: she lied calmly, saying she'd just received a letter from her father, in which he wrote that her brother had been badly wounded near Manchuria. Her father, a widower, was all alone in his grief. . . .

"Ah, of course—I understand," the general's wife said, having already learned everything from Marya Ilinishna. "You must go right away, of course. Just send a message from the station for Dr. Krivtsov. Tell him to come and stay with us until we find another nurse."

Then she knocked on the student's door and slipped him a little note: "It's all over. I'm leaving. The old lady saw your slippers by my bed. Don't think ill of me."

At breakfast his aunt was a little sad, but she spoke as if nothing were wrong. "Did you hear, the nurse is leaving for her father's house—he's all alone, and her brother's been terribly wounded. . . ."

"I heard, aunt. This wretched war's made everyone miserable. . . . What was wrong with uncle, anyway?"

"Oh, it was nothing, thank God. He's such a hypochondriac! He thought he was having a heart attack—but it was only indigestion."

At three o'clock they drove Antigone to the station in a troika. Pretending he was going out for a ride, the student ran onto the porch, as if by accident, just as she was leaving. He said goodbye without raising his eyes, ready to shout in despair. She waved her glove to him as she rode away in the carriage—her white kerchief was already gone, replaced by an elegant hat.

[1940]

Little Fool

D URING his vacation, the deacon's son, a seminarian, went to visit his parents in the country. One night he awoke to a sharp stirring in his body, and as he lay in the hot summer dark, his imagination aroused him even more: From behind a willow bush he watches girls go down to the river. It's late afternoon, and they have come from work. They pull their shirts over their heads, and sweat glistens on their white skin. They bend their backs and tip their faces to the sun. They laugh and shout, fling themselves into the blazing water. . . . No longer able to control himself, the seminarian left his bed and stole through the darkened hallway to the kitchen, which was as hot and black as a working oven. With his hands stretched out before him, he groped toward the plank bed where the cook lay sleeping. A destitute girl with no family, she was said to be an imbecile—a little fool—and she was too afraid to scream. The seminarian lived with her all summer, and soon she had a son, who spent his infancy beside his mother in the kitchen. The deacon and the constable and both their wives, the priest himself and his entire household, the shopkeeper's family—all of them knew where the little boy came from, and when the seminarian visited on holidays, he felt such bitter shame he couldn't stand to look upon his past: he'd slept with an imbecile!

After graduation—"A brilliant student," the deacon told every-one—the seminarian returned home for the summer before entering the academy. As soon as they could, his parents invited guests to tea in order to display the future academician. All the guests talked about his brilliant future, drank tea, ate different kinds of jam. The happy deacon wound up the gramophone; it was like a whispering that grew into a shout in the midst of the lively conversations—everyone fell silent and smiled with pleasure at the stirring notes of "On the Road." Suddenly the cook's little boy flew into the room and began a clumsy dance, stomping his feet out of time with the music. His mother had stupidly whispered to him, "Go and dance, my darling," thinking the guests would find it touching. But everyone was shocked by the boy's sudden appearance. The seminarian turned purple with rage, lunged at the child like a tiger, and sent him reeling into the hall.

On his demand, the deacon and the deacon's wife fired the cook the next day. They were kind, compassionate people, and they'd grown used to the cook—they loved her innocence and obedience—so they asked their son to forgive her. But he remained adamant, and they didn't dare disobey. The cook wept quietly as she left the yard that evening, holding a little bundle in one hand and leading her son with the other.

All summer she wandered with him through villages and towns, begging in the name of Christ. She wore out her shoes and her clothes; she was burnt by the sun and the wind; her body turned to skin and bones. But she did not stop. Leaning on a tall staff, she walked barefoot with a sackcloth bag on her shoulder. In the villages and towns she bowed silently before each house. The boy walked beside her with a bag on his shoulder as well; he wore his mother's old shoes, which were broken and stiff—the kind of shoes you'd see lying around in a ditch.

He was a freak. The broad, flat top of his head was covered with a shock of coarse, red hair; his nose lay almost flat on his face; his nostrils were too big; his walnut-colored eyes shone with a strange brilliance. But he was lovely when he smiled.

[1940]

Tanya

S HE WAS a maid in the house of one of his relatives—a petty landowner, a widow named Kazakova. She was sixteen. She was small and thin, and this became quite noticeable when she went barefoot or, in winter, wore felt boots and walked with her skirt gently swaying behind her, her small breasts slightly raised beneath her blouse. Her features were pleasant and appealing, but not striking. It was their youth alone that made her grey peasant eyes so lovely. During those years— now long passed—he led a particularly dissipated and aimless life, wasting himself in foolish ways. He had many trysts and chance affairs—and she was just one more.

She quickly came to terms with that fateful and surprising encounter that had taken place so suddenly one autumn night. She wept for several days but at the same time grew more and more convinced that this occurrence was not a cause for sorrow but for joy—and that he was growing ever closer to her heart. During moments of their intimacy, which soon began to repeat themselves with growing frequency, she even called him Petrusha, and sometimes she spoke of that first night the way she might have talked about a secret past they shared and cherished.

IVAN BUNIN

At first he both believed and didn't believe her version of events.

"You mean, you weren't just pretending to be asleep? You had to be pretending. . . ."

Her eyes widened with surprise.

"You really couldn't tell? Don't you know how heavy boys and girls can sleep?"

"I wouldn't have begun to touch you if I'd known that you were really sleeping."

"Well, I didn't feel anything. Nothing. Almost to the very end. But what sent you looking for me? What put a thought like that into your head? You had no time for me at first. When you came to the house, you didn't even turn your eyes to me. Only in the evening you said something like 'You must be the maid they hired recently. I believe your name is Tanya.' That was all you said. And after that you looked at me with no real interest. That's how it seemed at least. Were you pretending all that time?"

He told her that of course he'd been pretending not to notice her. But he was lying: he'd expected none of this to happen.

He'd spent the early fall in the Crimea, then stopped to visit Kazakova while returning home to Moscow. He'd stayed two weeks, rested in the quiet calm of her estate and those barren days that mark the beginning of November, then decided it was time to leave. He had one last ride on horseback—took a hunting dog and roamed with a gun on his shoulder all day through the empty fields and the barren thickets, found nothing, came back tired and hungry to the manor house. For dinner he ate an entire pan of rissole in sour cream and drank a small carafe of vodka and several cups of tea while Kazakova spoke, as she so often did, about her dead husband and her two sons, who were serving in Oryol. As usual, the entire house was dark by ten o'clock; just one candle burned in the study off the living room, where he always slept on an old ottoman when he visited. When he came into the room, she was kneeling on his bedding, running the candle's flame over the heavy, rough-hewn logs that formed the wall beside her. Seeing him, she thrust the candle back onto the nightstand, jumped to her feet, and bolted from the room.

"What's going on?" he said, almost dumbfounded. "Stop. What were you doing?"

"Burning a bedbug," she answered in a hurried whisper. "I was putting out your quilt and I saw a bedbug there, on the wall," she said—and laughing, ran away.

[316]

He stared after her, then took off his boots and lay down on the quilt without undressing, hoping to have another cigarette and do some thinking—he wasn't used to getting into bed so early—and immediately dozed off. Disturbed by its trembling light, he woke up long enough to blow out the candle, then dropped back into sleep. When he opened his eyes again, a bright autumn night stood outside the house, hushed and lovely in all its emptiness: he could see it through the two front windows that looked out on the courtyard, and the side window, which opened on the garden, and now was filled with brilliant moonlight. In its soft glow he found his slippers near the bed and went into the corridor beside the study. They had forgotten to give him everything necessary for the night, and now he had to step out onto the back porch. But the door had been latched shut from the outside: it was impossible to open it. He would have to go out through the *sentsy*, a large anteroom of rough-hewn logs that stood at the end of the main hall and opened onto the front porch. He started walking through the house, making his way carefully in that secret light from the courtyard. An old storage trunk stood below a high window in the main hall; across from it was a partition that formed the maids' room. The partition door had been left slightly ajar; beyond it there was only darkness. He lit a match and saw her sleeping there. She was lying on her back on a wooden bed, wearing just a shirt and cotton skirt. He could see the outlines of her small, round breasts beneath the shirt; her legs were bare up to her knees. Her face looked lifeless on her pillow, as did the arm she'd extended in her sleep toward the wall. . . . The match burned out. He stood there for a moment— then cautiously approached the bed.

He walked through the darkened *sentsy* to the front porch, thinking feverishly: How strange! How completely unexpected! Could she really have been sleeping?

He stood for a moment on the porch, then went out into the court-yard. . . . What a strange night. This courtyard spreading out beneath the high moon, all this empty space so brilliantly illuminated. Big sheds stood across from him—barns for horses and cattle, a carriage house, their thatch roofs turning hard as stone over time. The night's secret clouds were slowly parting in the northern sky, where they rose like lifeless mountains under snow. The clouds above his head, however, were thin and white, refulgent with that gemlike incandescence the moon poured into them as it slipped past, then plunged into the dark blue valleys, the starry

depths of sky, its unobstructed light seeming to grow stronger on the courtyard and the roofs. All the objects that surrounded him seemed strange in
their nocturnal forms, cut off from all human influence, shining with no
purpose. He felt as if he'd never seen this before, as if he were looking for
the first time at a world created by the night and the autumn moon. And
this sensation only added to the strangeness of the scene surrounding him.

Near the carriage house he sat down on the footboard of a *tarantass*
that was covered with dried mud. The air was filled with an autumnal
warmth, all the scents of a garden in the fall. And the night was solemn,
placid, beatific, linked somehow to all the feelings he had brought away
from that sudden, unexpected joining with a being still half woman and
half child. . . .

She'd sobbed quietly as she came to herself, seeming only then to
grasp fully everything that had occurred. And perhaps she really hadn't
understood until that moment?. . . Her entire body had surrendered to
him, as if it were completely lifeless. He had intended to wake her with
his whispering: "Listen, don't be afraid. . . ." But she hadn't heard him—
or she had pretended not to. He'd kissed her hot cheek tentatively, and
when she offered no response, he'd taken her silence as consent to anything that might follow such a kiss. He'd spread her legs, their tender
warmth, their heat—and she had only sighed in her sleep, stretched
weakly, tossed one arm behind her head. . . .

"But what if she wasn't just pretending?" he thought, getting up
from the footboard and looking anxiously into the night.

He'd responded to the touching grief with which she wept by kissing her neck and breasts, inhaling her intoxicating scents of country life
and girlish innocence. And there was something more to this than simple, animal appreciation for the unexpected happiness she'd unknowingly bestowed on him: he'd kissed her in a fit of ecstasy and love. And
even as she sobbed, she'd suddenly responded with an unconscious rush
of feminine emotion, pressing him more firmly to her body, embracing
him with gratitude, cradling his head. She was still half asleep, did not
yet understand exactly who he was—but it was all the same: he was the
one with whom she'd been fated to first share this secret, blissful, mortal
pairing. Now that it had happened, nothing could annul that shared intimacy. He would carry her inside himself forever. And the extraordinary
night received him into its bewildering and brilliant realm together with
her, with that link that lay between them.

How could he remember her only incidentally after his departure? How could he forget her sincere and tender voice, the devoted love her eyes expressed with sorrow and joy? How could he proceed to love other women, even grant to some of them far more importance than he'd ever given her?

She served them the next day without raising her eyes.

"Why so troubled today, Tanya?" Kazakova asked.

She answered dutifully. "You know my troubles, *Barynya*. Are they not enough?"

When she'd left the room, Kazakova said to him: "Of course, she's an orphan. No mother—and her father's worthless. Just a swindler."

Toward evening he passed her on the porch as she prepared the samovar.

"I've loved you for a long time," he said. "Don't think otherwise. And stop crying. All this sobbing doesn't help. . . ."

"If you really loved me—if that was true—it would all be easier to bear," she answered, sniffling as she inserted the lit kindling into the samovar.

Then she began to glance at him, as if asking, timidly: "Is it true?"

When she came into his room to make his bed that evening, he approached her, put his arms around her shoulders. She looked at him with alarm. "Please, for God's sake move away," she whispered, blushing deeply. "The old lady's going to see."

"What old lady?"

"The old housekeeper! As if you didn't know."

"I'll come to you tonight. . . ."

It was as if he'd touched her with a flame—she'd been in horror of the old housekeeper the first time he found her in bed.

"What are you saying! No, no—you can't. I'll lose my mind from fear."

"All right, calm down. I won't come," he told her hurriedly.

She began to serve with all her previous attentiveness and speed, racing through the courtyard to the kitchen just as she had done before, and now, from time to time, she'd seize an opportunity to glance at him with flustered joy.

One morning before dawn, while he was still asleep, she was sent to town for shopping.

"I'm not sure what to do," Kazakova said at lunch. "I sent the steward and his helper to the mill, and now I don't have anyone to pick up Tanya at the station. Could you, perhaps, drive there to meet her?"

He was careful to restrain his joy. "Well, all right. I don't mind a little drive," he said with affected nonchalance.

The old housekeeper was serving them at the table.

"Why, *Barynya*, do you want to stain a young girl's reputation for life?" she said, frowning. "What will they say about her in the village after this?"

"If you don't like it, go yourself," Kazakova told her. "What's the girl supposed to do, walk the whole way from the station?"

At around four he left in a cabriolet, drawn by a tall, black, aging mare. Fearing he'd be late for the train, he drove the horse at a hard run once he'd passed the village, the cabriolet leaping over bumps in the damp and slightly frozen surface of the road. The last few days had been wet and foggy, and now the fog was particularly heavy: even as he'd driven through the village, it had seemed that night was coming on, for smoky red lights were already visible in some of the windows of the peasant huts, glowing in the cold, dove-grey haze like preternatural fires. Farther on in the fields it grew almost completely dark, and the fog became impenetrable. Toward him streamed a cold, wet wind, but it didn't drive the fog away—just the opposite, it made that bluish, dark grey smoke so thick that he felt almost suffocated by its heavy scent of dampness, and soon it seemed that nothing lay beyond that murk, as if the world and every living thing were gone. His hat and coat, his moustache, his eyelashes—everything was covered with tiny beads of water. The black mare raced ahead with long, bold strides, and the cabriolet skipped over the road's slick ruts and bumps, its shuddering like a series of small blows to his chest. He managed to light a cigarette; the sweet, fragrant, warm and human smoke mixed with the primeval smell of fog, late fall, wet and barren fields. Straight ahead, behind, above, below—the darkness and the gloom grew deeper everywhere around him, and soon the horse was almost lost from sight: he could barely see her neck like a long, dark shadow, her ears turned forward apprehensively. And this spurred in him a deepening attachment to the mare, for she was the only living creature in that wasteland, engulfed by the lifeless enmity of everything around him—everything he couldn't see before him and behind him, to his left and right, hidden with such menace in the smoky darkness that raced toward him, growing only blacker and more dense.

When he drove into the next village where the train would stop, he exulted in the many signs of human habitation that surrounded him—the sad little lights in the impoverished windows of the huts, the gentle warmth that seemed to fill their rooms. With all its cheerful energy and city bustle, the station seemed like something from another world. He barely had time to tie his horse before the train came rumbling into the station, its bright windows flashing, the sulfurous smell of coal pouring from its engines. With the excitement of a man meeting his young wife, he ran into the station and immediately caught sight of her coming through the opposite doors. Well dressed for the city, she walked behind the stationmaster, who addressed her formally as "thou" as he carried her two large sacks of goods. The station was dirty and dimly lit by lamps that reeked of kerosene, but she was radiant, her eyes shining, her young face beaming with excitement from this rare outing to the city. And suddenly her eyes met his: she was so surprised and flustered that she stopped: What's happening? Why has he come here?

"Tanya," he told her hurriedly. "Hello, I've come to meet you. There was no one else to send."

Had there ever been, in all her life, an evening happier than this one? He came to meet me himself. And I am coming from the town, dressed up, prettier than he could ever have imagined after seeing me in nothing but an old skirt and a cheap cotton blouse. Now I look like a *modiste* with this headscarf of white silk. Now I'm here before him in a new brown dress of worsted wool, a cloth jacket, white cotton tights, new ladies' boots with copper on the heels. . . . Trembling inside, she spoke to him as if she were a guest as she picked up the hem of her skirt and followed him with the small steps of a refined lady.

"Oh, the floor's so slick," she said with almost condescending surprise. "The *mouzhiki* have tracked it up with mud."

She still quavered with joyful fear as she climbed into the cabriolet. To keep from wrinkling her dress, she raised it up and sat on her calico underskirt, then awkwardly arranged her legs around the two large sacks now lying on the floor beneath her. She sat beside him like his equal.

He flicked the reins without speaking and drove silently into the icy darkness of that foggy night, past the scattered, fleeting lights of the surrounding peasant huts and out along the bumps and ruts of that torturous November road. Terrified by his silence, she didn't dare speak: Was he angry about something? He understood this and deliberately kept silent. And then, once they'd passed the village and plunged deep into the total dark, he suddenly brought the horse to a walk and took the reins in his left hand. He slipped his free arm around her shoulder—her jacket already covered in tiny wet beads from the mist—and pressed her close to him, laughing, murmuring:

"Tanya, Tanechka. . . ."

All her body seemed to strain toward him. Against his cheek she pressed her silk headscarf, her flushed and tender face, her eyelashes filled with warm tears. When he found her lips, they too were wet from her joyful weeping, and for a long time he couldn't tear himself away from them. He stopped the horse. Seeing nothing in the fog and darkness, like a man completely blind, he climbed out of the cabriolet and threw his coat on the ground, pulled her toward him by her sleeve. She understood it all immediately, jumped down to him, carefully and quickly raised her new dress, her skirt, all her stylish garments, then felt her way onto the coat. She lay down and gave to him not only her entire body—which he possessed already—but all her soul as well.

He put off his departure yet again.

She knew she was the cause of his delay. She recognized the tenderness with which he treated her. She understood that he now spoke to her the way he would an intimate, a secret friend within the house, and thus she no longer trembled as she had at first whenever he came close to her. He grew calmer, simpler in the moments of their intimacy, and she adapted to him quickly. With that ease that youth allows, she'd changed completely, become carefree, routinely happy. It was easy now for her to call him Petrusha, and sometimes she even pretended to be tired of his kisses. "There's no resting now from you! Just catch a tiny glimpse of me alone—and here you come!"—such words gave her a particular rush of joy: this means he loves me; if I can speak to him this way, he must be mine! There was one more happiness: to express her jealousy, to assert her rights to him. "Thank God there's no work now at the threshing barn. Otherwise the girls would all be there. And if you started after them, well—I'd have to show you what that costs . . .," she said. And suddenly embarrassed, she added with a touching, tentative smile: "Maybe you need more than me?"

Winter began early. After the fogs came an icy northern wind that froze the muddy road's deep ruts and bumps, turned the ground to stone, scorched the last remaining grass in the courtyard and the garden. Whitish, lead-grey clouds began to fill the sky. The barren garden sounded agitated, ill-at-ease, as if it sought to run away. The white moon plunged in and out of cloud banks in the night with similar disquiet. The village and estate looked hopelessly run-down and poor. And then the snow began to fall, turning white the frozen mud, covering the grime with dry flakes like powdered sugar. The estate and all the fields that spread beyond it turned dove grey, seemed to grow broader in the snow. The peasants in the village were finishing their last work, sorting their potatoes for winter storage in the cellars. One day he decided to take a walk there; he put on a heavy winter coat lined with fox fur and a fur hat that he tugged down snugly over his ears. The northern wind whipped through his moustache, burned his cheeks. A morose sky hung over everything; the blue-grey fields that sloped beyond the river seemed strangely close. Mounds of potatoes lay on sacking on the ground beside the cellar of each hut. Young girls and women sat among the piles, sorting through them, removing all the rotten tubers. They were wrapped in hempen shawls and tattered coats, their feet in worn-out, broken boots of felt. Their faces and their hands were turning blue. "Their legs are bare under those skirts!" he thought with horror.

When he returned she was in the hallway, preparing a samovar for the table. The water inside it was already boiling as she wiped the surface clean with a cloth.

"You probably went out to the village," she said under her breath. "All the girls are there, sorting for the winter. . . . Well, what can I do? Go ahead. Just walk around and see which one's the best for you!" And holding back her tears, she ran out to the *sentsy*.

Snow began falling heavily toward evening. She glanced at him with unrestrained, childlike glee as she raced past him in the hall. "Still planning on another walk?" she whispered teasingly. "This is nothing. You should see how all the dogs are rolling on their backs. Soon such a blizzard's going to howl—you won't even poke your nose outside!"

"My God," he thought. "How can I tell her that I'm leaving? Where will I find the strength?"

He longed to be in Moscow as soon as possible. To see the snowfall there. To feel its heavy frosts. A pair of horses pulling a sleigh. The muttering of harness bells as they approach and pass the square by Iverskaya Chapel. And on Tverskaya, those tall electric lamps still burning in the swirling snow. . . . The brilliant light of chandeliers in the Bolshoi Moskovsky. And him there, tossing into the doorkeeper's arms a fur-lined coat covered with snow, drying his moustache with his handkerchief, then walking cheerfully down the red carpet to the warm and crowded hall, the hum of countless conversations, the smell of tobacco smoke and food, the bustle of the maître d's. And over all of it, the notes of those strings pouring forth in waves—impetuous and blithe at times, languid and voluptuous at others. . . .

He couldn't raise his eyes during dinner, couldn't watch her serving them with cheerful, earnest energy, couldn't look at her untroubled face.

Later in the evening he put on felt boots and the old raccoon coat that Kazakova's deceased husband used to wear, jammed his fur hat squarely onto his head, and walked out from the back porch into the blizzard. He wanted to breathe a little and see the storm. But a deep drift had already piled up beneath the porch's awning. He stumbled in it, filled his sleeves with snow: a pure, white hell clawed and raged before him. He struggled around the house, wading through the deep snow, sinking with every step until he reached the front porch. Stamping his feet, brushing off his coat and hat, he hurried into the dark *sentsy*, where the storm still droned, and then into the foyer, where it was warm and a lit candle stood on the trunk. She ran out from behind the partition, barefoot, wearing the same cotton skirt she always wore.

"God in heaven!" she cried, clapping her hands together in alarm. "Where have you come from?"

Scattering snow, he threw his hat and coat on the trunk, and in a delirium of tenderness and joy, lifted her into his arms. Equally transported, she broke free from him, snatched up a broom and brushed the snow from his boots, then pulled them from his feet.

"My God, these are full of snow too! You'll catch a killing cold!"

In his sleep that night he sometimes heard it: a constant drone, a constant pressure on the house, and then a sudden, furious assault as the storm flung its full weight against the walls, shook the window shutters, blasted them with snow that rattled sharp and hard as sand, and then abated slightly, moved away, lulled him back to sleep. . . . The night seemed sweet and endless—the warm bed in which he lay, the warm old house, alone in the white darkness of that roaring snow-sea.

In the morning it seemed the night's wind was still beating at the shutters, banging them against the walls. He opened his eyes: no, it was already light. All the snow-streaked windows were filled with the brilliant white of drifts the wind had mounded to their sills. The snow and droning wind had not yet stopped, but they were less violent now, as if the daylight had reined them in. From where he lay, he could see two windows facing the ottoman, each of their double panes comprised of tiny squares, their frames blackened by the years; a third window, to the left of the couch, was white and lighter than the others. The ceiling too was bathed in the white, reflected light of the snow. The damper tapped and trembled as the stove began to draw with a steady hum in the corner—how good it was: he'd slept, heard nothing, and she— Tanya, Tanechka—steadfast and beloved, she had opened the window shutters, then softly come into the room in her felt boots, all her body chilled. With snow still covering the hempen shawl she'd wrapped around her shoulders and her head, she'd knelt and made a fire in the stove. He hadn't finished this thought when she came in again, this time with a tea tray, and no headscarf covering her hair.

She smiled almost imperceptibly as she set the tray beside the couch, glancing at his eyes, which looked both clear from such a good night's sleep and slightly startled by the light of morning.

"Are you going to sleep all day?"

"What time is it?"

She looked at the clock on the desk but didn't answer immediately. She still had trouble telling time. "Ten . . . ten minutes to nine."

He glanced at the doorway, then pulled her toward him by her skirt. She stepped back, pushed his hand away.

"No. . . . Not a chance. . . . Everyone's awake."

"Just for a minute."

"The old lady will come in. . . ."

"No one's going to come in—just for a minute."

"Oh, it's like some kind of punishment being with you."

She quickly slipped one foot and then the other out of her felt boots and lay down in the bed in her wool tights, carefully watching the doorway. . . . The cool, apple-skin chill of her cheeks! The scents of peasant life that mingled in her hair and breath!

"You're kissing with your lips squeezed shut again!" he whispered angrily. "When will you learn?"

"I'm not a *baryshnya*. . . . Wait, let me move down. . . . Hurry. I'm scared to death. . . ."

They stared into one another's eyes, expectant and intent, uncomprehending.

"Petrusha. . . ."

"Be quiet. . . . Why do you always start talking now?"

"When am I supposed to talk to you, if not now? I won't squeeze my lips together anymore, I promise. . . . Swear to me you don't have anyone in Moscow."

"Don't press on my neck like that. . . ."

"No one in this life will love you the way I do. You fell in love with me. But it's like I fell in love with myself. . . . My joy in myself is almost more than I can bear. . . . But if you leave me. . . ."

Her cheeks were still flushed and hot when she hurried from the couch onto the back porch. She squatted for a moment beneath its awning, as if gathering her strength, then threw herself forward into the white whirlwind, sinking past her bare knees in the snow as she made her way around the house to the front porch.

The foyer smelled of charcoal from the samovar. Slurping tea from a saucer, the old housekeeper sat on the trunk under the high window, now plastered by the storm.

"Where have you been carried off to? All covered in snow . . .," she said, glancing askance at Tanya as she continued her noisy drinking.

"I took some tea to Pyotr Nikolaevich."

"Did you give it to him in the servants' quarters? Everybody knows what kind of tea you serve!"

"Well then—you know. May God grant you health. . . . Has the *Barynya* gotten up yet?"

"Now she remembers the *Barynya*!. . . She was up before you!"

"Always angry. . . . Angry all the time. . . ."

She sighed contentedly as she went behind the partition for her cup, singing in a voice that was barely audible:

One day into the garden I will go,
In the green, green garden I will walk
And there I'll meet my darling love at last . . .

Sitting in the study with a book that afternoon, he listened to the storm. It seemed to fade at times, only to resurge, turn menacing again, as it swirled around the house, which was sinking ever deeper in that milky whiteness, that constant snow that flew at it from every side. Once it settles down, he thought, I'll leave.

He managed to speak to her secretly in the evening. He told her to come to him much later, when everyone would be sound asleep. He wanted her to stay all night, until the morning. She shook her head, then thought it over and finally agreed. It was a terrifying prospect, and that terror made it even sweeter.

He was no less apprehensive. And at the same time a deep regret weighed heavily on his mind: she had no reason to suspect this night would be their last.

He periodically dozed off during the night, then woke up with alarm: will she make up her mind to come?. . . Darkness in the house. A constant noise surrounding it. The shutters bang. Again the wind begins to sough in the stove. . . . Suddenly he awoke in alarm. He hadn't heard her—she moved with such criminal stealth through the heavy darkness of the house that it was quite impossible to hear her—but he had some-how sensed that she now stood invisibly beside the ottoman. He stretched out his hand. Silently she slipped beneath the covers. He could hear the beating of her heart; he felt her chilled, bare feet. He whispered the most perfervid words he could find.

For a long time they lay facing each other, pressed close together, kissing so intently that their teeth began to hurt. She recalled that she was not allowed to squeeze her lips together, and in the hopes of pleas-ing him she held her mouth open like a fledgling jackdaw.

"You didn't sleep all night, no doubt," he said.

"Not a minute. I was waiting the whole time," she answered in a joyful whisper.

He groped around the nightstand for his matches, then lit a candle. She gasped in terror.

"Petrusha, what are you doing! What if the old lady wakes up and sees the light?"

"To hell with her," he said, looking at her small, flushed face. "To hell with her—I want to see you. . . ."

He took her in his arms and stared at her intently.

"I'm afraid," she whispered. "Why are you looking at me that way?"

"Because there is nothing on this earth that's better than you," he said. "That little braid wrapped around your head. Like the braid of Venus when she's young. . . ."

Her eyes shone with happiness and laughter. "Who's that—Venus?"

"No one, really. It doesn't matter. . . . And this sad little shirt of yours. . . ."

"Buy me one made of calico, then—a good one since you seem to love me so."

"I don't love you in the least. . . . You smell like quail again. . . . Or something. It's like dry hemp."

"Why do you like that so much?. . . You said I always start talking when we're together like this. But look—now it's you who's doing all the talking."

She began to press his body harder against hers. She wanted to say more, but now, already, it was impossible to speak. . . .

Later he put the candle out and lay silently for a long time, smoking in the dark and thinking: I have to tell her, all the same. Horrible . . . but I have to do it now.

His voice was practically inaudible when he began to speak. "Tanechka. . . ."

"What?" she answered, her voice as soft and secretive as his.

"You know . . . I have to leave. . . ."

She sat up in the bed. "When?"

"Soon, I'm afraid. . . . Very soon. There's something pressing that I have to tend to. . . ."

She fell back on the pillow. "My God!"

The idea of some important affair in some distant city known as Moscow produced in her a certain veneration. But how could they be parted for the sake of such affairs? She fell silent, searching desperately in her mind for some solution to this insoluble horror. There was none. She wanted to shout, "Take me with you!" But she didn't dare—was that even possible?

"I can't live here forever, after all. . . ."

She listened and agreed: yes, yes.

"And I can't take you with me. . . ."

Suddenly she spoke out of despair. "Why not?"

He thought quickly. Why not? Why not?

"I have no house, Tanya. All my life I've been moving constantly from one place to another," he answered hurriedly. "I live in a hotel room in Moscow. . . . And I'll never marry anyone."

"Why not?"

"Because I wasn't born that way."

"And you won't ever marry anyone?"

"No one, never. And I swear to you, I give you my honest word— there's something very important there that I have to do, something urgent. I'll come back at Christmas. Absolutely."

She pressed her face against him. Her warm tears fell on his hands. "Well, I'll go now," she whispered. "Soon it will be light."

She rose and made the sign of the cross over him in the darkness.

"Mother of God, protect him. Mother of God, keep him safe."

She ran back to her room behind the partition and sat there on the bed, pressing her arms to her chest, licking the tears from her lips.

"Heavenly father! Mother of God!" she whispered to the droning of the wind in the *sentsy*. "Please, let the storm continue now. Let it not pass for two more days. Two more days at least!"

Two days later he left. The weakening blizzard still swirled in the courtyard, but he couldn't stand to have their secret misery drag on any longer, so he refused all of Kazakova's urging that he wait.

The house and all the estate were empty then, abandoned, dead. And it was utterly impossible for her to imagine Moscow, him there, his life, the things that occupied his time.

He didn't come at Christmas. What days those were! Each one passed, from morning until night, in an agony of unresolved expectation while she performed a sad charade, pretending even to herself that she awaited no one. And from Christmas Eve until New Year's Day she put on her best clothes—the brown dress and ankle boots with copper on their heels that she was wearing when he met her at the station on an autumn night, a night she'd now carry forever in her memory.

For some reason on the day of the epiphany she fervently believed that he'd appear at any moment, cresting the last hill before the house in a *mouzhik*'s sleigh that he'd hired at the station, having sent no word of his arrival so that Kazakova didn't specially send her horses out for him. All day she sat on the trunk in the front hall, staring at the entranceway until her eyes began to ache. The house was empty—Kazakova had driven out to a neighbor's house, and the old woman had gone to eat lunch in the servants' hall; she was still sitting there, enjoying some bit of vicious gossip with the cook. Tanya didn't even go to eat, told them that her stomach hurt. . . .

And so the dusk began to fall. She looked again at the empty courtyard covered in a brilliant skein of ice, and told herself: It's over. I need no one now. I don't want to go on waiting anymore! Then she rose and strolled in all her finery through the main hall and the drawing room, the yellow light of winter sunset falling through the windows. She began to sing in a loud and carefree voice, a voice lightened by the knowledge that her life had passed:

One day into the garden I will go,
In the green, green garden I will walk
And there I'll meet my darling love at last . . .

And just as she sang those words about her darling love, she stepped into the study, saw his empty couch, the empty armchair by the desk—that armchair that he used to occupy with a book in his hands—and collapsed into it, laid her head against the desk, sobbing, shouting.

"Mother of God, please, send death to me!"

He arrived in February, when she'd already buried all vestiges of hope, resigned herself to never seeing him again.

And everything, it seemed, came back.

He was shocked when he saw her—how thin she'd grown, how thoroughly she'd faded, how sad and timorous her eyes had turned. And she had been astounded when he first arrived: he seemed to be some other person, older, unfamiliar—unpleasant, even. His moustache seemed to have grown larger, his voice coarser; when he was taking off his coat inside the foyer, she found both his laughter and his speech exceedingly contrived and loud. Every time his eyes met hers, she felt uncomfortable. But they sought to hide these thoughts from each other, and soon their past revived.

And then those awful days drew near—those days preceding his new departure. He swore on an icon that he could come at Holy Week and stay for the entire summer. She believed him. But she also wondered what would happen in the summer. Would it be the same as now? That was not enough for her anymore. She needed either a complete and absolute return to their first time together—instead of this attempted repetition—or a constant life with him, one with no more separations, no more vain hopes leading to humiliations, no more new agony. She tried to drive these thoughts away, tried to imagine the joy of summer when freedom would surround them . . . night and day in the garden, in the fields, in the threshing barn, and he would be beside her then for a long, long time.

His last evening at the estate was light and breezy, hinting at the first approach of spring. Behind the house the garden stirred and rustled anxiously. Kazakova's forestkeeper had trapped a fox earlier that day and brought it to the courtyard; he was keeping it now in a pit among the fir trees. The dogs couldn't reach it, but the fox's close proximity had brought them to a desperate frenzy. The wind was filled with their help-less, fitful barking as it streamed up from the grove toward the house.

He was lying on his back on the ottoman with his eyes closed. She lay on her side next to him, her cheek resting sadly on her palm. Neither of them spoke.

"Petrusha, are you asleep?" she whispered finally.

He opened his eyes and looked at the dusk that had gathered in the room, the golden light that still fell through the side window. "No, why?"

"It's all changed, though. . . . Both of us, after all, we know it. You don't love me anymore. You ruined me, in the end, for nothing," she said calmly.

"What do you mean for nothing? Don't say ridiculous things."

"It will be your sin. . . . But what will I do now?"

"Why should you do anything?"

"You're leaving again. Leaving for your Moscow—but what will I do here, all alone?"

"You'll do everything you did before. And then—I already told you positively—at Holy Week I'll come for the entire summer."

"Yes. Maybe you'll come for the summer. Only, before you never would have said, 'Why should you do anything?' like that. You really loved me then. You said you'd never seen a sweeter girl. . . . But I was dif-ferent then. . . ."

"Yes, you were," he thought. "So very different. How changed you are. Terribly. In almost every way."

"My time's passed," she said. "It used to be, when I snuck out to you, I was terrified to death and full of joy: Thank God the old woman's still asleep! But now I'm not afraid. Not even of her. . . ."

He shrugged. "I don't really understand you. Give me my ciga-rettes, could you? On the table there. . . ."

She passed them to him, and he lit one. "I don't know what's wrong. You're just unwell. . . ."

"That must be why I've grown so dull for you. But tell me, what is it? What made me unwell?"

"You don't follow me. I'm saying that you're unwell emotionally. Because just think for a moment, please—where did this come from?

What made you decide all of a sudden that I don't love you anymore? And why repeat the same thing over and over again: 'before, before, before. . . .' "

She didn't answer. The golden light hung in the window. The garden rustled in the wind. The hopeless whines of the ravening dogs rose again. . . . She got up quietly and wiped her eyes with her sleeve, tossed back her head in a momentary shudder, softly walked in her wool socks toward the doorway of the living room.

He called out to her softly, sternly: "Tanya."

She turned and answered in a voice almost inaudible: "What do you want?"

"Come here."

"What for?"

"I said come here."

She went to him compliantly, lowering her head to hide her tearful face.

"Well, what do you want?"

"Sit down. Come on, don't cry. Kiss me."

He raised himself on the couch; she sat down and hugged him, sobbing softly. "My God, what am I to do?" he thought with despair. "Again these warm childlike tears. This childlike face. She lacks the slightest understanding of my love for her, has no inkling of its strength. But what can I do? Take her with me? Where? To what kind of life? And what will come of it? Tie yourself down . . . destroy yourself for good?" He began to whisper rapidly, feeling his own tears trickle down his nose and lips.

"Tanechka, my darling. My joy. Don't cry. Listen, I will come in the spring and stay all summer. And then we really will go walking in the 'green, green garden.' I heard you singing that song and will remember it forever. . . . We'll take the cabriolet out to the forest. Remember how we drove the cabriolet from the train station?"

"No one will let me go with you!" she whispered bitterly, addressing him for the first time with informal "you." She shook her head against his chest. "And you won't go anywhere with me."

But in her voice he already heard a timid note of joy and hope.

"I will, I will go with you, Tanechka! And don't you dare speak to me with formal 'thou' again. Don't you dare weep anymore. . . ."

He put his arms under her legs and lifted her light frame onto his lap.

"Now repeat after me: 'Petrusha, I love you.'"

She repeated the words vacantly, still shuddering with sobs: "I love you very much. . . ."

That was in February, in the terrible year of 1917. He was in the countryside for the last time in his life.

[*October 20, 1940*]

First Class

A SUBURBAN TRAIN near Moscow—first- and second-class passengers only. It's been rolling steadily through the countryside, but now, suddenly, the train slows and something unheard of occurs: the conductor shoves a little *mouzhik* wearing clay-spattered rags into a first-class compartment.

"Forgive me, please, ladies and gentlemen," he says. "This worker has orders to go to Bykovo. He was supposed to ride with the engineer, but the fool didn't make it to the front of the train before we left. He'll only ride with you as far as Bykovo."

Everyone's astonished at first by this absurd situation. But the passengers keep calm, quickly recompose themselves. The train regains its speed, and the scene inside the compartment seems unchanged: the passengers smoke, converse, watch the scenery breeze by. But everyone's uncomfortable and out of sorts: the conversations are contrived, the cigarettes are smoked with fake insouciance. About the *mouzhik* there is nothing to say: he stands near the door, wishing the earth would open up and swallow him whole, hide him from these gentlemen in Tussore suits and Panama hats, these big, plump bodies and sated faces. He wipes the sweat from his forehead with one hand; with the other he holds a bag that stretches to the floor, weighted down with little iron bars, pliers, screws.

And it lasts a full thirty-five minutes, this torture, this nonsense.

[1930]

Cold Fall

I N JUNE of that year he was staying at our estate—we'd always considered him part of the family: his deceased father had been my father's friend and neighbor. On the 15th, Ferdinand was killed in Sarajevo; on the morning of the 16th, newspapers arrived in the mail. My mother and I were still drinking tea with him in the dining room when my father came from his study, the evening edition of a Moscow paper in hand.

"Well, friends," my father said. "It's war. The Austrian crown prince has been killed in Sarajevo. It is war."

On St. Peter's Day—my father's name day—many guests came to the house, and at lunch we announced our engagement. But on the 19th of July, Germany declared war on Russia.

In September he visited us for one more day to say goodbye before leaving for the front (everyone believed the war would end quickly; our wedding had been postponed until spring). And so began our last evening together. As usual, the samovar was brought into the dining room after dinner, and, watching the windows turn damp with its steam, my father said: "What a cold and early fall!"

The four of us sat quietly that evening and exchanged only a few meaningless words, concealing all our secret thoughts beneath an air of exaggerated calm. Even my father's words about the fall had been spoken with contrived simplicity. I went to the balcony doors, wiped the glass with my handkerchief, and looked out over the garden: sharp and icy stars were shining in the black sky. Leaning back in his armchair, my father smoked and stared absently at the hot lamp hanging over the table. In its light my mother wore her spectacles and carefully sewed a little silk pouch. Her work was both touching and terrible, for all of us knew what that pouch would hold.

"Do you still want to leave before breakfast?" my father asked.

"Yes, with your permission," he answered. "It's very sad, but I haven't taken care of everything at home."

My father sighed. "As you wish, my dear friend. But in that case, Mother and I must go to bed. We want to see you off in the morning. . . ."

Mother got up from her chair and made the sign of the cross over her future son. He bowed to her hand, and then to my father's. Left alone, we stayed a little while in the dining room—I played Patience distractedly at the table while he paced the floor.

"Would you like to take a little walk?" he asked.

Everything had turned heavy in my soul, and I answered with indifference. "Fine."

As we put on our coats in the hall, his thoughts seemed fixed on something far away. Then he smiled and recited from Fet: "*Such a cold fall! Put on your bonnet and your shawl.*"

"I don't have a bonnet," I said. "But how does it go on?"

"I don't remember. Something like: '*Look—between the blackening pines / A fire has begun. . . .*'"

"What fire?"

"The moonrise, of course. There's something wonderful about that poem. You can really feel the charm of autumn in the countryside. . . . 'Put on your bonnet and your shawl' . . . That was our grandparents' time. . . . God . . . dear God!"

"Are you all right?" I asked.

"I'm fine, it's just . . . It's sad. Beautiful and sad. I love you very much."

Wearing our coats, we walked through the dining room to the balcony, then down into the garden. At first it was so dark that I held his sleeve, but then black branches revealed themselves in the mineral shine of the scattered stars. He stopped and turned toward the house.

"Look at the light in those windows. That kind of glow comes only in the fall. . . . If I live, I'll remember this night all my life."

As I turned to look, he put his arms around me. I pulled my scarf aside and leaned toward him. We kissed and he stood staring at my face.

"Your eyes are shining," he said. "Are you cold? It feels like winter out tonight. . . . If I'm killed, will you remember me a little while?"

And I thought: "What if he's right? If he's killed, could I forget him—is it possible with time? Isn't everything forgotten in the end?" And frightened by my thoughts, I blurted out: "Don't say that. I won't survive your death!"

He was silent for a moment. Then slowly he said: "Listen, if I am killed, I will wait for you there. Live your life, rejoice in this earth, then come to me."

Bitterly, I began to cry.

In the morning he left. Mother put that fateful pouch around his neck, the one she'd sewn the night before. It contained a small gold icon that her father and her grandfather had worn in war. As each of us made the sign of the cross over him, our arms seemed to jerk with despair. Then we fell into that stupor that always comes when people say good-bye before long separations. Watching him go, we felt nothing but an astounding sense of incongruity between ourselves and the joyful morning that surrounded us with sunlight and shimmering frost. We stood there for a little while and then went back into the empty house. I walked through all the rooms with my hands behind my back, not knowing if I should sob or sing at the top of my lungs.

He was killed—how strange the word seems!—a month later in Galicia. Thirty years have passed since then, and when I sort through that dream called the past—that dream neither our hearts nor our minds can comprehend—when I separate the years and turn them over one by one in memory, then I begin to recognize how long I've lived, how much has been survived. By the spring of 1918 both my parents were dead, and I was living in a basement owned by a woman who traded at Smolensky Market. She loved to laugh at me and scoff, "Well, your lady-ship, how are your conditions?" as I too tried to survive in the market-place by selling a ring or a cross or a collar of moth-eaten fur. Like so many others, I sold whatever I owned to soldiers who wore fur hats and strolled through the market with their greatcoats unbuttoned. But some-how, on that corner where Smolensky intersects Arbat, I met an elderly, retired officer whose soul was rare and good. Soon we were married, and in April we left for Ekaterinodar with his nephew, a boy of seventeen who wanted to join the White Army. I dressed like a peasant woman and wore bast shoes; he put on a tattered Cossack coat, let his black and silver beard grow out—and for two weeks we traveled south until we reached the Don and the Kuban, where we stayed two years. And then, with countless other refugees, we set sail from Novorossysk for Turkey in a terrible winter storm: my husband died of typhus while we were still at sea. Of all the people on this earth, three remained who were close to me—my husband's nephew, his young wife, and their child, a baby girl of seven months. But the nephew and his wife soon left the child with me and joined Vrangel's regiment in the Crimea; there they disappeared without a trace. I lived a long time in Constantinople, supporting myself and the child through hard, demeaning work. And then, like so many others, we seemed to wander endlessly. Bulgaria, Serbia, Bohemia, Belgium, Paris, Nice. . . . The girl grew up and stayed in Paris, became French and beautiful and utterly uninterested in me. She found a job in a chocolate store near the Madeleine—with well-groomed hands and silver, manicured nails, she deftly wraps packages in satin paper and ties them up with golden thread. But I've remained in Nice and live here still on whatever God provides. . . . I first saw Nice in 1912, and in those happy days I never could have dreamed of what this place would come to mean!

Thus I survived his death, having said so recklessly that I could not. But when I remember everything that I've been through, I always ask myself: What really was your life? And I answer: Only that cold autumn night. Did that night exist? It did. And that is all there was in my life. The rest is an unnecessary dream. And I believe, fervently believe: he is waiting for me somewhere there with all the love and youth he had that night. "You live your life, rejoice in this earth, then come to me." I have lived. I have rejoiced. And soon, soon I will come.

[1944]

Raven

M Y FATHER looked like a raven. This dawned on me when I was still a boy. I was looking at a picture in *Niva* of Napoleon standing on a cliff. He wore buckskin pants and short black boots, and his belly protruded slightly under his white shirt. Remembering another picture from *Bogdanov's Polar Expeditions*, I laughed out loud with joy: Napoleon looked like a penguin! And then I thought sadly, but father looks like a raven.

My father held a very prominent position in the government of our provincial town, and this ruined him even more. I think no one in the society of bureaucrats to which he belonged was so taciturn, gloomy, and severe. None of them spoke so slowly and so cruelly, or acted with such cold reserve. Round-shouldered, short, thick-set—with his coarse black hair, his prominent nose, and his long, dark, clean-shaven face he looked exactly like a raven. The similarity was particularly striking when he wore a black tuxedo with tails to the charity balls sponsored by the governor's wife. Stooping beside a refreshment stand that had been decorated to resemble a little peasant hut, he would raise his big raven head to study the room, glance with his shiny raven eyes at the dancers, at the people coming to the hut for drinks, and at the woman dressed up to resemble a boyar's wife who would smile so charmingly as she served shallow glasses of cheap, yellow champagne—a sturdy woman wearing a brocade gown and a beaded, glittering headdress, her big hands heavy with jewels, her nose so pink and white with powder that it no longer resembled human flesh. My father had been a widower for a long time; my eight-year-old sister Lilya and I were his only children. The second-story apartment that the government provided us looked out on a boulevard of poplars between the cathedral and the main street, and all the huge, empty rooms had a cold, mirrorlike sheen. Fortunately I spent more than half the year studying at the Katkovsky Lyceum in Moscow, returning home only for Christmas and summer vacation. That year, however, I came back to something completely unexpected. . . .

In the spring I had graduated from the lyceum, and when I returned from Moscow I was simply amazed: Lilya's nanny, a tall, skinny old woman who looked like a wooden statue of some medieval saint, had been replaced by a young, graceful girl, and her presence had transformed the house: it was as if the sun had suddenly begun to shine in those rooms that were once so lifeless. The daughter of a poorly paid petty bureaucrat who served under my father, she was thrilled to have found good work immediately after graduating from high school, and when I arrived she was equally happy to have someone her own age in the household. But she was so cowed by my father that she trembled in his presence at our formal dinners while anxiously watching Lilya—an imperious little girl with black hair and black eyes, she was no less taciturn than our father, and she constantly turned her head from side to side as if waiting for something at the table, her silence as edgy as her movements. My father had become completely unrecognizable at these dinners. He no longer stared disapprovingly at old Gury as he served him with his hands in knitted gloves—instead he talked constantly, slowly enunciating his words and addressing only the new nanny. He called her ceremoniously by name and patronymic—"My dear Yelena Nikolayevna"—and even laughed and tried to joke. She was completely flustered by this display and responded only with a piteous smile—the smile of a thin, light-skinned girl whose delicate cheeks have begun to flush as sweat darkens the underarms of her white blouse, beneath which her breasts are barely noticeable. She never dared to look at me during those dinners: for her I was even more terrifying than my father. But the more she sought to avoid glancing at me, the more coldly my father looked in my direction: he and I both knew—sensed somehow—that she tried so painfully to hear only him and to serve only my ill-tempered, restless, and silent sister because she wanted desperately to hide another fear—a fear of the joy she and I felt in each other's presence. My father had always ordered tea in his study; he would drink it from a large cup edged in gold while working at his desk. But now he began to leave his study when Lilya was asleep and Yelena was free to sit at the samovar. Wearing a long, wide, double-breasted jacket with a red lining, he would appear in the dining room, settle into his armchair, and give his cup to her. She would fill it to the brim, just the way he liked, pass it back with trembling hands, and then, after filling a cup for me and for herself, she would lower her eyes and take up her embroidery while he launched into another slow, strange monologue:

"Dear Yelena Nikolayevna, I think fair-haired women like you look best in black or crimson. . . . A black satin dress with a stand-up, jagged collar a la Mary Stuart—one with little diamond studs—would look perfect on you. . . . Or a velvet, crimson dress in the medieval style— slightly *décolleté*, with a little ruby cross. . . . And a dark blue velvet coat with one of those Venetian berets—that would look splendid as well! But of course, that is all idle fantasy," he said, laughing. "Your father earns seventy-five rubles a month at our office, and he has five children in addition to you—'each one younger than the last'—and you, most likely, will be forced to live your entire life in poverty. But I will say this: what harm do dreams do? They enliven us, give us hope and strength. And does it really never happen that a dream comes true? Rarely, of course, very rarely—but sometimes, suddenly, a dream is brought to life. . . . Just recently, for instance, a simple cook at Kursk station won 200,000 rubles with a lottery ticket—a mere cook!"

She would force herself to look at him and smile, as if she understood these words to be a harmless joke, while I played Patience and pretended not to hear. Once he went even farther and nodded in my direction:

"And this young man—he too, of course, has dreams. 'One day,' he thinks, 'one day father will die, and then even my hens will grow tired of gold!' But he's quite mistaken. Papa does own a few things—an estate and several thousand acres of black soil in the Samara province, for instance, but there's little chance the boy will get his hands on that, for he has favored his father with decidedly little affection, and I see that he would make a first-class profligate. . . ."

That conversation took place just before St. Peter's Day—I remember it well. The next morning my father left for church, and from there he went to a luncheon in honor of the governor's name day. He was never home for weekday lunches anyway, so the three of us ate alone as usual. At the end of the meal, when Lilya was given cherry *blancmange* instead of her favorite pastries, she began to screech at Gury and pound her fists on the table. Shaking her head hysterically, she threw her plate on the floor and began choking with violent sobs. Somehow we managed to drag her to her room, begging her to calm down and promising to punish the cook severely while she kicked and bit at our hands. Eventually she grew quiet and fell asleep—but what fleeting tenderness Yelena and I had shared in that struggle! Again and again our hands had lightly touched as we carried Lilya away. The streets outside began to hiss with rain, lightning flashed in the darkening rooms, and thunder rattled the windowpanes. "It's the thunderstorm that made her act that way," she said joyfully when we went into the corridor; then she froze and listened apprehensively. "There's a fire!"

We ran into the dining room and threw open a window—a fire crew was roaring along the boulevard as the downpour streamed through the poplars; the lightning had already stopped, as if extinguished by the heavy rain. A bugler was sounding a warning as men in copper helmets rumbled past on long carts filled with ladders and hoses, and the notes he played seemed almost lighthearted, almost tender and mischievous amid the rattling wheels, the clattering hooves on the cobblestones, and the jingling harness bells that shook above the horses' black manes. . . . Then the city alarm rang out—again and again it clanged from the bell tower of the Warrior Ivan. . . . We were standing close to one another at the window; the fresh air smelled of water and damp dust, and it seemed we were only listening, only looking with excitement at the street. Hauling big red tanks, the last of the carts flashed by, and with my heart beating hard, with my forehead tightening from fear, I took the hand that she held limply by her side and stared imploringly at her cheek. She turned pale, parted her lips, and sighed so deeply that her chest rose. Her eyes were full of tears, as if she too were pleading. I caught her by the shoulder, and then, for the first time in my life, I tasted the tender, intoxicating cold of a young girl's lips. . . . From that point on, not a day passed without our meeting, as if by accident, in the parlor, the living room, or the corridor, sometimes even in my father's study before he came home in the evening. And each meeting was always too short; each forbidden, despairing, drawn-out kiss only made us long for more. . . . As if sensing something, my father soon stopped coming to tea and grew silent and gloomy again. But we paid him no attention; even at dinner she seemed calm and more composed.

Early in July, Lilya gorged herself on raspberries and wound up sick. She spent hours drawing in her room as she slowly recovered, coloring imaginary cities with bright pastels on a sheet of paper tacked to a board. Yelena spent every day embroidering a blouse while she sat by Lilya's bed. It was impossible for her to leave the room—with every minute, Lilya had a new demand. Left alone in that empty, silent house, I felt as if I were dying from the constant desire to see Yelena, to kiss and embrace her again. I passed the time by sitting at my father's desk, opening the first book I pulled off his shelf, and forcing myself to read. And then one evening I heard her light, quick steps approaching the study. I jumped to my feet as she entered.

"What happened? Is she asleep?"

She waved her hand. "Oh no—of course not. You have no idea— she can go for forty-eight hours without sleep and feel perfectly fine— like all lunatics! She has sent me here to find yellow and orange pastels. . . ."

Beginning to cry, she came closer and rested her head on my chest.

"My God, when will this end? Tell him once and for all that you love me, that nothing can separate us!"

She raised her tear-streaked face and suddenly embraced me, began to kiss me breathlessly. I pulled her body against mine and moved toward the couch—how, in such a moment, could I have thought more clearly? But suddenly I heard a cough, and, looking across her shoulder, I saw my father in the doorway. He stood and stared at us, then slouched away.

No one went to dinner. In the evening, Gury knocked on my door. "Your father wishes to see you." I went into the study and found him sitting at his desk. He began to speak without turning to see me:

"Tomorrow you leave for my estate in Samara. You will spend the summer there. In the autumn you will go to either Moscow or Saint Petersburg to apply for a position in the government. If you dare to disobey me, I will completely disown you forever. Furthermore, I am fully prepared to request that the governor send you to Samara under police escort if necessary. Now get out of my sight and don't let me see you again. You will receive money for your trip and your living expenses in the morning from the servant. In the fall I will tell my estate manager to provide for your move to the city. Do not even think of trying to see her before you leave. That's all, dear child. Be off."

That night I left for the Yaroslavl province, where a friend of mine from the lyceum lived. I stayed there until the fall. Then, under his father's patronage, I moved to Saint Petersburg, entered the ministry of foreign affairs, and wrote to my father, formally renouncing my inheritance and all other assistance from him. In the winter I learned that he had retired and moved to Saint Petersburg with, as I was told, "a charming little wife." And so it happened that I saw them one evening when I entered the Mariinsky Theatre just before the curtain rose. They were sitting in a box near the stage; on the barrier before them lay a pair of opera glasses made from mother-of-pearl. He still resembled a raven as he hunched in his seat, wearing a tuxedo and squinting one eye to read the program, while she, holding herself with elegance and poise, looked excitedly at the murmuring crowd that filled the hall below her, the glittering light of the chandeliers, the tuxedos, evening gowns, and uniforms of people entering their private boxes. Her light hair was arranged in an elaborate bouffant, and her bare arms, although still delicate, looked slightly heavier. She wore a cloak of crimson velvet, and it was fastened over her left shoulder with a ruby pin; she wore a little ruby cross around her neck, and it glowed like a dark red flame.

[1944]

Cleansing Monday

W HEN THE grey winter day was darkening; when the street lamps were freshly lit and their gas flames burned with a cold radiance while warm light filled the storefronts and the shops; when the day's demands finally let go and Moscow's evening life began to stir; when the cabbies drove with extra energy and bustle, and their horse-drawn sleds began to fill the streets; when the vague, dark figures of pedestrians moved with new vitality along the snowy walks; when the roar of packed trams plunging down the tracks grew stronger, and green stars were visible, already, as they fell hissing from the cables in the heavy dusk—always at that hour my driver whirled me through the streets, always at that hour I was sailing in a sled, pulled fast by a strong and spirited trotter from Krasnye Vorota to the Cathedral of Christ the Savior, which stood directly opposite the building where she lived. And every evening I took her to dinner at the Hermitage, the Prague, or the Metropol, then to the theatre or a concert, and finally to the Strelnya or the Yar. I didn't know where all of this would lead, and I didn't want to think about it, for I could come to no conclusion, and there was little point in trying—just as there was little point in asking her about the future: she'd ruled out all such conversations. She was enigmatic, at times inscrutable to me. Our intimacy was incomplete, and our relationship resisted definition: thus I was wracked by hope, suspended in a state of constant, painful expectation. And still, every hour spent near her brought me a joy beyond all words.

For some reason she was studying at the university. She rarely went to classes—but she went. When I asked her why, she shrugged and said: "Why do we do anything on this earth? Do we really understand anything about our actions?. . . And anyway—history interests me." She lived alone. Her widowed father, a cultured man from a distinguished merchant class, lived a quiet life in Tver, where, like all merchants, he collected something. Primarily for the view it afforded of Moscow, she rented a fifth-floor corner apartment in a building that faced the Cathedral of Christ the Savior; it consisted of only two rooms, but they were spacious and well furnished. The first was largely occupied by a wide ottoman; it also contained an expensive piano, on which she constantly practiced the beginning of the "Moonlight Sonata"—playing again and again those slow, enchanting, dreamlike notes, and nothing else. Elegant flowers stood in cut-glass vases on the piano and her dressing table; fresh bouquets were delivered to her every Saturday by my order, and when I arrived in the evening to find her lying on the couch, above which hung, for some reason, a portrait of Tolstoy in his bare feet, she would slowly extend her hand for me to kiss, and say distractedly, "Thank you for the flowers. . . ." I brought her boxes of chocolates, new books by Hofmannsthal, Schnitzler, Tetmajer, and Przybyszewski—and always I received the same "thank you," the same warm, extended hand, an occasional order to sit beside her on the couch without removing my coat. "I don't know why," she'd say pensively, looking at my beaver-fur collar, "but it seems there's nothing better than the smell of winter air that you bring into this room from the street." It seemed she needed none of this—not the flowers or the books, not the lunches or the theatre tickets or the dinners outside town—and yet she strongly preferred certain flowers to others, read every book I brought her, consumed each box of chocolates in no more than a day. At lunch and dinner she ate as much as I, having a particular affection for burbot pasties with eel-pout stew and pink hazel grouse in heavily fried sour cream. Sometimes she would say, "A whole lifetime of lunches and dinners—I don't understand it. Why don't people get tired of this?" And yet she ate her own lunches and dinners with all the zest and understanding of a seasoned

Muscovite. Her only glaring weakness was for clothes—expensive furs, velvet, silks.

We were both rich, healthy, and young—and so attractive that people often turned their heads to look at us in restaurants and concert halls. Although born in the Penza province, I for some reason possessed the flamboyant good looks of a southerner. Indeed, an acclaimed actor—a monstrously fat man who was famous for his wit and gluttony—once told me I was "obscenely handsome." "Only the devil knows what you are—some kind of Sicilian or something," he added in his drowsy voice. And it was true—there was something southern about my character, something prone to easy smiles and good-natured jokes. She possessed a kind of Indian or Persian beauty—a complexion like dark amber, hair so black and full it seemed almost sinister in its magnificence. Her eyebrows gleamed softly like sable; the rich blackness of velvet and coal filled her eyes. One had to overcome a small spell to look away from her mouth, her rich red lips, and the dark, delicate down above them. When we went out, she usually wore a garnet velvet dress and matching shoes with golden clasps, but she attended lectures dressed as modestly as any student, and afterward ate lunch for thirty kopecks in a vegetarian cafeteria on the Arbat. She was as taciturn and introspective as I was voluble and blithe—forever disappearing into her own thoughts, carefully exploring something deep inside her mind. As she lay reading on the couch, she'd often lower her book and stare meditatively into the distance: I observed her doing this several times when I stopped to see her in the afternoons, for each month she refused to leave her rooms for three or four entire days, and during these periods I was forced to sit beside her in an armchair, reading silently.

"You are awfully talkative, you know. And you fidget constantly," she'd say. "Just let me finish this chapter."

"If I weren't so talkative and fidgety, I might never have met you," I answered, reminding her of our first conversation. Sometime in December I'd wound up sitting next to her at a lecture by Andrey Bely, which he delivered in song as he ran and danced around the stage. I shifted in my seat and laughed so hard that she looked at me in surprise for some time, then also broke into laughter—and I immediately began to chat lightheartedly with her.

"True enough," she said. "But please be quiet for a little longer. Read a little more. Have a cigarette. . . ."

"I can't be quiet! You don't understand how intensely I love you—you have no idea! And you clearly don't love me. . . ."

"I do understand. And as for my love, you know perfectly well that I have no one on earth other than you and my father. You're my first and last—isn't that enough? But let's stop talking about this. Reading with you is clearly impossible, so let's have some tea."

I would get up then and put water on to boil in the electric teapot that stood on a small table beside the couch, take cups and saucers from the walnut cabinet in the corner—and all the while say whatever came into my head:

"Did you finish reading *The Fire Angel?*"

"I skimmed through it to the end. It's so pretentious I'm ashamed to read it."

"Why did you leave Chaliapin's concert so abruptly yesterday?"

"It was such a display—too much for me. And I've never been a great fan of all that dreck about 'Fair Haired Rus.'"

"You don't like anything."

"Not much."

"A strange love," I would think to myself, as I stood waiting for the water to boil and looked out the windows. The scent of flowers filled the room, a scent inextricably linked to her in my mind. Beyond one window, a huge panorama of the city sprawled far beyond the Moscow River, all of it blue-grey under snow. The other window, to the left of the first, looked out onto a section of the Kremlin, across from which stood the Cathedral of Christ the Savior: its white mass seemed excessively close to the fortress wall, and all of it looked too new. The reflections of jackdaws hung like blue spots in the golden cupola as they flew in endless circles around it. . . . "Such a strange city," I said to myself, thinking of Moscow's old streets, thinking of St. Basil's Cathedral and Iverskaya Chapel, thinking of the church known as Spas-Na-Boru, the Italian cathedrals inside the Kremlin—and then, those fortress walls before me, their guard towers and sharp points like something from Khirgizia.

Arriving at dusk, I sometimes found her on the couch wearing just a silk gown trimmed with sable fur—a gift she said her grandmother from Astrakhan had bequeathed her in her will. I'd leave the lights off and sit beside her in the half dark, kissing her arms and legs, her stunningly sleek and graceful body. . . . She resisted nothing but maintained a steadfast silence. Again and again I'd seek out her warm lips with my mouth, and she would give them to me, breathing fitfully—but never uttering a word. And when she finally sensed that I would soon lose all control, she'd push me aside and sit up, ask me to turn on the light, her voice completely calm. I'd do as she requested; she would rise and go into the bedroom while I sat on the piano stool, like someone waiting for a drug's hot flush and delirium to pass. Fifteen minutes later she'd come out dressed and ready to leave, calm and matter-of-fact, as if nothing ever happened.

"Where to today? The Metropol, perhaps?"

And again we'd talk all night about something unimportant and extraneous. Soon after our affair began, I'd spoken about marriage, and she'd said, "No—I'll be no good as a wife. I'll be no good at all. . . ."

But this did not eradicate my hopes. "We'll see," I told myself, and talked no more of marriage, hoping she would change her mind eventually. There were days when our incomplete intimacy seemed unbearable, but then, what remained for me, other than the hope held out by time? Once, sitting near her in the evening semi-dark and silence, I clutched my head in my hands. "No, this is beyond my strength," I said. "Why, why should you and I be tortured this way?"

She didn't speak.

"And really, all the same—this isn't love. This isn't love. . . ."

She answered calmly from the dark. "Maybe not. Who knows what love is?"

"I do! I know what love is—what happiness is," I exclaimed. "And I'll wait for you to recognize it too."

"Happiness . . .," she said. "Our happiness, friend, is like water in a fishing net. As you pull it in, the net seems full. But lift it out—and nothing's there."

"What's that supposed to mean?"

"Platon Karataev says that to Pierre."

I waved my hand. "Oh, please—spare me the Eastern wisdom. . . ."

And again I talked all night about something peripheral to our lives—a new production at the theatre, a new story by Andreev. . . . And again it was enough for me to know that I would sit close to her in the sleigh; that I would hold her in soft, rich furs as we rocked from side to side and the runners sailed along the snowy streets; to know that I would enter a crowded restaurant with her while an orchestra played the march from *Aida*; that I would eat and drink beside her; that I would hear her slow voice, look at her lips, remember how I kissed them an hour ago—*yes, I kissed them*, I would say to myself, looking with gratitude and joy at those lips and the soft down above them, looking at the rich red velvet of her dress and the slope of her shoulders, looking at the oval of her breasts as the light, almost spicy fragrance of her hair penetrated my senses, and I thought "Moscow, Astrakhan, India, Persia!". . . Sometimes in restaurants outside town, toward the evening's end, when the room was filled with smoke and noise—and she was tipsy, had herself begun to smoke—she'd lead me to a private room and ask to hear the gypsies sing. They'd come to us with a deliberate racket, overly familiar and relaxed. A woman with a low forehead and tar-black bangs would lead the small choir while before it stood an old man wearing a knee-length coat with galloons, a guitar on a blue ribbon over his shoulder, his dark, hairless scalp like cast iron, his blue-grey face resembling a drowning victim's. . . . She always listened with an enigmatic, languid, almost mocking smile. . . . At three or four in the morning I'd drive her home; on the steps of her house I would close my eyes from happiness and kiss the damp fur of her collar—and then, plunged into some strange mix of ecstasy and despair, I'd sail home to Krasnye Vorota. And it will be the same, I always thought, tomorrow and the day after and the day after that—the same torture and the same joy. . . . What else is there to say? It was happiness. Great happiness.

So January and February passed. So *Maslenitsa* came and went. On the Sunday of Forgiveness she told me to come to her after four in the evening. When I arrived, she was already wearing black felt boots and a hat and short coat made of dark astrakhan fur.

"All in black," I said, ecstatic as always.

A tender, quiet expression played in her eyes.

"Well, tomorrow's Cleansing Monday," she said, drawing her gloved hand from her muff to give to me. "Lord God, master of my life . . ." she said in Old Church Slavonic, reciting the first words of St. Yefrem Sirin's prayer. "Let's go to Novodevichy," she added suddenly. "I'd like to walk around the graveyard and the abbey. Will you go with me?"

I was surprised but answered hurriedly, "Yes, of course."

"What are we doing, after all?—every day another meal in some seedy tavern somewhere . . .," she added. "Yesterday morning I went to Rogozhskoe. . . ."

I was even more surprised. "The cemetery? For schismatics? Why?"

"Yes, the schismatics. It's old Russia—Rus before Peter. . . . They were burying an archbishop. Just try to imagine it: the coffin's made from the trunk of an oak, just the way they did it in ancient times; it has a gold brocade that looks like it's been hammered out. The dead man's face is covered by a white pall that's patterned with rough, black thread. . . . Everything about it's beautiful and terrifying. The deacons stand beside the coffin, holding *Ripidas* and *Trikirys*. . . ."

"How do you know all this? *Ripidas, Trikirys!*"

"You just don't know me—that's why you're surprised."

"I didn't know that you're so religious. . . ."

"It's not religiousness. . . . I don't know what it is, exactly. But, for instance, sometimes in the morning—or in the evening, if you aren't dragging me off to some restaurant—I go to the cathedrals in the Kremlin. You never suspected that, I'm sure. . . . But listen to the rest—about the funeral: you just can't imagine the deacons there. . . . It's like you're looking at those monks who drove the Tatars out five hundred years ago—it's as if Peresvet and Oslyabya themselves were standing in front of you! There were two, separate choirs, and all the singers were like Peresvet as well—tall and powerful, wearing long black caftans. They sang in answer to one another—first one choir, then the other. They sang in unison, but they weren't following the kind of musical notes you see today; they were singing by *kryuk*—those ancient notes without lines. . . . The grave was covered with fresh, bright branches from an evergreen. . . . And outside—a heavy frost, sunlight, blinding snow. . . . No, none of this makes any sense to you. . . . Let's go. . . ."

It was a peaceful, sunny evening, with frost hanging in the trees and jackdaws perched on the blood-red walls of the convent, lingering in the silence like little nuns. The sad and delicate chimes of the clock tower played over and again as we passed through the gates and set out along the silent paths between the graves, our shoes squeaking in the snow. The sun had recently set, but the evening was still bright. And it was stunning—how the icy boughs became grey coral before the gold enamel of the sky, how the undying flames of icon lamps glimmered all around us, like furtive, wistful lights scattered among the graves. Walking behind her, I looked at the small stars her new, black boots left in the snow, and a great tenderness welled up inside me: she felt it too, and turned.

"It's true, you really do love me," she said, shaking her head in quiet amazement.

We paused at the graves of Ertel and Chekhov. She stood for a long time, looking at Chekhov's headstone, holding her muff low, her hands clasped together inside it.

"The Moscow Art Theatre and a saccharine Russian style," she said, shrugging her shoulders. "What an irritating mix."

It began to grow dark and cold. We slowly left through the gates and found Fyodor, my driver, waiting patiently nearby with the sleigh.

"Let's drive around a little more," she said. "And then go to Yegorov's for our last *blini*. We'll take it slowly, though, all right Fyodor?"

"As you wish."

"Somewhere in Ordynka there's a house where Griboyedov lived. Let's go and look for it."

And so we went for some reason to Ordynka, where we drove for a long time along alleys that looked onto private gardens and backyards. We even came to Griboyedov Alley, but not a single passerby could point us to the house in which he'd lived. What did Griboyedov mean to them? It had grown completely dark a long time ago, and the lights of the rooms that we glimpsed through the trees glowed pink behind rime-covered glass.

"There's an abbey near here too," she said. "Marfo-Mariinskaya. . . ."

I laughed. "Again to the nunnery?"

"No, I just . . ."

The first floor of Yegorov's Inn at Okhotny Ryad was as hot as a sauna and completely packed with rough-looking cabbies wearing bulky coats as they cut into big stacks of *blini* drenched in butter and sour cream. The low-ceilinged rooms of the second floor were warm as well; there, old-style merchants ate their *blini* with large-grained caviar and cold champagne. We passed into the back and sat on a black leather couch before a long table; in one corner of the room an icon lamp hung before the blackened image of *The Virgin with Three Arms*. A delicate frost had gathered in the slight down above her lip, and a soft pink flush had risen in her amber cheeks; her pupils seemed to merge completely with the black rings of her irises. I couldn't take my ecstatic eyes from her.

"Just right," she said, drawing a handkerchief from her perfumed muff. "Completely savage *mouzhiki* downstairs, while here we have *blini* with champagne and *The Virgin with Three Arms*. Three Arms! It's India! You, my dear friend from the nobility—you cannot begin to understand this city the way I do."

"I can, and I do," I said. "And now let's order an *obed silen*."

"What's that?—'*silen*'?"

"'Mighty'—a 'mighty feast.' Don't you know that? It's Old Church Slavonic: 'So spake Gyurgy . . .'"

"Oh, that's nice—'Gyurgy . . .'"

"Yes, Prince Yury Dolgoruky—Gyurgy. 'So spake Gyurgy to Prince Svyatoslav: "Come to me, brother, in Moscow,"' and he commanded that they prepare an *obed silen*—a mighty feast."

"Oh, that's lovely. . . . Where can you hear words like that now? And you can find that old Rus only in a few monasteries in the north. And in the church songs. I went to Zachatyevsky Monastery the other day. You wouldn't believe how beautifully they sing there! It's breathtaking! And it's even better at Chudov. I went there every day during Holy Week last year. Oh, it was lovely. Puddles everywhere, the air already soft—already filled with spring. There's something tender and sad that enters your soul. And you sense all the time that this is your homeland—this is its ancient past. . . . All day the cathedral doors stand open; all day ordinary people come in and out; all day the services continue. . . . Oh, I'll put on the veil one day! I'll enter a convent in the middle of nowhere—some place deep in the heart of Vologda or Vyatka! . . ."

I wanted to tell her that then I too would enter a cloister—or slit someone's throat in order to be shipped away to Sakhalin. Distracted by the sudden surge of emotion her words brought on, I forgot where we were and started to light a cigarette—but the waiter came immediately.

"I'm very sorry, sir, but there's no smoking here," he said respectfully. He wore a white shirt and white pants, belted with a bright red braid. "What would you like with your *blini*?" he asked quickly, and launched into a complicated list with marked diffidence: "Herb vodka? Caviar? Salmon? We have an unusually good sherry to go with the fish stew, and for the cod. . . ."

"Sherry for the cod as well," she interjected, delighting me with this lighthearted banter, which she kept up all evening. I listened to her happily, not caring what she said. "I love Russian chronicles and legends," she continued, a quiet light playing in her eyes. "In fact, I'm rereading my particular favorites until I've learned them by heart: 'There once stood on Russian soil a city known as Murom. Over it reigned a prince named Pavel, a follower of God. The devil sent a winged serpent to tempt his wife with fornication. And as a man most alluring did the serpent come to her. . . .'"

I opened my eyes wide with mock horror. "Oh, how terrible!"

She ignored me and continued: "God tested her that way. 'And when the time of her passing came, that prince and his wife beseeched God to take them on the same day. Together they agreed to lie in one grave. They deemed that two chambers be carved in one tomb. They put on the clothes of the cloistered. . . .' "

Again my idle listening turned to sharp surprise, even alarm—what was going on with her?

I took her home that night sometime after ten, an extraordinarily early hour for us. As we parted, she suddenly called out from the steps to her house:

"Wait, wait. Don't come before ten tomorrow. There's an actors' party at the Art Theatre."

I was already sitting in the sleigh again. "And so? You mean—you want to go to a *kapustnik*?"

"Yes."

"But you've always said there's nothing more vulgar or more stupid than those actors getting drunk and acting like fools on stage. . . ."

"There isn't. But I want to go all the same."

I shook my head to myself: What caprice this city breeds! But I called out cheerfully in English: "All right."

At ten o'clock the next evening I took the elevator to her apartment, opened the door with my key, and paused in the darkened foyer: it was surprisingly bright in the rooms before me. Everything was lit: the chandeliers, the candelabra on the sides of the mirror, the tall lamp with the cloth shade that stood behind the ottoman. I could hear the beginning of the "Moonlight Sonata" being played on the piano—each slow, invocatory note unfolding with the mystic logic of a sleepwalker's steps, each growing stronger, almost overwhelming in its sorrow and its joy. I closed the foyer door heavily behind me: the music broke off and I heard the rustling of a dress. When I entered the room she was standing very straight and somewhat theatrically beside the piano in a black velvet dress that made her look even more slender than usual. She was radiant in all her finery, with her pitch black hair elaborately arranged, with the dark amber of her arms and shoulders and the delicate, full beginning of her breasts exposed, with the fractured light of diamond earrings playing on her lightly powdered cheeks—with the coal black velvet of her eyes, with the deep velvet-red of her mouth. Fine glossy braids hung from her temples, curling up toward her eyes like the hair of exotic, Eastern beauties in those simplistic prints so popular among the masses.

"If I were a singer on stage," she said, looking at my dazed expression, "this is how I'd answer the applause—a friendly smile, a light bow to the right and to the left, then to the balcony and the floor. . . . And at the same time I'd very carefully, very discreetly be using my foot to slide the train of my dress back a safe distance—to make sure I didn't step on it. . . ."

At the *kapustnik* she smoked a great deal and steadily sipped champagne, watching intently as the players on stage shouted and sang in little outbursts while performing something supposedly Parisian, and Stanislavsky, with his white hair and black eyebrows and big frame, performed a can-can with Moskvin, who was stocky and wore a pince-nez on his big washtub face: together they pretended to struggle desperately with the dance, eliciting loud, raucous laughter from the audience as they fell back from the stage. Pale from drink, Kachalov approached us with a wine glass in his hand. A lock of his Belarus hair fell across his forehead, which was damp with large beads of sweat.

"Queen Maiden Shamakhanskaya! Tsarina! To your health," he said in his low-pitched actor's voice, looking at her with an affected expression of gloom and greedy desire. She slowly smiled and touched glasses with him. He took her hand and almost toppled over as he lurched drunkenly toward her, then righted himself and shot a glance at me. "Who's this little beauty?" he said, clenching his teeth. "I can't stand him!"

A barrel organ began to wheeze and whistle, then broke into the driving rhythms of a polka: Sulerzhitsky came gliding through the crowd toward us, laughing and hurrying somewhere as always. He bent his short body low before her, like an obsequious little merchant at an outdoor market.

"Permit me to invite you to dance the polka," he mumbled hurriedly. Smiling, she rose and went with him, her diamond earrings, her dark arms and bare shoulders gleaming in the lights. Together they moved among the tables, where people clapped their hands or stared with rapt attention as she stepped lightly to the music's rhythm, and he threw back his head to shout like a bleating goat: "Come, come, my friend—it's time to dance the polka!"

Sometime after two she rose and put her hand over her eyes. As we dressed for the sleigh ride home, she looked at my beaver-skin hat, stroked the fur collar of my coat.

"Of course, you are a beauty. Kachalov's right," she said as she moved toward the exit, her voice equally serious and lighthearted. "'And as a man most alluring did the serpent come to her. . . .'"

During the ride home she sat without speaking, hiding her face as we drove into a bright stream of snow blowing through the moonlight.

"Like some kind of luminous skull," she said later, watching the half-moon plunge in and out of the clouds above the Kremlin. When the bells in Spasskaya Tower struck three, she spoke again:

"What an ancient sound. Some kind of tin and cast iron. They rang with the same sound when it was three o'clock in the fifteenth century. In Florence the bells sound exactly the same—they always reminded me of Moscow there. . . ."

When Fyodor stopped before her house, she said lifelessly: "Let him go. . . ."

I was stunned—she never allowed me upstairs at night.

"I'll walk home, Fyodor," I said, bewildered.

Without speaking we rode the elevator to her floor, entered the silence and dark warmth of her apartment, where little hammers tapped inside the radiators. I took off her snow-slick coat, and she cast into my hands the wet down shawl she'd used to cover her hair, then walked quickly to the bedroom, her silk slip rustling. I took off my coat and hat, went into the living room, and sat down on the ottoman, my heart going still, as if I'd come to the edge of an abyss. I could hear her every step through the open doors to the bedroom, where a light was burning—could hear her dress catching on her hairpins as she slid it over her head. . . . I got up and went toward the doors. Wearing only swan's-down slippers, she stood before the pier glass with her back to me, running a tortoiseshell comb through the long, black strands of hair that fell along her face.

"And all that time he kept complaining. Kept saying that I don't think of him enough," she said, dropping the comb on the table, tossing back her hair. "No, I thought of him," she said, and turned to me. . . .

I felt her moving at dawn and opened my eyes: she was staring fixedly at me. I raised myself up from the warmth of her body and the bed. She leaned closer.

"This evening I'm leaving for Tver," she said in a quiet, even voice. "God only knows for how long. . . ." She laid her cheek against mine. I felt the dampness of her lashes as she blinked.

"I'll write everything as soon as I arrive. I'll write everything about the future. But forgive me, I need to be alone now. I'm very tired. . . ." She laid her head back on the pillow.

Timidly I kissed her hair; carefully I dressed—and quietly stepped out into the stairwell, already bathed in pale sunlight. I walked in fresh, damp snow. The storm from last night had already passed, and now everything was calm. I could see far into the distance along the streets; the scent of the new snow mixed with the smell of baking from the nearby shops. I walked as far as Iverskaya Chapel: the heat inside was heavy, almost overpowering, and the candles blazed like banked fires before the icons. I knelt in the melting snow that had been tracked inside, knelt in the crowd of beggars and old women, removed my hat. . . . Someone reached out to my shoulder and I turned: a miserable old woman was staring at me, crying out of pity.

"No, no—you must not grieve this way," she said, her face contorted by her weeping. "Such black grieving is a sin. A sin!"

The brief letter I received some two weeks later was tender but unyielding in its request that I wait for her no longer—and make no attempt to find or see her. "I won't be coming back to Moscow. For now I'll serve as a lay sister, then, perhaps, put on the veil. . . . May God give you the strength to make no answer to this letter. It's pointless to intensify this suffering, to prolong our torture. . . ."

I complied with her request. I lost myself for a long time in the most squalid bars and taverns—drinking each day, letting myself sink deeper and deeper each day. And then, slowly, bit by bit, hopelessly, indifferently, I began to recover. Almost two years had passed since that Cleansing Monday, that first day of the Great Fast.

In 1914, just before the New Year, there was another quiet, sunny evening—much like that evening I cannot forget. My driver took me to the Kremlin. There I went inside Arkhangelsky Cathedral. It was empty; I stood for a long time without praying in the twilight, stood and looked at the dull gleam of the old gold in the iconostasis, the stone slabs above the graves of Moscow tsars: it seemed that I was waiting for something in the silence—that silence which occurs only in an empty church, when you're afraid to breathe. I climbed back into my sleigh, told the driver to continue at a walk to Ordynka—and slowly I followed the same little side streets as before, passing gardens and backyards beneath lit windows, traveling an alley named for Griboyedov while I wept and wept. . . .

At Ordynka I stopped the driver near the gate to Marfo-Mariinskaya Abbey. Black carriages stood in the courtyard; beyond them I could see the open doors of the small, brightly lit church, from which the singing of a female choir drifted mournfully into the open air. For some reason I felt an urge to go inside immediately. The groundskeeper blocked my way at the gate.

"It's closed, sir," he said in a soft, imploring voice.

"What do you mean 'closed'? The church is closed?"

"Well, you can go inside, sir, of course, but I'm begging you not to. Not now. The Grand Duchess Elzavet Fyodorovna is there, sir, with Grand Duke Mitry Palych. . . ."

I stuck a ruble in his hand; he sighed as if stricken with grief, and let me pass. But as I entered the courtyard, a procession carrying icons and holy banners came from the church, followed by the duchess, who wore long white robes and a white veil with a golden cross sewn into its front. Tall, thin-featured, she carried a large candle and walked slowly, devoutly, with lowered eyes. Behind her stretched a long row of women identically dressed in white, singing as they walked, their faces illuminated by the candles they held. I couldn't tell if they were nuns or women of the laity, and I didn't know where they were going. But for some reason I watched carefully as they passed. And suddenly, near the middle of that line, one of them raised her head in its white veil as she walked. Shielding the flame of her candle with one hand, she aimed her dark eyes into the darkness, as if staring straight at me. . . . What could she see in the darkness? How could she have felt my presence there? I turned. I went quietly back through the gate.

[*May 12, 1944*]

On One Familiar Street

I WAS WALKING in the twilight that fresh, green leaves create when street lamps glow metallically beneath them. It was a spring night in Paris; I felt young and easy with myself, thinking,

> *I remember one familiar street—*
> *One old house, its staircase steep and dark,*
> *A window with the curtain closed. . . .*

A wonderful poem! And how strange it is that I once lived those things. Moscow, Presnya—streets muffled by snow, a wooden, bourgeois little house—and I, a student, some kind of "I" immersed in a life that seems pure fiction now. . . .

> *A secret lamp still burning late at night . . .*

And there too—there was a light. Snow blew down like chalk dust from the roof; like smoke it was dispersed by the wind—and overhead, in the mezzanine, a light burned behind a red, calico curtain. . . .

She was beyond all words—the girl who waited
In that house, and met me at a secret hour
With her long hair already down. . . .

It was just the same. . . . A deacon's daughter. A girl who left her abject family in Serpukhov, came to study in Moscow. . . . And there I was: I went up to the wooden, snow-covered porch, pulled on the ring attached to a long, rustling wire that led into the vestibule—pulled until the bell clapped, and I could hear someone running down the steep wooden stairs: the door flew open, and she was there in the wind, snow blowing across her shawl and her white blouse. I rushed to kiss her, to shelter her from the wind, and we ran up through the freezing darkness of that stairwell to her room, where the air was just as cold and the light from the kerosene lamp was dull. A red curtain on the window, a lamp on a little table, a bed with an iron frame against the wall. . . . I dropped my coat and hat, sat down on the bed, pulled her into my lap. I could feel her body and its small, delicate bones through her skirt. . . . There was no "long hair already down"—only a simple braid of rather plain, light brown hair, and the face of a common girl that hunger had made translucent, only the translucent eyes of a peasant and those tender lips one finds among weak girls.

No longer like a child, she pressed her mouth
To mine. And later, trembling, she whispered
"Together, you and I, we'll run away. . . ."

We'll run away! Where to, for what, from whom? How charming it is—the earnest foolishness of children. There was no running away for us. There was the sweetness of those lips, a sweetness unknown in the rest of the world; there were tears that welled up in our eyes from too much happiness; there was a kind of exhaustion that settled like a weight on our young bodies and made us rest our heads on each other's shoulders—and her lips turning warm, as if she had a fever, as I unbuttoned her blouse, kissed her girlish breasts, their tips like wild, unripe strawberries. . . . Returning to her senses, she jumped up from the bed, lit a spirit lamp, warmed our weak tea—and we drank it with white bread and red-rind cheese, talking endlessly about our future and feeling the fresh, cold air of winter that streamed from behind the curtain while dry snow ticked against the window pane. "I remember one familiar street. . . ." What else do I remember? I remember how I went with her to Kursk station in the spring, how we hurried on the platform with her willow basket and her red blanket tied in a little bundle, fastened with a belt; I remember how we ran down the long chain of green cars, glancing at the crowds in the packed compartments as the train prepared to leave. . . . I remember how she finally climbed into the corridor of one of those cars, how we kissed each other's hands as we said goodbye, how I promised to go to her in Serpukhov in two weeks' time. . . . I remember nothing more. There was nothing more.

[1944]

Notes to the Stories

Antigone

Averchenko: Arkady Timofeyevich Averchenko, Russian writer and humorist, 1881–1925.

"This is my Antigone," the general joked. "Although I am not as blind as Oedipus . . .": Antigone is the daughter of Oedipus; she follows her father into exile from Thebes.

When he rode into the courtyard, a line from *Onegin* had been running through his head—*My uncle is a man of utmost principles . . .*: In A. S. Pushkin's famous work, *Evgeny Onegin*, the protagonist complains about the tedium of waiting for his uncle to die and leave him his inheritance. "My uncle is a man of utmost principles" is a rough translation of the first line of the poem's first chapter.

The current war against Japan: Fought from 1904 to 1905, the war was an embarrassing defeat for Russia.

Ballad

. . . every room glowed with the flames of lamps and wax candles that stood before the icons in the holy corners: Traditionally, each room in a Russian house would have a *krasny ugol*, literally a "beautiful corner," where an icon was hung.

"It all took place during the reign of the Great Tsarina": Catherine the Great.

Calling Cards

"That's how little children die, swimming in the summer months, near river-banks where Chechens hide." The protagonist is quoting incorrectly from A. S. Pushkin's poem "Prisoner of the Caucasus."

"A Chechen's what I'm waiting for," she answered with the same ebullience: The speaker's words are particularly provocative given the writer's "Eastern features."

kalach: a kind of white-meal loaf, similar in shape to a soft pretzel.

Caucasus

Gelendzhik and Gagry: Cities located on the coast of the Black Sea.

Narzan: A brand of mineral water, still popular today in Russia.

dukhan: A shop or a small inn with an inexpensive restaurant, in the Caucasus and the Middle East.

Chang's Dreams

Bunin was exceedingly well traveled. He made extended trips to Turkey, France, and Italy in 1903; Egypt, Syria, and Palestine in 1907; and North Africa, Turkey, Egypt, Ceylon, and Singapore from 1910 to 1911. In Ceylon he first encountered Buddhism, which developed into a lifelong interest and influenced many of his works, most notably "Chang's Dreams."

"Ve'y good dog, ve'y good!" Written in English in the original.

Perim: A rocky, barren island at the south entrance to the Red Sea.

Cleansing Monday

"Cleansing Monday": In Russian Orthodoxy, the longest of the three major fasts lasts for seven weeks, beginning on a Monday, usually in early March. This first day of the fast is known as *Chisty Ponedelnik*, or, as I've translated it, Cleansing Monday, and could be likened to Ash Wednesday, the first day of Lent in Western Christianity. But Cleansing Monday is not strictly a religious term; it apparently refers to the widespread practice of cleaning house on the first day of the fast. The week before Cleansing Monday is known as *Maslenitsa* and is traditionally celebrated by eating Russian pancakes, known as *blin* (plural, *blini*), similar to crepes.

Hugo von Hofmannsthal (1874–1929), Austrian playwright, essayist, and poet, probably best known for his collaborations with Richard Strauss.

Arthur Schnitzler (1862–1931), Austrian short-story writer, novelist, playwright, and critic.

Kazimierz Tetmajer (1865–1940), Polish romantic poet.

Stanislaw Przybyszewski (1868–1927), Polish symbolist poet, critic, and writer of fiction.

Andrey Bely: The pen name of Boris Bugaev (1880–1934), one of Russia's leading symbolist poets. Bunin detested the symbolists' aesthetics.

The Fire Angel: A novel by Valery Bryusov (1873–1924) about black magic in sixteenth-century Germany. Like Bely, Bryusov was a major figure in the symbolist movement.

Cathedral of Christ the Savior: Originally conceived by Aleksandr I to mark Russia's victory over France, the huge cathedral took several decades to build. It was completed in 1883. In 1933 Stalin leveled the cathedral and built in its place a large heated swimming pool for public use. The cathedral was later rebuilt from 1995 to 2000. Ironically the narrator's complaints about the building are voiced by many Muscovites today.

"Platon Karataev says that to Pierre": A reference to Tolstoy's *War and Peace.*

Sunday of Forgiveness: The last day of *Maslenitsa* and the day before Cleansing Monday. Traditionally a day when one asks forgiveness for transgressions.

St. Yefrem Sirin's prayer: The first line continues (roughly): "Lord and Master of my life, do not let come to me the spirit of idleness, despondency, domination, and vain talk. . . ."

Schismatics: In 1650 the Russian Orthodox church altered several of its religious rituals to correspond more closely to Greek Orthodox practices. The changes, which included altering the number of fingers one uses to make the sign of the cross, triggered a violent schism. Those who refused to accept the changes came to be known as Old Believers; many fled to remote areas of Russia or committed suicide. If Peter the Great is seen as the chief force of Westernization and modernization in Russia, the Old Believers could be said to represent the forces of mystical, archaic, non-Western Russia.

Ripida: A round, wooden icon of a cherub, waved by a deacon over the sacraments.

Trikiry: A candelabrum holding three candles, used in rituals involving high church officials.

Peresvet and Oslyabya: Monks remembered for battling fiercely against the Tatars in the fourteenth century.

kryuk: An ancient system of writing music in the Russian church, beginning in the eleventh century.

Aleksandr Ivanovich Ertel (1855–1908): Russian writer exiled to Tver for political activities. His work was highly esteemed by Tolstoy, Chekhov, and Maksim Gorky.

"The Moscow Art Theatre and a saccharine Russian style," she said, shrugging her shoulders. "What an irritating mix": The plays of Anton Chekhov (1860–1904) were first successfully produced by the Moscow Art Theatre. Although often critical of the theatre world, Bunin was fond of Chekhov and generally admired his work.

"Let's drive around a little more," she said. "And then go to Yegorov's for our last *blini*. We'll take it slowly, though, all right, Fyodor?": The speaker refers to "our last *blini*" because the Great Fast begins on the next day, Cleansing Monday.

Aleksandr Griboyedov (1725–1829) is best known for his play *Woe from Wit*, a satire of Moscow society written in verse.

The Virgin with Three Arms: According to legend, St. John of Damascus (676–754?) was once falsely accused of a crime, for which his hand was cut off. When the appendage miraculously grew back, John made an icon depicting the Virgin Mary with a third arm. A copy of the icon hung in a Moscow monastery. Apparently the speaker sees a similarity between this image and the Hindu God Shiva, who is often portrayed with four arms.

"You, my dear friend from the nobility—you cannot begin to understand this city the way I do": As a member of the merchant class, the speaker is a descendant of peasants while the narrator comes from the gentry. She implies that only the common people can fully understand Moscow's spirituality.

Zachatyevsky Monastery and Chudov Monastery: Founded in the sixteenth and fourteenth centuries respectively.

Sakhalin: An island for convicts in the Sea of Okhotsk, some four hundred miles north of Japan.

kapustnik: During a *kapustnik* (derived from the word for cabbage), actors and students would sing, dance, and perform informal skits that they themselves had written, often making fun of their colleagues and other artists.

Konstantin Stanislavsky (1863–1938): One of the founders of the Moscow Art Theatre. His "method acting," which emphasized a performer's identification with the character, influenced modern drama throughout the West.

V. Kachalov: An actor in the Moscow Art Theatre.

Leopold Sulerzhitsky (1872–1916) worked closely with Stanislavsky in the Moscow Art Theatre.

Shamakhanskaya: A beautiful tsarina in Pushkin's well-known poem "The Story of the Golden Rooster."

"The Grand Duchess Elzavet Fyodorovna is there, sir, with Grand Duke Mitry Palych": The groundskeeper condenses both names. Elizaveta Fyodorovna (1864–1918) was the sister of Tsarina Aleksandra (wife of Nicholas II); she was killed by the Bolsheviks after the revolution. Dmitry Pavlovich (1892–1942) was one of the few Romanovs to survive the revolution. Due to his involvement in the plot to murder Rasputin, he was sent abroad before the Bolsheviks came to power.

Cold Fall

"*Such a cold fall!*": From a poem by A. A. Fet (1820–1892), one of Bunin's favorite writers.

The Elagin Affair

"Op. Pulv.": powdered opium.

"*Quand même pour toujours*": And still, it is for eternity.

Alfred de Musset (1810–1857), French romantic poet and playwright credited with writing France's first modern dramas.

Zygmunt Krasinski (1812–1859), Polish poet, considered one of the country's most important Romantic writers.

Aleksandr Pushkin (1799–1837), Russian poet and prose writer, probably the single most important author in all of Russian literature.

Mariya Bashkirtseva (1860–1884), Russian painter and writer who lived in France and Italy. She is probably best known for her diary, which describes her thoughts and feelings with unflinching candor and was translated into several languages after her death from tuberculosis.

Mariya Vechyora: In 1889 the bodies of eighteen-year-old baroness Mariya Vechyora and Rudolph von Hapsburg, crown prince of Austria-Hungary, were found in a hunting lodge outside Vienna. It is believed that the prince shot Mariya Vechyora, his lover, and then himself. "Dear mama, forgive me for what I have done," Vechyora is said to have written in a note. "I could not overcome my love. . . . I will be happier in death than I was in life."

And so each of us listened once more in the hushed and crowded courtroom to those pages of the indictment that concluded Elagin's story—pages that the prosecutor wanted most to keep alive within our memories. It is not entirely clear why the prosecutor wants this passage to stay fresh in the court's memory, as much of it supports the defendant's claim to have only carried out Sosnovskaya's wishes. Perhaps all that matters to the prosecutor is that Elagin here admits openly to shooting the murder victim.

The Gentleman from San Francisco

tarantella: A fast, whirling dance performed in southern Italy.

tramontana: A cold northern wind that blows in the western Mediterranean.

Ischia and Capri: Islands just off the Italian coast.

"*Ha sonato, Signore?*": "You called, sir?"

"*Gia e morto*": "He is already dead."

"*Pronto?*": "Ready?"

"*Partenza!*": "Departure!"

Two thousand years ago that island was inhabited by a man who somehow held power over millions of people: Tiberius Claudius Nero Caesar, emperor of Rome from 14 B.C. to A.D. 37.

Ida

Bolshoy Moskovsky: A well-known Moscow restaurant. Literally "The Big Moscow Restaurant."

"Do you remember the magic tablecloth from all those fairy tales you read as a child?": The composer asks the waiter to cover their table with a *samobranaya* tablecloth, which appears in many popular folk tales and magically creates food for the prince who possesses it.

ukha: Fish soup.

"*Je veux un trésor qui les contient tous, je veux la jeunesse*": "I want to possess that treasure that contains within it everything, I want youth."

pirog: A small turnover, often with a filling of cabbage, potatoes, or meat.

verst: Russian measurement of distance equal to 3,500 feet.

"*Laissez-moi, laissez-moi contempler ton visage!*": "Let me, let me look at your face."

blinis: Russian pancakes, similar to crepes.

In Paris

"Rien n'est plus difficile que de reconnaître un bon melon et une femme de bien": "Nothing is more difficult than judging by sight the ripeness of a watermelon and the virtue of a woman."

zubrovka: Sweetgrass vodka.

"L'eau gâte le vin comme la charrette le chemin et la femme—l'âme": "Water ruins wine the way a cart ruins the road, and a woman—the soul."

"Caviar rouge, salad russe. . . . Deaux shashliks. . . .": "Red caviar, Russian salad. . . . Two shashliks."

The Great War: World War I.

"C'est moi qui vous remercie": "It is I who am grateful to you."

"Le bon Dieu envoie toujours des culottes à ceux qui n'ont pas de derrière. . . .": "Merciful God always gives pants to those who lack rear ends."

"Qui se marie par amour a bonnes nuits et mauvais jours": "He who marries for love has good nights and bad days."

"Patience—médecine des pauvres": "Patience is the medicine of the poor."

"L'amour fait danser les ânes": "Love makes even donkeys dance."

Late Hour

kolotushka: A kind of large wooden clapper or rattle used as an alarm.

Requiem aeternam dona eis, Domine, et lux perpetua luceat eis: Give them eternal peace, Lord, and let the eternal light shine for them.

Light Breathing

. . . she was bright but mischievous—and blithely indifferent to the admonitions of the *klassnaya dama*, that teacher charged with making future ladies understand the points of proper conduct: I have added the words that follow *klassnaya dama* to give English-language readers some understanding of this official's role in school. The term *klassnaya dama* (literally, class lady) might simply be translated as teacher, but it seems important to note that this particular teacher instructs young women about their conduct.

Mitya's Love

One could almost believe that the larks had returned, bringing warmth and joy: Larks are often associated with warm weather in Russian culture. A familiar proverb advises: "Warm days come with larks, cold days come with finches."

In the distance Pushkin's statue rose, pensive and benevolent . . . : A monument to A. S. Pushkin (1799–1837), Russia's greatest and most beloved poet, stands at the intersection of Tverskaya Street and Tverskoy Boulevard in downtown Moscow. It was erected in 1880, paid for with donations from the Russian public.

Kuznetsky Most: Literally "Ferrier's Bridge," this is still a major street in downtown Moscow.

Mitya accompanied Katya to the actors' studio at the Moscow Art Theatre: The theatre was founded in 1898 by Konstantin Stanislavsky and Vladimir Nemirovich-Danchenko. A young actress like Katya would have attended drama classes at the studio.

The spring fast: Similar to Lent, the spring fast lasts for seven weeks, usually beginning in March.

Domostroy . . .: Written in the late sixteenth century, the *Domostroy* offers instructions for daily conduct in keeping with principles of Orthodoxy. It states that a husband should maintain strict rule in his household, beating both his wife and children as necessary.

"Junker Schmidt, it's true—summer does return": From a poem by Kozma Prutkov.

The Asra: An operetta by Anton Rubinstein (1829–1894), based on the poem by Heinrich Heine (1797–1856); said to have made a deep impression on Bunin.

"Oh, darling, live and laugh," she said, quoting Griboyedov with a timid smile . . .: From Aleksandr Griboyedov's masterpiece, *Woe from Wit,* a play in verse written in 1822–1824 and considered one of the greatest plays in Russian.

mouzhik: A male peasant; plural, *mouzhiki.*

Tulsky Pryanik: A large, sweet, rectangular cookie, sometimes compared to gingerbread or spice bread.

My God, how forlorn he looks on the platform, the worker waiting for the owner's son—for me, the *barchuk*—to arrive . . .: The original text uses only the word "*barchuk,*" which literally means "little *barin*" or "little landowner." A Russian reader would understand immediately that this must be Mitya. I've added the words "for the owner's son, for me" to try to make it completely clear to an English reader that the *barchuk* is Mitya.

Maslenitsa: A weeklong celebration that precedes the spring fast, traditionally marked by eating *blini,* Russian crepes.

A *sych:* Literally translated as "little owl" in most dictionaries. I have chosen to leave the Russian name here as the English equivalent would be unintentionally comic.

drozhky: A light, four-wheeled, open carriage in which passengers sit on a thin bench.

. . . It was so close; its call was so distinct, so sharp and startling, that Mitya even heard the wheezing and the trembling of its small, sharp tongue as the cuckoo began to wail: A cuckoo's song is an important and frightening omen in Russian culture. The number of calls the bird makes is believed to equal the number of years remaining in the listener's life.

Faust: Charles Gounod's opera, based on Goethe's version of the famous legend, debuted in 1859.

Leonid Fyodorovich Sobinov (1872–1934) and Fyodor Ivanovich Chaliapin (1873–1938) were two of Russia's most acclaimed opera singers. They sang together in 1899 at the Bolshoi Theatre. Chaliapin left Russia in 1921; Sobinov remained in the country and supported the Bolshevik government as a performer and briefly as an administrator.

"There was a King of Thule . . .": The Ballad of the King of Thule is sung by Margaret in *Faust*. His dying mistress gives the king a golden chalice, which he keeps faithfully for years, weeping from the memory of his lost love whenever he drinks from it. His last act before dying is to drink from the cup and throw it into the sea.

verst: Russian measurement of distance equal to 3,500 feet.

He was riding down the main avenue, known by the local *mouzhiki* as Table Road: The word "table" in English is misleading here. The Russian word *tabel'ny* probably refers to a government registry rather than a piece of furniture. The idea, apparently, is that the (private) road on which Mitya is riding is actually large enough to be listed among the country's major thoroughfares.

Sevastopol: A major city in the Crimea, founded in 1783 as a military port and fortress.

The Baidar Gates: The gates mark the chief pass through the Crimean Mountains to the Black Sea.

The gardens of Alupka and Livadiya: Elaborate estates and gardens built in the early nineteenth century on the Crimean coast of the Black Sea.

Mitry Palych: Mitya is a short form of the name Dmitry. The full, formal name of the story's hero is Dmitry Pavlovich. The steward shortens this to "Mitry Palych."

kvass: A dark, fermented, nonalcoholic drink made from rye or barley.

salo: Pork fat, sometimes salted or smoked.

Aleksey Feofilaktovich Pisemsky (1821–1881) was a Russian novelist and playwright. He wrote extensively and sympathetically about the peasantry.

Muza

Muza: The names in this story have obvious connotations for a Russian reader. Muza is literally "Muse." Zavistovsky's name comes from the Russian word for envy, *zavist.*

Prague Restaurant: A very fashionable and expensive Moscow restaurant.

fortochka: A small, hinged pane of glass set inside a window, which can be opened for ventilation in winter.

"I saw you at Shor's concert": David Solomonovich Shor (1867–1942), a pianist and professor at the Moscow Conservatory whom Bunin knew personally.

"I was just sitting here in the twilight, enjoying a night without lamps": In Russian a single verb describes this process: *sumernichat.*

On One Familiar Street

"*I remember one familiar street . . .*": Bunin quotes loosely from "The Hermit" by Ya. P. Polonsky (1819–1889).

Serpukhov: A city roughly fifty miles southeast of Moscow.

Raven

Niva: A popular illustrated journal, published in Saint Petersburg from 1870 to 1918.

patronymic: Referring to someone by first name and patronymic is a sign of respect and deference. One's patronymic is formed from the first name of one's father—Yelena's father is Nikolay; her patronymic consists of a feminine ending, *evna*, attached to this name.

Patience: A card game similar to solitaire.

Rusya

sarafan: A peasant dress without sleeves, buttoning in front.

vareniki: A kind of dumpling made with fruit or curds.

okroshka: A cold soup made with chopped vegetables, meat, and *kvass.*

"It's no wonder the devil took the form of a snake": The Russian word for grass snake is *uzh*; the Russian word for horror is *uzhas.* Rusya actually says, "It's no wonder the word for 'horror' comes from the word for 'grass snake'"—a statement that cannot be rendered in English for obvious reasons.

Marya Viktorovna: Rusya's formal name and patronymic.

"Amata nobis quantum amabitur nulla!": "Beloved by us as no other shall be."

The Scent of Apples

mouzhik: A male Russian peasant; plural, *mouzhiki*.

babye leto: Literally "the women's summer," this term signifies the last warm days of September before the onset of fall. Often translated in English as "Indian summer."

odnodvortsy: a class of free people who had the right to own serfs as well as other limited privileges, but who were themselves often no wealthier than the peasantry. The word literally means "one yard," a reference to the limited landholdings most *odnodvortsy* were able to amass.

barchuk: the word might be literally translated as "little master." In *Mitya's Love* the protagonist is also referred to as *barchuk*.

It wasn't customary for married sons to split off land from their fathers' plots in Vyselki: In much of Russia it was common practice for peasant sons to divide evenly their fathers' land. This resulted in ever smaller plots being held by different members of a single family, often making it impossible for anyone to farm effectively.

The Gentleman Philosopher: An anti-utopian novel by Fyodor Dmitriev-Mamonov (1728–1805). The author later used the title as his pseudonym. The novel tells of a landowner who builds a model sun and solar system on his estate.

The Secrets of Aleksis; Victor, or a Child in the Forest: Novels by the French sentimentalist François-Guillaume Ducray-Dumenil (1761–1819).

Styopa

Kislovodsk: A city in southern Russia, not far from the Georgian border.

Maly Theatre: One of Moscow's best-known drama theatres.

Sukhodol

Sukhodol: The name combines two words that would convey to a Russian reader the idea of "Dry Valley."

Natalya: Her first name can be shortened to Natasha or Natashka, as it often is when the narrator speaks about her in her youth.

Her mother was my father's wet nurse: It was customary for a serf to breast-feed the offspring of nobility. Wet nurses were generally well treated as their health directly affected that of the owner's child. The use of wet nurses continued in Russia long after it had ended in Western Europe.

Could she be the witch Baba-Yaga?: A popular figure in Russian children's stories.

In the servants' quarters hung a large dark icon of St. Merkury—the same saint whose helmet and iron sandals lie before the iconostasis in the ancient cathedral of Smolensk: The Bunin family reportedly had such an icon, passed down from Ivan Aleksandrovich's grandfather. But the story behind the icon, as told in "Sukhodol," seems to combine the histories of two separate martyrs. According to legend, St. Merkury of Smolensk heard a voice from an icon that called on him to fight the Tatars in 1239. He defeated them but was killed in battle. The people of Smolensk buried him in the city's main cathedral, where his sandals remained on display before the iconostasis. An earlier St. Merkury lived in Rome in roughly 249 A.D. He won a major victory over the barbarians but then declared himself a Christian before the emperor and refused to accept the pagan gods. He was tortured cruelly for several days and eventually killed by decapitation.

"Ou etes-vous, mes enfants?": "Where are you, my children?"

Nyanechka: an affectionate, diminutive form of the word for Nanny.

odnodvortsy: A class of free people who enjoyed limited privileges, including the right to own serfs, but who were often only slightly better off than the peasantry. Odnodvortsy were often settlers in outer regions of Russia, particularly in borderlands with Ukraine. Still, it is surprising that Natalya, a serf, would imply that she is more frail than they.

"Maître corbeau sur un arbre perché": Raven, perched in a tree . . .

sentsy: a small room without insulation leading to the entranceway or vestibule of a house. Used for shaking off snow and dirt before one enters even the outermost part of a building. Comparable perhaps to a "mudroom" in English.

She lived in a daze, stunned by her crime, spellbound by her terrifying secret and her treasure, like the girl in the tale of the scarlet flower: A reference to the story by Sergey Aksakov (1791–1859), in which a girl asks her father to bring her nothing but a scarlet flower from his journeys while her sisters plead for expensive gifts. The flower turns out to be magical.

kalach: a kind of white-meal loaf, similar in shape to a soft pretzel.

The Nogais: an ethnic group residing primarily in the Caucasus and some areas of the Crimea. Traditionally nomads who survived by fishing and raising cattle.

Oginsky's polonaise: M. K. Oginsky (1765–1831), Polish composer.

The Feast of Pokrov: Held on October 14 (October 1 old-style calendar), it celebrates the appearance of the Virgin Mary before the Holy Fool Andrew in Constantinople in the tenth century. According to legend, the Virgin appeared holding a veil (*pokrov*). Peasants traditionally sought to complete their harvesting and other preparations for winter by the time of this holiday.

Aunt Olga Kirillovna: Olga Kirillovna is the aunt of Pyotr Petrovich and Arkady Petrovich. This would make her the great aunt of the narrator and his sister, but in Russian tradition they refer to her as grandmother.

"Your sacred word has bound you to a dead man": an inexact quotation from Mikhail Lermontov's "The Dead Man's Love."

"Martyn Zadeka already predicted this in my future": a reference to a well-known book for the interpretation of dreams.

Crimean War: Fought between 1853 and 1856, the war pitted Russia against the Ottoman Empire, France, England, and Sardinia. It stemmed in part from disputes over the Palestinian holy lands.

"No, Uncle Yevsey. I won't ever go to the altar": Here "uncle" is used as a term of respect and affection.

She crossed herself and bowed to the icon in the corner, then to the mistress and Miss Tonya, and stood waiting for questions and instructions: In pre-revolutionary Russian houses, one corner of each room was dedicated to an icon; it was customary to bow to this "beautiful corner" of the room upon entering.

Sometimes when she worked, she would narrow her eyes and sing in a deep, strong voice about the infidels laying siege to Pochaev, and the Mother of God defending the monastery as "the evening sunset burned above the walls": During the Tatar-Mongol invasions of Kiev, monks and priests took refuge in the Pochaev Mountains beginning in roughly 1240. According to legend, the Virgin Mary appeared in a column of flames in that year. A church was built on the site where the vision was said to have occurred.

In the fall, Russian peasant women from Kaluga were brought in for the harvest and the threshing, but Natashka stayed away from them: Because they are Russian (as opposed to Ukrainian) it would have been natural for Natashka to strike up a friendship with the women from Kaluga. In the Russian text they are given the nickname *raspashonki*, a word for a loose-fitting jacket for small babies that can be easily removed.

"Holy Saint! Pray to God for me, a sinner, Mariya of Egypt!": St. Mariya of Egypt led a young life of promiscuity in Alexandria toward the end of the fifth century. She traveled to Jerusalem with a group of pilgrims and was prevented by an invisible force from passing with a crowd into Christ's tomb. She repented and began a life of solitary fasting in the desert for fifty years.

Patronymic: see notes to "Raven," p. 372.

"So I headed home, to Rus. . . . I'm not going to waste away, I told myself": The Kiev Monastery is in Ukraine; Yushka returns from there to Russia (Rus), his original home.

It was the eve of St. Ilya, the ancient fire-thrower's day: celebrated on August 2. St. Ilya is associated with thunder, lightning, and rain as well as fertility.

They took Aunt Tonya to a saint's remains in Voronezh: The remains of saints were believed to have both physical and spiritual healing powers.

Various rumors came about emancipation, triggering alarm among the house serfs and the field hands: Serfdom would be abolished in Russia in 1861.

Tanya

Kazakova: The feminine ending ("a") on this name would immediately inform the Russian reader that the owner of the estate is a woman.

Petrusha: an affectionate, intimate form of Pyotr, the name of the male protagonist.

They had forgotten to give him everything necessary for the night: a chamber pot.

Barynya: A barin is a male member of the gentry, comparable perhaps to a lord in English. "Barynya" could be translated as "the wife of the barin" or "a female barin." It is often used by peasants to refer to the female head of an estate. A baryshnya is a young, unmarried noblewoman. When Tanya later says, "I'm not a baryshnya," she means she is not a member of the upper classes (who know how to kiss with their mouths open).

Toward evening he passed her on the porch as she prepared the samovar: Coals would have to be lit inside a small chimney that heated the water in traditional samovars. A servant would prepare kindling and light the coals outside, then bring the samovar to the table.

Well dressed for the city, she walked behind the stationmaster, who addressed her formally as "thou" as he carried her two large sacks of goods: There are two forms of "you" in Russian: roughly speaking, vy (thou) is used to address formal associates and to show respect. Ty (you) is used when speaking to close friends, family members, and children. It was also customary for members of the upper classes to speak to menials and peasants with ty while servants and workers always addressed their superiors with vy. The stationmaster would ordinarily speak to Tanya with ty, but he has evidently mistaken her for a member of some class other than the peasantry because of her packages and good clothes.

Tanechka: an affectionate form of Tanya.

Bolshoi Moskovsky: an expensive, popular restaurant for Moscow's upper classes, literally "The Big Moscow (Restaurant)."

Pyotr Nikolaevich: the first name and patronymic of the male protagonist.

Wolves

"Events of days long passed," a quotation from Pushkin's poem "Ruslan and Lyudmila."

Zoyka and Valeriya

The Kazan railway line: A Russian reader familiar with Moscow would recognize this as a sign of prosperity. The Kazan line runs south from the city to pleasant countryside with a temperate summer climate—a prime spot for dachas.

Still recovering from typhus, she wore a little cap of black silk as she half sat and half lay in an armchair nearby: It was common practice to shave the heads of people suffering from typhus in order to combat the lice that carry the disease.

"May we call you Valechka?" A diminutive, affectionate form of Valeriya.

"The dark woods smell of pitch and wild berries. . . ." From A. K. Tolstoy's "Ilya Muromets."

Why did she call him "thou" one day and "you" the next? In Russian there are two forms of the word "you": the formal *vy*, and the informal *ty*. Addressing someone as *ty* would imply greater intimacy than the *vy* form.

tvorog: A kind of curd.

Valya: The short, familiar variant of Valeriya.